the
MAIN
CHARACTER

ALSO BY JACLYN GOLDIS

The Chateau
When We Were Young

the

MAIN
CHARACTER

a novel

JACLYN GOLDIS

EMILY BESTLER BOOKS

ATRIA

New York | London | Toronto | Sydney | New Delhi

EMILY
BESTLER
BOOKS

ATRIA

An Imprint of Simon & Schuster, LLC
1230 Avenue of the Americas
New York, NY 10020

First Emily Bestler Books/Atria Books hardcover edition May 2024

EMILY BESTLER BOOKS/ATRIA BOOKS and colophon are trademarks of Simon & Schuster, LLC

Simon & Schuster: Celebrating 100 Years of Publishing in 2024

For information about special discounts for bulk purchases, please contact Simon & Schuster Special Sales at 1-866-506-1949 or business@simonandschuster.com.

The Simon & Schuster Speakers Bureau can bring authors to your live event. For more information or to book an event, contact the Simon & Schuster Speakers Bureau at 1-866-248-3049 or visit our website at www.simonspeakers.com.

Interior design by Joy O'Meara

Manufactured in the United States of America

1 3 5 7 9 10 8 6 4 2

Library of Congress Cataloging-in-Publication Data has been applied for.

ISBN 978-1-6680-1304-5
ISBN 978-1-6680-1306-9 (ebook)

For my wonderful parents, Cheryl and Alex Goldis

the
MAIN
CHARACTER

CHAPTER ONE

Ginevra

For Ginevra Ex, bloody, murdered bodies were par for the course. Ginevra had poisoned and stabbed with the best of them. She'd decapitated, shot, and even had a victim killed while skydiving (framed as an accident). The *New Yorker* had called that one "ingenious." But a murder conducted by pen—blood contained to a page that was summarily flipped—well, that was quite different from standing over the dead body of someone you loved.

Ginevra averted her eyes from the face caught midscream. How had it come to this? *How?*

Ginevra had been especially proud of her latest book. She'd spun pages with characters still tangy on her tongue. Characters closely inspired by people who existed in real life. Then she'd arranged those unsuspecting people on this very train. She had awaited this moment, the end of their journey in sight. The perfect trip. Culminating in the sweet, sweet End.

In the end, it wasn't as she'd intended. Not even close.

Because *dead*. Not alive.

The train chugged along, the treetops whizzing by in a black, bushy haze, and in the darkness and her grief, Ginevra felt her footing give way. She was fifty-nine, but she lumbered as someone decades older, her limbs laden in flesh, not sprightly enough to quickly catch herself. Instead she toppled down onto the body, cheek to blood. She gagged a bit, but still she reached over, grappling across the still chest. For a hug.

Their first.

Her own flesh and blood.

She clutched the body to hers. Still disbelieving. How in the world had it come to *this*?

Ginevra was a plotter, after all. Not a *pantser*. Plotting versus *pantsing*—that eternal vociferous debate used by writers to distract themselves from just sitting down and doing the damn thing. While all those midlist authors, whose names no one would ever know, bandied about pros and cons of writing methods, Ginevra—the wealthiest author in the world after J. K. Rowling—simply wrote. Furiously. Successfully. Stratospherically. One book a year, starring her main character du jour. Always an instant #1 *New York Times* bestseller, except for her most recent publication, a disappointing launch that had hardly taken the literary world by storm and had even left her off the bestseller lists. The book had garnered a barrage of angry, critical reviews alleging the murder was flawed, the twists too obvious, the main character a cardboard cutout. Worse yet—that Ginevra was losing her golden touch. But oh, how she'd planned to redeem herself with her latest manuscript and its grand finale: this trip on the Orient Express. Ginevra had assembled all her characters, meticulously dropped clues, laid all the traps. Tightened the noose.

But she hadn't foreseen this.

She scooted back from the body. Tears mingled with her heavy black winged eyeliner and mascara, applied always from the middle of her eye rather than the inner corner, exactly like her idol, Sophia Loren. Although in every other way, Ginevra was the opposite of Sophia Loren. Ginevra was tubby and short, barely grazing five foot, with hair once chestnut but now her signature purple red. Her skin was mottled, and her nose crooked—like a rugby player, her twin sister, Orsola, had once said, wriggling her own pert nose. Orsola also had warm brown eyes with tiger flecks. Ginevra's eyes were black, the color of those deep foreboding lakes that policemen trawl for dead bodies in the movies.

Ginevra's vision clouded as minuscule mascara flecks irritated her pupils. Again, she wrangled herself across the parquet and caressed the forehead—still warm.

She strangled a sob.

She'd been so certain it would work, her meticulous plan to give

Rory—and the rest of them—the perfect trip. Ambitious, fiercely protective Rory. An old soul. Occasionally too determined and bighearted for her own good. Ginevra's latest, and finest, main character.

All Ginevra had wanted to do was save Rory. To make decades of wrongs, right.

And so Ginevra had plotted and planned, but somewhere along the way, her eagerness, her confidence, her old but raw pain had bested her. Run roughshod over her clarity of mind.

Ginevra had forgotten the cardinal rule: Often characters have a mind of their own.

And characters are prone to hiding secrets—from the author and from each other. Secrets that take pages to untangle. The majority of the book to tease out until you yelp a little surprise.

Oh!

Sometimes it doesn't matter that you've lined it up perfectly, all the acts, all the beats—the twisty, perfect lead-up to that critical character's final zig.

Because instead of zigging, they zag.

CHAPTER TWO

Rory

Three Days Before

"Benvenuto," says the impeccable man in a starched royal blue uniform with yellow braided trim, his white-gloved hand outstretched. Behind him looms the Venice Simplon-Orient-Express—a behemoth, glossy navy train meticulously restored to replicate its early-twentieth-century predecessors that traversed Europe in unfathomable luxury. The train has long been lodged in my imagination as the setting for the most glamorous Agatha Christie novel. A place inexplicably of both fun and murder.

Let's be honest—nowhere has murder seemed more alluring than on the Orient Express.

Quite the leaving bonus, this train trip. Insanely extravagant, is more like it. Almost . . . strange, to be honest. And for hands-down the easiest job I've ever had in my life. Three months in magnificent Rome, where I was paid a small fortune to simply talk endlessly about myself. But Ginevra Ex is rolling in money, without a husband or children to spoil. Besides, we got along well, Ginevra and I. And the bestselling author does everything extra, indeed.

Still, when I looked up the price of a ticket, my mouth dropped so far down into my chin that I was basically a cartoon character. Thirty thousand dollars, at least if I were staying in one of the nicest suites. I'm sure my cabin will be less grand, but still, that won't quite knock the last zero off the price.

"Your ticket, signorina."

I fumble in my purse, a slick of perspiration on my forehead. "I . . . it's . . . oh. Here!"

I clasp my fingers around the smooth ticket, relieved that my mouth can still eject speech, however clunky. In the past ten days, until now, I've spoken approximately five sentences. All to various people helping to transport me here: the Monte Carlo train station.

I'm not a freak—I was just on a ten-day silent meditation retreat.

After I finished my work for Ginevra, I took a train to an ashram in northern Italy to satisfy a long-held curiosity as to whether the whole meditation thing is all it was cracked up to be. For ten days, I meditated and practiced mindfulness and listened to dharma talks, all the while eating the same medley of vegetables cooked in different conglomerations, staring at the dingy eggshell walls, and walking the stunningly overgrown paths, with views out into Piacenza.

Verdict? I can see why people decide to become monks. It's all a bit clearer, nicer, without the noise. Without your phone as a fifth appendage. But now, with this Technicolor train saturating my senses, the scent of honeysuckle permeating the swollen July heat, and the people milling about dressed outlandishly with printed Gucci totes and candy-pink stiletto mules and stiff Panama hats, I feel a bit like a baby who's been birthed on Mars.

The porter lifts my luggage as if it is made of air and not the entirety of my belongings I've been hefting around ever since I left LA over three months ago. I follow him up the steps, running my fingers over my phone in my purse. I haven't switched it back on yet, not since the start of the meditation retreat. It's the longest I haven't talked to my father my entire life.

But my phone means questions. The people closest to me want to know about my plans and when I'm coming back. I thought by now I'd have answers, but I don't. That's what this train trip is for, I suppose. Why Ginevra gifted it to me. A reintegration, to figure out what comes next. Time to decompress.

Time—both a blessing and a curse. In my prior existence as a news anchor, I salivated for more of it. But now I have *endless* time to ponder how my boyfriend of ten years broke off our engagement, and how I screwed up my career, and how I found out a life-changing secret while working for Ginevra—a secret that those closest to me knowingly kept. Infinite time to think about how, even when I call my father, he probably won't know who I am (Alzheimer's). And to top it off, in need of quick cash, I agreed to serve as the main character for Ginevra's upcoming book. While a fun and once-in-a-lifetime experience, it also means that my failures and traumas will soon be splashed out for basically the entire world to judge.

The porter leads me down a narrow corridor and my thoughts blur as I wander after him, mouth agape. It's all that high-gloss lacquer wood-work and art deco style that makes you feel like you've stepped straight into a smoky-air Hitchcock film. The pale yellow carpet is smattered in squiggly geometrics punctured with scarlet red lines all slashing out in different directions. Piano music wafts from invisible speakers, the air cool and heady with musk and neroli. One side of the corridor is all win-dows, and the other is lined with doors in the ubiquitous gleaming wood. At one, the porter stops and gestures.

"Your cabin, signorina. The Roma Suite. One of our newest."

The Roma Suite. A thrill sweeps over me. I read about this suite—done by the premier design firm in Rome. It's basically the most coveted accommodation on this train.

No *freaking* way.

The porter opens the door to a room that, while small, is the fanci-est I've seen in my entire life. The walls are covered in the same intricate marquetry as in the hall, alongside Roman accents like mosaic flooring, slick bronze fixtures, and a frescoed ceiling. A full bed nestled in the window nook is styled in white bedding embroidered with lilies, and a gold baroque bed frame is set against emerald brocade wallpaper. On the wall opposite is a mosaic of colored glass, and astride it is the bathroom, where I glimpse a charming pale pink pedestal sink. I turn in disbelief, taking in the view toward the door. To my right, a small banquette table and forest-green velvet chairs line the windows. On the table rests a sil-ver tray with artfully arranged fruit, cheese, and bread. At the end of the banquette, mounted on the wall, is a gold bar lined with crystal barware, aglow in the late afternoon sun. Then, to my left, a narrow walkway sepa-rates the banquette from a cream couch piped in green. Beside the couch is a brass side table with a malachite top. And beside the table is a man.

I yelp. I can't help it. He's inches from me but camouflaged somehow—the gold braid on his uniform melding with the room's metal accents.

"This is your steward," says the porter. "Meet Marco. Marco is here for all your needs, however big or small. Twenty-four hours of the day." With a flourish, the porter gives a little bow and then leaves.

"*Benvenuto, signorina*," says Marco.

"*Grazie.*"

Marco's smile reaches all corners of his face, and I smile back my winning smile, the one my father has always told me reveals nothing. When Papa's thoughts were still crystalline, capable of expression, he'd point out that I can smile brightly on the worst day of my life, and you would never know that anything other than pots of gold at the ends of rainbows percolated below my surface. Papa and my brother, Max, are different—they are incapable of masking their emotions. Prone to demonstrations of both great enthusiasm and great rage.

"*Buon* . . . uh . . . good afternoon." I fumble for something, anything, to say to my twenty-four-hour steward, feeling weird and exposed. "You're—you're very kind to . . ." Kind to *what*? All he said was welcome. What am I even babbling? I should be able to engage normally and effortlessly.

Engage, Rory. Ask him politely to leave so you can sink into that bed and . . . do what?

Sleep? I'm not tired. I slept more in the past ten days than I've probably slept in the entirety of my adult life.

Meditate? I've already completed my new daily routine, both my twenty-minute meditations, one in the morning before leaving the ashram and one in the car en route to the station.

Cry? I'm not a big crier. I wish I were—the cries feel buried deep, denied their release.

"You will notice a tray of snacks." Marco points pleasantly to the food. "If you are hungry from your travels. Then, a welcome letter." He gestures to the chair. "Along with a travel kit, robe, and slippers, and a guard's whistle."

"A guard's whistle?" I step closer and identify, indeed, a silver whistle on a chain. "Meant for what?"

Marco smiles. "A guard's whistle," he repeats, as if that explains it. I nod. I bounce the whistle in my palm, wonder vaguely if I'm supposed to wear it as a necklace. Is this like on a cruise ship, when you have to participate in some sort of drill? Eventually, for lack of anything else to do, I loop it around my neck.

Marco places his hands behind his back and straightens up, standing a bit like a statue who is about to pitch himself onto a pedestal and remain in this room forevermore. He's sweet, but right now I could really do with one of those futuristic AI robot stewards, instead of having to make small talk with the real thing.

"Would you like me to unpack for you, signorina?"

"No," I say quickly. I haven't even washed the stuff I wore at the retreat. I cringe, imagining Marco handling one of my dirty tank tops and doubtfully arranging it on a silk padded hanger. "Thank you, but I'll do it. There's not much to unpack anyway."

I point, forcing a laugh at my beat-up black suitcase with the busted wheel. I'm still so proud of myself for fitting everything into one suitcase for this extended three-plus-month trip to Italy. Admittedly, though, my suitcase certainly stands out amid the other passengers' matching designer luggage. I watched it all file onto the train as I approached: trunks and other carryalls without wheels, uniformly spun out of silk and other impractical materials. Luggage with an almost ominous tenor, like the type the upper class took on the *Titanic*.

"A welcome cocktail? Perhaps you would like one?" Marco offers. "You would like me to show you to the bar car?"

A welcome cocktail. Now, that's an idea. There was no alcohol on the vipassana retreat. No meat. No sex. No pleasure. We were supposed to find the bliss within ourselves.

I'm still searching.

"You know, a cocktail in the bar car sounds like just the ticket, Marco."

He nods discreetly and starts toward the door. I glance around again, still in awe of this decadent room. A room fit for romance, if I ever saw one. I can't believe this is the level of trip Ginevra sent me on. I'm basically on someone's honeymoon. Well, I suppose I'm on *my* honeymoon.

Through our interviews, Ginevra discovered that Nate and I once dreamed of taking this very trip together: the Orient Express's first foray into special trips that include overnight stops, rather than just traveling nonstop between destinations. So Ginevra decided to send me here on one of the train's inaugural trips along the western Italian coast, all expenses paid, by myself. A gesture exceedingly kind and wildly generous. But as my eyes rove back to the bed, I can't help but think about all the things I could be doing on that bed, with Nate. Or with Gabriele.

God, where did *Gabriele* come from? He was a fling, I remind myself. A fleeting Roman indulgence, like tiramisu.

Right. To the bar car we'll go. I anticipate I'll be spending a lot of time there, table for one.

Should I change first? Freshen up?

I bend down to give myself a quick once-over in the bar cart's mirrored panel, wedging my face up beside a crystal decanter. My normally chestnut hair looks almost haloed in blond—crazy how quickly my strands turned in the Italian sun. My hair was previously accustomed to fluorescent lights, not endless walks around the vipassana property, and before that, on gorgeous spring days, exploring Rome in my ample free time when Ginevra was writing and didn't need me for interviews. I'm tan, I realize. A tan I haven't been since I was a kid, spending the summer boating on Orchard Lake with Max and my best friend, Caroline.

I peer closer at the freckles clustered by my nose, at my green eyes surprisingly soft and rested, at my ears that stick out a little bit, endearingly I now think, even though as a child I was teased for them (especially around Christmas, when there was an uptick in elf jokes). I'm makeup free, in a floaty white cotton dress and platform jute espadrilles adding four necessary inches to my five foot two. Then there's the whistle, which almost looks like a cool dangly necklace. It sinks in that I look different from when I was a news anchor, all pale and buttoned up in a severe suit or sheath, with a slash of red lipstick, juggling fifteen tasks at once. I smile at myself, pleased that the smile finally travels to my eyes. I can see the years on my face—all thirty-three of them, present in the new spider lines that are setting off stubbornly toward uncharted frontiers. But I can also see the little girl in me, the one who used to spend full summers barefoot, living in her imagination far more than in reality. I realize that's what I was doing the past ten days—living in a pretend world. And I suppose this train is an extension of it.

Three last days of make-believe before I have to face reality again.

I nod at Marco, suddenly self-conscious that he's been watching my self-inventory.

Marco sets off out the door, and I follow him back down the corridor, past the blur of mahogany doors, once more throttled a hundred years back in time. After thirty seconds' worth of steps and passing through a corridor connection, we arrive before a plaque that reads Carriage 3674. The bar car. I step inside to rows of sumptuous velvet sofas and matching ottomans, all upholstered in a luxe royal blue zebra print. There are gleaming brass fixtures and plush navy curtains and the now-familiar glossy wood polished to within an inch of its life, with lacquer tables interspersed among all the cozy, opulent seating. A buffet of antipasti flanks the bar, and a photographer is capturing shots with a vintage Polaroid. Off to the side, along the windows, a man is swaying on a bench, his tuxedo-ed back to me, playing pleasant notes on the grand piano by the bar. I feel as though I'm in some bootleg speakeasy, about to witness F. Scott Fitzgerald and Ernest Hemingway clink their gin rickeys.

Chin-chin!

Nope, not the old literati, but a silver-haired man in a white dinner jacket and a woman in a floor-length red-sequined evening dress, whose face defies gravity, clinking their flutes of champagne. Tiny boxes of caviar and mother-of-pearl spoons litter their table. I consult my phone, see that I still haven't switched off Airplane Mode.

Five thirty-five in the evening, and we've already got sequins and caviar.

If I had a hat, I'd tip it to them.

My mind conjures Nate in a white tuxedo. He has soft blond curls and almond brown eyes, almost prep-school boyish until your eyes lower to check out his hard-exercised body. Nate in a white tuxedo . . .

Swoon.

God, I hate Nate, though. I *hate* him. And I still love him. Ugh. I thought meditation would expunge all that heavy emotion. It did, for those drifty, unreal days at the retreat, but now it's back. Somehow, almost sharper.

"*Buona serata, signorina.* What can I get you?" A waitress in the signature royal blue has materialized.

"I'll have . . . what it looks like she's having." I point to the table to my right, to a girl whose back is to me, her hand cradling a crystal goblet with clear liquid and a single giant ice cube.

"A vodka neat?" the waitress asks, eyebrow raised. "*Davvero?* You are certain? Not an Aperol spritz?" She says it like she's identified my type—bumbling American, who comes to Italy and downs them like water.

"Yes. I mean, no. Not Aperol spritz. Vodka neat, *per favore.*" I'm a bit surprised, too, but only because I'm not the lone woman drinking it here. "I'll take Zyr, if you have it."

I used to drink vodkas neat with Max when I was in college and he was in grad school, both of us together in Ann Arbor. When Papa found out I was downing Franzia wine in a box with my similarly broke friends, he shuddered and said a lesson in premier vodka was in order, given our Soviet roots. We Aronovs could—and certainly did—scrimp money in other ways, but with food and alcohol, the fine stuff was warranted. Before he got sick, Papa, Max, and I used to drink vodkas neat by the fireplace in winter, and in the summer out in the Adirondack chairs by the lake.

To us, Papa would say. *The three musketeers.* Then he'd clink our glasses and give us each a solemn gaze, holding my eyes with his for a few long moments that made me feel startlingly transparent.

Max and I got Caroline into nice vodka, too. And Nate, when he joined our trio. Made us a quad. I allow myself a brief moment to slip back inside those memories. The closest people I have in this world. *Had.*

Then the girl with the goblet turns.

"Holy shit." I hear the words come out of me, but I don't feel myself saying them.

It's Caroline.

I clap my hand over my mouth, my heart thumping fast. "Wha— Caro . . . what are you—"

"Ror!" Caroline runs a hand through her ice-blond hair, cut shorter now than when I last saw her a few months ago, in a piecey bob with wispy face-framing bangs. She's thinner, too—not in a way anyone else would notice, only a best friend. Her oval face is surprisingly wan, deflated, almost elongating her already long forehead. A pseudo friend of ours in high school once nicknamed Caro "Horsey"; she declared that Caro had a five head—five fingers could fit comfortably above each other, she said, demonstrating. It was a cruel nickname concealed in that breezy teenage in-crowd way. Caro has always been acutely sensitive to outside opinions, so the critique stuck; she's worn bangs of varied lengths ever since.

We always want what we don't have, isn't that the truth? Because to me, Caro is stunningly beautiful. Tall, regal, solid, with a butt and thighs way before TikTok made them aspirational. She's got zingy curves where I can feel rectangular, like SpongeBob. Caro's not the most intoxicating, maybe, not a conventional star—but in her quiet, unassuming way, in her kindness, her softness, she shines like the sun, and you find yourself wanting to launch into her orbit.

"Ror!" Caro's face animates with a giant smile. She grabs my hand and dances it around. "We were wondering when you were gonna show up!"

We?

I'm still poleaxed with shock as my best friend—the closet thing I have to a sister—folds me into a hug, and my eyes catch upon the "we" she was eclipsing.

What in the world. . . .

It's Max, my only sibling, my older brother, with his piercing blue eyes like Papa's, his shaggy dark hair in that familiar threadbare navy baseball cap. Only Max could get away with a baseball hat in a place like this. In fact, he's sprawled on the bar's sofa, lanky legs outstretched, looking just like the nonchalant CEO in his recent *Detroit Magazine* cover ("Maximillions" was the headline, and below it, "The Thirtysomething CEO Whose Much-Anticipated Alzheimer's Vaccine Is Spearheading Detroit's Resurgence"). Although contrary to the cover, where he probably had makeup done and, now that I think of it, Photoshop, at this moment his eyes are bloodshot and the bags beneath them evident, almost bruised. He hasn't exaggerated about those long hours; he wears them on his face. Max was a nerdy child, always buried in his science books, awkward. Bullied. He still is all those things, other than bullied, thank goodness, but he's grown into his tendencies, certainly fills them out with more confidence now. My brother grins sheepishly as he stands up to hug me.

"LS!" Max has called me LS—Little Sister—since day one. He extracts me from Caro's arms, pins me to his chest. "I missed you. You've been massively MIA. I would take it personally if . . . well, I *do* take it personally."

I can't bring myself to apologize, not now. But I'm unsurprised by his greeting. Max's equilibrium is always throttled if someone in his inner circle is mad at him. And he realizes I am mad at him, evidenced by my not responding to his many calls and emails, but he doesn't know why. Even though I'm furious at him, and hurt, I relax into my brother with a degree of comfort as if we were once in the same womb instead of born four years apart. I clutch his familiar back, not Nate's jacked but Max's teddy-bear soft, the worn cloth of Max's turquoise Polo, his ever-minty smell. He's eternally self-conscious about his breath, swigs mouthwash a good five times a day.

Then my eyes flicker behind Max. And my breath leaves my body as my eyes lock onto Nate.

I don't understand. I don't understand anything at all.

They've all crashed my solo trip? But . . . how? Why?

My ex-fiancé sits ramrod straight, massaging his forehead, avoiding my gaze. Nate, sturdy Nate, five-foot-ten to Max's six-four, but with far more gravitas than my brother. Unless you know him intimately, and then he can be witty and silly. It's *Nate*—the guy you'd trust with your life. Indeed, in his professional life, many in the most high-stakes scenarios do. God, it's actually *Nate*, with his golden hair untamed and the mole above his left brow that he used to claim would grant me any wish I desired if I rubbed it right. *Any wish at all! Just like a genie, Ror. I'm your genie in a bottle.* Then he'd dance around like Christina Aguilera. Making me pee with laughter.

I can't believe it. That Nate is actually here, in white slacks and an olive-green collared shirt, far more appropriate to the atmosphere than Max's rumpled casual. Nate's wearing the shirt I got him for his last birthday, I realize, the same one he wore four months ago, when I was still drowsy with sleep and he began breaking up with me. Swiftly, calmly, ending all the big things but the little ones, too—our little routines and traditions, our plans. All the little dirt paths of our life together that spanned a decade, the paths that wouldn't appear on any maps but were the only routes I knew how to navigate, I realized after the fact. In a few sentences, Nate made all our little paths dead ends.

What the *hell* are they all doing here?

CHAPTER THREE

Caroline

I have a million thoughts when I hug Rory—and I can't tell her any of them.

"Oh my gosh, Ror. I missed you so insanely much," is what I finally settle upon. That, at least, is the truth. I hug her harder, harder than she likes. I'm the touchy-feely one between us. The one who insisted on sleepovers together in her bed when we were ten, which she'd indulge until around midnight, when she'd deliver a series of "bad dream" kicks to my leg so that eventually I'd flop down onto her trundle.

She stays in my embrace longer than I expect. "I don't get what you're doing here, but aah! This is seriously crazy."

"Crazy good?" I ask.

"Crazy good!" Then she whispers, "At least with you." Rory sets me back at arm's length. She looks different—less severe in a way, her bare arms not as chiseled after weeks of not going to Pilates every morning, her skin a degree of tan I haven't seen since we were kids.

"Why are you guys all here, though? I seriously don't get it." She lowers her voice. "Why is *Nate* here?"

"Your author invited us. . . ."

"My author?" Rory's strangely dazed. All that adventure, freedom, meditation has painted over her somehow, made slow, round corners where there were once hard edges.

"Ginevra," I say. "How many Ginevras do you know? Ginevra *Ex*."

"I don't get it." Rory absently rubs at her arms. "I—"

"She wanted us to surprise you. God, it was so hard to keep the surprise! Even though it's not like you've been great at answering my calls." I smile, but I know it underscores the raw accusation behind my nonchalance. That Rory has been MIA. That I've wanted to tell her so much, but it all spiraled so horribly, so now it's past the point where I can say anything at all.

"Ginevra wanted to surprise me. . . ." Rory stares at me, then at Max, ignoring my passive-aggressiveness. Then Rory's eyes dart toward Nate, before her gaze snaps back at me. She crosses her arms over her chest. "I just don't . . . Ginevra wanted *all* of you to surprise me? And *all* of you wanted to?"

"All of us did," I tell her. "A lot." I nod, trying to reinforce the statement, trying to convey to her that, yes, Nate *really* wanted to be here.

"I . . ." Rory accepts her drink from the waitress, sinks listlessly to a seat. "I don't get it. She, like, paid for you guys to come on the Orient Express?"

"Yep," Nate says, finally piping in. He stands, inches toward Rory, and I move back to give him berth. "I tried to insist on covering my way, but she refused. And I thought about not coming, Ror, because this all felt too much, too deceptive, surprising you. In case you didn't want . . . in case you—shit." He puts a hand on Rory's knee, and I inhale sharply, wondering if Rory will shove it off. She has every right to. But she doesn't. Just stares up at him blankly. "I have so much I want to tell you, Ror. Stuff I really want to explain . . . make right. Make *us* right."

Rory opens her mouth, but then closes it, eyes bewildered.

Nate frowns. He was clearly hoping for more of an exuberant reaction. Some indication that his gesture will ultimately be reciprocated. But Rory must be shocked at our arrival. At Nate's declaration. For nearly the first time in our friendship, I can't identify what she's thinking. She and Nate were together forever. Practically our entire adulthood. He got scared. He went through a beyond shitty time. He knows what he wants now, what he had. He messed up, plain and simple.

We've all made mistakes. Some of ours worse than others.

He's the love of her life, though. Rory will take Nate back now, won't she?

Rory downs half her drink in one go. She swallows, twines her hands in her lap. "I don't really get it. I don't get why Ginevra . . . why she wanted . . ."

"We didn't necessarily, either," I admit.

Six weeks ago, I agreed to a few Zoom interviews with the quirky author—sitting there with her jarring purplish hair, her makeup Kardashian caked, asking me inane questions. She wanted me to catalog all the times I saw Rory cry (a grand total of once, when in our midtwenties a doctor diagnosed Ansel's memory issues as Alzheimer's, and a one-two punch ensued: first a brain scan revealing moderate to severe plaque deposits, followed by a genetic test showing Ansel to be positive for a variant associated with more rapid progression of the disease). Then Ginevra asked me if, marshaling my background as a fashion stylist, I could opine on whether Rory's optimal color palette is a winter, spring, summer, or fall. (I don't subscribe to that old-fashioned model, but if I did, Rory is clearly an autumn, although maybe borderline spring with her new blond streaks.)

Still, despite having spent a few relatively painless interview sessions with Ginevra, I was shocked when she called me a couple of weeks ago. Offered up this trip. When she said that Nate and Max would be included, as well.

"But the trip sounded fun, Ror." I think how to put the other part delicately. "You just went through so much. And it meant the four of us together again. Even if things have changed in our dynamic, we still love each other. That's a given, right?"

I look at Rory for confirmation, but she's quiet.

"And how often does it happen that we're all together? With us divided, Michigan and LA. Or . . . actually—now you're in Italy. You're not *staying* in Italy, are you?"

Rory gives a tiny shrug. "I have no idea. It's not like . . . there's not much tying me to LA anymore." She doesn't look at Nate, but the pointed way she says it is an obvious dig. "I know I want to spend a lot more time in Michigan, at least, with Papa."

I nod, digest that. Michigan for Ansel, not for me or Max. I know Rory didn't mean it to be an insult; but it stings, probably more so because of all the things I'm grappling with now. Decisions I still need to make that will have deep repercussions not only for me but for all of us.

I shove all that out of my mind. "Well, besides coming here to see you, it was a free luxury trip on a silver platter. So how could we turn it down?"

Rory finally smiles. "Even Maximillions got a free ride?"

"You know me." I can feel Max's smile boring into my back, sending an unexpected zing of fury through my bones. "I can't resist a freebie."

"We heard you got the Roma Suite, Ror," Max continues. "I got the new Istanbul one. Your author must love the Aronov siblings. The other two are slumming it in regular-people cabins."

Rory nods, her lips barely parted. Interesting. She's angry at Max. Clearly. I'm angry at her brother for my own reasons. But I wonder why she is.

Rory shakes her head. "I really can't believe you're all here."

I laugh. Hard. Devolve into giggles. The rest of them laugh, too, with far less fervor. It's hard not to laugh when someone else is—that's what I've discovered about this quirk of mine and what it rouses in others. I laugh when I'm uncomfortable, when I'm scared, when I'm angry. Basically, I laugh at all the inappropriate times, and usually not at the things people generally find hilarious.

"I can hardly believe we're here, either," I finally say, when I can form words again.

Other than a conference I attended in Dubai two months ago, I haven't taken a trip in a year. That's what I signed up for, though, as a member of the sales team for one of the fastest-growing biotech start-ups. It's called Hippoheal: a play on *healing* and *Hippocrates*, the father of modern medicine. Our Alzheimer's vaccine—the first to be fast-tracked by the FDA—is approaching phase IIb clinical trials. Our successful earlier trials garnered international attention, as has our patented device to detect signs of Alzheimer's through the breath, which is undergoing clinical trials itself. Hippoheal is Max's company. Max's brainchild. Maximillions. My close friend since childhood. My boss. Like a brother—sort of.

Since I met Rory, and then in short order Max, I've known that Max harbored a not-so-secret crush on me. One drunken night in college, he confirmed it, and we tumbled into bed together like you see on coming-of-age TV. It was wonderful, to be honest. Our chemistry, the softness of his embrace. But it was *Max*. I couldn't sleep after, my heart thumping at what it all meant. In the morning, I told him that I loved him too much to risk dating him. That I *needed* him too much. I wouldn't be able to handle it if we broke up. And we were too young to make a go of it. After all, Max, Rory, and Ansel are the only family I really have.

Sometimes, though—often, truly—I've reconsidered my firm decline, after facing the ashes of yet another situationship, after getting set up on yet another tepid date. Let's say it how it is—after being rejected by yet another man. Although I know I'm part of—really a catalyst for—the rejection. As my therapist once told me, when I attract emotionally unavailable men, I have to look at the parts of me that are unavailable. And when you analyze the way I grew up, it makes sense. What I witnessed of love wasn't anything desirable. It was yelling and cheating and gambling. It was locking my door, slipping under my covers with earplugs, and eating tubs of frosting that I bought from the supermarket with money my mother occasionally gave me to get groceries. (She wasn't making any birthday cakes, let's make that clear.)

And I was never the girl dreaming of becoming a mother. My ovaries didn't start screaming at thirty. I suppose my family of origin, dysfunctional as all get-out, has played a ready part in that. But I've always adored Max, thought of him as a romantic prospect, maybe in recent years more than ever. He's soft, brilliant, endlessly supportive. And now, filled out with a confidence he didn't have when we were kids, perhaps part the growth that comes with age, and of course his surging business success, too. His star is on the rise. Lately, Max has had a string of supermodel girlfriends—dumb, twentysomething PR girls, if you ask me. Not surprisingly, they haven't held his interest. Until recently, I always felt like I could have Max if I wanted him, which was a thrill, a certain kind of power. A relief. My plan B I always kept tucked in my pocket.

I think I hoped one day I would feel safe enough to use it.

In fact, a little over a year ago Max made a plea for me again. That it's me he wants. That the two of us are inevitable, and I need to face it. For the first time, I considered it seriously. Imagined, even, what it would be, to have a partner to really rely on. Max—wonderful Max. Someone I trusted, someone who would truly try to make me happy, even when the world dealt up its surprises and horrors. Then Max didn't blink twice about bailing me out of a bit of financial trouble, and he even generously offered me a job with his burgeoning company. One day I absently doodled *Caroline Aronov* on my notepad, and then and there I resolved to speak to him. I remember how excited I was that day, imagining our future unfolding. Thinking that, perhaps, we were actually destined. That we might have a happily-ever-after awaiting us. Imagining what it would mean to Rory and Ansel. But then . . .

Then the most unexpected, terrible thing happened.

I feel the pressure bloom in my chest again, like an elephant has come to rest atop it.

Plan B is shot to hell. Never can be.

It's painful having Max here with me on this vacation. I almost bailed on coming. But there are reasons I didn't bail, beyond just fun and games and old friends and the Tyrrhenian Sea.

"Is it okay that I'm here?" Nate finally asks Rory. His voice catches, a blip on his typical assured.

"I don't know why you're here," Rory says, taking a deep sip of her vodka and then smacking the glass back down on the table with such force that vodka sloshes over the brim. A ruddy-faced elderly man in a pressed navy blazer and a fairly absurd pom-pom beret shoots us a sour, disapproving look. A glamorous fortysomething Italian couple across the aisle—the wife bedecked in the serpent Bulgari necklace I positively covet—merely appear amused at the spectacle. But Rory doesn't seem to notice any of them or care that they're all watching. "Seriously, I really don't get why any of you are here."

Nate flinches. Rory looks away, squeezes my hand. "I'm so happy *you're* here, Caro," she whispers.

My body relaxes against her touch. "Oh my gosh, babe. You can't imagine. Me, too. We have so much to—"

"Ror, I just have to tell you, to make this clear, because I feel like I'm dancing around it. . . ." Nate wrestles his hands in his lap, twists his big silver-face watch on a black leather strap. "I really regret breaking up with you. It was crazy, that time for me." His eyes roll back a bit, remembering. "I felt like such a fuckup, such a . . . I don't know. You know what it was like for me when—"

"You know what it was like for me, too," Rory fires back, oblivious to another scowl from the man in the beret and his muttered epithet that I don't catch. Meanwhile, our other compatriots on the train are flitting more restrained glances our way; Rory has become something of a spectacle. A group of Scandis murmur their surprise over fizzy coupes, and a spectacular Indian woman in a burnt-orange silk dress clucks her tongue, her back straight like a mannequin's in the most impressive display of posture I've ever witnessed.

"Ror." I flick my head sideways toward our onlookers, and Rory seems to come to and notice all eyes trained upon us.

"Oh." Her face is still splotchy and fired up, but she eases into a low hiss. "You know what, Nate? It's not like it was all sunshine and rainbows for me. I lost my job. Then I lost you. And that's not all. I lost . . ." But she stares at her hands, doesn't continue.

Lost what? It feels so foreign, not to hear the sentences echo in my head before they tumble out of my best friend's mouth.

"Will you talk to me? Will you at least give me a chance to explain?" Nate asks.

"I . . . I don't—"

"*Ciao!*" Suddenly a man is before us—around my and Rory's age, I guess. Or maybe a bit older, like Max and Nate. Later thirties, perhaps. He's tall and tanned, with warm brown eyes, dark sweeping hair, and a scruffy beard. He has a confident air with obvious charm, but there's a noticeable softer element to him, too. He looks like a dad, in a way that I can't exactly pinpoint, the protective kind. Not that I'd know about protective dads personally, but I grew up with Max and Rory, and so their dad was kind of like mine. Yes, that's it. There's something in this man that reminds me of Ansel Aronov. Compassionate, kind. The type to make you raspberry blintzes when you're sad, then tell you grand bedtime stories with creative twists to cheer you up.

"*Ciao,*" I say slowly, but the man is staring at Rory, and I notice she is staring back. Staring like she knows him.

"Gabriele," Rory says, and there is a raw element in her tone I can't decipher. "What in the world are *you* doing here?"

CHAPTER FOUR

Rory

I'm in a bizarro land where, poof! People from my past suddenly appear. Clearly orchestrated appearances over which I was given zero input.

"Why are you here?" I ask again, a sudden tornado of anger in my chest.

"Ginevra sent me." He smooths the lapel of his gorgeous beige linen suit that he's paired with cognac loafers, and despite myself, a swell of attraction washes over me.

Still, I maintain my brick-wall facade. "I figured that much." Gabriele is Ginevra's lawyer, so of course she sent him—but why?

"Well . . ." Gabriele shifts uncomfortably back and forth. "*Scialla*. Everything is okay, Rory. Calm down."

My anger intensifies. Telling me to calm down has the effect of tightening every single one of my organs, on the precipice of explosion. I restrain myself from the explosion, though—unlike the other two Aronovs, I am quite good at restraining myself.

"You must be Max, Nate, and Caroline?" Gabriele says pleasantly.

"Reporting for duty." If eyes could spit fire, Nate's would.

"Yes, the whole crew is here," I say, my sarcasm crackling more than I intended. "But I have no real idea *why* the whole crew is here. Maybe you can clear that up."

Gabriele nods. "Well, please know that Ginevra wants this to be the best three days of all of your lives. She sent me here for two reasons. One, because she made an itinerary for your trip. Really, all she wants is for it to be the most perfect time. That the four of you see the most exclusive, exciting spots and eat the most delicious meals that Cinque Terre, Rome, and Positano have to offer. Price being no limitation at all. That you are happy with the service on the train. That your rooms are to your liking. That—"

"And she couldn't just send photocopies of this magical itinerary to a staff member here?" Nate interjects. It's a fair question, but his jealousy is obvious, his glaring suspicion at this man—a man he does not know but that he recognizes *I* do. Well, serves him right. I may have gotten more spiritual and Zen, but still, I have to be honest, there is something primally satisfying about Nate's jealousy. Even as his presence here—his potentially wanting me back—confounds me.

Nate isn't aware of it, but his jealousy of Gabriele is, in fact, warranted.

I met Gabriele through Ginevra, when I signed a litany of contracts at the beginning of my employment. Then Gabriele and I kept crossing paths, as I was staying in Trastevere, in an apartment Ginevra arranged for me, an apartment in a building that he manages and in which he also lives. Once we wound up sitting beside each other at the bar downstairs during lunchtime, when I was hunched over my guidebook. We decided to split a pizza and got to talking. Gabriele explained how he'd married at thirty— rare for Italians, who typically settle down later, in their later thirties or early forties. So, he explained, he wasn't the typical *mammone*—a mama's boy, who lives at home far beyond his youth. Sure, Gabriele said he was devoted to his mother, tried to make it to his parents' outside the city every other week for *il pranzo della domenica*, the sacred family occasion of Sunday lunch. But he didn't *need* his mother. Certainly not to do his laundry—he grimaced—and he could cook well on his own. And after his divorce, when his ex-wife absconded to Australia with her new boy- friend, he was raising his daughter, Chiara, on his own. I could see then how much was riding on Gabriele's shoulders but how much he wanted to rise to the occasion. How he *was* rising to the occasion.

I thought he was deeply sexy. And I liked him immediately, or the flut- ter in my stomach told me I did. It was strange and new to think a man other than Nate was cute, to even *look* at a man who wasn't Nate.

After that lunch, Gabriele offered to show me the less touristy sides of Rome. I accepted. He took me to explore Mercato Testaccio, where he got me to try a hot tripe sandwich (absurdly good), and to the Aventine Hill, where we peeked through the keyhole to the most picturesque view of the city. Gabriele knew I was getting over a broken engagement. That I was only looking for light and fun. And light and fun it was, until Gabriele told me he was starting to have feelings for me. That he was looking for something more. I understood, of course. We parted as friends, although I suppose you never really know what a person thinks of you after you've sort of dated.

"Well, think of me like your concierge." Gabriele smiles, and I am reminded how genuine his smile is. Strangely, how much I trust him.

"Who's staying with Cannoli?" I ask.

If you want to know who Gabriele is at his core, you need know only the story of his dog, Cannoli—a terrifyingly ugly mutt. Cannoli is jumpy and needy and pees everywhere and doesn't stop barking. He'd been adopted four times, by different families, and they always wound up giving him up. They couldn't handle him. They wanted a cuter dog. An easier dog. But Gabriele saw something lovable in wounded, acting-out Cannoli. He told me he'd never give Cannoli up, even when Cannoli drives him absolutely nuts. Because Cannoli needs a family that promises him forever.

Gabriele grins. "The most difficult part of this trip, I admit. Logistically speaking, at least. Nino."

Ah, Nino—our cantankerous upstairs neighbor. But he loves Gabriele, because Gabriele is always bringing him ribbolita or steak, claiming he accidentally made extra. It's not extra, I know. It's intentional. Gabriele—lawyer, real estate manager, Super Dad, good-deed doer. And hottie. Can't forget hottie.

"Extra ribbolita for Nino, I presume," I say, my heart thumping noticeably faster.

"Ribbolita for all of eternity, more like it." Gabriele groans, then his face goes businesslike again. "But listen, what I began to say is that Ginevra doesn't want any of you to pay for anything or worry about figuring out the best restaurant, the perfect vista. She's planned it all. The best of the best. She wants this to be the trip of a lifetime. The most perfect trip of all of your lives."

I nod, but I still don't get it. Not even close.

"She also wanted you to have these." Gabriele clicks open his tan leather briefcase and pulls out books.

Shit. My heart grinds to a halt. Not books, but *the* book. The one about me.

I can tell it's not a finished copy because there's no elaborate cover, and it's not Ginevra's usual hardcover. Instead it says *Bound Manuscript* and the title: *The Cabin on the Lake.*

A shiver springs down my spine. I hear a gasp. It's Max, his face gone startlingly white. Then my eyes travel to Caro, her knuckles white where she grips her glass. Even Nate's shoulders have shot up to his ears. Strange—they all look as anxious about this book as I feel.

The Cabin on the Lake. Of course, that's what Ginevra's titled it. Makes perfect sense, but I didn't know it till now. The title clearly references the shared trenches of our childhood. Our rickety cabin on Orchard Lake— the lake Papa adored, property around which he could hardly afford though sprung for all the same. The title conjures my first memory, in fact, knees knocking in terror, as Papa cajoled me to jump into the water off our dock. He said to pretend I was a tree. *Chop, chop.* He made the motions on my calf. *Now, timber, Rory. After it's cut, the tree is meant to fall down.*

Papa wanted me to fall, so fall I did. I crashed onto the water. I still remember my body's slap against the surface. Then Papa's arms, embracing me. But first, the slap.

The fall without catching me was pure Papa. He lived a harrowing life filled with tragedy in the former Soviet Union. He emigrated to the United States, to freedom, with great risk and by the sheer force of his perseverance and will. So, yes, he was always there for us, always, always, and truly, the best father I could imagine, but Max and I were raised to know we were each responsible for ourselves. We had to pull ourselves up by our bootstraps. No one was going to clean up our own poop. (Papa had some catchy eye-rolling sayings.)

In other words: chop, chop, timber. I had to fall, and swim, and save myself. And then Papa would be waiting there, arms wide open. Kisses and love and support galore.

Except now he sometimes doesn't even know who I am.

Could Ginevra have set the book in Michigan?

Our hometown in southeast Michigan, in the suburbs of Detroit, is a world away from Ginevra's native Rome. What does Ginevra know of Michigan anyway? I didn't tell her all that much about my home state, really. As far as I know, she's never been there before. She did ask to go in person, to interview Max and Caro, and Papa. But I didn't like the idea of signing the people in my life up for days of interviews. They could certainly consent to Zoom—that was reasonable. Anyway, it wouldn't be right to subject Papa to an interview with a person he didn't know, not in his current state. So I politely declined Ginevra's request to interview Papa, and said she could talk to the rest remotely. Ginevra accepted what I offered without a fight.

A frisson of nervous energy comes over me now, worrying that perhaps Ginevra will have set this book in my hometown. Sullying or exploiting it. It's a possibility I hadn't contemplated. I thought for sure she'd throw me on a Zimbabwean safari or an expedition in the Arctic.

No. It can't be. Ginevra won't have set the book in *Michigan*. Her settings are always exotic: Istanbul, Iceland. Siberia, even. Murder in a place that oozes with intrigue, ripe with atmospheric and natural elements, the more brutal the better. Extreme heat, extreme cold. Sharp ravines to hide dead bodies. The kind of places UNESCO canvasses, appealing to armchair travelers worldwide. That's Ginevra's specialty. Employing—as the critics often marvel—characters who feel eerily real.

To call Ginevra's writing method quirky is spectacularly understating it. For each book, she uses a new real-life person as her main character. She then mines that main character for handsome reward, delving into the most minute corners of their past, using their genuine tics and traumas to craft an otherwise fictional tale. When my job crashed and burned, and Nate broke off our engagement, she offered me the gig. One hundred thousand dollars for a few months of answering questions about my life and submitting to private investigators and psychological evaluations and the like. Plus full room and board in Rome. And unexpectedly, this train trip leaving bonus.

Once the book comes out, I'll have to do press with her, too. Easy enough. I know how to operate in front of a camera, even though the shame of my derailed career as a news anchor is still fresh—a constant sour sloshing in my stomach. Anyway, I knew Ginevra from my news days. I interviewed her a few times, about her creative process, about her latest bestseller. She was one of my most high-profile gets. We got along. That's how she wound up offering me the job as main character. I never imagined I'd do something like this, but then, why not?

When I signed up as main character, I figured that I didn't have any secrets. Nothing to hide. Just some hardships. Some regrets. Who walking on this planet doesn't?

What did I mind if Ginevra sifted through my life? Talked to my family and friends? Crafted fiction from my truth?

But so much has happened since I agreed to be the main character. Now I stare uneasily at the books—saying what? Painting me how? And an even more gnawing worry: What secrets are buried in these pages? What messages lurk between the lines, or explicitly within them? Will Ginevra have revealed—

"Ginevra wanted you each to have one of her books," Gabriele says cheerfully, interrupting my spinning thoughts. "She told me it's the proudest she's ever been of a story." He distributes a thick copy to each of us. No one speaks. Nate palms his book between his hands, his face screwed in confusion.

"You all contributed, of course. Consented to interviews, agreed not to sue if Ginevra used certain elements of your likenesses, too. These are rough drafts. Ginevra's process is to write furiously as she interviews her main character. To let the story reveal itself as the main character does, too. She's still making final edits as we speak. She thought it would be fun—a bonding experience for you all to read it. She apologizes in advance, though. One of you had to die." He winks. "She does write murder mysteries, after all."

My heart is now a bass drum, battering my chest. "So you came to give us itineraries and the books?"

"Well, and . . ." Gabriele's smile strains. "Ginevra had one other request. For Rory, in particular."

"Okay?" I arch an eyebrow at him. God, this is weird. Pretending we weren't at the Spanish Steps together a couple of months ago, eating gelato, my head on his shoulder as the sun crept toward the horizon, setting aglow all the terra-cotta facades of the Piazza di Spagna.

Gabriele frowns almost apologetically. He hands me an envelope.

"It's a note from Ginevra. You can read it in your room, if you'd like. And then I'm happy to discuss any questions that come up as a result."

The envelope sizzles at my skin. It's puffy, like it contains multiple sheets of paper. How can she possibly have that much to say to me, especially after we've spent three months in each other's company? Does she finally tell me about . . . I mean, will she finally reveal the truth?

"Her intentions are good." Gabriele pins down my eyes with his. "I really think her intentions are good, Rory. That this can be the trip of a lifetime, if you allow it to be."

I nod, suddenly sapped of all life force. "I'll read it later."

"And you're joining our trip, Gabriele?" Nate asks. "Like, you'll be hanging out with us in Italy? You're not just dropping this stuff off?"

"I'm here to stay," Gabriele says pleasantly. "With my daughter, in fact." He motions across the room to a nine-year-old girl with round pink eyeglasses, legs primly crossed, sipping from a glass bottle of Fanta.

Chiara. I never met her, of course, only saw her in passing. Gabriele wouldn't introduce us unless it was serious. But I heard lots about her— how brilliant she is, how precocious. In the accelerated path for genius kids. How, because she's so smart, acts almost like an adult, she's had trouble making friends.

"Ginevra thought it would be fun for me to have my daughter here, for the trip. She's generous like that. You won't even notice us. I'll be in the background, making sure everything runs smoothly."

"She's really a puppeteer, isn't she?" Nate shakes his head. "Ginevra *Ex*. What is that name even? Was she born with that last name? *Ex*. So strange. Gathering us all here . . ."

Gabriele frowns. "I wouldn't call her a *puppeteer*."

"Really?" Nate glances around at us to galvanize support. "Am I really wrong? And now, giving us these crazy books!" He waves it in his hand, something flashing in his eyes that I can't decipher. "What are we supposed to do, decode them? Figure out what's truth and what's fiction? Is this all part of a diabolical plan, writing about us and then throwing us all into her train blender of crazy?"

Nate's tirade settles like cement in my stomach. He's being sarcastic, but his rant strikes a chord. What *is* Ginevra's plan? Could she actually have something diabolical up her sleeve?

"You're wrong." Gabriele shakes his head. "You're totally wr—"

"Is he, though?" I ask, a realization suddenly dawning on me. "Ginevra's last book totally bombed. I overheard her with her publicist, with the publisher. Readers thought the last main character was dim-witted, a dud. They said Ginevra's losing her magic touch. She's worried. *They're* worried, her whole team. There's a lot riding on this new book. Is having us all here—with the books—some kind of publicity stunt?"

"No!" Gabriele says. "Really, you're off here. Truly, Ginevra has pure intentions. She—"

"She's a puppeteer," Nate says again. "Pure intentions or not. And I understand why you may not share my view, Gabriele. Because if she's the puppeteer, then I guess that makes you her puppet."

"Nate." Now I frown. "Don't be rude. Gabriele's not trying—"

"No," interrupts Max. "Gabriele's not the author's puppet, Nate. He's almost irrelevant to the equation."

Signature Max tact.

Max waves a hand at Gabriele. "No offense, man. I'm just trying to say, *we're* Ginevra's puppets."

I absorb that. Are we Ginevra's puppets? Is that what I've been the past few months, after all? I take in this weird, weird trip. My life shattering and now inexplicably sitting before me again, all in shards. With a bottle of glue placed in my hands—perhaps the means to cobble parts of it back together, if I want.

Do I want? I have zero freaking clue. Anyway, I can't even contemplate that yet, not until I can get into my cabin, alone, and read the letter and the book. The envelope is hot on my lap; the book nudges almost portentously against my thigh. All of my thoughts are a thicket in my brain, obfuscating me from any truth.

Now Max leans back on the sofa, his lips quirking in a smile. "You know what, guys? Let's give Gabriele a break. So the author wants to pay for us all to enjoy Italy? Well then, let's enjoy Italy. It's been ages since I've had a vacation. I had to move a shit ton around to even get here on such short notice, and Caro and Nate did, too. Besides, when do we ever get a vacation, let alone together? And I for one am not complaining about this setup your author arranged, Ror."

Max raises his glass. "If we're gonna be puppets, guys, then I say let's drink to being well-fed, well-liquored-up ones!"

CHAPTER FIVE

Max

Rory is sitting across from me in the dining car, riveted to her celeriac-artichoke stuffed crepe. Her eyes have barely grazed mine. She's obviously mad at me, and I have zero clue why. The not knowing . . . the excruciating not knowing . . .

She *knows* it is excruciating for me, and yet she cuts her crepe with surgical precision, deliberately not telling me what I've possibly done wrong. Fork into mouth with a slug's speed. Chewing, fucking chewing . . .

I twine my fingers into the linen napkin on my lap, trying to keep my own anger at bay, trying, trying. "Why are you mad at me?" I finally ask.

Okay, maybe I bark it.

The clatter of cutlery, din of conversation, waiters doing their deliberate circles and deliveries and inspections of tablecloths and the clarity of glassware—all of it immediately halts.

"*Max.*" Caro presses her fingers to her temples, clearly embarrassed by my minor outburst. That's Caro—proper to a tee. Formal. One of the many things I love about her—Caro's Miss Manners to the general Aronov philosophy of better messy than perfect.

"Sorry, sorry! *Scusi!*" I smile at the patrons to my right, an elderly couple dabbing their napkins to their mouths, eyes shooting beams of judgment.

"Ror, you know you're driving me insane."

"I don't mean to drive you insane." Her calm, sure tone somehow intensifies my feelings of insanity. "We'll talk later. When I'm ready. In private. Okay? Please chill out."

"So you *are* mad at me. Why? What did I do? What do you *think* that I did?"

She says nothing. Keeps chewing in her irritating, silent way.

I try again. "Why have you been ignoring me? Papa would hate that you were giving me the silent treatment."

Rory scowls. "Don't bring Papa into this. He's already in it, anyhow."

She's mad at Papa, too? How could she possibly be? He has Alzheimer's—impossible to be angry at him or, at least, for him to deserve, or feel, her anger. "I don't know what that means."

She nods, doesn't elaborate. "Anyway, *you're* the ones who surprised me on this train."

"No, that's your author. Your *author* is the one who surprised you."

"My author," she says pointedly, "is nowhere in sight."

At that we dovetail into quiet.

"You're different, Ror." I shake my head. "There's something different about you."

To my surprise, she doesn't get insulted. Doesn't say *I'm just the same person I always was, and I'm gonna be top of my game again as a news anchor, you'll see.* "I do feel pretty Zen" is all she says calmly.

"Zen?" I don't think the word has ever once come out of my sister's mouth. It's the opposite of the way we were raised: Scorch earth with your passions. Make a mark. Work hard. Give it your absolute all. Don't give up. Don't ever give up.

"Yes." Her eyes practically shimmer with earnestness. "Zen. Like I can breathe again."

"You couldn't breathe before?"

"No, I couldn't breathe, not really, and I never stopped to watch the leaves. . . ."

"The leaves?" I'm not following.

"The leaves?" Caroline begins to laugh. She claps her hand over her mouth. "Sorry, Ror." Still, her laugh increases in intensity.

I notice, though, that Nate has arched an eyebrow at my sister's Zen leaves thing, too.

"The *leaves*." As ever, Rory's eyes resemble the murky green, glittery surface of the lake we grew up on. "You know? Leaves blowing in the wind. I never had time to watch them."

"Watch what?" Nate shakes his head, fork hovering over his Magret duck with red cabbage puree. "Sorry, I'm not following, Ror. What's there to watch?"

Rory's eyes widen. "Oh, so much. You could spend your whole life watching the leaves blow in the wind, and you wouldn't have even seen a thing."

"Really?" I try to sound interested and supportive as I simultaneously nudge Caroline's leg under the table.

"Yep. Try it. You'll never feel as happy as when you're watching leaves in the wind. Give it five minutes, and your fingertips get a little hot. Ten minutes, and your whole body feels tingly. It's your soul. You feel it, I swear, like *alive* inside you. Try it, Maxie."

Maxie. Thank God, she can't hate me, if she's still calling me Maxie.

"Mmm, I'll be sure to." I swig from my vodka glass.

"She's lost it, bro," I whisper to Nate when Rory's not looking.

Nate doesn't smile; his shoulders budge up almost apologetically. Sheesh. I know he wants my sister back, but he's gotta admit: She's lost it. We should have intervened sooner. Good we've come here when we did. We need to get Rory back on track. Have her sending out résumés again. If she doesn't want to go back to LA, she doesn't have to. Maybe Detroit, an easier, kinder market, where she'll be close to me and Caro, and Papa. If she needs some money to get started, I'll lend it to her. Hell, I can just give it to her. I'm happy to give it to her.

"So," says Nate.

"So," echoes Caro. Then she gets out her phone to snap photos. "I should have remembered before we started eating."

"I have a feeling picturesque things won't be hard to come by on this trip." Rory smiles.

Caro sighs. "I know, more like I'm trying to keep up with the Gram."

"Yeah?" Rory frowns. "Are you still trying to grow? Or is there less . . . I mean, do you feel like there's less pressure now, with your audience and stuff?"

I wince, because I know clearly what my sister's trying to say, and I'm sure Caro will, too. Does it matter less that Caro has only six thousand followers now that she has a job? A wonderful job, at my company. Still, she's been trying to build her platform for over a decade.

"It doesn't matter less. No. I still want . . . I guess I don't know what I want *exactly*. But I see what you're saying. In a way, working with Max . . ." Caro's eyes flit over at me. "Yeah, sure. It takes some of the pressure off. I just—I like posting my outfits and trips. However shallow that sounds."

"It doesn't sound shallow! You're amazing at it." Rory looks fondly at her.

"You are. Hippoheal is lucky to have you now, too." And I wholeheartedly mean it. I couldn't do it without Caro—business or life. My heart does the thing it always does, pitters faster as I watch her, so unassumingly beautiful in the soft light from the tulip-shaped chandeliers.

"Yeah." Caro smiles, but it's clear it's an effort. "I mean, maybe I should fully throw in the towel with the influencer thing. I dunno. Gen Z, man. They're just different. I'm like a dinosaur when I try to TikTok. My millennial pause is practically an hour long."

"Your *what?*" I ask. Sometimes, when Caro talks, I surreptitiously consult Urban Dictionary.

"Never mind." She waves a hand. "My skinny jeans are out. I look more Elderly Fisherman in a bucket hat than Hailey Bieber cool. Maybe it's getting time to admit this whole influencer thing didn't really pan out."

"No," Rory says, more fervently than I expect. "No way. You can't look at it as failing. You have to look at it as you're in the middle of succeeding."

"Did you come up with that?" I ask, immediately resolving to use it at an inspirational team meeting.

"I heard it somewhere, I think."

Caro laughs dryly. "Thanks for the reframe." But she and Rory lean into each other. I feel a warm glow pass over me. This is the stuff. Being with the three of them. The closest people I have in the world, other than Papa. I'm so glad we all shuffled things around, to come. We needed this. And the trip is ripe with potential—Nate and Rory back together.

Maybe things will finally spark with me and Caro, too.

"So, Ror." Nate smiles. "Want all the dirt you've missed?"

Rory doesn't smile, and I can tell it's too soon for her thaw, at least toward Nate. "Sure," she says without enthusiasm.

Nate's smile fades a twinge, but gotta give him credit, he plows on. "Well, Maximillions here"—Nate points to me and winks—"*Maximillions is all, like, It's been forever since I was on a vacation.* Ror, wanna know what your brother did a few weeks ago?"

I blush. "It was actually two months ago."

"No, what?" Rory sounds about as interested as if Nate had mentioned he switched his toothpaste brand.

"Went yachting with Jay-Z."

"I didn't go yachting with Jay-Z," I correct Nate, unable to excise the note of pride from my voice. "I did, *however*, fly out to Saint-Tropez for five days to meet with one of our investors. Jay-Z, on his yacht, true. But it *has* been years since I've been on an actual vaca—"

"Did you get the money?" Rory asks.

"He got a shit ton of money," Caro says quietly.

"I did. *We* did, I mean. The company."

"Wow. Congratulations," my sister says, but I notice her smile is weary, doesn't travel to her eyes. "And what about the vaccine? Is it getting close to—"

"Closer," Caro says before I can answer. "But we're still a bunch of steps from full approval. After phase two b we'll move to phase three, and then still—"

"But soon," I interrupt. "I'm very optimistic. The new trials are going well."

"And Papa . . . what about . . . ? I mean, will he . . . ?"

It's the pivotal question after all, isn't it? The question that is never, ever, not assaulting my mind. Will the vaccine work on Papa? Will he be able to get it in time? See, Papa has a variant of Alzheimer's that is more resistant to common treatments. Sure, he takes donepezil and memantine, and does weekly off-label transcranial magnetic stimulation treatments, but has any of it slowed his deterioration? Only slightly.

Years ago, Papa was enrolled in trials for a different Alzheimer's vaccine, while I was still entrenched in the research that enabled ours. So as I sped along as fast as humanly possible, researching and formulating, assembling a team, Papa was eligible for a now-defunct vaccine. Mine is somewhat similar; both target the amyloid protein that denatures with age and catalyzes the disease. Both could be used to prevent the onset of the disease, but most critically to cure it: to reverse memory loss and plaque formations once already formed. But the vaccine Papa received was later terminated due to issues with its safety profile. Papa was one of the nearly six percent of participants enrolled in the trials to develop meningoencephalitis—an inflammation of the membrane surrounding the brain.

He could have died. In fact, he nearly did.

Which is why his doctors have all uniformly said he is ineligible for any further vaccine trials. Once our vaccine is approved by the FDA, however, it's a different story. . . .

So time is of the essence, quite literally.

"We hope," I finally say. "We hope Papa will get it in time. That's all I've been working toward." *Practically my entire adult life*, I nearly add.

"I know." Rory softens, and it's almost like the whole thing between us, that I don't understand, disappears. "How is he?"

I shrug. "The same, I guess. More or less."

"But . . . ?"

I know what she wants to know. The little things. That he can't shave anymore. Now I do it for him. The aides are there around the clock, and his saintly nurse, Suzette, but I prefer to take care of the little dignities I can, when I visit. Which is nearly every day. Does my sister really want to know that Papa can dovetail into incoherent babbling, talking about things that make zero sense. That he has a difficult time walking on his own now. That he often stops speaking midstream, his words evaporating, and then switches into increasingly agitated Russian, which is the primary language he learned in school, even though he lived in Ukraine. But I can't understand him, because he never taught us Russian—after he immigrated to America, all he wanted to do was be an American.

Does Rory really want to know that recently Papa didn't recognize me? That he asked Suzette if I was her son.

"He's getting worse. Is that what you really want to hear?"

"He'll still know you," Caro puts in, shooting me a frown. "Ror, it's not exactly as bad as your brother makes it sound. A lot of times when I visit, he still bursts out with *Caroline!* in his thick accent. Never have I felt like anyone was as excited to see me in my whole life as Ansel Aronov. And his hugs. He still gives you the tightest, biggest, longest hug."

She smiles, a sad smile, though. Sometimes I forget that Papa is the only father Caro ever really had. She sees him more than Rory these days, although I have to give Rory credit—she was diligent about visiting from LA, once every six weeks like clockwork. It's only since coming to Italy that she hasn't seen Papa, but I know from Suzette that Rory calls frequently.

Rory grimaces. "After this trip, I'm gonna go to Michigan and see him."

"I know he'd like that," I say. "But, Ror, he wants you to live your life. He's always wanted us to live our lives."

"Easier for you to say. You get to see him all the time."

I shrug. "We all make our choices, I guess."

"I wish I could be at peace with mine," Rory whispers.

"Maybe you'll move to Michigan."

"Hell, no. Sorry, guys. Sorry. But *no*."

"Got it. So that would be a no, then." I try to say it lightly, but I feel something stiffen in my chest. "Michigan has always been like a shoe that's too tight on you," I say, mimicking a phrase she's said several times. My tone carries a sarcastic scorch that I feel powerless to squelch.

I could have left Michigan after college, too—the mass exodus to Chicago, to New York City, to LA. But Papa was already having memory issues when I was in grad school. I decided to stay. Switch my research to Alzheimer's. Put down roots in Detroit. To believe in the city's renaissance—ultimately, with my company, to participate pivotally in it. But Rory's dreams took her across the country, to the bigger news stations in LA. Justifiably for her career, but maybe she also wanted to escape. Not take a front-row seat at Papa's decline.

I get it, and sometimes I resent it. But I'm always happy I stayed. Especially because now, I'm on the cusp of saving Papa. If our vaccine works—it works!—it could reverse his disease to a degree. Revert him to a sixty-five-year-old who can function in society. Even if it doesn't expunge the Alzheimer's completely, and we get more lucid windows . . . more lucid moments . . . everything I've devoted, everything I've sacrificed, will have been worth it.

"So what's on tap for tomorrow, guys?" Nate asks.

"Yeah, let's check out this exalted itinerary." I run my eyes over the stapled packet Gabriele distributed. "Hiking Cinque Terre. Followed by lunch in Vernazza and seaside relaxation in Monterosso."

"I've always wanted to go to Cinque Terre," Rory says. "Wander the five towns. It's supposed to be one of the most stunning places on earth."

This is my very first time in Italy. We didn't travel much as kids, certainly not across the globe, and my adulthood has involved totally bananas work hours, with very few days off. "It sounds amazing, but it's all Greek to me."

"You mean, it's all *Italian*." Caro twists her Cartier panther ring around her finger. It's new, I know. More than twenty thousand dollars. I looked up the cost. The finest gold, the panther studded with emeralds.

"*Sì, signorina*," I say.

Caro doesn't smile.

God, we got old and uptight, all of us.

Suddenly Rory rises and says, "Guys," in a way that I suddenly know, *know*, is an attempt to leave. It's an indisputable truth that endings aren't a collective decision. The first person to go begins the unraveling.

"Not yet. Don't leave yet," I hear myself plead, and hate myself for it, for needing my sister this much, for being this rocked by her moods and indignances. "We have to talk first! Seriously, enough is enough!" My chest flames with anger. This isn't fair of Rory. This isn't fair at all!

"Ror, we need to talk, too," says Nate. "Please."

"Ror . . . no," Caro says, quietly pleading. "Don't leave yet."

Rory's eyes dart around at each of us. "I . . ." All of a sudden there's a lurch, and Rory falters for a step, then catches herself.

We're moving. We're on our way.

Applause breaks out in the dining carriage as the train rolls forward. Even the man with the ridiculous pom-pom beret is raising his glass for a toast, if not overtly smiling. He clinks it against his neighbor's proffered glass, the husband from the Italian couple in the bar car with us earlier. Then the husband inches back over to his wife, slides his meaty hand down her thigh. They make an alluring, handsome pair, and I realize now they are joined by the two preteen kids across, with lush hair and smart attire, who win the award of being the first kids I've seen in ages whose faces aren't buried in their smartphones. I feel myself arch toward this picture-perfect family, like I have my entire life toward people who seem to epitomize the ideal. Old habits, and all. When you were a nerd, decidedly uncool, it's difficult to excise that instinctive reaction. No matter that I've become a respected biotech CEO, you are always, in some part, that little kid version of yourself.

Suddenly there's champagne popping, and the intoxicating communal cheer ratchets up in volume. My gaze flitters to Rory. She gives me a small smile, and I feel a surge in my chest, like a breeze, clearing up all the cobwebs. Rory will stay for champagne, at least. I realize how anxious I've been, how everything's been tied in the thorniest knots, and here, with the people I love most in the world besides Papa, I can finally relax. Rory will finally tell me why she is angry, and I will apologize, for whatever it is—no need to save face. Relief is on the horizon. I can finally see blue sky from the tops of the trees, and gosh, it's spectacular.

It's stressful running a company with such a critical lifesaving mission, stressful running a company that is worth eight figures and soaring, no matter the lack of sympathy that statement can arouse. Still, I'm about to express it, not bemoaning the fruits of my success but rather something cheesy about the meaning of life and what really matters, and everyone will groan but agree.

But then instead, right as my mouth has pitched open, Rory shoves in her chair. "Guys, I need to . . . I'm so tired. It's been a long day. I'm sorry. I'll see you tomorrow. We'll start fresh, okay?"

It's a bucket of ice water sloshed on my head, and I'm suddenly very cold as my sister gathers up her purse and her early copy of Ginevra Ex's book and rushes off, leaving all of us staring listlessly after her. Eventually we resume eating and talking with the countryside whizzing by in the waning sun—wheat fields, sheep, and churches sprouting unexpectedly around corners. We are on a trip of a lifetime, after all, so no use letting Rory sour our night, even if by leaving, she intractably does. It was only the three of us last night, too, in Monaco, dining at the casino. Gambling. Having ostensible fun. But still, the fact of it builds in my throat, simmers below the surface: It is Rory who made us a foursome. She's the glue, and now our evening—our trip—is on pause. And we're just the three idiots waiting for her to deign to press Play again.

My sister, ladies and gentlemen—always, *always*, the star of the show.

CHAPTER SIX

Rory

God, I had to leave. I couldn't breathe with them all there, needing things from me.

With reassurances to Marco—yes, everything is so beyond fine, I swear, grand smile—I'm finally alone, sprawled out on my silk cocoon of a bed. Beside me is the mysterious letter from Ginevra that Gabriele gave me, and the book. Jesus, the book.

My heart squeezes as I imagine what the book contains. No, the letter first. Like ripping off a bandage, I think. I slide my finger under the flap and tear, then pull out several sheets of paper. The top is simple notepaper with neat edges. I surmise it's from one of those yellow legal pads Ginevra was always writing on, signing her name over and over, the same beautiful, loopy way, up and down the margins, the way some might doodle hearts or 3D shapes. She might have all the money and a grand apartment by the Spanish Steps, but she is simple, unpretentious. Not the monogrammed stationery type.

I peek below the notepaper to the other sheets—bank statements? Bizarre. I turn back to the notepaper and take in the haphazard scrawl.

Rory,

By now, you've seen whom I've assembled on the train. Forgive me for springing them on you, but I was afraid you might not agree to go if I told you what I'd planned. Please trust me, Rory. Truly, I only want to give you the most magical trip. You, Max, Caro, and Nate. Each of you is here for a very specific reason.

I know you are angry at Max, for what you discovered inadvertently from me. He was a child, though, Rory. Only four when you were adopted. He loves you so much, however hurt you are. Trust me, I too have a sibling. A sister. I spoke to Max, you know, in interviews for this book. It is quite clear to me that Max loves you—would die for you—just like my sister would for me, and I for her. Siblings are the most powerful of relationships, the longest of our lives. Try to enjoy this trip with Max, and ultimately try to make amends.

Perhaps you are most surprised that I invited Nate. Please don't be angry with me for doing it. Trust I had good reasons. He told me quite clearly that he is still in love with you. That breaking up with you was the biggest mistake of his life. Rory, I try to stay out of the lives of my main characters, but in your case, I have felt the impetus to intrude. I have seen in my life love stories interrupted. People destined for each other, whose paths run apart, and each wanders off with righteous indignation into their own eternal unhappiness. I don't want that for you. I want you to have the love of your life. People make mistakes. People get scared and curl up like snails. Don't let your pride get in the way of your love story. I implore you, Rory. Come back out of your shell and give Nate another chance.

Now, Caroline. She is your best friend. But as you are aware, I dive deep into the life of my main character. I find out everything. Oftentimes I discover things that people don't want me to know. You see what I'm getting at, no? I found out something about Caroline you may not want to know. But you must.

Caroline is embezzling from your brother's company.

I read that last line again, then a third time, my heart in my throat. What? No fucking way. Caro? She would never. I would put my life assuredly in her hands. I've known her since I was nine.

The letter skates out my hand onto the bed. For a while I stare out the window into the dark, with a picture of Caro at dinner filling my head: her aristocratic profile, her pale skin with hardly a freckle, as she moved her ring round and round on her finger. It's new: a Cartier panther ring.

They're wildly expensive; I know this because I, too, have champagne taste—but not the champagne salary to afford one.

Well, Caro can afford a Cartier panther ring, I suppose, with her salary from Hippoheal.

I mean, can she?

Caroline is embezzling from your brother's company.

I blink, shake my head. Impossible. Utterly impossible. Max is family to Caro. Plus, he's been in love with her since we were kids. And she loves him, too. She would never do this to him.

In fact, I was thrilled for Caro that Max offered her the opportunity to work at his company. Caro floundered after college, trying to indulge in her love of fashion and travel as a career, working as a stylist at Nordstrom, with a fledgling blog and Instagram account on the side. She used to pack up a carry-on with her latest purchases, then jet to offbeat places, documenting outfits and pyramids and beachscapes on Instagram—Guatemala, Bhutan, Lebanon. I was always in awe of her verve, her adventurousness, maybe her recklessness, too. She once hitchhiked across Lebanon just to reach this obscure Roman temple. I thought her photographs were inspiring and entertaining, but her account never really took off. And she always had money problems, but they never seemed to faze her. Whereas for me, security, having enough, has been my foremost guiding principle.

We both come from families with precarious finances, but where Caro is more trusting that things will work out, I always feel like the bottom is always about to drop out from beneath me. Indeed, it did.

After my stint for Ginevra, I have no more money coming through, and I feel the familiar pinging sensation in my chest that, while I'm fine just now, there's no more income on the horizon. That soon in the future I may not be, fundamentally, okay. Caro has never seemed to share the same fears, opting to glide close to her zero point, even accrue debt, in a way that has often seemed to me irresponsibly nonchalant. Once, I lent her two thousand dollars, and it took her several years to repay it. I thought about that loan every day, irrationally wondering if she'd abscond with the money, even though I had enough then, and I knew she was good for it. Eventually she did come through. And maybe it's unfair to revisit those times, because Caro is infinitely more grounded now, building something with Hippoheal that could finally have roots. Gone are the days of her last-minute travels. Now she's the high-flying businesswoman, in a chic pink linen suit and white cat-eye sunglasses, on her international business trip, with the Burj Khalifa as the backdrop. And she's finally making bank, more money than I suspect she has ever raked in.

She would never embezzle from Max, from anyone. She would *never*. And besides, does Caro even know *how* to embezzle? I mean, I'd have zero clue. It sounds inordinately complicated, like Madoff and that whole crypto FTX catastrophe. Caro's smart, for sure, but embezzling? It's so farfetched. . . .

Reluctantly, I force myself to retrieve the letter and keep reading.

You won't want to believe it, but I'm including the proof. Bank statements. Transfers—huge transfers—from Hippoheal that are not part of Caroline's compensation or bonus structure. Transfers shuttled through intermediary shells. Gabriele has informed me that it's quite a complicated crime. Others in the company may be involved. Be careful, Rory. I didn't pass this on to the authorities because I wanted you to know of it first. I wanted you to be the last word on how to handle it. You understand what you must do, though, right? You need to tell Max. There must be a way of remedying things without further damage—to get Caroline to see the wrong in what she is doing. To admit to the full scheme, repay the funds. To get Hippoheal back on track, to ensure its important mission is unobstructed. I thought it most certain that you would want to be the one to help fix things.

I'm sorry to lump it all together in this letter—the good with the bad. Truly, I apologize for springing everyone on you. I wouldn't have done so if I didn't strongly believe that gathering them all here was in your best interests. Despite the situation with Caroline, I feel certain you can have a wonderful, fruitful trip, especially after you patch things up with Max and Nate. Three days of luxuries lie ahead, three days of anything you wish coming true. Truly, whatever it is that you desire, tell Gabriele. He will make it happen.

And please, Rory dear, do not worry about your career. You are an incredible interviewer and a talented news anchor. I have the connections to get you another job—an even better one. We will speak after the trip. Indeed, I have already put things in motion. So please, don't worry one bit about your future livelihood, about all the hard work you have put in to achieve your dreams.

They will certainly, no doubt, come true. If you don't know it already, I am firmly—eternally—in your corner.

I do have one last request which I hope you will indulge. In three days, when the Orient Express arrives in Positano, I ask that you go to Le Sirenuse. It is the best hotel in town. You have a reservation at the restaurant there at one in the afternoon. Please bring the others. I can't tell you whom you are set to meet there, only that it is a surprise worth showing up for.

Things may seem confusing. You might question my motives. I promise you, at Le Sirenuse all will become clear.

I realize everything I am asking of you and telling you is substantial. You may be irritated with me. You may be more than irritated. But, please, if you can, think of me like your fairy godmother. You've had some tough breaks this year. Your career. Your relationship. Your father's illness. This trip can resolve everything capable of resolution. I hope that you will take my advice and allow it to do so.

With fond regards,
Ginevra Ex

When I finish the letter, I feel the dizziness of being spun around and around on one of those teacup rides at a fair, unsure exactly where I've landed when it's stopped.

I'm on the crazy caboose. That's what this is. This whole wonky train trip, and now Caroline embezzling from Max's company? How is that even possible?

I riffle through the bank statements that accompanied Ginevra's letter, my mind churning. Okay, so it's Caroline's account at UBS, and on the first of every month . . . going back June . . . May . . . April . . . shit. Ginevra's right. For almost a year, one hundred thousand dollars has been deposited into Caroline's account, like clockwork, on the first of each month. I trace through the papers, showing LLCs and offshore accounts, entirely disbelieving. If Caroline were the CFO, or CMO, or even the director of HR, this could possibly be in the realm of plausible for monthly compensation. But she's not—she's on the sales team, that's it. Rising up the ranks, sure; Max always says she's doing a stellar job. But I see there are other deposits into her account, direct, not routed from anywhere strange, for $12,666 a month, which must be her monthly salary after taxes. I do mental mathematics and decide that $12,666 per month on its own is quite generous, in my mind, for a woman who until a couple of years ago was barely scraping by, who had no formal sales skills.

I feel something acrid rise up in my throat. If this is true, how could Caro do it to Max? To his company? To Papa? To *me*?

Lately, I've wondered if Caro and Max would finally find their way toward each other. My brother's infatuation with her has been a foundational fact since the moment I brought her home. Max has always adored Caro, full stop, even trailed around us, sitting on my bed, long legs dangling impatiently, just to hang out with us when we'd give each other makeovers. He simply liked being around Caroline's energy. Well, most people do. Caro's enthralling—she could sell dust to a shepherd in the Sahara. Somehow she flashes her smile; focuses her still, shrewd attention on you, and everything she describes sounds immensely appealing, everything she offers sounds legitimate.

Maybe it's the prospect, however slim, that she can turn all your shit into her clear brand of gold.

Max and Caro hooked up when Caro and I were in college and Max in grad school, and the hookup was good, from what I understand from Caro (although, *ew*). And it seemed to me in the last couple of years that Caro was increasingly opening to the idea of a relationship with Max. But then when I lightheartedly tossed out the question mark of her and Max a couple of months ago, she was in a different mindset altogether—they would never, *ever* be. It was like overnight she threw up a brick wall, both between her and Max but also weirdly between her and me. Like the prospect of her and Max was a ridiculous notion that she'd never truly considered.

But she had truly considered it. I know she had.

Is this why she gave up on her and Max? She didn't want him to question her latest indulgences? She would find it easier to embezzle from my brother if there were no romantic entanglements between them?

I roll over on my side as the contents of the letter reverberate through my brain, knocking against my skull. It hurts—it all hurts, and I don't understand any of it. At some point, there's a rap at my door, and I hear, "Ror? Are you still up? It's just me."

Just her. My supposed best friend.

The closest thing I have—have ever had—to a sister.

I close my eyes and feign sleep, as if Caro can see through the peep-hole, and eventually, when I hear footsteps retreating into the distance, I feel my breathing shakily resume.

I shift onto my stomach and prop myself up on my elbows, staring out the window, at a glistening pool that has now eclipsed the trees. My eyes focus, and I realize it's not a pool, it's inky sea. We're crossing south toward Cinque Terre, a place I've long had on my vision board. Somewhere I always dreamed of going, when I had the elusive time and money. I should sleep so I can enjoy it tomorrow.

Try to enjoy this once-in-a-lifetime trip.

But I'm not tired. I'm *so* not tired. I need a distraction. Something for my brain to do, other than ruminate on Caro stealing from my brother, and Nate potentially wanting me back, and Max champing at the bit to know why I'm mad at him—to ruminate on the reason *why* I am mad at him.

I suppose I could watch TV. I could— My ankle nudges against a hard edge. Oh. Ginevra's book.

The Cabin on the Lake.

I could suck it up and read the book about me. See what Ginevra's created out of my life and the lives of those closest to me. I recall Max, Caro, and Nate on the train, when Gabriele gave us the books. They all looked sort of . . . anxious, didn't they? I wonder why.

Well, buckle up, Rory. You can't avoid this. I take a deep breath and crack open the book.

CHAPTER SEVEN

Rory

The clock glows 2:24 when I finally toss the book aside and switch off the bedside lamp. I'm still in my dress but too exhausted to change into pajamas, to wash my face, any of it. Instead I slip under the cool, silky covers, everything in a whirl.

Shocking to see myself in ink. On a page. Reduced to a limited number of words that are supposed to convey who I am, what I care about. *Whom* I care about.

I read it fast—skimmed a lot, especially the second half, as exhaustion began to descend, but I certainly got the gist. In some ways, Ginevra was kind—to me, at least. My alter ego, Laci Starling (leaving the porn-star name aside for now), is bighearted, endearing. As a child, she's putting on performances, commandeering her older brother to participate in her shows. He, Benedict Starling, is shyer. Brilliant, always embroiled in a science project, bullied by the neighborhood kids. They plucked off his eyeglasses and shoved him into water fountains. They started a rumor that he'd been born with both a vagina and a penis and had to undergo reconstructive surgery. They drew penis signs all over his locker in permanent marker, over which they wrote in huge script *Benedick*.

Maxie'sTinyOne—the clear real-life inspiration.

In the book, Laci goes to school and locates the bullies, four years older than her, and tells them that if they ever fuck with her brother again, they will have to fuck with her. And to drive the threat home, she pulls out a butcher knife and holds it menacingly an inch from the head bully's cheek.

The bully says, "I'll tell the principal."

And Laci just replaces the knife in the pocket of her overalls, so it's no longer visible, and says, "Who will believe you? I'm only a puny fourth grader."

Crazy to think now that I was that steely fourth grader, defending Max's honor. Actually threatening kids so much older with a knife.

I wonder how I got to be so brave. I suspect it was that we were a unit, the three of us: Max, Papa, and me. Max wasn't just my brother but like an extension of myself, my arm, my leg. He was always needy, so sensitive. And I was stronger, braver. That's what Papa told me, like he was confiding a secret, and I wanted to live up to it, to make sure he'd never retract those words. The one time Max confided in Papa a snippet of how the kids were bullying him, and that the principal wasn't cracking down, Papa lost it. He told us this story about how when he was a kid, ten or eleven, a gang of kids on horses came to attack him with iron bars, screaming at him that he was a dirty Jew. Papa told us how he made a whip out of rabbit skin; how he kept a blade in his bag to defend himself. I remember Max staring at the peeling yellow wallpaper in the kitchen, his body rigid, saying that those Soviet Union–type defenses probably wouldn't go over well at Ely Middle School.

And I remember how Papa half smiled and said, "No, probably not. We'll solve this." But he didn't say how. Not a single idea. It struck me then that Papa was resigned, a different Papa than the one he described in his youth. When had he given up the fight? When had he realized he couldn't take on the world? When his mother died? When our mother did? Or maybe when he realized the life he'd fought for was a quiet one, without riches, without even security? Parenting two small children, alone?

I think I understood then that Papa wasn't going to be able to fix things for Max. A plan formed in my head. And, indeed, those kids had never fucked with Max again. At least not as blatantly as with Maxie'sTinyOne, although they still bullied him in all the soft but pointed ways I was incapable of preventing: picking him last for any team, making him the butt of all their inside jokes.

Anyway, I never told Max or Papa what I'd done.

Now, when Max reads *The Cabin on the Lake,* he'll know. I wonder if Max thought it was Papa who'd protected him. Who'd gotten rid of the bullies. No way did he think it was me—his scrawny little sister.

Max always underestimated me.

The book percolates through my mind. The descriptions of Michigan, like they were pulled from my memories, which I suppose they were. But still, Ginevra described the summer morning dew like she'd dug it out of my soul.

I'm still processing all the characters, figuring out who's who. Most resemblances are obvious. There's Misha, the brilliant Soviet immigrant dad with Alzheimer's, who worked long hours as the chef at the local Russian diner, who aspired to greatness, to being a famous violinist, but never quite made it like he hoped. Laci: the actress who returns from LA to the ashes of her old life in Michigan after a scandal torpedoes her career. Her arrival back in Detroit sets off a series of events that leads to a body plunging face down into an icy lake. That's the opening image of the novel, and the second chapter flashes back a few months prior. The prodigal daughter, Laci, fresh off the plane, running into her old child-hood love, Eddie (Nate), at the Russian diner, and reuniting with the brother who has catapulted from a bullied kid into the CEO darling of the biotech world, plastered on the cover of every major magazine. And then there's the former best friend, Candace, who wants what Laci has. Every last thing.

Caro, obviously. And she got a bit of a smear job. Although I can see how the embezzling allegations might have colored Ginevra's creativity.

In the end, Candace holds Laci captive in her childhood home in a wintry storm. *Fresh drifts smothered branches and the whole world spun into a snow globe, with Laci in its center. One good shake, and it would all be over. No one would miss Laci. No one would find her. The ice consumes.*

Ultimately, Candance forces Laci to walk down to the lake, down the dock, like in a pirate movie, threatening to chop, chop, chop Laci into timber with an axe. A clear allusion to my childhood game with Papa—warped. It's early in the winter; the lake isn't yet thickly frozen. But Benedict figures out the plan and there's a struggle atop the dock. In the end, he rescues his sister by plunging the axe into Candace, whereupon she falls face-first into the lake. Then the fragile lake cracks and the icy water engulfs her.

And the villain is, ultimately, the murdered.

Candace. Caro. Whatever.

There's a lot I'm thinking about now, in the dark, in the train lurching along. So many tidbits for my mind to chew on, to decipher what is moldy truth and what is truth spun off into something different, far enough removed from the kernels I provided so as not to nudge against an old pain point or a treasured memory. The line between truth and fiction seems flimsy and precarious, like walking on a tightrope, with easy slips into the abyss.

Truth: Caro is extravagant; she likes rare, beautiful things.

Truth: Papa is the most optimistic person ever, the most grateful—probably put down to the hardships and traumas he overcame in his youth. When we were kids, he'd spend eons extolling the brilliance of the sunrise, admiring the maple tree out back as its leaves transitioned through the spectrum of crisp to faded orange. Anytime someone asked Papa how he was doing, he'd declare, "Near perfect!" I once asked him why he always used *near* as a modifier, and he smiled and said because it was good to leave yourself a little gap to reach for.

Truth: Nate has an older brother with Down syndrome.

Truth: Nate isn't very good with illness or failures or being unhappy—even being around unhappy people. That's not to say Nate can't spearhead the fight and assuage the troops and give rousing speeches; he can—anything in the aim of a win. But in the end, if things don't successfully resolve, all of that exertion will have consumed the last of Nate's energy reservoirs. In the novel, Eddie broke up with Laci after he bombed the law school entrance exams. Although that's not a truth—Nate went the international diplomacy route and has aced anything he ever attempted—it does mirror the way Nate broke up with me, in the doldrums of a professional failure, when I was down in the dumps, too.

Truth: When I threw a party in high school and discovered Papa was coming home early, Max declared it Operation Kazuka and helped me gather up the hundreds of red Solo cups and other party detritus so that Papa wouldn't find out. I don't even remember telling Ginevra that story, and I don't think Max would have—we pinkie swore on keeping the terminology secret forever. Anyhow, the full story didn't make it in, just the resulting phrase. Operation Kazuka, what we said to each other anytime we needed to run a little cover-up. Interesting how Ginevra twisted our reality, made it suit her ends. . . .

Truth: Both Max and Papa can go from zero to one-eighty in anger. Sometimes the strangest things provoke them—Papa once lost it when a customer criticized his borscht. (It was his mother's recipe, so his borscht had milk-of-God's status in our household. I absolutely despise the taste and texture of beets; however I've always kept that fact to myself and forced Papa's borscht down with a radiant smile on my face.)

Lie: I crave the attention. Lie: I try to be the star of every show, sucking the light from everyone else.

Or maybe those are truths—that I am a moth to the limelight. Am I?

Max has accused me of such my whole life, usually in good humor, but ringing of resentment. He's claimed I divert Papa's attention, have the tendency of monopolizing all of it.

But something more is bothering me, something I read that doesn't feel right. I sift my mind, but only grapple at fumes.

What is it? What? Something odd . . . something that disturbs me . . . *What?*

Maybe it's just that my whole life is bleeding in ink, and I can't see in the dark, to discern what I'm supposed to do next.

Well, I thrive under pressure—that's what Papa always used to say proudly. I wonder, though, did he say it because I actually naturally do, or because he needed me to? Because, in our family, one of us three had to be the get-shit-done type. The take-care-of-things person. But Papa was more the let-bills-expire-on-the-counter, let-life-happen-and-it-will-likely-work-out type.

So I became the take-care-of-things one.

What do I do next? *What?*

Sleep. I could go to sleep. I'll read it all over again tomorrow in the light of day, and piece together what's nagging me.

The dark obliges and swallows me whole.

CHAPTER EIGHT

Nate

In my whole life, I've never been so nervous waiting for a person to open a door—and yet a few months ago, I stood outside a suite in one of Dubai's premier hotels, awaiting a six-foot-five hulking Syrian arms dealer.

But at last the glossy wood door cracks opens, and Rory peeks out, her cheeks rosy, wearing olive-green linen trousers with a matching flowy tank that shows a sliver of tanned stomach—my favorite outfit of hers, which she purchased before our trip to Mexico City a couple of years ago.

My heart soars. I love her so damn much.

"Hi," she says flatly. "What's up?"

My heart stops its soar, stills in my chest, begins to deflate. "Uh . . . it's on the schedule?"

"The schedule?"

"The itinerary, you know, the one Ginevra made? Breakfast in your room, just the two of us. Caro and Max are in the dining car already. I'm staying right next door to you actually." I hear the clearing of a throat behind me, then servers holding silver trays weave a path between us.

"Oh." The servers set down the trays and stream back out. "Okay. I guess—Wait, you're staying *next* next door to me?"

"Next next door," I confirm.

"Okay. Well, come in, then." We are impossibly formal, like two peo-ple who have never met, let alone laughed together, lain together, once served as each other's emergency contacts.

"Ror, I . . . Jesus." My eyes take a wander. "This room is insane."

"I know." She avoids meeting my gaze. "I'm in the middle of my makeup."

"Oh, sure. Don't stop on my account. Even though you look gorgeous without."

"Thanks."

But her voice is clipped. She returns to the bathroom and I sit before the trays wafting their yeasty aromas. I stare out the window at the sea lapping calmly against the cliffs, the sun casting early lazy beams against the surface of the Gulf of Tigullio. The Italian Riviera—crazy that not so long ago, Rory and I dreamed of coming here. I glimpse Rory in the bathroom now, her familiar movements, the way she purses her lips when she curls her eyelashes, how she cocks her head at herself at the end of the whole procedure and gives herself a little smile. I used to sneak up from behind and wrap my arms around her waist and say, "The *Mona Lisa* is complete." She'd groan, but still she'd kiss my cheek before telling me the million things she had to accomplish in the next hour and then strik-ing off in a whirl.

Now she finishes dabbing on her lip gloss and sits on the velvet chair across from me, half smiles. "Hi. Ready."

"You're in the Roman theme colors." I indicate her green outfit.

"What?" She glances down.

"I mean, you match the room." I laugh, even though it's not funny, and why did I even say it in the first place?

"Oh." She glances around perfunctorily. "Yeah, I guess I do."

"You don't want to wear . . . ?"

"What?"

"No, but I . . ."

"What? You don't like what I'm wearing?"

"It's not that I don't like it. I do. I *really* like it. It's just, we're hiking today."

"Oh." She nods. "I'm gonna wear sneakers. This is my hiking outfit."

"Okay." Drop it, Nate. "Perfect."

She narrows her eyes. "Like, we're *hiking*, hiking? In all the Instagram pictures of Cinque Terre, people look cute."

"You look cute in hiking gear. Very cute."

"When did we go hiking last?"

The *we* does something to me, calms things. "Hollywood Bowl!"

She half smiles. "That wasn't hiking gear. We wore athleisure. And I'd venture that linen is even more breathable."

I raise my hands in surrender, find myself smiling genuinely. This feels like a conversation we've had many times before, and its normalcy untangles a few knots in my chest. "Your outfit is Indiana Jones approved, then."

She nods, doesn't give me another smile. "I just feel like wearing this."

My chest tightens. I wonder if she's trying to look cute for a special reason. For Gabriele?

"So wear that." I try to imbue my tone with nonchalance. "Eggs?" I pass her the poached ones, her favorite.

"Yeah. Thanks."

We serve ourselves, the gap between the people we once were and these new strange ones widening with every silent pour of coffee from the silver pot, every quiet spear of an avocado slice.

"You're wearing the bracelet?" she asks, her eyes flitting toward my wrist.

"Oh." I twist it around—woven blue, orange, and green threads, like kids in summer camp movies use to seal their friendship. "Yeah, why wouldn't I?"

"You didn't wear it when I gave it to you. That was like—"

"Two years ago."

"Two years." She shakes her head. "It's atrocious."

"It's not! I like it. And I like the memory of it even more, how you were sitting by the coffee table, making it, trying to be mindful."

That coaxes a smile out of her. "Right, my mindfulness phase. I must have spent a hundred bucks at the art store. And all that came of it was that awful bracelet. You can take it off now. Burn it. I give you full permission."

I play with the end strands, knot them through my fingers. "Sorry. I'm attached now."

"I can't believe you kept it," she says quietly.

"Ror, of course I did. You know, when you left . . . I mean, when we broke up, and the apartment was empty, and all I had anymore was your smell—"

"My smell?" She frowns.

"Your amazing smell! Like a fireplace. Like a sexy fireplace," I hurry on. God, I'm bad at this. "It was really hard and—I don't know—I was looking through old stuff, and I found the bracelet. And I haven't taken it off since. I meant what I said yesterday, Ror. I have so many regrets. I'm so sorry for hurting you. So sorry. *So*."

She puts down her fork. It feels like for the first time since we broke up, she really looks at me. Her eyes narrow, not angry per se but certainly not inviting either. "We had vendors, Nate. We had a date. I had to cancel it all, negotiate refunds. You remember that, right? I packed up every last dish in tissue paper for *you*. So you could take them to . . . I have no idea where you went after our lease ended, to be honest. Where you're sleeping now, with that hideous painting that used to be in our bedroom—"

"Hey," I say weakly. "You said you liked it." She's referring to my first and only art purchase that I got at a networking event gallery exhibition. Carting it home made me feel like a bona fide adult.

"I lied." A hint of a smile curls her lips. "I was more than happy to concede it to you in our breakup. If I never have to see those creepy dancing people again, it will be too soon."

"Well, you're in good company. Garrett said the same thing." That's my little brother, who also didn't mince words telling me I was a fucking idiot breaking up with Rory.

Rory nods. "I always liked Garrett."

I swallow a perfect bite of egg, finding it impossible to savor. "I'm in therapy now, Ror."

"Oh, yeah?" She says it with exaggerated nonchalance, like she hadn't been suggesting it to me for years.

"Yeah. I finally did it."

"Well, that's good. That's . . . I'm happy for you. So what is showing up here? Part of your treatment?"

"It's not part of my treatment, no, although Owen—that's my therapist—was supportive. I've learned so much from him. It's kind of wild, Ror, a new language. And it's not fun, really. Seeing the parts of myself I'm not proud of. Having to feel the triggers behind them. I'm not great with feelings. Hearing them, feeling them."

"I know. I do know that."

I nod. "Like, do you know about avoidant attachment?"

She stares at me like I have two heads.

I hurry forward before I lose my nerve. "Owen thinks that me being the middle child had a lot of implications, considering Mark has Down syndrome, and Garrett had all his addiction issues."

"Sure." Rory softens. "You were the kid who did everything perfectly. Your mom always says you didn't give them an ounce of worry."

"Yeah, but Owen has made me see that I closed something off inside me, had to ignore my own problems, my own needs, because my brothers had greater ones. Avoidant attachment means you're always putting up barriers, creating distance. Denying your feelings. Denying mine, I mean."

Rory tears off the corner of a crispy waffle and pops it in her mouth. "I can see that," she finally says.

"When I feel needy, I want to push everyone away. That's what I understand now. I needed space after everything that happened in Dubai. So I pushed you away. I was so stupid. I pushed you away right when you needed me the most."

Rory blinks a few times. "I hardly even know what happened in Dubai. You barely told me."

I chew on my lip, on a place that is tender from lots of previous chewing. "I lost him. Cesar. I was too late."

She nods, her expression shifting into one more compassionate. "That much I knew."

I continue to stare out the window because if I look at her, something will happen that can't happen, something will break in me that I need to keep contained. Cesar was an idealistic nineteen-year-old kid who crossed from Turkey into Syria because he wanted to make a difference, wanted to help people in the most dangerous and depraved place on earth. The day after he arrived in Syria, he was kidnapped by a courier he trusted to ferret him from the border. Soon after, his parents got word of the demanded ransom.

How did I get involved? Well, it starts from my childhood, really. My father is a diplomat, and growing up, we lived in various places across the Middle East and Africa, with our home base in DC. I was always around people of different cultures, learning new languages. And my grandmother is a Syrian Jew; when I was a kid, she lived with us in DC and spoke only Arabic with me, which proved immensely useful later in my career. I knew I wanted to work in the international sphere, like my father. I got my master's in international relations, then spent the first few years post graduation in big-firm project-finance practice in DC, where most of my work was in developing nations, helping them to emerge from poverty; pay down debt; and develop new political, economic, and judicial systems. Soon I transitioned to working for an international foundation, helping developing nations create democratic structures, and even mediating in war zones.

I travel often—though crisis mediation is anything but glamorous. And when the Arab Spring erupted, I got involved in mediating between the war sides. In 2012 and 2013, I traveled to Syria a few times a year, trying to negotiate a cease-fire; but later, when the Russians got involved and Assad had the upper hand, I worked from afar. People are often surprised I don't still live in DC, or at least make it my base. I did for a while, but then the long distance between Rory and me became too hard, and I moved to LA, because it was important for Rory to be there for her own career aspirations. And I've always supported Rory's rising star, been her biggest cheerleader. Plus, even if I'd lived in DC, I would have been on an airplane most of the time, anyhow. It's strange work, difficult to explain to people on the outside of it, but deeply fulfilling.

Then, six months ago, I received a call from a colleague: "My friend's son is missing in Syria. You have experience in Syria. You know the lay of the land. Will you help?"

What did I know of hostage negotiation? After a sleepless night, though, of course I said yes. I could make zero promises, and I wouldn't be involved in the payment of ransom or trading favors with terrorists, but I would try my absolute hardest to get Cesar out. What ensued was the wildest two months of my life. I conducted meetings in Paris, in Istanbul, in Dubai. I chased leads throughout the Middle East. I met with sheikhs, drug lords, and arms dealers to pursue the truth. To find Cesar, dead or alive.

In the end, it was dead.

Cesar didn't make it. Which absolutely wrecked me. And it was more than just Cesar—it was also the teenage girls I met in Dubai, who were sold by their Syrian fathers into the sex trade and transported to Dubai by the drug lord who ordered Cesar's kidnapping. They met with me at great risk to their lives. They gave me crucial information that ultimately led me to discover what happened to Cesar. After it was all done, I spent every waking moment trying to extract the girls from their horrific circumstances—but doing so required coordination with several governments and organizations.

Finally, two weeks ago, it happened. The girls have new identities and homes in Europe. They're safe.

"Rima and Youmna, we got them out," I tell Rory.

"The girls. God, I've thought about them a lot."

I nod. "They're safe."

Rory exhales deeply. "That's incredible news."

"I can finally sleep again."

"Wow. So—"

"I was a total asshole, Ror. I was so caught in my own storm that I didn't see what you were going through."

She puts her fork down, stares at her lap. "What happened with Cesar and Rima and Youmna . . . I get how awful it all was. But you shut down, Nate. You completely shut me out. You'd barely speak to me. Barely look at me. I felt like everything I did infuriated you. When I was humming while doing our laundry, you acted as if I was, like, trying to deliberately irritate you."

I nod, remember it. The whole world felt like a bleak, black hole. I took it out on her. I realize it now. "I'm so—"

"And it's more than that. I know that you were going through something crazy and horrible, but at the same time, I feel like—I don't know how to say this without being a jerk, but it wasn't a solitary incident. You were always, I mean—"

"I was always involved in one crazy work situation or another. That's what you mean? I get it, Ror. You have every right to say it. I can be too . . . involved, I guess. Emotionally, maybe." I manage a wry smile. "Can't say I'm not *ever* emotional, hey?"

But instead of taking the easy entrée onto a bash-Nate train, to my surprise Rory says, "I get it. Like the world is on your shoulders alone."

I nod and feel a ballooning in my chest, how she knows and accepts me so completely. And I'm not always an easy person to live with, to get. I can't believe I let it go—let her go.

I can't believe I made so many mistakes.

"I feel it, too," Rory says, "like when the horrible news is pummeling, and it's all so urgent and important, and I feel like maybe I can make a difference. Or at least, that's how I used to feel."

"You'll be back there in the newsroom again soon. They were total assholes to fire you over such a stupid mistake."

She shrugs. "I deserved to be fired. I didn't check my source. That's, like, rule number one. I broadcasted a story that wasn't accurate at all."

"People make mistakes! It's not the end of the road, Ror. Trust me." I know how hard she is on herself, because it's how hard I am on myself, too. We're perfectionists, both of us. Driven to excel. Hate—*hate*—when we let anyone down. It's why I blew us apart so spectacularly, I suppose. In hindsight I see it, how I couldn't face her, or face myself, when I failed.

"Things have a way of working themselves out," I tell her, and I feel like I'm telling it to myself, too. Hoping it. "It's not the end."

"Maybe it *is* the end." Her face adopts a strange, calm look. "Maybe I *want* it to be."

"With your career? Or with us?"

She stares at me blankly. "I don't know."

I feel fear rise up my throat that my apologies, my promises—even this incredibly romantic trip—won't be sufficient to fix the things I've torpedoed. "Ror, I was an idiot. A total and complete idiot, to ruin what we had."

"What *did* we have?"

I study her, to see if she's being angry or sarcastic, but she just cocks her head at me, curious.

"We had love. So much love, Ror. I love you. It's always been you. And we had fire! We both have passion in spades. We chase success. We go after what we want, and we try to change the world for the better. You make me want to be a better person, Ror. And I hope I did the same for you. And we had all these plans. I know I fucked them up, but I want the . . . What's that show you like?"

Shit. I feel like I'm messing it up, misremembering it. Rory always loved these wholesome TV Land black-and-white sitcoms. There was one about a saccharine family and this perfect, ideal mother that Rory always watched, but I'm forgetting its name. With kids embroiled in the most PG of scrapes, with parents who kissed perfunctorily when the husband came home from work. It always surprised me a little that Rory wanted something so simple. So trite. She loves all those kinds of shows—*Get Smart*, *I Dream of Jeannie*, *I Love Lucy*. Almost aggressively wholesome.

"*Leave It to Beaver*." I can tell she's peeved I've forgotten it—that there's a minus in some column she's using to keep tallies on me now, when I was aiming for a check.

"I want that kind of family," I tell her. "With you."

She grimaces. "I don't want that kind of perfect family. It's a show. It's an act! You're misunderstanding why I like that show. It's just simple. It makes me think of pure, simple times. I just think there are a lot of hard things in the world. We know that."

I frown. I do know that.

"And I wanted kids with you," she said. "I wanted a family with you."

"And now?" I feel myself hold my breath.

"I don't know." She smiles at me, but I can see it's an effort. "I think what I miss most are the quiet moments. You know? Like the meme of let's look at our phones, but next to each other. Sometimes, in the middle of all our craziness, we could just sit and not talk. I think I need more of that in my life. And you know . . . what you said before, about how we both want to be better? Well, maybe I don't want to be better. Maybe I don't want to succeed anymore. Maybe I want to live a quiet life in the country somewhere and stare at the leaves in the wind and have a couple of kids and live a life that's not so complicated."

I laugh—the leaves-in-the-wind thing again—but when she doesn't join me, I shut my smile down. "Okay. You're serious." I try to wrap my head around that, get my bearings, that Rory who loves—loves!—being on air, the adrenaline and the bustle and making a difference, suddenly wants to retreat to nowheresville and become one with trees. "I can do quiet. I can do country. I can do trees." I summon conviction.

Rory gives me a humored smile. "Sure. Sure, you can, Mr. Negotiating with Syrian Arms Dealers. Look, I appreciate your coming on this trip.

Apologizing for what happened with us. Telling me what's been going on with you, but my head is spinning a bit. It's not just you; it's everything. Did you read the book?"

"The book?" My shoulders stiffen. I meant to read it last night, but then after the first page I nodded off. Jet lag, but also the weeks of sleepless nights, missing Rory, wondering how I'll ever make it right. And I slept past my alarm this morning, with barely enough time to get ready, let alone read the book.

I need to read it. Obviously, I do. "The author's book?" I ask, still playing for time. Has she read it? Fuck. Does she know?

No, can't be, I reassure myself. If she knew, she'd have said so right off the bat.

"Yes." Rory looks at me curiously. Not accusatorily. Thank the Lord. "Ginevra's book."

"Haven't read it yet." I try to sound nonchalant. "I think I passed out the second I got back to my room last night."

"Oh."

"What? Did she write something . . . bad?" To be honest, I thought it was insane, Rory agreeing to be this main character. I mean, lots of people read Ginevra's books. Even lawyers I know, and diplomats, who hardly ever read anything but dry biographies. I'm not inclined to fiction myself, but I've seen Ginevra's books in every airport, the star of every massive display.

Still, ever since I agreed to be interviewed, I've lost sleep about it. Could Ginevra have figured out . . . put in a line about . . . ?

No. I didn't say anything, so how would she know? But then, she did all those interviews, with each of us. No, no chance. But still, I should read this book immediately. Maybe I'll have a quick flip through before our hike.

"I don't know if bad, just weird. Something struck me as . . . I don't know, off. I mean, you haven't read it, so never mind."

Off. Shit. I feel heat creep up my neck. "I'll bring it to the beach today. I want to read it."

She nods. "No pressure."

"It's a book about you, Ror. Of course, I want to read it."

"Okay. Just look, Nate, I—I need you to give me time. I need to think.

I didn't expect you to show up here, say these things. You were . . . *we* were, well, great, you know? And then you ended it, and I had to make peace with that."

"And you did? You made peace with it?" My voice has fallen to a whisper.

"I don't know. I need time."

"Okay. Of course." I feel sick. Angry at myself for how severely I've messed things up.

Rory nods, uncrosses her legs, looking supremely huggable. God, I want to hug her so badly, but I don't feel entitled to.

"Nate . . ."

I feel a sweep of hope. "Yeah?"

"Can you . . . I need a few minutes before we go." She motions to the door.

"I . . . oh. Yeah, of course. Sure." I fumble up to a stand. "I'll just . . . so . . ."

"I'll see you out for the hike in a little. We have the whole day ahead of us. The whole trip. Try to be patient with me, okay?"

"Okay," I agree, because what else is there to say? "I'm really sorry."

"I know." She shakes her head sadly.

And suddenly the door inches open and then Rory isn't banishing me from her suite, exactly, but still I feel an invisible wave of energy propelling me to step back and back some more until I pass the threshold, holding my breath, hoping she will say *Wait. Don't go.* But her mouth doesn't eject words. Instead, it morphs into a firm but soft smile—her master of ceremonies smile, the smile that kindly, assuredly deters anyone from getting too close. I've seen her give it to colleagues, acquaintances, the guy at our regular coffee shop who could skew excessively chatty and personal.

And now, with one last flex of her master of ceremonies smile, Rory closes the door in my face.

CHAPTER NINE

Rory

A driver takes us the short distance from the La Spezia train station to Portovenere, and then we board a boat over to stunning Riomaggiore, the southernmost of the five fishing villages that comprise Cinque Terre.

Before we departed, Gabriele distributed sunscreen and bottled water, his thick dark hair in particularly fine swooping shape. He asked if we'd like him to accompany us, and I said no, thank you. There is only so much tension one group can hold—the four of us reunited already feels like a peak tornado tunnel, seconds away from plowing everything over.

Anyway, Nate was quite the eager volunteer to navigate us through the five towns, instead of Gabriele.

"Fabrizio Salvatore will be your tour guide on the Sentiero Azzurro!" he keeps announcing, thoroughly butchering the Italian, wearing his brand-new panama hat for which he paid far too many euros from the first vendor we encountered. Fabrizio Salvatore is in fine form and mood, warbling "Volare" as the boat speeds along, seawater spritzing our faces. Nate adopts a new alter ego anywhere we travel together—it's totally dorky and not PC and contrary to his typical staid composure. I'm grateful for it now, though, lightening the mood after his breakfast revelations.

We pull ashore to the most charming village that I am certain has ever existed: a pebble beach flanked by a harbor of colorful boats lolling in the tranquil sea, and above, pastel houses climbing skyward up the towering cliff. We file into a line to exit the boat, and in the standstill, Nate gives my shoulders a little rub. Maybe because we're not making eye contact, I allow myself to sink into it with unexpected pleasure. One of the things I enjoyed most about life with Nate was when we'd stay in and watch *Curb Your Enthusiasm*, and Nate would rub my feet on the sofa. *This is it*, I'd think, surprising myself. *This is the life I want.* The next evening, though, we'd be on the hamster wheel again, me at a gala, him packing up suit-cases again—the stillness, the quiet, extinguished.

When Nate ended our engagement, Max, ever the sensitive older brother, sent me one of those expensive shiatsu massage contraptions. *Here is a substitute fiancé*, the gift communicated without words. The note said, *I'm here for you always, whenever you want to talk. But I draw the line at foot massage.*

As Nate continues warbling his awful rendition of the Italian classic, the four of us stream off the boat and begin to roam the narrow medieval lanes. Up the steep stone hill we go, wrought-iron balconies clinging to pale yellow apartment buildings, villagers' laundry languid on the bars.

Max gets gelato; it's not yet ten.

"Where does it go?" Nate marvels, in an exaggerated Fabrizio accent, eyes flickering from the scoop of stracciatella to Max's long, thin limbs. I stifle a laugh at my brother all Gumby-like in his hefty hiking boots and technical shorts with what look like a thousand zippers, like he informed the REI salesman he was readying to trek the Himalayas. Although, more likely, his assistant did the REI run.

"Sugar powers the brain." Max licks up a beelining stream before it plops onto his forearm.

"That magnificent brain," Caro says, and I am surprised to detect something acerbic in her tone.

We pop into stores selling olive oil and pesto, admire waxy produce in wooden crates outside little mom-and-pop shops, walking up and up the hilly town that, despite the heavy influence of tourism, still evinces a fisher-man's village at heart. Occasionally we pass our fellow train-goers, some of whom we boated over with—the photogenic Italian family kitted out in chic hiking gear; the red-faced man in his pom-pom beret, an eternal grimace on his face; the chatty couple from California on their fortieth-anniversary trip, who were seated beside us on the boat and told us *all* about their magnificent therapist—Ira—who saved their marriage and to whom they are dedicating this trip. "To Ira," they declared in unison, completely serious, their hiking poles spearing the air in punctuation.

"To Ira!" Nate whispers in my ear as they pass, and I can't squelch a giggle.

As we ascend into the town, I pant with each step, sweating from every pore, cursing the Superga sneakers I wore in lieu of something more athletic like Nate suggested. Meanwhile, elderly ladies zip past with the light assistance of canes, shopping bags cradled in elbow nooks. I marvel that they walk this route every single day, farther even, up punishing steps to their houses hugging the cliffs.

Gabriele posited two options for our day: either leisurely exploring the five towns, stopping for limoncello and lunch whenever it strikes our fancies, taking the train between a couple of towns to minimize the mileage—or else forgoing the train, hiking the whole eight miles, and adding a rugged detour into the highlands to the mix to boot. Nate was for the rugged hike, no surprise. Max vacillated, I suspect both because of his sporty outfit, and because he always likes to impress Nate. To Max, Nate epitomizes cool, like some sort of James Bond.

Still, in the end, Caro and I cast the deciding votes, opting for leisurely exploring. So after walking up the main thoroughfare, we wander back down to the peninsula that juts into the sea, rounding the bay, where fishing boats bob in tranquil waters, and above us, multicolored houses are baked into cliffs. There are houses in ochre and sherbet and salmon pink, weathered and storm beaten, climbing up toward azure sky.

"This place is insane." Caro applies lip gloss, then returns it to her Gucci crossbody bag. No surprise—Caro has also opted for the cute end of hiking gear.

"Insane." I slip on my round Ray-Bans, which Max told me look like I stole from John Lennon. It wasn't said lovingly—he's clearly pissed, fairly rightfully so, that I haven't told him yet why I'm upset.

Every Italian wears sunglasses. I first noticed it in Rome, amid my observation that Italians are uniformly well turned out. Men endure this heavy heat in suits and trousers, eschewing short sleeves, opting for proper socks. God forbid Italian men reveal an anklebone. Women, too—no sign of athleisure, except for the tourists, only locals in figure-hugging tops and skirts. It is important to them to *fare una bella figura*—make a positive impression. I learned that expression from Ginevra, of all people. Though you wouldn't think it on first appraisal, with her wild purple hair and black caftans, Ginevra quite cares about her appearance. She applies her eyeliner with militant precision, has an entire dressing room devoted to her extensive makeup collection, all the latest and hottest stuff. She's unexpectedly vain, even if the package she pulls together somehow misses the mark—heavy, aging powder, cakey foundation, spidery false eyelashes that weigh down her eyelids.

My sunglasses are using my nose as a slip and slide. I push them up, grateful for the reprieve they give my eyes. Not from the sun alone, but from having to turn out. Maintain my poker face. With everyone showing up to surprise me on this trip, I need that cover now, that concealment.

Successfully sunglassed, my eyes flicker on over at Nate. God, does he actually want me back?

It's still so shocking, to process him here, this person who used to be synonymous for me with home. LA was never home for me—even though it was the right place to pursue being a news anchor, I always found the city too sterile, too superficial.

After Nate ended things with us, I remember staring numbly at the ceiling for so many nights, conjuring this dream scenario, not the train but his return. In the past couple of months, though, something in me shifted, began to scab over the wound. At the start of our relationship, we talked for hours, about every subject. I felt like I let Nate inside my soul, and he splayed his out for me, too. But maybe over the years, we both put up our little orange traffic cones: *Don't come this way; veer around there.* Annoyances grew and fermented. I would say, *You're on your phone all the time when we're together.* I didn't vocalize the hurt underneath. *I miss when we're just quiet together. When you're paying attention to nothing but me.* Were those realistic expectations after ten years, though? In the end, we both retreated into our hurts. We made little corners for our traumas, our pains.

The difference is, I wanted to stay. And Nate decided to go.

Interesting, though, what he revealed, that he's started therapy, is assessing his childhood. Nate has two parents who love each other, who love him; but still, his childhood broke him, in the small ways that are the big ways, in the end. I always thought two loving parents were the ticket, but maybe I was wrong. If I'd had a mother, would it have made me a different person? Catalyzed different, somehow better choices? Or is even wondering about it a kind of crutch, a forever excuse? There's always someone who has it better, after all. And usually many someones who have it worse. I know that intimately, from years of reporting on the greatest tragedies on earth. I think we humans are all just variations of Humpty-Dumpty, forever trying to put ourselves back together again.

Now Nate announces in his American Nate accent that he's guiding us to Manarola, the next town, a mile or so. Then he switches to Fabrizio Salvatore, starts warbling "Volare" again.

"*Nel blu,*" he sings, horridly off-key. "*Dipinto di blu.*"

Somehow he's still sexy when he channels Fabrizio Salvatore. It makes him even more sexy, maybe, that he isn't good at everything and can laugh at himself.

"*Dipinto di bluuu.*"

The pianist in the dinner car played "Volare" last night, and Nate Shazamed it. There's no chance the lyrics will leave him, or us, for the duration of the trip.

"You know the song's about a man who dreamed of painting himself blue and flying?" I ask. I don't mention that Gabriele told me that.

"*Nel blue, dipinto di blu,*" Nate sings louder, smiling. He's as handsome and charming as ever, but something's itching at me, like Nate's going overboard in his effort at endearing himself to me. I used to find his impressions purely cute. But I'm almost . . . am I . . . starting to find the bit annoying?

"You know one line, but you do rock that one line," I finally say.

"*Come sei dolce!*" he says. It means, "You're sweet." He's got lines, Nate. And leave it to him to already have a dangerous grasp on Italian hours after arriving in the country.

He smiles, wraps a quick arm around me, but instead of stiffening, for the first time since we broke up, my body relents, accepts a real embrace. I stare down at his hand that's absently stroking my arm, at the blond hairs dusting his forearm. This is Nate, not Fabrizio. And I do miss him. I do miss us. I feel myself liquefying, melding back into him, my organs gone to mush, my head misty.

It can't be this easy to just start again——or can it?

We round the bend, descend a steep hill, and pause to drink from our water bottles. I gaze back at the distance we've traversed, then detach from Nate's arm and head over to the wooden guardrail at the cliff. I tip forward a bit, mesmerized by the waves crashing against the dramatic rock formations that jut out of the sea. For what seems like many minutes, thoughts slosh around my brain, but I can't seem to unpick any of them, make them fit, make them make sense.

Suddenly, I hear my name. It's said sharply in a frantic tone. "Rory!"

That's Max, I register, my eyes flickering back. Then all of a sudden, I am shoved sideways, right as a boulder whizzes toward me.

CHAPTER TEN

Rory

"Ror! Ror!"

My knees crunch down onto the gravel as the boulder scrapes my biceps, then sails over the cliff. My shoulder bashes against the guardrail. Dust sprays my face, and my eyes clamp shut, but not before sealing particles inside. I probe my shoulder, test out moving it, rolling it, relieved that I can. Then I rub my eyes and flicker them open. I look up.

Three concerned faces break the line of pure blue sky.

"Wha-what happened?" My voice is shaky, my pulse still racing.

"I don't know," Max says, his body still covering—protecting—mine. "It just came . . . that huge rock, out of nowhere."

"It almost crashed into you," Caro says breathlessly. "If Max hadn't . . . I mean, what the hell was that?"

Now I hear a flurry of indistinct chatter; and other people swim into my vision, all huddled together, faces pinched in unease. That glamorous Italian family we passed on the way up; a youngish hipster guy with this cool silver arrow earring who's also on the train, who took the boat over with us to the first town; his girlfriend, I think, pink hair in a pixie cut, speaking what I infer is Russian, as evidenced by a few vaguely familiar words.

"Ror." It's Nate now, kneeling down. "Ror, are you okay?"

"Yeah," I say hastily. I let Nate pop me up. I brush off my pants, now shredded at the knee. "Yeah. I'm fine. Thanks."

I turn and assess the highland from where the boulder must have come—dense, scrubby brush. Parts of the path are protected overhead by concrete, but this section wasn't. Still, how in the world did such a big thing get dislodged?

Everyone encircles me, closing me off, proffering their water bottles and even a clove of garlic from the Russian lady. I know that people from that part of the world religiously believe in the healing properties of garlic. Papa was known to eat cloves raw, usually right before our friends were due to come over, to my and Max's childhood chagrin.

"No thank you, but *spasiba*." I hope that means *thanks*, and not goodbye. I must have gotten it right, because she smiles and unleashes a torrent of Russian.

"No, no, I don't speak Russian. And you can have . . . here." I thrust the garlic toward her, but she pulls her hands back like it's a hot potato.

She says something again in insistent Russian, and her boyfriend says, "It is the Russian penicillin. To heal wound."

"I know. But no thank you. I'm fine. Please." I stuff the garlic clove into his hand with slight aggression. The stench of garlic wafts up from my fingers, curdling my stomach. I edge back, the adrenaline of what just happened still whisking through me.

"*Coraggio!*" the Italian dad says, peering down from my circle of now groupies, his voice as booming as a subwoofer.

"I'm fine, really." *Can everyone get the fuck away?* But my mouth refuses to voice it, stays frozen in a rictus smile. And then everyone squeezes even closer to me, making way for a gaggle of German trekkers with their massive backpacks and walking sticks that nearly spear my elbow.

After the Germans pass, our train friends slowly disperse, leaving only us four. "I'm fine," I say, as much to them as to myself. I lick my forefinger and massage it over a cut on my knee that's visible through the hole.

"Should we get you to a doctor?" Caro frowns.

"No. I'm fine."

"Well, at least we should bandage that up," Nate says. "We should stop at a pharmacy."

"Where? At the pharmacy around the corner?" Now I'm irritated. "A cut's not going to kill me. The *boulder*—now that could have killed me." I hear myself say it in an odd jokey tone. "Come on." I step a tentative foot forward. "Let's just keep on."

"You sure?" Max asks, eyes crinkling in brotherly concern.

"Yeah. Thanks, Maxie. Honestly, you saved me." I squeeze his forearm.

Max shrugs. "Right place, right time."

"No, really. You seriously saved me."

"Anytime, LS." He looks surprised.

"Was it a rockslide?" Nate asks, gazing back up toward the high ground. "I feel like I read about that happening here."

"Only in rainy season, I'd assume," Max says. "Not in summer."

"But this part of the path is the most treacherous," Caro says. "I read it in my guidebook. See." I follow her finger point to a sign with a red triangle, inside of which is a stick figure of a person falling.

"But I didn't fall."

"No," Caro agrees. "You didn't."

The four of us traipse back along the dusty path. My gait is unsteady, but I soldier on, my heart still in my throat as I ponder how close I came. If the boulder had crashed into me, it could have swept me through the guardrail. Hundreds of feet above punishing rock . . .

We pass lemon and olive trees nestled in lush foliage, then flowering agaves and cacti sprouting from the earth at every twist—as if placed for maximal delight by an expert gardener. I try to focus on the beauty, let it temper the fear. But I can't stop my eyes from flittering back every few feet.

"You sure you're okay?" Nate asks, filing in beside me. "That was weird. I mean . . ."

"I'm fine. I'm okay."

"Ror?" he says, his gaze penetrating.

"Really."

We walk on in silence, but eventually the landscape compels us to resume proclamations—*I'm never leaving!* (Max) *Bury me here.* (Caro)

Only Nate is still quiet. I wonder if he's thinking the same thing I am. That it's probably rare for boulders to dislodge for no reason. . . in the middle of summer. . . .

The route is blessedly flat now, the air perfumed with juniper and oregano. Occasionally we pass terraces festooned in magenta bougain-villea, with clusters of people drinking slushy granitas and eating twirly forks of pasta, some bites green with what I suspect is pesto, some red. Caro walks slightly ahead, marveling at the scenery, snapping pictures that I know I'll see soon on Instagram. It's a little bizarre that she's not hovering close, especially after the weird boulder thing. Typically, Caro and I are conjoined, not a bit of space between us to hide a secret, to store a lie. But we haven't seen each other in a while. We haven't yet had that thaw, where one of us says something that pings our history, our shared language, and I'm right back into the thick of our sisterhood. Instead I'm a fritzing light, on and off, on and off, stuck on Ginevra's allegations of Caro embezzling from Max.

"Watch it," Nate says when I get close to the seaward edge. He skirts around me, so he's next to the sea.

"What?"

"Look. I don't think they're great at maintenance. There are places where the supporting soil looks like it's eroded."

"I should have worn better shoes like you said." I muster a smile.

He smiles back. "It's taking huge restraint for me not to say *I told you so*."

"I applaud your restraint."

"Hey, let me take a breather." Max pauses to gulp from his bottle of Evian. Nate wanders ahead to an overlook, and I stop with Max, leaning against the stone wall, on vigilant lookout in case another boulder comes flying toward me.

Okay, I've got to tackle something, deal with one of them. Might as well begin with my brother. Especially after he saved me, now that I feel my anger toward him loosening.

I let out a deep exhale. "Max, you know your first memory?"

Caro watches us from ahead. Somehow, I know she attunes, gets that this conversation is important. She whispers something to Nate. Nate's glance flickers between Max and me, then the two of them slip farther ahead.

Max finishes his water and swipes at his mouth. "Yeah, of course." He pulls off his sunglasses—ancient Oakleys that really should be tossed. He eyes me wearily as we pass a cluster of olive trees. I slow to give Nate and Caro more time to get significantly ahead. "Why?"

"Well . . . it's why I'm upset with you. And I'm sorry I didn't tell you sooner. I needed to process it first myself."

"You're upset me with me about my first memory?" Max's voice tunes up. "You mean, like when I was *four*? You haven't answered my calls for weeks . . . because of something from when I was *four*? How could that possibly upset you? All I've ever said was you were pink and scrunchy and I loved you instantly."

My heart swishes over itself. "I know you love me. But honestly that doesn't have anything to do with what I'm trying to say now."

"Okay." He nods, swallows. I can tell he's trying hard to keep it friendly and together. Not lose it. CEO Max tries not to lose it, but my brother, Max? I've seen him lose it many times. "Then what? This is because of the book, isn't it? The author? I started it last night, Ror. Or should I say, Laci Starling?"

I eke out a smile. "It's horrible, isn't it? Thankfully one hundred thousand dollars makes it easier to swallow."

"It's horrible," he confirms, smiling. "You belong swinging on poles."

"But she's good, huh? Ginevra? I mean, objectively, as a storyteller. How she took me and turned me into—"

"Yeah. She's good." He indicates his backpack. "Got it in there to finish on the beach. I'm dying to know which one of us is murdered. And who did it." His smile fades. "Okay, Ror. Just tell me already."

I know he's talking about why I'm angry, not the murderer in a fake story.

"Well, look, Ginevra's methods for creating her main character aren't exactly orthodox. She hired a private investigator to, like, look into my life. Our lives, I guess. And then she informed me that I was adopted."

Max stops. I watch it dawn. "She told you that you were . . ."

"*Adopted*. Ring a bell?"

"And she hired private investigators? Seriously?"

"That's not the newsworthy thing here."

He's quiet as we continue along a bridge with a little stone statue that looks like birds kissing, with thousands of locks attached to the guardrails. Couples are kissing and fastening new locks as we pass. It's clearly a lovers' bridge, where you attach a lock and toss the key away to assure the eternal strength of your bond. I see Nate and Caro as dots in the distance, having the same idea as I do—bolting right past. Nothing to memorialize.

No lovers now, not among us four.

"She told me I'm adopted, Max. And of course I thought instantly of your first memory when you were four. You tell it to me on every birthday—I was pink and wrinkly and you loved me from the start. You said you remembered everything from that moment, when I came home. That it was sunny, and Papa made borscht."

"It's what happened," he says quietly. "I didn't make it up."

"But implied in that memory was the fact that I was a newborn, not *seven* months old. Apparently I was seven months! Sitting up, maybe even crawling. And now I realize, how would Papa have had time to make borscht if he was in the hospital? You made it sound like I came home from the hospital, with Papa and Mom."

"Mom." Max winces, looks away.

"But I didn't," I continue, feeling tears press at the corners of my eyes. "I didn't because Papa *adopted* me. A blind adoption, at least as far as the paperwork goes. Crystal clear from what Ginevra showed me that Papa isn't my father, not genetically. And the woman I've always thought of as Mom was apparently never mine. And you knew. I just know it—you *knew*."

Max chews his lip as we walk. I know we're both thinking of her. Mom, who as the story goes, as Papa has always said, as we've treated as the foundational fact of our family, died a month after I was born, from a brain aneurysm. We have a single photograph of her—stunning and windswept, with a kind, toothy smile.

Papa always said there was a flood in the attic that ruined all the photos, and that Mom didn't have any family besides us. I was never suspicious of his explanation. I didn't have a mother—what did it matter if there were pictures to cling to, or not? Or maybe that was what I told myself to keep on coasting, not have to face the lies.

"She shouldn't have told you that," Max finally says.

"Who? You're blaming Ginevra? For what Papa did?"

"What did Papa do?" Max erupts. "Bring you home and love you? Love the hell out of you? Love you more than he even loved me?" He's panting, his face pained. "That's all he did, Ror. That's his crime."

We both stop, stare at each other. There it is—a firm tenet of Max's existence, that somehow Papa loved me more. It's not true, not in the least. But I was always confident of Papa's love, and Max always doubting. Who can say why? Max didn't need much attention—he could play on his own for hours at a time, hunched over test tubes conducting obscure experiments, reading Benjamin Franklin's autobiography at age ten. He could drift off into his imagination, scribble endless ideas in a notebook.

I was different. I preferred being with people. I liked tasks. Ride a bike, bake a cake—but with people watching, people helping. Usually Papa.

"I remember once, you were playing in puddles outside," Max says. "You were six, maybe, and I was ten. And you were jumping in all the biggest ones, so muddy, so . . . I don't know, gleeful. And Papa was watching you from the deck. We were both watching you. And Papa had this look on his face. Such a weird look. Like he was sad or something. I said, *Papa, what's wrong?* And he said, *It's scary how much I love you and your sister.* I didn't know what he meant. He shook his head and said, *Sometimes I watch you both with a little bit of dread. One day, you'll go. One day, this will end.* And I just remember—all I could hear in his whole speech was your name in it! *It's scary how much I love you and your sister,* but he was watching you! I was standing right beside him, but his eyes were on *you.* It took you to make him feel that way. Always you."

I blow my baby hairs off my forehead, feeling frustrated at the trotting out of this memory, one Max clearly has selected to make me feel guilty. Cacti lining the edge of the path prick my ankles. The air feels as scorching as our words.

"I *know* he loved me. Of course, I know that. But honestly, Max, you have a revisionist memory. He loves both of us the same. And back to the adoption—" My tone is icy, but that's because he's steered things away from what we're supposed to be addressing. "He should have told me. *You* should have told me."

Max is silent.

"Like, I remember my birthday when I was, I don't know, maybe eight," I say. "How I'd been asking about Mom. Who her parents were and stuff. If we could at least visit the house she grew up in. See something that would clue me in on who she was. And I heard Papa and you in the kitchen. He told you that I could never find out. I remember asking you about it after, because you would tell me anything, wouldn't you? You wouldn't hide things from me. It was us against the world, even against Papa. Always, or that's what I thought. And you just said that he was talking about a big surprise he'd planned, which was true, in a way. He'd rented the ice rink for the afternoon—"

"The Zamboni!" Max smiles. "All you wanted to do was ride the Zamboni. And get nachos. Those were by far the exciting parts of the rink, over actual skating."

I smile, too, despite myself, despite this conversation. "It was the best birthday gift, riding the Zamboni with Papa across empty ice. Even though I remember thinking your explanation didn't really make sense. I remember Papa's exact words. *She can never find out.* That didn't really jibe with a surprise I was soon going to discover. But you were a good liar."

"Papa never wanted you to feel different. To feel less his," Max finally says.

I feel a crushing pain in my chest, that Max is confirming it. Confirming that I am not who I thought I was, that the entire life that has been fashioned for me is a lie.

"How did Papa get me? Who are my birth parents?" I whisper.

"I don't know." Max's face is ashen now, the pink flush expunged. We stop overlooking a picturesque harbor, hundreds of sailboats and yachts dotting the water like confetti. "Papa never said. And I didn't lie about the memory. I remember the day he brought you home, exactly like I said. He had made me borscht earlier. It was all true. You were pink and scrunchy and I loved you instantly. We both did. I wonder if . . ." Max's face shades. "No."

"What?"

"I don't know, I guess I wondered for a second, if your author, if the reason she brought it up was because . . ."

"What?" Then it hits me, what he's suggesting. "No." My breath hitches in my throat.

"But—"

"*No.* I mean, there's no way, there's no . . . She's Italian. And besides, she didn't bring it up like that. She was asking about Mom . . . I mean, your mom, I guess. Sandra Lowenstein. And we talked about her, and what it was like to grow up without a mother." I avoid looking at Max. It wasn't easy for either of us, even though Papa was wonderful, and tried his best to be two parents in one.

But one person can never be two people. Math doesn't work that way.

"And then Ginevra asked, *What about your birth mother, then?* Obviously I froze. And she got it immediately—that I didn't know. She felt guilty, I think." I recall it, how she handed me tissues and even came over to me on the couch. I thought at first she'd hug me, and I didn't really want her to. She's not the huggy type—more witty and terse, with a frenetic sort of energy atypical of the superrich. But she's kind. Somehow I trust her. I did, at least. Anyway, she put a hand atop mine, but we didn't hug. Maybe because I used to interview her, and now she was my boss. Keep some good barriers. Even when we parted in Rome, my last day working for her, we just shared a firm handshake.

"Did you ask who . . . ?"

I stop, out of breath and keel over, hands to my shins. I notice the blood has congealed on my knee, on its way to a scab. I stand, dizzy. We've been walking on a ledge of sorts, one side of which is hewn into a mountain, the other side scrubby with vegetation, a veritable free fall if I were to misstep. I inch over to the mountain side, put a hand on the earth to steady myself. I watch Max over at one of the ubiquitous water fountains, filling up our bottles. He returns, hands one to me, and I chug, squinting, trying to make out ahead. Finally I pinpoint them—Caro and Nate, still specks in the distance.

"Of course I asked." I swipe water from my lips. "I think I went through the five stages of grief or whatever all at once. Anger, mostly. Well, everything other than acceptance. It still feels absurd, Max. Like it can't be real. Like Papa had this whole hidden life . . ."

I don't tell him that it made me think about Sandra Lowenstein, and wonder which parts Papa invented. Just that she was my mother? Or more?

When you identify one lie, it's difficult not to wonder what others supported it.

"I asked Ginevra who my birth mother was, and she said she didn't know her name, but that she thought it could be a waitress who worked at Papa's restaurant. A girl who had drug problems, who couldn't be the mother her baby—me—deserved."

"Really?" Max's eyebrows flick up. "Huh. I guess that's possible."

"Yeah." Papa was always helping everyone, especially the Eastern European immigrants who worked at his diner—looking over résumés, giving our old clothes to the ones who had children. We didn't have much, but we had more than a lot of them. Is it a stretch to think that if someone needed to give up a child, Papa wouldn't have stepped in to take her? To take *me*?

"Ginevra could have lied, though," Max says. "I mean, if it's her . . . if she . . ."

I swallow hard. "But how would her and Papa's paths have ever crossed? It makes no sense. But . . ." I remember how Ginevra was kind of evasive when I pressed for details. She seemed shocked I didn't know. Maybe she just regretted telling me, when it wasn't her place to dig and share.

"And if Ginevra is actually my . . ." I can't say it. It's too crazy. "Then why would she have told me I was adopted but lied about who gave me up?"

"I don't know. I have no idea, and, like, yeah. There's no way she would know Papa. He was in the Soviet Union and then Michigan his whole life."

"Right. There's no way," I agree, even though something heavy sits in my stomach—the feeling that I am not very sure about anything right now.

CHAPTER ELEVEN

Ginevra

Three Months Before

Ginevra Ex sat across her dining room table from Rory Aronov and watched her twenty-sixth main character sip Acqua Panna from a crystal goblet.

Twenty-six main characters, and Rory was without a doubt Ginevra's favorite, even though they'd yet to begin.

Ginevra had published one book a year since her early thirties. She'd written other books before—as a child, as a teenager, in her twenties. Those books she'd long ago torched, turned to quite literal ashes. They were about her. Fiction, but really truth masquerading as fiction. It was common sentiment that an author's first main character most acutely resembles herself. And in Ginevra's case, this was true for her first book, her second, her third. She had a world to work out in ink, but in the end, she couldn't untangle any of it. Everything she wrote was awful sludge—attempting and not succeeding to parse her guilt and shame, to make it up to her father, to her mother, to her sister. Especially to her sister.

Ginevra had loved writing since she was a child. Writing was how she made sense of the world. Or tried to.

Her solution was to stop. Full stop. For a year she didn't write a word. Occasionally she picked up a pen, hovered it over a notebook, and tried to summon something. But she couldn't. Couldn't face herself on the pages anymore.

Maybe if she were braver, she'd often thought. But if there was anything her life had proven to her, it was that she was not.

And then one day, working at the Biblioteca Nazionale Centrale di Roma, Ginevra was shelving books and came across a teenage girl in one of the aisles. Propped on her knees, pages furiously turned, was *La Coscienze di Zeno. Zeno's Conscience*—the book that had touched Ginevra more than any other. It featured Zeno, a neurotic businessman, forever trying and failing to stop smoking. He narrates his memoirs to his psychologist, revealing his many faults, as life throws him one punch after another. Or perhaps Zeno courts those punches. For instance, he has the choice among three sisters to marry—two beautiful, one ugly. He chooses the ugly one. And he lusts after the other two thereafter.

Yes, Ginevra related to Zeno and to the story so much that she had a copy by her bedside, pages worn and dog-eared. Zeno fascinated her—at once he could reflect on his actions and habits, yet be tricked into repeating his mistakes again and again.

The girl saw Ginevra examining her book. She smiled. "Have you read this?"

"Many times," Ginevra answered.

"Does he ever quit smoking?" the girl asked.

"Never manages to."

"Ah." The girl frowned.

Ginevra understood it: If Zeno could succeed at his hardest mission, then the girl—and Ginevra—might feel they, too, could succeed at the thing that vexed them. But life wasn't as even as that. Sometimes it was better to stop trying.

"I smoke, too. Drink, also."

"Me too," Ginevra admitted.

And suddenly the girl was closing the book and confiding in Ginevra about how a few months ago she was riding a *motorino* and the crosswalk, as in all of Rome, was faded and not entirely visible, and so the girl didn't see an old man crossing the street, and accidentally she careened into him. He died instantly. And Ginevra heard, and understood, the girl's pain. But it was a different story—different facts. A different person. The girl's mother was wealthy and tried to cover it up, and the girl was apparently a burgeoning artist, but after the accident, she said she threw red paint on all her canvases.

As the girl spoke, Ginevra listened, and asked the questions that sprouted in her mind. She was curious about this girl, for sure, but even more, she thought, *You.You would be an excellent main character.*

And that was how it was all born. With a new person—a person not Ginevra herself—fanning out fascinating quirks and thoughts and feelings, Ginevra found her creativity flowing again, able to run wild. To devise crazy scenarios in which to place her characters. But they were not her. That was the freedom of it. She didn't have to delve into her own past for backstory or pain points. Main characters were a surfeit, a spout that didn't stop streaming.

Ginevra's first book was an international sensation. It was still difficult for Ginevra to believe that she'd created a career of what was first and foremost the pure joy in her life. Imagining, creating. Her fingers always trembled, poised over her notebook, as a new person began to speak. What might be birthed.

And as yet, the past—Ginevra's past—would lay dormant. Festering, sure. But on the whole, blessedly undisturbed.

So many readers told Ginevra that she changed their lives. That she inspired them. Entertained them. Distracted them from their troubles. Illuminated pockets of light in their rooms full of darkness.

Still, for as long as she could remember, Ginevra had felt the world would be better off without her. She nearly did something about it after that treacherous time in her early twenties. But her readers—they convinced her to stay in this world.

And besides, there was Orsola. Ginevra would forever be making it up to her sister. It was Ginevra's well-due punishment to stay and care for Orsola, provide for her. To stay and try to make it up to her.

Ginevra always fell in love with her main characters. How could you not? When you saw the whole of a person—sometimes their hatred of themselves or their pride. The fleeting, flickering shadows that conjured their innocent child selves. The secrets not even their parents or spouses knew. When a person showed you everything, turned their insides out, it was impossible not to love them. This was what Ginevra had learned in her long life.

With one exception. The rule did not extend to herself.

Ginevra knew everything she had done. Everything she was. And it was not lovable. Yes, she had spent a lifetime repenting for it—but she'd need lifetimes more.

Now Ginevra watched Rory drink her water, tentatively, unsure. It was early days together. There was much to get to, parts that wouldn't be fun. Main characters usually anticipated this, arrived anxious to Ginevra's apartment on the first day, accepted her extension of limoncello shots. But Rory was sticking to water now, which made Ginevra respect her even more—that Rory didn't need to bury her nerves in order to face what would come next.

"Let this be fun, too," Ginevra always said. She meant it, but alcohol was medicine, too.

Ginevra certainly imbibed. Italians in general are not big drinkers. In fact, the Italian language has no single word for a hangover. But in this way, Ginevra did not typify Italian stereotypes. She needed to drink to survive life. Occasionally, after a bottle of wine, she could feel almost happy.

Of course, in other ways, Ginevra was very Italian. Take the Italian children's character of Pinocchio—the story beloved worldwide. Not the versions bastardized by Walt Disney but the one by Carlo Collodi. It is a story not about the perils of lying, like everyone thinks. In fact, in the original story, Pinocchio tells several lies, but in none of those instances does his nose grow even a smidge. Disney created the moral tie-in. But Collodi's version epitomized the Italian way—in Italy, lying amuses; it doesn't elicit the same degree of contempt or condemnation as in other societies.

Ginevra was comfortable with lying. Especially about herself.

"Do you need anything? Do you feel at home?" she asked Rory, caring very much about the answer.

"Yes. Thank you. Your home is so beautiful."

Ginevra gazed around with pride. Her home was beautiful, it was true. Italian frescoes adorned the walls, tree-filled country vistas hand painted by acclaimed Italian artists. The living area boasted silver brocade sofas; a gold baroque chandelier; twisted silver lamps with red shades; and on the jade dining table, at which Ginevra and Rory were sitting, a jardiniere brimming with wild poppies. Ginevra didn't allow many people into her apartment—it was her safe space, to retreat from the world, to share with her main characters and her sister, when Orsola visited from Positano.

"Thank you. The decor is inspired by Sophia Loren. She was my idol when I was a girl. Still is."

Rory nodded politely. She wasn't the generation, of course, of Sophia

Loren. Neither was Ginevra, but though she was fifty-nine, not exactly ancient, she'd always felt older than her biological age.

"Shall we get started?"

"Sure," Rory said nervously. "Where do you want to start?"

Ginevra considered this. She preferred to be spontaneous in the moment, to follow her instincts. Now she sifted for question number one. It should be easy. Day one was for easy. Even though everything was riding on this new book. It had to succeed. Ginevra was acutely aware of the pressure, on her and on Rory, to turn out a memorable main character. Absolutely everything was pinned upon it.

But easy day one, Ginevra reminded herself, trying to quell the knots in her chest. "What inspired you to become a news anchor?" she finally asked.

"Oh." Rory smiled in a way that Ginevra couldn't parse—half smile, half grimace. "It's funny, but I've thought of this more recently. After . . ."

It hung in the air. After she was fired, though Ginevra didn't want to pursue it, not now. There was time for that—much time to explore every last crevice of Rory's life.

"My father always said I'd be an excellent news anchor. I'm curious, I love people's stories, figuring out what's behind the masks everyone wears. And to be honest . . ."

Ginevra smiled, tried to make her at ease. "Yes, please do be honest. Brutally so."

Rory nodded. "I suppose I do like being the star. My brother's always said so, at least. And so anchoring, reporting, it made sense. But maybe the real reason is that Papa slipped the idea in my head as a child."

Ginevra nodded, transcribing it. Ansel. She would ask more about him—she definitely would. But not now.

"Makes sense." Ginevra nodded. "You're beautiful. Very dynamic. Wonderful with people, attuned to them, to ask the right question. I have personal experience with you, of course. And you were sharp. Asked incisive questions. I'm not only saying so. I felt it firsthand."

Rory blushed. "Thanks. I guess I've always been interested in people. Their stories. What makes them how they are. Some anchors love the headlines, the adrenaline, but I preferred the interviews, especially with someone new. Making them comfortable. Finding out the small things that are really the big things. And the rush of the studio—I'd lose all sense of time, all sense of myself, really."

Ginevra recorded it and thought, *Funny, how we all try in different ways to make ourselves disappear.*

"But there were negatives to the job, too. I don't want you to only know the positive slant. Because then you're missing how I was basically never off my phone, scrolling through the endless international horror stories on our network Slack."

"That was hard?"

"Not hard as in laborious, per se, but it sucks your energy, all that bad, sad news. Although I guess you could say it is . . . was . . . laborious work, too. Because I'd be doing fifty things at once, absorbing all the news pouring in while conferring with my producers, and researching stories, and manically weaving it all together in something palatable for our audience while a producer was shouting at me that I needed to get into hair and makeup. And then of course I'd smile big as I was cued onto air." Rory demonstrated, a wide, beautiful smile that Ginevra noticed for the first time had nothing real behind it. "It was important to smile in just the right way. Likably, for likability ratings, and credibly, so our viewers would feel like they could rely on me."

Ginevra recorded it, absorbed it—the elements of anchoring that Rory didn't love, that didn't spark her with joy. In her own way, Ginevra related. Even writing, which Ginevra adored, entailed the necessary evils of interviews and social media.

Ginevra pondered where to take the conversation next. A new question hovered on the tip of her tongue. It was more provocative than she usually asked on day one, but this wasn't a typical interview, nor was Rory a typical main character. And Ginevra found that she couldn't wait anymore—her eagerness was overflowing.

"What was it like, as a child, with your father and Max?"

"Oh." Rory flushed, then smiled wide and, Ginevra thought, genuinely. "I had the best childhood, truly."

Ginevra felt a puzzle piece she didn't know she was missing slot back into her heart. "You felt loved?"

"Very." Rory's voice trembled, the way a main character's usually did when Ginevra had hit on someone or something important.

"I mean, don't get me wrong, I wanted a mom. It was hard sometimes without a mom." Rory stopped, remembering, and Ginevra felt an ocean of pain in her chest. Ginevra wanted to ask when Ansel told her she was adopted. What that was like, reconciling it? Whether Max ever longed for his mother, too?

Piano, piano, Ginevra reminded herself. Slowly, slowly.

She didn't want to scare the girl or hurt her. In all likelihood, Rory would raise the fact of her adoption on her own volition. And if not, then in a few weeks, Ginevra would gently inquire about it. Not now.

She exhaled deeply, prodding the words back into her throat.

Not now.

"Of course, there were times I ached for a mom, like when I got my period or saw other girls running into their moms' arms after school. Their moms would, like, take out their pigtails that were rumpled from the school day and fix them and make them perfect. Whereas my hair was awful. A bowl cut, basically. Papa took me to the Ukrainian barber." Rory laughed softly.

Ginevra's hand flew across her page, transcribing every word. She knew later that day she would read the pages again, savor them. She didn't know yet how she'd spin the novel, what fiction she'd make of Rory's truth, but those things were of less importance than what would emerge from these interviews. And this day, talking about Ansel, was something Ginevra had eagerly anticipated for oh so long.

She took a breath. She must not let on about her eagerness.

"I mean, yeah, I would have loved to have a mother," Rory continued, "but I'm not sure I felt the lack as much as I felt . . . so happy to have Papa. Because my dad, he totally adored us. He's—well, he *was*—so much fun. And we were the center of his world. We didn't have a lot of money, but made do, and he was big on activities—skating on our lake in winter, sledding, swimming. We did everything together. The three musketeers." She smiled sadly. "That's what he called us. He worked hard—he was the chef at the local Russian restaurant. It wasn't how he was trained. He's a violinist. Hugely talented."

She sighed, something painful in her eyes. "But he didn't make it into the local orchestras. I guess Americans don't appreciate classical music like Eastern Europeans do. Often I wondered, though, if he was disappointed. . . ."

"Disappointed?"

"In how his life turned out, I guess. He never married. Not after . . ."

Ginevra waited for the rest of the sentence, but it didn't come.

"I don't know. I guess he'd had the real love of his life. He once said that his mother had told him to only be with someone if you can't live without them. My grandfather, Papa's father, died suddenly when Papa was young, and his mother was content with just Papa. She didn't want someone as a placeholder, I guess. But I don't know. . . . I've always wondered . . ."

"Yes?"

"If he missed out. You know?"

Ginevra felt her breath suck in. She placed her pen onto the table and tried to quietly collect herself. Then she took a big sip from her glass. In the morning, it was limoncello. Normally she could pace herself, but right now her nerves were so jangly; she needed a bigger fix. She would switch to lower-alcohol wine soon.

"In vino veritas" was the saying. Ginevra found it funny and incorrect. For her, wine obfuscated the truth. Wine helped Ginevra to withstand life—to conceal herself, all her horrible truths.

With her main characters, of course, it was different. Ginevra's very goal was to get to *veritá*. Truth.

Truth made for interesting fiction, when you spun it how you wanted. That was where Ginevra's imagination could take root, then blossom.

You had to start with truth, though. Someone's truth, at least.

But in Italian, *veritá* also meant a version. Ginevra knew that, in the interviews to come, there would be Ginevra's *veritá* and Rory's *veritá*. And Rory was here, after all, because Ginevra needed to understand Rory's *veritá* before Ginevra revealed hers.

"Oh, I forgot!" Ginevra said, opting not to pick up the conversation thread about Ansel and his first love. His only love. "We forgot to toast."

"Toast?" Rory asked.

"Yes. Doesn't matter— you can do it with water. But I like to toast on the first day, to set the tone for our whole experience."

"Okay," Rory said uncertainly, raising her water glass.

Ginevra closed her eyes. "To a fruitful partnership. To truth flowing freely. To love and sunshine in Rome."

When Ginevra opened her eyes, Rory was smiling, her sweet, glittery smile that made Ginevra smile in her heart, too.

"To you, Rory. You will be a wonderful main character." Ginevra felt strangely happy and also sad, nostalgic. Unexpected words glided out over her tongue. "'All the world's a stage, and all the men and women merely players.'"

Rory looked at Ginevra quizzically. "Shakespeare, right?"

"Yes." Ginevra sighed. "'And so he plays his part.'"

Rory nodded politely, and Ginevra could tell Rory was trying to indulge her. That, to Rory, Ginevra was a quirky old ugly lady babbling unimportant stuff. Ginevra was reminded of the vitriolic note she once received from a reader, accusing Ginevra of masking her "obvious loneliness" by buying off people as main characters, to pay her attention foremost, essentially hiring a friend under the pretense of filling a story. Ginevra received tons of fan mail—hundreds of letters a week, most resoundingly positive, with the exception of her last book, which both the critics and readers had panned. But alongside the failure of her last book, that one old note had hurt—had dug itself a place in the loop of Ginevra's thoughts.

Maybe it was true in some ways. Maybe it was especially true here.

Ginevra clinked Rory's glass. "*Alla famiglia*," she said, taking a long sip of her limoncello.

"To family?" Rory's nose crinkled up. "Is that what that means?"

"Oh. Yes. It's how my father used to toast. *La famiglia è tutto*. Family is everything. *Il sangue non è acqua*. Blood is thicker than water. It's a very Italian saying. But it is at the very core of our being, as Italians."

Rory nodded uncertainly.

"Old habit," Ginevra said, seeing that she'd gone a bit too far, needed to tone it down, to not raise Rory's suspicions. "Although main characters do indeed become my family. That's what I always say."

In fact, it was not a thing Ginevra always said.

But with Rory, Ginevra did mean it.

CHAPTER TWELVE

Rory

Max and I continue along the path between Riomaggiore and Manarola, down a steep rocky way that makes me rethink my questionable hiking attire again. Caro and Nate are far ahead, not even visible from my current vantage point, where all that exists is a panorama of waves swirling in white froth, then smacking the cliffs dizzyingly far below. Max scrambles to the bottom of the path and I follow more tentatively. He reaches out his hand, and I take it, jittery from the heights and exertion and the still-present adrenaline rush of the boulder rolling at me.

"I got you," Max says, which teases out my smile. It occurs to me that our roles were reversed as kids—it was I who had him. Had Papa, too.

Papa always said, "My tough girl. My bulldog. My strong one." Something pulls at my heart, wrings it up like a rag, when I remember him calling me those things, his voice filled with pride, but maybe also with need.

I feel Max bear some of my weight, and finally I leap. I smile at my brother, dust my pants off.

"You've changed," I tell him.

"What do you mean?"

"Just . . . you've got it all together." I give him a weak smile. "And I've got nothing together."

"I wouldn't say that," he says breezily, but not at all convincing.

We stop to look out over the peninsula jutting into the sea, with what appears to be ruins of a medieval castle at the far end and a mélange of tin rooftops, nestled close. Orchids mingle with the thick brush, and ginormous yachts litter the water, anchored as far along the coastline as I can see. The silence between us now is stretching, yawning; I think we'd both rather it engulfs us. That we can continue to pretend there weren't so many lies. Lies told by Max, but more pivotally by Papa.

"I'm thinking about Ginevra still," Max says. "Like, Ror, why this trip? Why you? Does she do this for every main character she hires?"

I consider it, the surprise, the extravagance. All the subterfuge. Her note—the stuff about Caro, and the lunch reservation at Le Sirenuse after the trip. So bizarrely mysterious.

"You think she . . ." My lips begin to form a theory, running ahead of my brain.

"I don't know, Ror. I hardly know her. Just our couple chats on Zoom. Which were kind of strange in themselves. But I mean, I was happy to do them for you." I nod. "How do you even know this author in the first place?"

I think about five years back, how I didn't even have my own show yet but was part of a team building a new network from scratch. How exciting that felt to be creating something that was going to make a mark, make a difference. Insane hours, so much enthusiasm, the magic of the studio—the lights, the frenzy, how in but one day, you could prepare and interview and then produce something tangible. I was only doing field reporting and filling in when other anchors were out, but I was thrilled, because all of it was a step up from my radio days. It was happening—it was all happening, the dreams I was bent toward achieving. And Ginevra Ex—the private, bestselling author—decided to give an interview to our brand spanking new network to launch her latest book. It was a huge get, teasing the infamously reclusive author out of her cave. It meant we were creating the kind of prestige we desired, attracting good guests and talent, of which I was one. The talent. Crazy to believe, and how it stoked my ego, too. Somehow I was assigned the gig to interview Ginevra, and we hit it off—even though she was a hard person to probe. Since I was a child, I've noticed that people naturally open up in my presence, that I'm a good listener—both important qualities of a successful anchor.

Ginevra, though, was a challenge. She evaded personal questions. She wanted to talk writing, the process, her courting of the muse, even fashion and design, subjects in which she was interested, although her taste ran to the frankly garish. She decidedly did not want to talk about her past or her personal motivations—only those of her main characters. Which still proved fascinating, both to me and to our audience. The first interview was a rousing success, and so others followed. Each time Ginevra released a new book, it became my thing to invite her on air along with her main character. To talk about what was truth and what was fiction, and how she achieved the dance between them both.

Now, though, I wonder, why me? Why I was the chosen one, of all anchors she could have picked?

I tell Max the backstory. He exhales slowly, clearly skeptical. "Huh."

"She's never even lived in Michigan. It's impossible she'd—"

"It's weird, though, LS."

"But then why would she have told me about my adoption in such a strange way? If she gave me up for adoption, if she orchestrated my main character thing because she's—I don't know—curious about me, or wants to reunite, then why wouldn't she have just told me so?"

"I'm probably off, then." Max shrugs.

But I don't feel so confident either, about any of it. "I could ask Papa."

"You could. But, Ror—"

"I know. It's unlikely that he'll be able to give me clarity."

Max is quiet. Finally, he says, "Sometimes it's like he's the old Papa. For a few minutes we have him fully. But a huge thing like this, this emotional—a secret he's clearly kept for his own reasons, well, I just think you have to be careful about approaching him with something like this."

"Yeah, I know. I need to call him anyway. God, sometimes, though . . . sometimes I dread it."

Max nods. He of anyone gets it—the little stabs I feel in my chest when I notice Papa has deteriorated, that a skill he used to have mastered has now disappeared through his fist like sand. Or when I have an entire conversation with him that I find almost shockingly nice and connected, and then when we say goodbye, he smiles and says, "You are a very wonderful lady. Now, who are you again?"

"I haven't talked to him since right before the silent retreat," I admit.

"Well, if it's any consolation, he won't remember." Max smiles, the smile of a person who sees Papa all the time, who can actually joke about these things.

I grimace. "It's harder for the person who's always far, I think."

"I don't know about that, Ror." Max's tone is sharp. "Could be harder for the person who's right there. Who has to rush over when Papa wanders out for a walk and doesn't return. Who has to drive across Farmington like a maniac, trying to find him."

I nod, ashamed. That was a couple of months ago. Max told me only after he'd found Papa, at a park where we used to play as kids. "Sorry. I know."

"You don't know, though. Not really."

I bristle, but don't want to argue. "I appreciate your being there. I really do. If you weren't . . ."

If you weren't, I would have to be. And I don't think I could do it.

Aloud I say, "I'm calling Papa later."

It might not solve any mysteries. He might not even know it's me. But I know I need to.

We walk in quiet for a while, occasionally peel a few purple grapes off dangling vines from the vineyard and munch on them. Two kids pass ahead of us, giggling. Kids, because they look to be in their early twenties, their pale arms unblemished by the spots and freckles that the years seem to hoard.

"Were we ever that young?" I ask Max.

He laughs, then snorts, a classic Max move. "*I* was. You had the soul of an eighty-year-old as a newborn."

He didn't know me as a newborn, I almost say, but decide to take the high road. "I always had it together, huh?"

"Always."

"Guess I was due a breakdown at some point," I say cheerfully.

"Is this the breakdown?" He gestures at my outfit. "If so, you make breakdown look good."

I laugh. "Thanks. I got that going for me, at least."

We've nearly caught back up to Nate and Caro. They've stopped at a terraced lookout on a cliff high over Riomaggiore and the coastline, with endless vineyards to their backs, wedged against mountains covered in shrubby Mediterranean macchia. They're in what looks like an intense conversation, all terse hand motions and pinched faces. When Caro spots us, she suddenly stops midstream.

"What's . . . um, you guys okay?" I call out.

Caro nods. Her lips crater into a wide salesy smile. "Great."

"Yeah, all good." Nate dusts his hands of invisible dirt and goes to stare out over the guardrail. I wonder if they've been talking about me.

In a few moments, Nate is back, poring over his map. "Okay, I say we take the train to Corniglia. Otherwise it's three miles, a lot of that uphill. Or do you guys want to hike it?"

"Train," Caro and I say in unison.

"Right. Okay. It's supposed to be the least exciting town, set away from the sea but with incredible views. Then we'll hike to Vernazza. That's an easier one. Flat terrain. We can explore the castle there, go to a lunch place Ginevra put on the itinerary. Ristorante Belforte. Then we'll hop on the train again to Monterosso, explore the town a bit, and spend the rest of the afternoon lounging at a *bagno*." He says the Italian word for beach club proudly, in his Fabrizio voice.

"What do you guys say?" Then his eyes crease with concern. "How you doing, Ror? I didn't even ask."

"Perfect. But can we add a coffee stop in the mix in the foreseeable future?"

"*Sì, signorina.*" Then Nate sings, again, "*Dipinto di blu.*" I groan, but he winks at me, a wink I well know. Still, I can feel something in me that's hardened—stiff where it would usually soften.

Then Nate, Max, and Caro set off toward the train. I pause for a moment, drop my attention into my body, like they taught us on the retreat, and watch them—Max and Nate chattering, Caro off to the side, scrolling on her phone, her expression weirdly gloomy.

"Coming, Ror?" Nate glances back, and the rest of them do, too.

"Yep." I slowly walk over.

"Ror." Caro's at my side. "Hi." She says it softly, almost afraid.

"Hi yourself."

"Look . . . maybe I'm off, but gonna say it anyway. If I didn't know better, I'd think you were avoiding me." I hear the implication in her tone—that this is weird, that we are weird. We aren't ourselves, our typical Rory and Caro.

"I'm not avoiding you. It's just . . . a lot. This trip. Nate." I think how to sum up our breakfast conversation, then don't have the energy to. "That boulder. Stuff with Max. God, I have stuff to tell you. Not now, though."

I have stuff to *ask* her, too.

"I have stuff to tell you, too."

"Yeah?" I cock my head at her, trying to get a sense of what's going on. Her eyes flit over to the guys. "Not here."

"Okay. Later, then."

She squeezes my hand as we wait to board the train to Corniglia. I squeeze hers back, and appraise her panther ring, running my finger over the emeralds.

"This new?" I ask. "I'm obsessed."

"You want it?" She pulls it off and plops it in my palm.

"Shut up." I laugh.

"No, I'm serious. You can have it. I *want* you to have it."

"I don't want it." I push it back at her, slide it on her finger. "You're crazy. You're way too generous."

She shrugs, pushes the ring back down past her knuckle. "What's mine is yours. And you don't have a job at the moment, so I thought . . ."

"Well, buy me a sandwich, not a Cartier panther ring!"

"I'm happy to buy you both." Then Caro smiles at me, her wide, warm smile, and a thousand memories lodge themselves like little pillows propping up my heart. Caro, aged nine: a girl in my class I didn't know well, quiet, head down, the only one, other than me, who never had money for a hot school lunch. She approached me on the playground one afternoon and said shyly, "I like your shorts." I looked down, confused. They were brown cloth with faded daisies and a bleach stain in the back. Then I saw the hopeful tilt of her chin and understood. She'd chosen me. Needed me. Later I discovered why. Caro's father was always gambling over the border in Windsor, and Caro's mother was obsessed with horses. Some winters, her mom chose to fund the horse's keep instead of paying their heating bill. Caro once overheard her mom say to a friend that she loved her horse more than she loved her daughter.

Caro always says that the person she is, and all she has achieved in life, is a credit to me, Max, and Papa. We took her in. We gave her a family when the one she had royally sucked. And in return, she's the most loyal friend to me and Max, and to Papa. And the most thoughtful, like making scrapbooks for my birthday with ticket stubs she saved from when we were twelve, organizing a blowout surprise party for my thirtieth, and randomly buying me a shirt she got herself, too, because she knew I'd love it. She's also beyond generous. Offering up her Cartier ring is typical Caro. It's probably one of the reasons her finances haven't been tip-top. But it's not just money—she's attuned to the littlest needs of those she loves. Whenever I come to Michigan, she picks me up at the airport with bottles of water and my favorite snacks. She insists on filling our cabin ahead of time with all my favorite foods, and then stays with us at Papa's, putting out fresh peonies and the wafers I love on the nightstand. She does that kind of stuff for Papa even when I'm not there—replenishes his stock of halvah, takes him to his longtime barber. She sends me videos of Papa, hugs him extra for me.

Caro is the best. Ginevra simply has to be wrong. Caro can't be embezzling from Max. She just can't.

The train pulls into the station, and once we're ensconced inside with a crush of tourists all yammering in a tangle of languages, I spontaneously hug my best friend.

"I love you so much. We'll talk later, okay?"

"Later," Caro agrees, her breath a tunnel on my neck, her tone odd, though, prickling all my little hairs. It feels like some kind of promise.

CHAPTER THIRTEEN

Caroline

Sometimes Max can be especially eye-roll-inducing—like when he tries to order his Zhitomir salad at a luxe chef restaurant.

We are at the spectacular Ristorante Belforte in Vernazza, carved high up into the cliffs, rope railings navigating the stone walls and tables shrouded in white linens, with navy umbrellas overhead. At first there was a mishap about our reservation; they had us down for an hour later. Max began to get heated, raising his voice at the poor, meek maître d'. Hungry Max is a phenomenon best to avoid. I could tell that old Aronov temper was about to geyser out, but thankfully right then the manager arrived, patting a hand on Max's shoulder, saying we were VIPs, and they would fit us in, *nessun problema*. So here we are, miraculously at the best table in the house. There is no fight for the good seat—every seat is a good one, with three-sixty views of the sea. I've ordered the trofie pasta in Ligurian pesto. Rory and Nate have each opted for squid ink tagliolini. And Max is issuing his precise specifications for his Zhitomir salad.

What is a Zhitomir salad, you might rightfully ask? Zhitomir is the small town in Ukraine from which Ansel Aronov hails. It's a few hours southeast of Kiev, a fertile place in summer—endless green—and in winter, it's one long cold that seizes your bones. With antisemitic bullies lurking around frozen corners.

But apparently, they had delicious salads. Salads made of radishes and green onions and tomatoes, chopped small. At the Russian diner next to the Jewish Community Center in our hometown where Ansel was chef, one of the salads on the menu was called the Zhitomir salad. (Not many people other than Max ordered it. The blintzes, on the other hand . . . chef's kiss.) But I understand why Max loves it, why he orders it on vacations, even. The salad ties Max to Ansel, and of all his identities—brother, CEO, friend—Max cherishes his title as Ansel's son the most.

Max is still describing the salad to our patient and incredibly attractive bronzed waiter, Alessandro, with swoopy dark hair. Historically, I'm a sucker for swoopy dark hair. Gabriele's got it, too—and I definitely noticed Rory eyeing his up. Max's got the swoopy hair gene as well. His lack of swoopy dark hair has never been our problem. Max drones on with his precise specifications, down to the dressing of olive oil and red vinegar—but not too much vinegar. I feel my chest tighten with each ingredient addition.

When Max finishes, Alessandro smiles good-naturedly. "Sir, you are in Italy. How about you order an Italian salad?"

That's it—I devolve into giggles. It's not just me, though—Nate and Rory erupt, too. A shadow passes over Max's face, and for a tense moment, I wonder if he's going to unleash. But he clears his throat, and his eyes go light again.

"An Italian salad. Okay, I'll have an Italian salad." He throws up his hand in congenial surrender. Then he points to our water glasses. "Can we get some ice for the waters, though, please?"

The waiter chuckles. "You are American, no?" Then he ambles away, his laughs still audible.

"Is it really that weird to ask for ice?" Max asks, his irritation obvious.

Rory shrugs. "Italians like water room temperature."

"Fine. But is it that egregious to ask? And what is an Italian salad exactly?"

"A caprese, Max." I roll my eyes. "Progress, though. I remember a time not so long ago that you would have lost it. Insisted on your Zhitomir salad."

Rory bellows out a laugh. "Gone full-out chess pieces."

"Ha ha," Max says dryly.

No need to rehash, we all remember the incident Rory means. Rory and I were in middle school, and the three of us would play casual im-promptu chess tournaments. One time it ended in Max and me for the championship. But Max lost; I still remember that sweet final checkmate. And how suddenly, he was throwing Rory's board and all the pieces into the lake.

"I apologized," Max grumbles. "I brought you guys Dairy Queen after, didn't I? And bought you a new set, Ror. And honestly, that happened ages ago. That's the problem about being around people who've known you since you were a kid. They don't notice your evolution. They want to remember you like you were."

"Maxie, I haven't known you since you were a kid, and I still think you are a character, my man." Nate slaps Max on the back good-naturedly. "But I guess if Maximillions wants a Zhitomir salad, Maximillions can have a Zhitomir salad. You can hire someone to be your full-time Zhito-mir salad man. I mean, why not?"

"I don't quite have the funds for that yet," Max says, cheerfully now. "But isn't that the dream?"

"You can't find the funds in your millions?" Nate fans out his red-and-white-checked linen napkin on his lap and removes that dorky panama hat that ages him a couple of decades into a goofy tourist dad. Or bum-bling American. Same vibe.

Max smiles. He turns out his pockets, demonstrating their emptiness. "My millions are all on paper now. Nothing to see here, until we turn a profit. One day, I'll have my Zhitomir salad man."

"That's when you'll know you've made it, huh?" Rory smiles genu-inely, and I know something has been smoothed out with her brother. Even though I don't know what. It bothers me, not knowing. I always need to know where I stand with the two of them. I suppose it's because of how I needed them, how I've relied on them to be my family. How I still do. It's why . . .

Let's just say it's informed everything in my life. And I don't know what to do. I truly don't. . . . . My eyes fizz with the blue of the water. It's strange to feel so utterly hopeless in a place as majestic as this.

"I'll know I've made it when I've cured Papa," Max says as our waiter returns, pen poised over pad. "Hey, what are we drinking?" Max asks.

"White wine? Something local?" Nate asks. "Franciacorta?"

"What's that?" Max asks.

"Like prosecco, but from the Lombardy region." Nate pulls something out of his pocket—two interlinked metal circles. His fidget toy. His fingers begin working it. He's on edge. We all are, I guess. I can almost feel the vibration of his knee bumping up and down under the table, too.

"Franciacorta, then." Max shuts the menu, his Italian accent so abysmal normally I would smile. Or laugh.

I don't.

"I'll have a vodka neat," Rory says, then negotiates with Alessandro about which kind of vodka is their best. Alessandro says he'll have to go check; he'll be right back.

Into the void, I say, "Ror, how you feeling after that rock attack?"

"Oh." Rory spins out a smile. "I'm fine. Must have been one of those things."

"One of those things. I mean, I guess? Rocks getting dislodged. Barreling right toward you? Another day in paradise."

"Yeah." Rory shifts in her chair, looks uneasily at the water.

"You know what I was thinking, though?"

"No, what?" Now Nate cocks his head at me.

"If I were the author, I mean. Just putting myself in her shoes. Her last book bombed, didn't it?"

"Yeah. What does that matter, though?" Rory flickers uncertain eyes at me.

"Well, if I wanted to make sure my next book was on the map, I'd arrange some PR stunt with my new main character." I cough, clear my throat. "I mean, if I were psychotic. I was just thinking, is all. If that boulder had hit Ror . . ."

"It would have been all over every newspaper," Max says slowly.

"That's insane," Nate says. "There's no way the author is that diabolical. Rory could have *died*."

"Insane," I agree. "But is it out of the realm of possibility that she could have leveraged this trip for her ends?"

"*Leveraged* this trip?" Rory says, her face pale, but I'm not sure if she's angry at me or at what I'm suggesting, or both. "You're being so corporate, C. *Leveraged* this trip? She sent me—she sent *us*—on this ridiculously luxe vacation, and you're suggesting she, what? I mean, what *exactly* are you suggesting? Ginevra can barely walk up a flight of stairs without struggling to breathe properly, but somehow she located this massive rock and pushed it down a mountain right when we were passing, in exactly the right direction to hit *me*?"

"No! I mean, it's not like I really think *she* pushed the boulder. But isn't it possible she was behind it? Like, she could have other minions on the train. Besides Gabriele, I mean. Look at the people on the train who were on the trail, too. Probably others we didn't notice."

Silence, as that lands with a thud. Probably they didn't contemplate that, but I have. I've contemplated a lot of things.

"And another thing." I'm on a roll, but I can't stop. "Wasn't there something in the book? A rock through the window . . . that narrowly missed you, Ror. I mean . . . *Laci*."

"Oh, wow," Rory says. "Yeah, actually. During the snowstorm, when they lose power. She's looking through old journals, trying to find that pivotal clue, when—"

"The rock crashes in. If she hadn't been crouched on the floor, it would have smashed into her skull. I haven't finished yet. Don't know who did it."

"You did." Rory doesn't smile.

"I'm the villain? I'm the murderer? Candace?" Well then. Interesting, that.

"How about that? Caro's the murderer?" Max asks. "Funny."

"Is it?" I ask.

"I mean, it sort of is." Max smiles. "But back to reality, huh? The book isn't real. No one's trying to take Rory out."

The table is now stiflingly quiet. My bag is heavy in my lap—the book. That damn book. Fiction doesn't grip me like nonfiction. I'd be far more riveted by Roman history or a travelogue, and *The Cabin on the Lake* is absurdly long. I'm halfway through, though. I should have stayed up to finish, and now I'm deeply regretting that I didn't. So I'm the villain? Then maybe Ginevra knows. Both things. Both my dirty secrets. Max confided to me now, on the last portion of our hike, that Rory told him Ginevra hired private investigators. To look into us all, apparently. Wild. And now I can't stop wondering whether this trip is more than simply a frivolous gift. What Ginevra has truly planned for Rory. For us all.

I'm in the most beautiful place on earth, with the most important people in my life, and all I want is to escape. I feel quite like jumping off that rail into the sweet blue water and sinking down into oblivion. Throwing in the proverbial towel.

Suddenly, Alessandro is back, chirpy and oblivious. "We don't have Zyr, but we do have Grey Goose, signorina."

"Great," Rory says. "Thanks."

I busy myself staring at my nails as I feel the waiter's eyes move to me. I communicate my decline silently. Hope he'll get the hint, mosey on.

"C?" Rory asks. "You didn't order yet."

Usually I'm the drinker of us all—I can throw back four vodkas in a row, easy. Once in a while I black out, sure, but more in my twenties than now. For the past couple of months, though, I've stopped drinking, but if I said so now, I'd invite questions I don't want. It's required a bit of subterfuge on my part, like asking the waitress yesterday for a vodka on the rocks when we boarded the train, but then excusing myself for a feigned bathroom break and waving the waitress aside, asking her to please substitute water for the vodka but to make it look like a cocktail. And to keep those coming throughout the trip.

"My stomach feels weird," I say, adding a bright smile. "Drinking will commence later. For now, mineral water, *per favore*."

e

Indeed, I am aggressively sober when we arrive at the beach in Monterosso, the final stop on Ginevra's itinerary for the afternoon. On our way into the last of the five towns, we crossed a stone bridge, and a man popped out from a hole in the side; I still have no clue from where. Turns out he was selling limoncello shots, and the rest of them went overboard, toasting to God knows what. My mind was buzzing too fast to listen properly.

Something settles in me, though, when we descend the steps along the sea. My eyes mop up the uniform rows of striped orange and green umbrellas and lime-green lounge chairs, the sand sweeping out to the turquoise sea, with several rock formations close to shore, that people are climbing and leaping off.

"Oh my God, it's like that movie," Rory says as we all beeline to the sand and strip off our shoes. "You know? What's it called?"

"*The Talented Mr. Ripley?*"

"Oh, right, I almost said *Life Is Beautiful*."

"Definitely not that one." I grimace. "That's a Holocaust movie." I still remember watching it, even though it must have been twenty years ago. How painful I found it, for so many reasons. Because I am Jewish, and the Holocaust lives in our collective DNA. But also because I am sensitive and find it horrific to witness anyone being mistreated. Or perhaps it's simpler—that the movie was memorably excruciating because the little boy in it had such a spectacular father.

My therapist says I am always playing out my father wound.

But I don't say any of that.

"*The Talented Mr. Ripley* had striped umbrellas," I agree. "I'll order up a young Matt Damon, too, if they're offering."

"Really, is Matt Damon your thing, C?" Max asks. "I would have said Ben Affleck."

"What, because he's got hair more like yours?"

Max gives me a hint of a smile. I don't return it.

One of the young bronzed beach guys runs up to us, and Max doles out euros for four beach loungers. The last ones available, it looks like, in the row farthest from the water's edge.

"I want to explore a bit first." My eyes flitter back toward the shopping area that, by the looks of it, is more substantial than the main streets in the other four towns.

"By explore, she means shop," Max says.

"What's wrong with that?" My voice, my chest, flush with anger.

"Nothing." But Max's judgy tone conveys otherwise, and the fact that he's said it so matter-of-factly to Nate and Rory feels like a betrayal.

"I want to take a walk along the shore first," Rory says.

"I have to call the office," Max says.

"Who?" I ask.

"Katerina."

Katerina. Right. The head of the lab.

"I'll . . ." Nate wavers. "I need a new belt."

"A new belt? Here?" Rory asks.

"It's Italy," he says. "They have good leather belts."

"Okay," I say, deciding to take charge. "So let's all meet back here in an hour, why don't we say? Should we put something down, to save our seats?"

"We just paid for them," Rory says.

"Yeah, but still, they seem like a hot commodity. And the beach guys don't look like they're paying much attention." I motion to a cluster of them, half flirting with tourist girls, half riveted to their smartphones. "Here." I riffle in my bag, which was large enough to stuff the book Rory's author wrote at the top. "I'll leave this. No one's gonna steal a book."

"Good call." Max unloads his book from his backpack and places it on another chair.

"Oh," says Rory. "You guys all brought them? So you *are* reading them?" I can't tell if she sounds irritated or pleased. She pulls her copy from her canvas backpack. "Lightens the load, anyway."

"I got mine, too." Nate riffles in his backpack and deposits his on the fourth chair.

I can't help but smile at the sight of the four books, all propped up on the chairs. "Your author needs this shot for Instagram."

"Right." Rory laughs. "Actually she'd probably like it. She has a rabid following." Rory takes a quick photo. "All right, I'm gonna walk a bit."

I know that, despite our conversation earlier, Rory is avoiding me. The two of us love shopping, exploring. Another day we'd squeal around town, me trying to convince her to buy stuff, and her stating all the ways a shirt or jacket didn't quite work, how it could be improved. And then her trying to convince me not to get the shirt or jacket, that I didn't need it, advocating that it wasn't special enough. That I needed to pare back— plus now that she's been traveling in a single suitcase for months, she's also become the poster child of minimalism.

It's okay. I need to think. I guess I'm avoiding her, too.

"See you in a little, guys." And I head off toward the shops, think-ing that I will buy myself something—something really nice. That always works to perk up my mood, to take my mind off things. And, hell, there are *a lot* of those things.

CHAPTER FOURTEEN

Rory

When I locate our chairs after my mindful beachside walk, the Italian family from the train is ensconced in them. At first I think I'm in the wrong place.

Eventually I orient myself, determine that these are indeed our chairs. I clear my throat. "Excuse me, I think . . . these are ours."

The woman slides her ginormous black sunglasses down the bridge of her nose. For the first time, I assess her up close—midforties, with an angular black bob, curtain bangs, and dark eyes rimmed in black kohl. "*Quale?*"

"Hi, ehrm, you're on the train with us, right? I'm—"

"Oh, yes. It's you." She has a melodic voice that doesn't jibe with her angular frame and oozing irritation at having been interrupted from her sun nap. "The girl who fell on the trail."

"I didn't fall. I was almost hit by . . . oh. Whatever. Doesn't matter. But these are our chairs. Sorry, my Italian's not great. And have you seen— I mean . . . where are our books?"

"*Che problema c'è?*" The husband joins in, his chest so orange and slick with oil that I feel like I'm staring blindly at the sun.

"What?" I drop to my knees, moving aside the woman's straw tote to see . . . nothing under her chair.

"He said, *What is your problem?*" The woman still hasn't budged, is sprawled out on our chairs without a seeming care.

"The problem is . . . these are *our* chairs. And my book is missing!"

"Your book? What do you mean, *book*? I didn't see any book. And these are our chairs. My husband has paid for them."

Suddenly, Max is at my side, and then Nate and Caro stagger back, all three confirming that I have not misremembered the location of our chairs. And we argue with the Italians, or spiritedly discuss—which one I'm not sure because we don't exactly understand one another—the Italians with increasingly vigorous hand motions that I can't decode. At some point in our discord, it emerges that Max and I are staying in the Istanbul and Roma suites, respectively. Suddenly there is an about-face—"*Ma non mi dire, we are in the Paris suite!*" They appraise us with newfound interest, their indignation abating.

"Once we meet the people in the Venice Suite, the circle will be complete," the husband says.

"There is a Do Not Disturb sign on the door." The wife winks. "They are having too much sex to come out!"

"Ah." I force a laugh. "But the books? You don't know anything about the books?"

"Books? Again, the books? Buy new books, how about." And with that the wife slips her sunglasses back on and reclines, dismissing us.

So Max flags the beach boys, and there ensues a flurry of activity that involves us all, minus the sunbathing Italians, scavenging beneath and around the chairs, knees in scorching sand. Searching for the elusive books. Our tenuous bond with the Italians by virtue of being wealthy suite goers has dissolved, and now they are mincing no words, eyes full of disdain: They want us gone. Their kids return from the sea, lithe golden bodies dripping in seawater, equally disinterested in our plight, confirming with flicks of wet hair in my face, that no, *niente libri*.

And so, *finalmente*, it is crystal clear—the books are gone. All four copies of *The Cabin on the Lake* vanished without a trace.

After the hubbub, we are ensconced in a different four chairs, recently vacated nearer the shore. The beach boys are triumphant—*sedie migliore!* Best chairs! When I mention that, yes, best chairs but no books, they return triumphantly proffering scuffed paperbacks, apparently from their lost and found.

A pink-covered Susan Mallery and a thick tome with an Italian title.

"*Grazie.*" I muster a smile, accepting the books, whose pages cough up dust.

For a while, we all lay not speaking, staring out at the water nearly as still as a swimming pool, nary a wave, just occasional tiny blurps from the sea that flatten into shell-smattered sand.

"I don't get it—why would anyone take the books?" Max asks. "Especially all four of them."

"Maybe it was an accident," Nate says.

Silence as we all ponder the fitting accident that would result in four identical books being deposited inadvertently in someone else's beach bag. My chest feels knotted tight. The whole hike, I was envisioning the moment I'd lie on the beach and flip the book open again. I still can't shake it, this nagging sensation that I missed a crucial detail on the first read. I just know if I still had the book, I'd find it—it would all click into place.

"She's popular, the author. So probably a fan just took them," Nate says, his tone decisive and curt, like he wants to end this conversation. Why would he want to end this conversation?

"You think it was a fan? I mean . . . doubtful," Caro says. I'm doubtful of that myself, but something in her tone, and the set of her jaw, seems tense.

She lifts her gauzy white cover-up over her head, revealing a neon yellow one-piece in crinkled spandex. Then she stands, showing off her pert round butt, with her birthmark shaped like a crescent moon at the tip-top of her thigh. She digs through her bag, fishes out a canvas bucket hat, plops it on, and eases back onto the lounger, her leg flexing in a pose that could leap out of the pages of an Assouline coffee table book. Predictably, Max is watching her. I smile, and then he blushes and looks away when he sees that I notice.

Things may change, but one thing will always stay the same: Max loves Caro.

I stiffen when I remember that Caro may be embezzling from him. Is probably embezzling from him. Ginevra provided evidence. Bank statements. And what motive would the author have for forging them?

"I guess I agree with Caro on the fan theory," I eventually say. "What are the chances a fan took all four?"

Max slides on a pair of stylish sunglasses—blond plastic frames with brown lenses. What happened to his Oakleys? "You never know. People are weird. Maybe an enterprising person is going to throw them all up on eBay."

"If that's the case, Ginevra will be pissed," I say. "She'll want to control the narrative and obviously the release. It doesn't make any sense." Quiet lingers for a bit, just the dive and squawk of gulls now converging on the chairs to our right, beelining to a three-year-old who is gleefully dispersing a loaf of bread.

"Or maybe . . ." I say, a thought circling my brain.

"The Italians?" Max asks. "Like Caro said earlier. Ginevra could have minions around. Doing this stuff for nefarious—"

"I think you guys are bonkers," Nate says. "You're being paranoid. There's no way this author orchestrated the theft of her own books. Why would she give them to us in the first place? It's not like this theft is going to make front-page news, or any page news, at that. And they're basically worthless—they're early editions, not even hardcovers!"

We all absorb the sense Nate is making. Right. So Ginevra wouldn't have had her own books stolen, but the boulder? Caro's accusation earlier, that there was something sinister behind that boulder rolling at me, still has me off-kilter. And now the books. It's all so bizarre, and I can't help feeling like someone—someone close to me—is burying, or concealing, the lede.

"Hey, new sunglasses?" I ask Max.

"Oh." Max slides them down the bridge of his nose and smiles. "Yeah, whaddya think? I just picked them up."

"You bought yourself sunglasses?" Caro asks incredulously.

My thoughts exactly. Max never shops for himself. Could really care less what he wears, how old his shirts are. If they lose buttons, he takes them to the cheap tailor around the corner from where we grew up. Even with his newfound wealth and success, it doesn't occur to him to splurge for new ones.

"Oh yeah. I called the office quickly and then had a little time. Tried to find Nate and Caro, but couldn't. And no one responded to my texts. I'm in Italy, thought I'd try some Italian sunglasses." Max grins, feigning our waiter at lunch. "The town is pretty cool. Did you find your belt, Nate?"

"What?" Nate is staring out at the sea, lost in thought.

"Your belt," I say.

"Oh." He rubs his eyes and blinks. "No, didn't find one. Did see the church, though. With the black and white stripes."

The church. Right. I saw it described in the glossy magazine on my banquette table. It's one of the landmarks in town, but is Nate bringing it up with some kind of hidden agenda? To prove he was in town—not here, stealing books?

No. I'm being irrational.

Still, I say, "What about you, C? Get anything in town?" I make my voice light, but suddenly I am curious. Curious because of the embezzle-ment stuff, but also because . . . oh God. I can't stop thinking down this route. Thinking that . . . well, a stranger, or someone from the train—the Italians, for instance—could have taken the books, accidentally or in-tentionally, for a variety of reasons. But also, one of us could have taken them. One of us who pretended to mosey around Monterosso but then scrambled back to the chairs when everyone left . . .

"I didn't get anything." Caro shrugs. "I didn't find anything I liked."

Caro could find something she likes in places as far ranging and un-likely as a Chico's and Colonial Williamsburg. So the fact that she didn't find anything in Italy is . . . bizarre.

"Trying to trim the fat, you know?" Caro adds.

I roll my eyes to myself. Does she realize how everything she says now is peppered with corporate speak? And does buying a Cartier pan-ther ring really qualify as your trimming-the-fat phase? Besides, I saw her eyeing the shops right outside the station where our train is docked. No doubt, she's planning to barrage them when we return this afternoon. She can't fool me; we've been best friends far too long.

"I did go to the pharmacy, though." She brightens. "Why are European pharmacies so much cuter than ours?"

"Totally. I love all the creams over here. What did you get? Lemme see!"

Maybe I'm being a bit overkill, but I do love skin care, Caro knows that. And more so, I want to see if she actually did go to a pharmacy . . . or if she was doing something else in that time. . . .

"Ror, I didn't take the books. Can you turn off journalist mode, please?" She's peeved, but is it my imagination that she clutches tighter to her purse strap?

"I'm not saying you took the books," I say carefully. "And I'm not in journalist mode. Really, I just want to see the cute Italian lotions. C'mon, show me!"

"Later. I don't want to hunt through my bag right now." She stares at the sea, still gripping her bag like she's liable to be pickpocketed.

Now I am really doubtful. Starting to feel certain she wasn't even *in* a pharmacy.

I wonder if I should vocalize what's looping through my mind. Maybe not lay the blame on Caro alone, but suggest we all open up our bags? See if anyone has the books? Although whoever took the books could have easily tossed them. But why?

Again I run my brain over what in the book struck me as odd. *What?* I can't summon it, but is there a connection to them all going missing? I shouldn't have skimmed, should have read more carefully, or started over again, no matter if it meant not sleeping a wink.

I watch a few kids squealing into the shallows and then splashing back to shore, digging through all the shells and coral fragments for treasures.

"What if . . . ?" I probe around for the words but ultimately can't bring myself to voice my suspicions. "Hey, anyway, who had a chance to read the book?"

Nate nods slowly. "I got a few chapters in before we left this morning. Interesting, that Eddie character . . ." He makes a face.

"'Knows he's handsome, and yet, it doesn't alter the fact of it. Some people, like Eddie, cruise through the world, life made ever easier when you are genetically blessed,'" Caro says, quoting. "Let's just say, she didn't eviscerate you like she did me."

"Felt pretty eviscerating to me," Nate says. "I didn't have it easy."

"She goes into it, though. Eddie's complex," I say. "I mean, she humanizes you. You just didn't read far enough to see it."

"Great," Nate says, not sounding thrilled, which I guess I get. Who wants to be both eviscerated and humanized in a book that's likely to sit on the bestseller lists for months or years on end?

"You read some of it too, huh, C?" I ask. "Enough to be able to quote the Nate lines and get past the rock-through-the-window scene?"

"Some." She doesn't elaborate.

"Maxie?" I say.

Max nods. "A couple of chapters. You know, I'm not the biggest fiction person, probably haven't read a novel since high school, I guess. *Lord of the Flies*? But it was tense. Juicy, too—how we were all sort of in there."

"Sort of?" Caro says dryly. "How about very, very, *completely* in there."

"How far did you get, C?" I try again. "What scene?"

She eyes me oddly. "Why?"

"Well . . ." My brain keeps sifting, sifting for that little thread that I might use to unravel things. I strain, reaching for it, but as anything does if you grasp for it too hard, it drifts obstinately away.

"Something was off in the book," I finally admit. "Something weird."

Max smiles. "Don't you think the whole thing is foundationally weird? Like the meta-est meta. Reading about yourself in Michigan with people who are basically us—and a murder."

"Yeah." I try to gather the words to explain it more, to reveal my exact fears, but I don't want them to interpret anything as accusations.

I try to push my thoughts away for now, dissolve them in the sea. "I guess it's just a fluke then, the books disappearing."

"Must be," says Nate cheerfully.

"Maybe Gabriele has extras," Max says.

"I don't think so," I say. "I saw inside his briefcase—only four."

"Well," Max says briskly, "this trip will be over soon enough. I'm sure Ginevra can get you another."

I shift on my chaise so the sun isn't beating on my chest.

"I'm sure," I eventually reply, feeling anything but.

CHAPTER FIFTEEN

Max

Back on the train, I pass the lounge car that's swarmed for afternoon tea, the atmosphere like New Year's, with patrons already turned out in satins and silks, certainly not in their finest REI like me. I mosey down the hall, doling out smiles to passing guests and waitstaff—must be the Midwesterner in me, but I love a wholesome stranger smile exchange. At my suite, I greet my steward, who is standing outside the ornate door, lifting his blue cap to scratch an itch on his scalp.

"Francesco!" I clap his shoulder, and he swiftly returns his cap to his head. Then he launches his shoulders back and beams, as I've learned that a person does when you speak his name aloud, showing you've remembered it, showing him you value his individuality, that his name is worth paying attention to, even if—especially if—he is working for you.

It was once difficult for me to remember faces, names. Perhaps because there is often a lot going on in my head that diverts me from the things right in front of me. Papa was always pushing me to get out of my comfort zone—he convinced me to enroll in a Dale Carnegie class after graduating college. In one memorable class, we each had to pretend to be a wild animal in front of our silent, seated, watching cohort. I drew a tiger and had to roar, roar, roar around the room.

It was awkward as fuck. I felt all eyes deboning me, judging me. I decided right then and there that one day I would be the boss, so no one would ever be able to tell me I needed to fake being a tiger again to prove I had what it takes.

It's more than that, probably. I was fated to be the boss from the start. From when Papa started calling me Maximillions long before a magazine splashed it across its cover.

"You have cornetti inside." Francesco holds the door open for me. "With local citrus jam."

"Amazing! Thanks! I really appreciate it."

"Anything else I can do for you? You have dinner later in Palmaria, I understand."

"Yes, thank you, Francesco. I'll freshen up a bit now. Check in with the office. *Ciao*."

The door clicks behind me. I cross the room and flake off a cornetto. Yum. It's almost a cross between a croissant and a brioche, with flecks of vanilla bean that dance on my tongue. Amazing to have your smallest satisfactions anticipated, pursued.

Yes, I have millions to my name now, on paper at least, so one might think I was practiced at luxuries in the vein of the nouveau riche. I can't say I dislike the money that comes along with my company. I've worked for years, hundred-hour workweeks, high stress. I deserve it. But money does not drive me. I am happy wearing the same shirt over and over. I don't need five houses or yachts.

What drives me is expunging a horrific disease from the face of the earth. It is being the person who did it. Who saved Papa. Like Jonas Salk before me. Louis Pasteur.

Maximillian Aronov.

I quickly text Katerina in the office, then unload my backpack and continue to munch on the cornetto. Then I shed all my clothes, deposit them in the laundry bag Francesco pointed out yesterday, and change into the luxe white robe hanging in my bathroom.

It's even softer than the one on Jay-Z's yacht.

I head to the bathroom, swish mouthwash for my usual ten count, and then sprawl out on my bed and think about the day. It's wild that Rory knows she is adopted—a fact I'd pushed to the recesses of my mind so that mostly I'd forgotten it's even true. Uncanny how brains can do that, compartmentalize things, ingenious storage facilities of pretty crazy shit.

I feel guilty that I kept it from her. Even though she's forgiven me, I'm not sure I've forgiven myself. It never sat right with me that Papa asked me to keep it from her. I figured he had good reasons, though, so I let his own judgment substitute for mine.

Maybe it's better it's in the open. I am curious, like Rory, who her birth mother is. I wonder if it's in that book—*The Cabin on the Lake*. It wasn't in the part I read, but I didn't get through the whole thing. I still don't get how Ginevra even knows. And if it is indeed in the book, it's going to be painful for Rory. I didn't tell Rory—didn't want to make the whole thing more painful—but I'm furious at the author for opening this can of worms. She's dangerous. She's playing Rory, and Rory doesn't even see it. And we don't know what's coming next.

Still, despite my misgivings about Rory's being clued in as to her adoption, for a moment I experience a twinge of jealousy that Rory's birth mother might be out there now for her to find. I know my mother—have one picture at least, gorgeous, her smile unassuming but warm, like she would have held me and kissed me and loved me, her hair dark like mine, her brown eyes big and curious. And I know her name. Sandra Lowenstein. But I never got to have her. Somehow it feels like Rory gets yet another leg up—a mysterious birth mother who might be alive to boot.

It's the worst shame to feel jealous of someone you love. But I'd love to have a mother alive right now, to help me, to hug me. To tell me she was proud of me. That she was certain things were going to work out.

When we were kids, Papa would always imagine our futures, like he had a great, infallible crystal ball. Really, he had a conch shell, found on the one international vacation he took us on, when I was twelve and Rory eight, and he scrounged up some money—I have no clue how—for tickets to Jamaica.

Papa would pretend to listen to the conch.

"Max will be a scientist—one of the names that go down in history. Curing an important disease, like Jonas Salk."

Jonas Salk featured prominently in the lore of our household because Papa's father died of polio when Papa was seven. He'd been sick, but still, in the cruel laws of the Soviet Union, workers had to report to their employment in any condition, unless endowed with a doctor's note, otherwise risk being sent to jail or Siberia. My grandfather's doctor misdiagnosed him and refused to excuse him from work, so my grandfather reported to his blacksmith shop and collapsed under his horse at the collective farm at which he was employed. My father's family—really just consisting of him and his mother now—already very poor, was made destitute.

So Jonas Salk acquired a reputation of legend in our home. Did I desire to follow in his footsteps because Papa planted the seeds? Or by my own natural volition—because I gravitated toward the sciences? Or was it later, when I began to associate the first of Papa's symptoms with dementia?

As with anything in life, it is difficult to parse the root.

For Rory, Papa's conch shell had markedly different predictions. "You will be an actress, like Elizabeth Taylor."

For Papa, Elizabeth Taylor personified the pinnacle of success and stardom, first glimpsed in illegal movies he managed to watch in the Soviet Union. He had many American idols, mythical as they were in the Soviet Union, where anything Western was verboten. You could be shuttled to Siberia if found with a copy of the American Constitution in your possession. Papa was always good, though, at working under and around the system. He wanted to be a cowboy like John Wayne, a photographer like Ansel Adams—the latter of whom became Papa's chosen namesake.

"I want to be something more important than an actress," Rory said. "Something that helps people."

I remember being surprised at Rory's conviction at age eight, to know she aspired to more. Even to contradict Papa, whose word was gospel in my head. And maybe I burned a bit inside that Papa found Rory so magnetic and beautiful as to be able to be a famous actress if she wanted.

Then Papa groaned, shook his head. "Yes! Of course. You're right! I was wrong. Rory, you are destined for something much greater than Elizabeth Taylor. You'll achieve far more than fame alone—acting is too small for you. You *could* be an actress, though, because you are a natural star."

At this I bristled further. Does any child ever hear a compliment to his sibling without internalizing the negative—that the compliment was not bestowed upon him?

"You'll be a news anchor," Papa said decisively. "You love the limelight, you shine in it. But your most beautiful quality is that you have such a tender heart. You want to help people. In the Soviet Union, the press wasn't free. You will bring truth to the people. You will tell the stories that sit in your heart, that will inspire others and get them through dark times."

Rory beamed as Papa filled her up with all his fluff, making her sound like Mother Teresa. But that's how Papa always saw Rory, I guess.

"And, Max . . . I named you Maximillian for a reason. Maxi*millions*, that's what you'll be, my son. One day you'll be supremely wealthy."

I sank into the prediction, felt how much I wanted it to come true, not for the money in itself, not for the stuff—but for the power money provided, which at age twelve I already understood. "The block party, that's what I'll do."

"The block party?" Rory asked.

"Yeah! I read about it. There's this hockey player or—"

"Basketball," Papa said. "I read about it, too."

"Oh." I blushed. I didn't really follow or get the appeal of sports, but still I was embarrassed I'd mixed it up. "But anyway, when this guy became rich, he bought houses on the same block for all of his family and friends. That's what I'll do one day."

"Cool!" Rory said. "I'll take a free house."

Papa looked bursting with pride, as if his imaginings had already contracted with the future, locked it in place. He surveyed us both tenderly. I remember exactly where we were—in the bare-bones hotel room that felt like a palace because we were on vacation. A concept that rolled off the tongue of the rich kids at school but was impossibly foreign to me. We were all sitting eating beef patties that Papa had picked up from one of the street stands, as always, declaring it the best meal he'd ever eaten. Even when we all got food poisoning the next day from said patties, Papa still declared them worth the consequence!

Perhaps it was blind optimism. When overdue bills filled our mailbox, and Papa would sing that the little money fairies would take care of things, don't you worry, kids, Rory would bite her nails down to nubbins. No matter what, though, I trusted in Papa. Trusted in good people getting taken care of. Things working out. That if you were essentially kindhearted, if you tried your relative best, little troubles would fritter away, be subsumed by good intentions.

My mind tugs Jamaica back to the forefront, pans in on the two double beds with eighties-floral coverlets, the three of us eating our empanadas, moaning with pleasure. Papa then continued orating his lecture on our futures, mine and Rory's. "Whatever you both do, you will be successful. But remember, sometimes you have to take risks. Get out of your circle of comfort. So if I'm not around to remind you—"

"You'll always be around," Rory said, licking her fingers of grease.

Papa smiled sadly, like he knew something we didn't. "I won't always be around, Rory. And I can't sugarcoat that for you. That's why you have to try the thing you're scared to do. Dare to love. Take risks. Take the risks that feel right in your soul. And whatever happens, you will always have each other. I never had a sibling, you know? You both are so lucky to have each other. Always be honest with each other." His eyes got faraway, sad. "As long as you don't lie or mislead, you will always be a safe harbor for each other, even after I am gone. Promise me," he said, transfixing my eyes with his. "Promise me you will always tell each other the truth."

"Promise!" I remember how Rory said it cheerily, tossing her plate in the trash can like a Frisbee, raising her arms in a *V* when it swooshed in.

"Promise," I said, too.

Suddenly my phone buzzes with a call, blinking me back from the memory. I don't answer, just stare at the screen with mounting dread. Then I quickly text, *Call you back in a few.*

I roll my eyes toward the ceiling, hoping a piece of wisdom will drop into my head. Tell me what to do.

What do I do, Papa?

My whole life I relied on him to give me sage advice that I would inevitably follow. I trusted him, but maybe even more—I found it easier to listen to his yes or no than mine.

And now he can't tell me.

I need to help people, too.

Maybe Papa knew always, though, that my greatest motivation would not be the limelight or conventional success, things I have inadvertently now conjured. I'm grateful for them—enjoying them, too—but still my motivation remains quite simply, him.

Making Papa proud. Saving him and protecting him, like always he did me.

But guilt and shame and love all flow together in the same stream.

They can't be separated, no matter how Hallmark movies try to convince us they are separate beasts.

Then there's a knock—three terse raps—that I've been expecting.

I open the door. Sure enough, it's Caro, hair damp and rumpled, no makeup, her blue eyes like arctic lakes I have always wanted to sink inside.

I smile, feeling my anxieties settle. "What brings you to these parts—me or this insane suite?" I ease the door open farther, and I notice her eyes flit behind me, taking in all the hand-carved timber, embossed leather, and sumptuous rugs.

Caro doesn't answer, and I try to remain calm. I know she wants to tell me a lot of things, and I'm readying myself to listen, but I already quite know the entirety of what she'll say. We've been playing tug-of-war, and it's inevitable. She knows it, and I know it: I'm going to win.

I open the door wider and her bare arm brushes against mine as she slips inside.

CHAPTER SIXTEEN

Rory

Back from the beach, still sandy and sunburned on my shoulders, I recline on my bed, the white linens pressed and taut. I know I'm going to end up sleeping in a sandbox, but Current Me is too lazy to go shower off for Future Me. Nate would despise that—any crumb he encounters in bed is treated as though he's sleeping atop fifteen hoagie sandwiches.

I run my eyes over this heavenly suite and grab the aloe from the glossy wooden panel set into the wall right below the window that acts as my nightstand. Marco fetched the aloe for me when he spotted my sunburn, declaring that "any wish is yours, any wish at all!" So I asked if it wouldn't be too much trouble to bring me a caffè shakerato—my Italian addiction that is espresso mixed with sugar and ice. Now I set the aloe back on the table, rub my sticky hands on a napkin, and reach for my fluted crystal shakerato. I sip, savoring the sweet foam crema on top, and sigh.

Out my window, the Mediterranean is a now-familiar show-off. Man. This is the life.

Okay, I need to finally do the thing I've been putting off.

I grab my phone, thumb to FaceTime, dial, then hold the phone above my head. A familiar unease roils my stomach—that I hope Papa's nurse, Suzette, will answer, that I hope Suzette will *not* answer.

One ring—two—three. I wonder if today is the day that I will ask Papa whether I'm adopted. I haven't gathered up the courage yet on any prior call. I suppose because I've been grappling with whether it's even fair to confront him with the past when he remembers it only indiscriminately now.

Finally, the rings abate and Suzette's head fuzzes into view: boingy brown curls, red lips, and a smile like sunshine that I am grateful is bequeathed to my father every day.

"Hi, Suzette!" I say, summoning cheer.

"Hi, Rory!" She waves exuberantly. "It's been a while! How was the meditation retreat?"

"Amazing, actually. I'm meditating twice a day now. Twenty minutes each time."

"Really? Tell me everything! What is all that *quiet* like? I can't even imagine it." Suzette has thirteen grandchildren, four of whom used to live with her, before she began to provide live-in patient home care. She once joked she suffered from overtouch syndrome.

"Honestly, I couldn't imagine it before, either. You know what I was like. . . ."

"The best anchor in the world." Suzette smiles proudly, a smile that immediately sears all my little pockets of shame.

"Thank you." I can feel she's about to ask me about it—when I'm going back to LA and where I'll work next—so I rush on. "It's crazy how something so boring as a silent meditation retreat could be so . . . I don't know, transcendent."

I feel instantly stupid to use such a grand word to describe it, but there was something indisputably sacred about the retreat that I am still struggling to define. Failing to slot into place how ten days when, quite literally, *nothing* happened except birds sang and food was eaten and sleep was had, the moments nonetheless feel elongated in my mind, crystal clear. I felt such love for the birds that it nearly brought me to my knees. I found myself rubbing the trunks of trees with reverence. Digging my toes into the grass and sighing because I felt like my skin connected with the ions in the earth, or something.

And the memories are sharp, lingering, like cream rising to the top, displacing the arguably far bigger and more important things I've done and lived.

My whole life I've tried to be strong, persevere, work hard—at my career, at my relationships. Because I checked those boxes, I believed that of course things would work out for me. How hilarious! But then Papa got sick, and my job and relationship imploded, and now I get it. That life is one huge mind fuck, and you can do everything right but still wind up in the muck.

Maybe some of it is salvageable. And all the things Max and Caro and Nate have said swirl around me—*Get back on the horse. Go get 'em, again!*

Second chances, blah, blah, blah.

But this strange feeling has clung to me since I lost my dream job— the sense that in any event, I was just marching toward the end. And not really enjoying any of it, certainly not savoring the sour-coffee-perfumed windowless prison of my television studio. Maybe there's something easier, something that feels lighter, like meditation, for me to pursue. It's weird, though, imagining deviating from the path that has felt pre-destined. By God or by Papa, I've never been entirely sure.

"Anyway, how's Papa doing?"

"He's okay today, sweetheart. Been asking about you."

"Really? That's a good sign. Each time I get worried . . ." I trail off, suddenly not wanting to vocalize my deepest fear: that one day soon I will become a permanent stranger to my father. Unless Max can cure him.

I squeeze my eyes shut, praying hard, like I do anytime I think of Hippoheal and the incredible stuff Max is doing. If it's at all possible to save Papa, Max won't give up until he does. That comforts me some. It does.

"Here," Suzette says. "I'll bring you over to your dad."

The view gets bumpy as she moves across the hall, panning the phone over the dusty Oriental rugs and paintings of ships navigating stormy seas. Papa loves our home in Michigan. Used to love swimming in the lake and all the green and the fact that a poor kid from the Soviet Union, who'd only ever lived in cramped rooms without indoor plumbing, sud-denly had space and relative luxuries.

It pangs me that Papa could one day need to leave our beloved home. That his Alzheimer's may progress to a point that even Suzette living in full time couldn't care for him all on her own. Papa's been adamant that he wants us to live our lives, that he doesn't want either Max or me to forsake our dreams to care for him. But I would—in a heartbeat. I will. I want him always at home, where he prefers to be. And thankfully having Papa at home, even with Suzette, is cheaper now than a care home. Though Papa doesn't have the funds to pay for Suzette. So Max took out loans against his equity in his company and is paying for it, by and large. I know he can afford it, especially once his drug is on the market, but still. I do feel guilt that Max is not only financially responsible for Papa's care but physically there, too. And what am I doing or providing? I'm just floundering. If Papa understood, if I told him I'd lost my job, he wouldn't approve of my path. He would tell me to get back in the game. He would scoff at main characters, at meditation, at silence, at giving up on all my dreams.

Is that what's happening now? Am I giving up on my dreams?

I can't ruminate too hard on that depressing thought because the top of Papa's head pops into the screen. His hair is silver now, still thick and gleaming, brushed to the side. He's sixty-five, but his forehead is that of someone twenty years younger, hardly marred by a crease. He's still vigorous and youthful, strong—visible facts that are even more jarring given his memory loss, constant knife-in-the-chest reminders of all the time we have lost. Suzette tilts the phone down and there he is, my father.

I don't care if I'm adopted. This is my father. Whatever the story behind it—maybe I'll never know—but he chose me, and he wanted me. And he was the best dad I could ever imagine.

"Papa." Tears well in my eyes.

His small blue eyes are warm and happy, the whites of his eyes so bright they add to his air of virility. He smiles, his familiar sweet smile, with teeth crowded and a bit yellowed. He was always self-conscious about that. Seven years ago, Max and I saved up and got him a fancy dental whitening package for his birthday, right before he was diagnosed with Alzheimer's. He never used it—developed a fear of the dentist, or maybe just doctors in general—and couldn't be cajoled to go.

"MW . . . my wonderful . . ."

"Daughter," I supply, the last part of his nickname. He calls me MWD; Papa can create an acronym from anything. Max is MWS. But lately Papa often just conjures the first part, and I can always see the moment exactly when his brain loses the neural connection in the middle and his expression goes bleak.

He knows me. He still does, at least.

"Rory, is that you? Where are you?"

I swallow hard and smile. "I'm in Italy, Papa."

"Italiya? Finally, you took a vacation."

I force a smile. "I did."

He nods. "You deserve it. How hard you work. Are you on the sea?"

"Yes! I collected seashells on my walk today, like we used to do when we'd go up north."

His eyes twinkle. "Was the water wet?"

I smile. "You've still got jokes, Papa."

His eyes dart around, suddenly confused.

No, not yet, I silently pray. He has lucid periods, and then sometimes he goes.

"Very wet, I can confirm," I say, regretting having not answered more simply. "I'm here with Max, too. Traveling on a really fancy train."

"I'm glad you are together with your brother. It's so important, Rory, that you and your brother are always good to each other. Some siblings . . . they aren't good to each other."

"We are. I promise, Papa," I say, glad I can say that honestly now that Max and I have discussed things.

"Where are you?" he asks, face scrunched in confusion.

"Italy, Papa," I say again. "On a train."

"You're on a train." He nods, and my heart sinks. He's just repeating the word, trying to give the pretense of understanding, which is what he did a lot before we finally convinced him to go see a specialist. Before his diagnosis.

I debate what to say, whether to wait patiently for him to talk more, or comfort him somehow, or change the subject. The specialist Max and I paid to help us navigate Papa's decline said other techniques to calm and comfort him could be resting a hand on his forearm or maintaining eye contact, both of which are difficult to do from afar.

I'm agonizing over what to say when Papa says, "I took a train to Kyrgyzstan—did I ever tell you that?"

I feel my chest surge with relief that Papa can still continue the conversation, even if it's patchy. Maybe Max was exaggerating Papa's deterioration, if he can still pull a memory out of his pocket of which I wasn't aware.

"No, but I'd love to hear."

"It was a horrible train, in the military." Papa's military years are a black hole—I know nothing. He never liked sharing, going back to his past. He was an only child, his parents long gone. *What is the point? I have my wonderful children, living in freedom in America. Life can only be lived forward, not backward.*

It's something I grieved after he was diagnosed with Alzheimer's, that I hadn't asked sufficient questions, tasted the marrow of Papa's wisdom and experience. That maybe I'd never get access to all that history—his and ours.

Back when I thought Papa's ancestry was actually mine.

The phone clips to spotlight just his forehead, and Suzette's fingers overtake the screen. She shifts the camera back to encompass all of Papa's face, now pinched, from anger or pain I'm not sure. "I took this train after basic training. That was hell on earth. I ever tell you about it? They beat me because I was Jewish."

"Who beat you, Papa?"

"Yes." He nods. "They beat me bad. Ten on one, in the night, screaming 'dirty Jew' and stuff like that. We drank vodka and slept on wooden slabs. The train was going to . . ."

"Kyrgyzstan?" I remind him.

"Yes. It was pretty country. A lot of evergreens. I could have just slept and looked out the window, but the other soldiers wanted booze. One night, I woke up to a fellow soldier taking off my pants and selling them for vodka."

"No way!" I clap my hand over my mouth, and in that moment, Papa smiles his glittery smile, and it is just like BA (Before Alzheimer's—that acronym is only mine and Max's).

"Yes!" Now he's laughing, too. "It was so crazy. They convinced me to sell everything—shirts, jackets, extra boots. When we arrived at our base after four weeks on the train, we stumbled out in only our boots and underwear. Our officer was pissed!"

"Oh God, I can't believe I didn't know that." I'm giggling; Papa seems so with it now. I wonder if I can ask him about the adoption, after all. I probably should have broached it with Suzette first.

"Papa, I—"

"You're in Kyrgyzstan?" Papa frowns. "Be very careful about your watch, Rory."

"My watch?" I glance at it, a small gold face with a brown leather strap. Papa surprised me with it when I got my first reporting job, so that I'd always be on time on air.

"They'll steal it!" Papa's eyes crease with alarm. "In the middle of the night, they could take it!"

"I'm okay, Papa. No one's taking my watch."

"A knife to your throat!" He makes a slashing motion at his neck. "That's what they'll do. Thieves!"

"There aren't thieves on this train," I say gently, though it flashes, the boulder careening at me as Max shoved me aside. The missing books. I wiggle my torso, to shake out the anxieties. "Hey, Papa, can I ask you a question?"

It takes him a few moments to calm. "Anything. Anything and everything."

I hold my breath. "Do you know a woman named Ginevra Ex?"

I mentioned her once to him, before I came to Italy, when I visited him in Michigan. I told him I'd be working for a famous author, and I said her name. His face took on this peculiar look, and he said, "The good one and the evil one. Of course."

He was obviously confused. Babbling, like he is prone to sometimes. I tried to change the subject, but then he became agitated, erupting in Russian. I was a bundle of nerves, tried to divert his attention to a deer trotting across the fresh snow outside, and then we had hot cocoa in the kitchen looking out on the frozen lake.

Eventually he relaxed. And I didn't dare mention her name again. I thought it a random trigger, though—not anything meaningful. And thankfully now, Papa's face is perplexed. Relief washes over me. He doesn't know her. I'm inventing crazy links in my head.

But then he says, quite strongly, "Ginevra Efrati." Still, he looks unsure. Efrati? "No, Ginevra Ex." But my heart spasms.

Who is Ginevra Efrati? I sift my memories, parsing my past. Is that a name with significance, or something completely random his brain has conjured up? My heart has begun to beat quicker, a weird sensation stirring in my chest.

Is he talking about Ginevra Ex?

Is she my mother? The question dangles off my tongue. In any moment it could career off. I need to get the book back; I was so focused on figuring out the embezzling thing, so sure that's what struck me as odd. But now I wonder if the odd thing is that Ginevra could have dropped a clue about, or revealed, my birth mother.

"Ginevra Efrati," Papa repeats. "Yes. The good one and the evil one. The evil one!"

It's the second time he's said the name Ginevra Efrati. And now he's made the second strange association with good and evil. Something sling-shots at me, a memory.

"Are you talking about the story you used to tell us? About the sisters?" Yes, I know it as a certainty now, deep down; Papa means the fable he used to tell Max and me when we were kids. It even came up in my interviews with Ginevra—a moment I remember clearly because Ginevra shifted from slow, professional interviewer to a more feverish pace, abandoning her notes, pressing me for details, like the story was somehow important. I couldn't conjure all the details, but the bones of the bedtime story, I do remember.

Papa nods solemnly. "The good one was the beautiful one. So very beautiful. It's not fair! It was never fair. The evil one. She ruined it all. She lied to me. I never . . . I never should have walked away. Where is she? *Where?*"

"Where is who, Papa?" I'm completely confused, but I want to keep him talking. It feels like I'm on the precipice of understanding something significant.

"Ginevra!" Papa lurches closer to the camera. "Where is she?"

"Ginevra *Ex* is in Italy, Papa. I'm not sure it's the same person you're talking about. She's the author, the one I told you I'm working—"

"Ginevra, where . . . ?" The phone clatters to the ground, and I hear him shout something unintelligible.

Suzette pokes her head back in the frame with an apologetic frown. "Rory, darling, we need to go."

I'm breathing so fast. "But—"

"Try us tomorrow, sweetheart." Her eyes are compassionate but firm. The call clicks off.

The phone flops out of my hand. I stare at the ceiling, trying to make sense of our conversation. Did Papa know Ginevra? But how?

I summon back his bedtime story, try to recall all the contours. It was about a duke who meets two sisters by a lake. One sister is very beautiful but oblivious, and one is very ugly and brilliant. The duke is in love with the beautiful sister and makes valiant efforts to be with her. I would always press Papa—*More, more!* Laughing hysterically at all the duke's endeavors and failures. He skates across the lake, but then he plunges through the ice! He climbs the highest mountain, but then he falls off a cliff! He hikes through the desert, but in the end, he doesn't have enough water! Basically, the duke never succeeds.

Because, as Papa would say, the ugly sister is evil and controls the beautiful sister. The ugly sister keeps moving the beautiful sister farther and farther away from the duke. For a while, the ugly sister even deludes the duke into believing the beautiful sister doesn't love him in return. And in the end, the duke and the sisters all wind up alone, because eventually the evil sister locks the beautiful one up in a tower and throws away the key.

How strange are the stories told to children. I wonder if Max remembers more than I do. But what could this story possibly have to do with Ginevra? I think back to the first time I interviewed Ginevra. I was pretty low ranking to score such a get. Now I wonder, did she request me specifically? Because of Papa?

I shiver—because if she's one of the sisters, she's obviously the ugly, evil one.

No, that's impossible. There has to be another explanation. I don't want to believe the story could be true, that Ginevra could have horrible motives—evil ones—in sending us all on this trip.

My fingers run over my knee now, the cuts en route to scabs. I think about Caro's accusation—about Ginevra leveraging this trip. Could she be targeting me? Is this all a publicity stunt? Or maybe the book's not even done, maybe she's still scripting things, playing us like her puppets to cultivate more story lines. Okay, I admit that speculation is out there, but I can't discount Caro's idea that Ginevra has people planted on the train, besides Gabriele. I consider everyone we've met—the chirpy Californians; the Russians wafting that garlic stench; Mr. sourpuss Pom-Pom;

the Italian family seemingly popping up around every turn. Could one of them have pushed the boulder or taken the books? But why? If Ginevra were picking anyone to be her minion, would she really pick a couple or a family? Or maybe she'd figure unlikely culprits would present the perfect cover . . .

I shake my head, feel like I'm inventing monsters under the bed who aren't at all real. The thing is, despite all this craziness, I like Ginevra. I've always liked her. There's something about Ginevra that is down-to-earth, kind. Compassionate. Flamboyant, sure, and occasionally self-important, although I get the sense it's all masking deep-seated insecurities. A few times she spoke about her sister, Orsola, who lives . . . where again? Some Italian city . . . not Rome, I don't think. They're twins, identical. Close, I think.

Beautiful, Ginevra once told me. Orsola was the beauty.

I feel sick.

It can't be true. I'm inventing things. How would Papa even know them?

And if Ginevra is my mother, does that mean I'm not exactly adopted but that she had some warped relationship with Papa? And why would she tell me the earth-shattering information that I'm adopted but lie about her role in things?

Why would she send me on this trip with so many instructions, so many strange setups?

It's like I'm still her main character, and she's scripting the show.

I could get off the train right now, I remind myself. No one—not even the famous Ginevra Ex—can keep me on board, riding a crazy train against my will. My eyes flitter out the window, at the outside world that seems far now, out of reach. My life narrowed to this box on wheels, and the people who exist upon it. This luxury train is starting to feel like a gilded cage. As beautiful as it is claustrophobic . . .

I don't want to leave, though. I can admit that to myself. It's not just Nate coming back into my life. It's Max, Nate, and Caro, and even Gabriele. So many unfinished things. I realize I need to see how this all ends. Stories can't really be aborted in the middle.

But I need to take back control. Of my life, of this trip. I have so many questions, and I've texted Ginevra, asking them, but so far she hasn't responded. Tomorrow, we'll be in Rome, and I'll go see her. I'll resort to ambushing her at her apartment, if I must. She can't avoid me. Enough is enough.

I need answers. And another copy of the book. I rub my hands on my forehead, feeling absolutely . . . bewildered. I wish I could talk it over with my brother, with my ex-love, with my best friend, but I can't fully trust anyone now.

I should meditate, but I don't feel like it. The thing is, it's easier to meditate when your mind's not spinning out. At the retreat, I had so many moments of rebirth, thinking, *Why doesn't everyone on earth do this? Drink this Kool-Aid? If people knew silent meditation retreats existed, the entire drug industry would collapse.* I felt like a junior Dalai Lama, needing to spread the message near and far, with the conviction that if only people knew that you could do absolutely nothing at all and experience the greatest bliss that exists, then world peace would be easily had. I imagined teaching people the wisdom of life: *You get to choose how you feel. You can decide to feel joyful and observe all the wonderful blessings around you.*

But now, back in the real world, it all feels a bit foolish. I'm facing *real* problems that I can't avoid. I'm not going to stare out the window at the trees and solve everything.

Am I?

Papa would say, "There is nothing that a walk cannot cure." If Max and I were fighting, Papa would shove us both out the door. "Go for a walk and don't come back until you're smiling-diling."

I miss Papa's dumb rhymes and optimism that things would work out. I imagine his strong arms around me—but I am struck with the melancholy realization that I am putting a halo around his memory that isn't exactly warranted. His were never strong arms that promised to protect me from everything. I realize suddenly, sadly, that as wonderful as Papa was, *is*, he never promised to cushion me from life's cruelties. It's like chop, chop, timber—he wanted me to learn to jump and survive in the water alone, before I found his arms. He had to persevere through so much in his young life that he wanted Max and me to be prepared to do the same. On our own. Because in the end, you were always on your own. I remember the times—many times—that Papa would suddenly well up in tears. I never understood his triggers, often innocuous—an ambulance siren, the season's first snow. As an explanation of his tears, he would tell me, "They're all gone," and I know he was talking about the people he loved before me—his mother, his father, and the woman I thought was my mother. "But I have you and Max," he would say. I knew he meant it, but I think I also wondered if he was forever trying to convince himself we were enough.

The train doesn't leave until midnight. Dinner isn't for a few more hours.

I'll shower, change, and then go for a walk—channel new energy. I summon some of Papa's courage, tick through the things he overcame, like this new train-to-Kyrgyzstan story.

No one's selling my stuff for vodka, at least. But even though Ginevra's just paid me enough to last a good while, I don't feel very abundant. Because until I find another job, nothing more is coming in, which triggers me in a deep place after the money worries of my childhood. Still, I can admit my situation is not quite at the selling-for-vodka level of dire. Not yet.

And how difficult is it, after all, to endure a luxury trip on the Orient Express?

To be honest—more difficult than I would have thought.

CHAPTER SEVENTEEN

Rory

I'm on my way out of the train when I stop and decide on a quick detour. Caro's room—214, according to the itinerary.

I walk rapidly over there, then rap on the door. No answer. I rap again. Nothing.

As I hoped. I'd wager anything Caro's gone off to town to shop.

Am I really going to do this? I shuffle in front of her room, as a woman with majestic hip-length gray hair and a floor-length beige silk duster coat passes by, staring at me quizzically. I smile, then study my watch, hoping she doesn't find me suspect. I mean, I haven't done anything wrong. Not yet.

After she's gone, I hasten down the hall, through the connection corridor back toward my carriage, and find Marco right where I left him, in his usual vigilant perch outside my room.

"Marco!"

His face lights up at the prospect of doing something to serve me. "*Sì, signorina?* I thought you were going out for a *passeggiare*. Did you forget something? Need a glass of water?"

If any more water is foisted upon me, I'm liable to float away. "No, I didn't forget anything. I realized . . . well, my friend, Caroline. Do you know her? She's with our group."

"Yes, of course. Signorina Caroline is"—Marco consults his iPad— "room 214."

"Yes. Caroline's not in her room at the moment, and she has something of mine."

"Something?" Marco's kind, dark eyes flicker uncertainly.

"My mascara." That banal claim shoots out of me.

"Mascara? Mascara . . . for your eyelashes?"

"Well . . . yes. I lent it to Caroline, and so it's in her room, and I forgot to get it back. . . ."

I hope he is like 99.9 percent of men and doesn't notice that I'm already wearing it.

"And you *need* this . . . mascara?"

"Yes! I want to go into town, but first, I really want to put mascara on. Can you let me into Caroline's cabin real quick?"

Marco opens his mouth, then closes it again. Mascara, so freaking dumb, I berate myself inside. Couldn't I have thought of anything—literally *anything*—more urgent? He's probably going to say he has to check with his higher-ups, or that actually, he knows where Caro is, and he'll guide me there right away. But then to my relief, he says, "I really shouldn't, but you are an important guest. I trust you that you need this . . . mascara. And that Signorina Caroline would not mind."

"I do," I assure him. "And she wouldn't." I flush at the abject lie.

Marco nods. He fiddles in his pocket with uncharacteristic clumsiness—clearly he'd far rather be fetching me a platter of exotic fruits. But he leads me down the hall, as it occurs to me that Caro could at any moment stroll by. She'll see instantly through my lie. Obviously, I own mascara. I mean, I'm wearing it.

But thankfully, no Caro lurking around corners. We reach 214, Marco brandishes a key, and within a few moments, the door clicks open. I slip inside the cabin, expressing profuse thanks. I shut the door, then on instinct, I peer through the keyhole to spot Marco still out there, standing guard.

I pry open the door and peek my head out. "You don't need to wait. I'll be done shortly. I know my way out."

"Oh. Ehrm . . ." He looks disconcerted, but what with the customer is always right being advocated on steroids on this train, he eventually starts down the hall, gazing doubtfully back.

When Marco disappears from sight, I duck back inside, shut the door, and replenish my breath. Then I take stock of Caro's room. Tidy and far smaller than mine—a navy banquette by the window, which converts to a twin bed in the evening. Despite the postage-stamp size, there are no sunglasses littering the countertop, not a remote out of place. No surprise; Caro has a militant attention to details and order that always pleased Papa, caused him to jokingly label her the most Soviet of his children. Her cream hard-shell luggage is on a folding stand, zipped shut. I jigger the zipper open with a guilty gnaw, then flip open the top to find a lavender lace bra and panty set, carefully folded. I smile. No one loves luxurious, matching lingerie like Caro.

Okay, go time. I rifle through her suitcase, come across several gorgeous pieces: a crossbody Celine bag, spangly lavender heels, and a blue knit cutout dress. I peep the label—Staud. Aka four hundred bucks for a few yards of fabric. I suppose Caro can afford all this stuff on her Hippoheal salary; after all, she's never been much of a saver. But I can't help thinking that all her new designer everything could also be courtesy of her embezzling from the company, like Ginevra alleged.

In quick order I finish sifting through Caro's suitcase. Verdict: no books. I peer under the banquette. Nothing, not even a stray piece of lint. Then I glance around again, wondering where I've forsaken the search. There's no bathroom to search in, at least not one attached. She shares one down the hall, allocated to passengers without suites. Aha. I spot a handle on the wall by the window, half-eclipsed by gauzy drapes. I cross the room eagerly and open what turns out to be a tiny cupboard that could be called a closet, in the most generous sense of the word. Three shallow shelves hold nothing but a robe, several towels, and a few neatly folded scarves and belts perfectly curled. There's not even a hanging rail.

I shut the closet, cross the room in two steps, and slump down on the banquette. I really thought it was Caro who stole the books. The embezzlement allegations—that *must* be what struck me as odd in the book. It's the only thing that makes sense. Caro must have read something that would implicate herself. She must have been freaked out Max would decode it. Besides, Caro's been acting weird this whole trip. Like offering me her Cartier ring—she's generous, but was that overboard, a gesture out of guilt? Except, if Caro took the books, where are they? She must have tossed them. Unless I'm wrong about this . . . unless I'm sniffing the wrong scent . . . There's something else disturbing me about what I read, something I can't quite remember. . . .

I'm flying through other possibilities and discarding them when suddenly I hear a click and watch in horror as the doorknob turns.

Shit, shit, shit, shit, *shit*.

"Ror!" In as much time as it takes me to draw my next breath, Caro's through the doorway.

"What in the— Rory!" She glances behind her, as if she's being punked, then returns her gaze to me, confused, cheeks abnormally pink. "What—what are you—"

"I wanted a dress! To borrow a dress." I paste a smile on my face, hoping it flies as genuine. "I'm going into town, and, yeah, I thought I could borrow a dress."

"You're wearing a dress," she says flatly.

I look down, realize that yes, I did change out of my hiking outfit into a dress. When I glance back at Caro, expecting her to call me out on my blatant lie, instead her eyes are bobbing around the room, like she can suss out invisible traces of what I've been up to.

"I've gotten so sick of my dresses since I've been living out of a suitcase for months. Yours are amazing," I babble. "Like that new blue knit one." I realize too late that I've just copped to looking in her suitcase.

"You opened my suitcase?"

"I needed to—to find a dress!"

"Right." She cocks her head at me thoughtfully, her face smileless, her hair unusually mussed.

"Yeah." I smile again, but I'm not sure I'm selling it. "Where are you coming from?"

"Just now? Nowhere. Getting coffee. I don't have a butler to fetch it for me."

"Oh." She had, like, three espressos at lunch while the rest of us were drinking. But it's plausible, I guess. Like me, she's a zealot for caffeination. Still, with another espresso, she should be levitating, and yet she's decidedly not buzzy. Was she really getting coffee?

"Well, you're welcome to borrow my butler anytime," I finally say.

"I don't think it works like that." Her face softens a tad, and she sighs. She meets my eyes, almost ekes out a smile.

"Wanna come into town with me?" I ask. "I'm gonna go walk around."

"What? Oh, no. No, thanks. I'll stay here. I'm tired from all the walking we did today, you know?"

"Okay. Well, rest up. See you at dinner."

This is weird. *So* weird. She doesn't want to shop together? She must suspect I've been snooping. There's so much subtext to our conversation. So much it feels like we're both not saying.

"So you want a dress?" Caro finally says.

"Yes, please."

In short order, I'm newly cloaked in Caro's blue cutout dress that is no doubt sexy on her, but decidedly not on me. Caro's far taller than me, so the dress pools at my ankles instead of skimming mid-calf like it should, and my boobs are molehills compared to Caro's Everests; mine look saggy, not filling out the triangles up top. I catch a glimpse of my reflection in the half mirror above the sink; I look like a child wearing a grown-up's outfit. But it was the best of the lot, and I couldn't exactly refuse it.

Now I remember why I never borrow clothes from Caro, only accessories—because our proportions are completely different. Before we both acknowledge I looked way better in *my* dress, and there's no way I legitimately came here for hers, I make toward the door.

"See you at dinner," I say. "And thanks for the dress. I'll leave mine here and grab it later, 'kay?"

She opens the door, cracks a small smile. "Sure. We're meeting to get the boat at seven, yeah?"

"Yep."

Then I step into the hall and turn, my eyes grazing upon Caro's crossbody bag—and onto the unmistakable object wedged at the top. The door clicks shut, but not before I saw it. Not before my eyes registered that cover with just the title, and the declaration that it's a bound manuscript.

Caro took the books. No question. *The Cabin on the Lake.*

e~

"Caro!" I bang the door with my fist.

"One second," comes her trill. But the door remains shut.

I bang again. "Open back up! We need to talk!"

The pom-pom man—still in his jaunty beret—saunters past. I move aside to let him by, his tense face and murmured epithets as ever communicating his distaste for me and my newfound propensity toward public spectacles.

Caro cracks open the door and peers out. "Did you forget something?"

"*The Cabin on the Lake*! I just saw it in your bag. I know you took the copies, C. Why did you take them?"

"Take what?" She looks genuinely confused.

"The *books*. The ones that went missing at the beach. The only four copies in—I don't know—on this train, at least."

Her face is a study in apathy. "I don't know what you're talking about. I didn't take the books."

"I just saw one," I say evenly. "In your bag."

"In my bag? This one?" She slides the Gucci bag through the door, turning it sideways to fit in the small window she's allowed. "Where? Show me what you saw."

I riffle through quickly, but it's clearly not there, already gone. I try to edge the door open with my hip, slip back inside, but her grip is firm and unwavering.

"You've obviously hid it."

"Ror, I'm tired." Her voice is kind but firm. "I don't know what you think you saw, but you didn't. You want the book back—I get that. I'm sure the author, or Gabriele, will get you another copy in two days, when we're off the train. But you're inventing things that aren't real. I don't have the books."

"Yes, you do." I'm trembling, astounded at her casual lie. "I know you do."

"I don't." And then, to my shock, Caro pries my fingers from the door and shuts it in my face.

CHAPTER EIGHTEEN

Ginevra

Three Months Before

Day three of interviews, the day in which cracks in the perfect surface typically began to show.

Day one was usually: *My childhood was pretty uneventful. Normal.*

Or else it was: *Oh God, my parents were crazy.* Followed by affairs and varied chaos that streamed out fast and tangled as Ginevra would note it, murmur soothing refrains, and sift for the gems that lay under the debris.

Ginevra knew: You had to tease out the good stuff. You had to ask questions from many angles. But only at the right time, in the right way. *Piano, piano.* Ginevra was unusually patient. And she was usually uncannily good at picking main characters who yielded riches, once she prodded them to peel the onion layers back. Ginevra had no dearth of offers for main characters. Thousands of would-be main characters sent letters and emails, begging to be chosen. Bombarded her DMs. Shuttled missives and flowers to her manager, promoting their zaniest stories and quirks and dark thoughts.

But there was an art to choosing a main character. You had to pick someone emotionally stable, capable of great insight and reflection, able to acknowledge their missteps, but also possessing a baseline confidence. Readers didn't want a flimsy, self-hating character.

Ginevra could admit she'd faltered with her last main character, but

Rory would redeem Ginevra—a no-brainer, in every way. Never had Ginevra desired a main character more.

"Tell me more about your father," Ginevra said, not able to help the sigh that heaved out of her, a release of that sentence that had been stirring around for a while, crying out to be asked.

Daylight streamed in from the wide windows onto Via Borgognona toward the Spanish Steps, Hotel d'Inghilterra, and Palazzo Torlonia. Ginevra loved the view, loved watching the palace softly lit in the night, the people bustling below, finely dressed, young invincible teens on *motorini*. There was something safe about it—observing life but not exactly participating in it.

"Obviously, your father has been pivotal in your story. It's important that I get a sense of him, what kind of life he had, because this book isn't about you alone. It's about everyone who shaped you and matters in your life. You don't have to start at the beginning, either. For instance, you can start with one story that your father told you about his life, one that really stuck with you."

Rory broke off one of the pizzelle Ginevra had set out on a cheery dish she'd gotten ages ago in Capri. Ginevra made a note in her head. Pizzelle—check. Ginevra liked to make her main characters feel comfortable, have their favorite things on hand.

"Papa didn't talk much about his past. I know he had a very hard life. The Soviet Union was a brutal place, even harder for Jews. It's difficult for me to imagine him as a child, having lost his father, not having enough to eat. He started a business killing rabbits when he was not even nine just to be able to eat the meat, to sell the skins. His mother mixed potatoes with sawdust to bulk it up. I wish I'd asked him more about it. I really wish . . ."

Ginevra could tell Rory—highly empathetic as she was—was sinking into painful places, that she was almost uniting with the child version of her father, becoming him.

"We can talk about your father's childhood later," Ginevra said gently. "But for now, it will help me to understand, how did he leave the Soviet Union? How did he get out?"

"Ah." Rory visibly straightened, returned to herself. "He was a refusenik, do you know what that means?"

"No," Ginevra lied.

Rory nodded. "In the Soviet Union, Jews were discriminated against. On my father's passport, it didn't say he was Ukrainian. It said he was Jewish. He wasn't allowed to practice his religion. Jews were kept out of the best universities. Bullies beat him as a child, because he was a Jew. They beat him when he was in the military, too." Rory winced, and Ginevra did, too. For Ansel, and also for Ginevra's father, Domenico, who was a Holocaust survivor.

"But then by his late twenties, Papa was doing well. He'd finished music school, was a violinist in a Moscow symphony, and was sending decent money to his mom back in Ukraine. He visited her a lot. But then she had a sudden stroke and died. He wasn't there, and he suffered from that enormously, from the guilt, I think, but also the loss. After she was gone, he felt he had nothing left there. So he began to imagine getting out. There was something then . . . this new law in the late seventies. I forget it. . . ."

"The Helsinki Accords?" Ginevra supplied. "I study history," she explained, even though that wasn't how she knew it. "The West finally recognized the inviolability of the borders of post–World War Two frontiers in Europe. So they no longer challenged the Soviet Union's grip on its occupied Eastern European countries. In turn, the Soviet Union committed to allow *family reunification*."

"Right." Rory nodded. "It meant that Jews could finally get out, to Israel, if they had relatives there. In practice, all they needed was someone on the outside to send them an invitation, usually manufactured, from relatives apparently in Israel. Once they were out, Jews could then choose to go to other friendly nations, not just to Israel. Papa only knew these things because he listened to this illegal radio station Voice of America, and discussed stuff in quiet among his friends. He used to go to a synagogue in Moscow. . . . I forget the name. . . ."

The Moscow Choral Synagogue. But Ginevra bit her tongue to keep quiet.

"Jews used to go to this synagogue, and tourists would go, too. It was very historic. The KGB was always watching, but sometimes a tourist would smuggle an illegal book to Papa, or postcards of menorahs. Usually Jewish foreigners came expressly to help Jews behind the Iron Curtain. Local Jews would go to the synagogue to mingle with the tourists. That's how Papa ultimately got an invitation to leave. He found . . . I'm not sure. Two foreign girls, maybe."

Rory's face contorted in recollection, then she sighed. "Or maybe an older man. I wish I could ask him. Regardless. They took his address and finagled an invitation to Israel from fake relatives there. And so he applied to leave, but he was refused. Denied by the government. It's what happened to many Jews during that time—they became refuseniks. Sharansky, the activist, is the most famous one, I guess. He was before Papa's time, but Papa saw Sharansky protesting and carted away by the KGB. Papa had a good job. But once he became a refusenik, he was considered like an enemy of the state. He was immediately fired from the symphony. They made him go up on the stage and everyone threw food and sour milk on him."

Rory winced. "He could have been jailed or sent to Siberia on any fake pretext. The government could have invented a crime he'd perpetrated, locked him away. You didn't ask to leave the Soviet Union and then get the red carpet rolled out for you. Eventually, though, after a lot more turmoil, he did get out—do you want to hear it all now?"

Ginevra could tell it was a lot for Rory, this story. It was a lot for Ginevra, too. The emotional weight of one's past was best distributed over sessions. It couldn't all diffuse and process in a single go. "You can save that part for later."

Rory nodded. "Once he got out, Papa decided on the United States, in the end. He wanted to go to Texas." Rory smiled. "He'd seen John Wayne movies and dreamed of being a cowboy. But they said the wait for Texas was longer, and Detroit would take him, so he went to Detroit. And soon after he got there, he met my mother and had Max. Then me. He always said we helped him forget everything in his past."

And Ginevra nodded and scrawled in her notepad. *Forget everything in his past*, she wrote and underlined it, her heart beating so fast she feared it might fly out of her chest.

He hadn't forgotten everything. He couldn't have. Because those tourists, the ones who got Ansel out, who mingled with him outside the Moscow Choral Synagogue—he wouldn't forget them.

He wouldn't forget the Italian identical twins named Ginevra and Orsola Efrati.

e〜

With identical twins, the embryo splits shortly after conception. Once they are separated, the embryos keep on splitting. With each new split comes the increasing chance that the DNA of the end result is different from the DNA from which it came.

Thus, identical twins can look quite different.

Orsola Efrati was born first—as family lore goes, pink and lovely. Then the heart-rate monitor began to beep wildly, according to the twins' father, Domenico. The second baby was in distress. The twins' mother was shuttled into surgery. Eventually, the second baby was born—another girl, but ugly, the cord strangling her neck. She was blue, not getting air. Her nose, even then, looked a little squashed. They called her Ginevra.

Orsola and Ginevra's mother did not survive their birth.

Ginevra knew that her mother had died birthing the twins, but it wasn't until Ginevra was seven, when she was coming down the hall to breakfast, that she overheard Orsola say to their father, "I wish Mamma was here on Festa della mamma."

Ginevra stilled in the hall, didn't meander on.

"I know," their father said. "I wish that every day."

"It's not fair," said Orsola, in a voice uncharacteristically down. "Sometimes I feel . . . oh, I shouldn't say it. But it's so hard, not having a mother. And sometimes I even . . . I know this is vicious, but I feel angry that Ginevra is here, instead of Mamma. Like, Ginevra killed Mamma! Because Mamma was fine—fine, you always say—until it was Ginevra's turn to come out. . . ."

Ginevra would never forget it—how she stayed frozen in place, waiting out the infinity until her father responded. Hoping, praying, that he would admonish Orsola. Tell her in no uncertain terms that it wasn't Ginevra's fault that their mother had died.

But instead their father just sighed. "Sometimes I feel angry, too. But anger is futile, *mia ragazza bellissima*. We must accept the cards life has dealt us."

Ginevra blacked out the moments after. All she remembered was that Orsola had made biscotti and presented them to Ginevra with a smile on her face, like the entire conversation had never even happened. Ginevra couldn't eat them. She didn't eat anything for at least an entire week. Just pushed things around on her plate.

And neither her father nor her sister noticed.

The Efratis lived in Rome, in Trastevere by the Tiber, where Domenico was a professor of Jewish studies. He was older already when the twins were born, sparse hair white from Ginevra's earliest memory. He had survived the Holocaust—ten when he entered the concentration camps, twelve when he was liberated, his entire family erased. He was smart and kind but beaten by life, weary; conversations with him ended by guttural sighs, nights frequently punctured by his awaking in terror.

Orsola was his favorite. Well, she was beautiful, with long dark hair, big brown eyes, and a slim figure. Yes, they were twins, but Ginevra had been spackled with the ugly wand in utero, and Orsola with the pretty one. Ginevra's hair was coarse to Orsola's silky, her body was more filled out—a butt where Orsola had none, breasts that surged where Orsola's were pert and petite. Ginevra's nose that sat a bit more prominently on her face. Orsola was kind, outside of that conversation Ginevra had once overheard. More than kind, she was easy. Life went her way, whereas Ginevra often felt she was swimming upstream. Ginevra fought with her father—about the clothes she wanted to wear, not as colorful and feminine as those Orsola favored; about cooking, the bulk of the responsibility of which fell on Ginevra because Orsola, ever perfect, took extra Hebrew studies around dinnertime; about reading secular books on the Sabbath, because her father insisted the day was for reset and worship and books strictly of the religious kind. Orsola didn't give one hoot about reading books, secular or religious alike.

Subtle differences, but important ones. They were twins, and the resemblance was there, but Ginevra grew up knowing she was the tainted one.

Were an outsider to hear Ginevra's scathing assessment of herself, it might rouse pity. But Ginevra harbored no anger over her lackluster looks; at some point in her childhood she'd accepted it. She did her best with what she had—her later wealth bought her the best facials and creams, dark sunglasses and wide-brim hats, and flowing black dresses made of sumptuous silks and wools to cloak her bulk. Sometimes, though, when she was alone and sad, she stood in front of her bedroom's gold baroque mirror and shimmied her favorite dress over her frame. She'd bid upon it at auction—once Sophia Loren's, made of pale pink taffeta, impeccably tailored. It didn't fit Ginevra, but that wasn't the point—when Ginevra closed her eyes and the silk caressed her skin, she could imagine for an instant that she was that beautiful and beloved.

As a child, she escaped into books. Her father indulged her with books; outside of the Sabbath he found them a worthy indulgence. She'd hide in the attic, away from her father and Orsola, devouring them. Dark and dank up there. Just a flashlight, and her father always grumbled when Ginevra needed new batteries. The thing Ginevra hated most about reading was the last page, when all of a sudden she'd feel a tidal ache. They were gone, all of them. All her friends, all the pages she'd lost herself inside. As an adult, she thought of it as a little death. That's what the French call an orgasm. And she supposed that was what it was—the height of pleasure, and then nothingness again, just Ginevra all alone with herself. The End.

She began to study books, how the authors pulled it off. How they got you to care about people in ink. How they surprised you—you were certain one person died, but then you figured out it was someone else. The guy you suspected was bad was the good one all along.

Ginevra tried her hand at stories and found a passion in writing. In seventh grade, she wrote about a woman on her honeymoon who runs off with another man. She wrote about women kidnapped in forests. Her father allowed her to enroll in a creative writing class, and Ginevra was so excited to share her stories, but absolutely devastated when her teacher tore them apart. She said the characters lacked soul. That you could only know your characters as deeply as you knew yourself.

So Ginevra began to write herself into the pages, and her teacher showered her with praise. But even then, Ginevra looked for ways to write around herself. To fully write herself meant excavating great pain. It meant sadness and loneliness and guilt and shame and ugliness. Still, until her early twenties, she wrote. Incessantly. And then for ten years she didn't. Not a single word. And then Ginevra met the girl in the library. And she realized she didn't have to write about herself to access emotion, to find real traumas to exploit.

She'd proven her formula, hadn't she? Ginevra Ex was one of the

most successful authors to ever walk the earth. Was she in there somewhere, anywhere, in her books? Maybe. Had to be, she supposed. If you
sifted around in corners, probably a couple of shards kicking around.
But for the most part, Ginevra didn't need to access her wounds, her
heartaches.

That was what she had main characters for.

CHAPTER NINETEEN

Rory

I'm still seething as I head out in my ludicrous, ill-fitting dress from the station at La Spezia, where the Orient Express has parked for the day. A porter guides me in the direction of town, and I follow a walkway wedged between the sea and idyllic pastel-colored facades—my mind rolling over the insanity of seeing the book and of Caro denying it to my face, zero shame.

The sun torches my already-crisp shoulders. I reapply sunscreen, walking fast, my anger swirling at Caro, obviously, but also at myself for not forcing my way in, for not telling her I know exactly what she's done, that I know all about the embezzlement. I'm orating in my head, giving the speech I'm going to issue when I'm back on the train. How I'm going to demand my book back, demand that Caro own up to everything to Max, when I pass a little girl singing like an angel beside an upturned straw hat into which people are plopping coins. She's crooning some Italian love ballad in a way that is super heartfelt, a thick Romeo and Juliet vibe. I pause, my spiraling outrage losing a bit of charge at the wholesome, sweet scene. It's kind of comical, after all, to see a child acting like a heartsick—

Wait a minute. My head executes a near-complete swivel. That's not *any* little girl. It's Chiara, Gabriele's daughter. I glance around but don't spot Gabriele anywhere.

I stay until the end of the song, still peering around for Gabriele. Italy is safer than America, probably, but surely you don't permit your nine-year-old to roam around aimlessly? Despite my uncertainty, I find myself sinking into the song—Chiara is brilliant, a radiant talent. She's small, with toothpick limbs that belie her big voice, clad in pink shorts and a red top that clashes with her red hair. It's a gorgeous rich red—the type of hair you admire as an adult but probably wouldn't choose to be saddled with as a child, especially in Italy, where the majority of girls have dark hair. I can tell Chiara is self-conscious of hers, because she keeps smoothing the frizzy parts as she sings. Gabriele's ex-wife disappeared from their lives, so Chiara doesn't have a mother to show her what a good pump of smoothing serum can do.

My heart swells as I watch this brave little girl, belting her heart out.

"Bravo," I shout when Chiara ends on a lingering note, stretching it out, pandering to her fans. "Bravo! Bravo!"

Her eyes flutter open. They register me.

"Oh," she says. "It's you."

"I'm Rory." I wave. "I'm friends with your father."

Chiara smirks. Her green eyes survey me with surprising accusation and subtext.

I blush. "Hey, where's your dad?"

"Oh." She gives a glittery smile to a few fans who drop more euros into her hat. Then she scoops up all the change and deposits it into her purse. "I ran away," she says blithely.

"You ran away?" I repeat. "Like . . . from your father."

Chiara shrugs. "Yeah." Then she turns and abruptly takes off, down the route toward the castle where I was planning to head. "You can come if you want," she tosses over her shoulder.

I stare after her for a few beats, disbelieving. Then I trot ahead. "Wait, yeah! I'm coming!"

e

"So, why did you run away?" I ask her.

"Oh, Papa is *irritante*. Very, very *irritante*. And I've had enough. *Basta!*"

Irritante. I get that gist easy enough. I digest her complaint, summon back being nine, and all I can remember is how much I idolized my father.

But I suppose he did annoy me a good deal, too—like how he insisted I wear a hat to cover my ears when I went to meet my friends in the winter, even in the fall, and even though hats were decidedly uncool. He hadn't had a hat in the Soviet Union. Still, back then, I didn't see how it tracked. Fitting in was the important thing.

"Does your dad know you ran away?" I ask Chiara.

She shoots me a death stare. "No, *obviously*. And if you tell him, I'll run away from *you!*"

At that, I slip my phone back in my bag that I'd been trying to clandestinely pull out to text Gabriele. I'll have to do it when she's preoccupied.

"Is this your first time running away?"

"No." As we walk, Chiara ticks off on her fingers. "I've run away one time, two, three, four . . ." When she gets to eleven, she stops. "Eleven times."

I choke back a giggle. Poor Gabriele.

"Wow, well . . . eleven, gosh. That's a lot of times."

Chiara crosses her arms over her chest. "Well, Papa's done a lot of *irritante* stuff. *Cioè*, today, he told me he made plans with the boy across the street for me when we get back. Like I'm a baby! Like a playdate or something. Tommaso doesn't even like me! He barely looks at me at school. *Allora,* Papa talked to his mother, and now Tommaso will be forced to hang out with me. And he plays the stupidest games! Like, with toys and stuff."

"Hmm, well, toys can be fun?" I venture.

Chiara shoots me a withering glare. "Mozart conducted his first symphony when he was eight. I'm *nine*."

"Really? Mozart? At age eight?"

"Yes. He wasn't playing with squirt guns and yo-yos." The intonation she gives to "yo-yos" makes them sound equivalent to baby rattles.

"Right. Mozart." What a kid. I squelch a smile. Gabriele has his hands full, for sure, but she's such a personality. So clearly special. I just need to talk her down. Get her back on the train somehow.

"You know, I was raised by a single dad, too," I finally say. "So I get it."

"You don't get it." Chiara blows her bangs off her forehead. "There's no way you do. Because you were born in the olden days."

"The olden days, huh? You're right. I was knee-deep in cow poop, milking them at dawn. All the Tommasos of my generation were heading off to war."

No smile. Tough audience.

"How about gelato?" I finally venture.

"I like gelato." She smiles—looks like such a kid when she does.

"Great, gelato it is, then! Hey, that's the castle. From the sixteenth century, I think." I point to the large crumbly building with moss clinging in patches to the side.

Chiara gives it about a second's worth of her eyeballs' time before rolling them. "Cooooool," she says, her tone conveying aggressive un-excitement. "Adults get so excited about old stuff."

"What do you get excited about?"

Her face lights up. "Experiments. I love doing science experiments! Like, I did this one where you add things to water and it explodes!" Her face darkens. "Papa didn't like it. It ran all over his papers on the table. That was seriously *irritante*."

She shakes her head, and I think she's saying that it was seriously *irritante* that her dad had the gall to put his papers there. Not seriously *irritante* for him! I bite my lip. Poor Gabriele. But also lucky Gabriele. What a spirited, sassy kid.

"My brother is a scientist," I tell Chiara as we join the gelato line. "He's on the train actually, too. So I can introduce you, if you want to ask questions. He has a pretty big company."

"*If* I go back to the train."

"If," I agree. "It's probably not fun, though, to be homeless."

"Oh, I don't know about that."

"How would you get ice cream, though?"

"Easy." Chiara jingles the coins in her purse. "People love to give money to a kid who's singing."

Oh. She's right, I suppose. "But after a while, you won't be exciting anymore. People will have seen you often and already given you their money."

She considers it. "Well, if that happens, it's not a big deal. It's different when you're a kid. I could just stand here, and someone will buy me ice cream and give me money. People feel sorry for a kid." She puckers her lips, then affects a sob. "*I lost my papa, and I haven't eaten all afternoon.*

I want some ice cream." It's an Academy Award performance. Then her face brightens. "Like that!"

She's got a point, this kid. We advance to the front and Chiara surveys the ice creams. While she isn't paying attention to me, I quickly text Gabriele. I send him our location and tell him Chiara is fine. That I'm getting her gelato.

Chiara is already talking to the boy scooping out cones, speaking to him in a stream of Italian. I watch him smile, then shake his head and respond in a flurry of Italian.

"Oh." Chiara turns to me. "They don't have the flavor I want."

"What's that?" I ask.

"Earl Grey lavender."

I squelch a laugh. "That sounds highly specific. And not exactly Italian."

Chiara shrugs. "Papa and I have an ice cream maker and we experiment with different flavors. That was our best experiment. Papa suggested the combination, and I said *che schifo!* But it wasn't gross, it was actually delicious."

"Well, maybe try something else this time."

"Yeah." She ends up ordering gelato alle mandorle and gives me a taste.

"Yum!" It's almondy, with crushed almonds sprinkled atop.

I consider getting pistachio, my favorite, but then I opt for something more Italian. I order *bacio*—chocolate and hazelnut.

We move to the side as I dole out euros to the ice cream guy. Of course, Chiara doesn't offer to pay with the coins she collected for singing, which makes me smile. The glory of childhood, that coins can be hoarded and feel much like Monopoly money.

But then my smile fades at the memory of bills collecting on our dining room table, scary words embossed in red on the envelopes. *Overdue. Last Notice. Collections.*

Papa was wonderful, but mastery of our finances was never his top skill. Or maybe he was just always stretched. Being a diner chef wasn't exactly lucrative. And he certainly didn't make a living off his violin playing. Still, whatever his financial stress, he never let it show. He would want to take us to get new skis when we'd outgrown our old ones, and I would say, like it had only now occurred to me, "I don't love skiing. Maybe we don't need to ski this year."

He always pinned me down with his piercing eyes. "You are a child, Rory. You don't have to worry about if we can afford it. I am handling it."

And I would bite my lip and nod. But I did worry about it. A lot. Papa did admittedly pull things off, paying for field trips and clothes and any excursions and extracurriculars Max and I desired, but the bills weighed on me. And Papa certainly didn't have the salary of a lawyer, like Mr. Robinson next door, or of a businessperson, like other kids' parents I knew. He was a cook at a diner, where the seat cushions were yellow pleather and torn in places, with stuffing poking through. Papa gave me money often, insistently, for ice cream, for the Doc Martens I coveted— but instead of spending it like he wanted me to, I would save it. I used to babysit the Robinson kids and I would save my babysitting money, too, and mail it all to the address in the bills, stuffing in my crinkled dollars and coins. I don't think Papa ever knew.

Papa believed God took care of things. God. Me. He was right, wasn't he? We always skated by—other than his credit score, perhaps, the fears that kept me up at night were the only real casualty of my childhood.

Chiara and I sit on a bench, and I steal a glance at my phone. Gabriele has texted me back that he was working and didn't even realize Chiara had run away, with a face-palm emoji. Followed by the fact that he's leaving immediately and will be here in ten minutes. And he's added a *grazie mille* followed by three prayer-hand emojis.

"Your brother is a scientist?" Chiara asks, slurping up a trail of ice cream fleeing down her wrist.

I nod. "He created an Alzheimer's vaccine. To prevent the disease, and also cure it. It's going to be really huge when it finally comes out. Do you know what Alzheimer's is?"

"Of course," Chiara says. "Like Nino, who's losing his mind. That's what happens when you're old. You know, old old. Like, you're just old. But you're not *old* old, not yet."

"Thank you for that." I smile.

"Is your brother the blond guy? The one who doesn't smile?"

I blurt with a laugh. "No, that's Nate. He's—he's had a lot going on lately." I was about to tell her about how Nate wants me back and all that, because I've started to feel like Chiara is a miniature adult, but I stop myself, thank goodness. She's *nine*, I remind myself. And I've dated her father. I can't go to her for romantic advice, no matter how much I'd like to hear what she'd say, which would probably be hilarious and even useful.

Chiara nods. "So Nate . . . he's with that other girl?"

"Other girl?" I shake my head. "You mean Caroline?"

She shrugs. "I don't know her name."

"The blond girl?" I ask. "She's really pretty."

"She's really pretty," Chiara confirms. "Sort of like a Barbie girl."

I smile. "Yeah. That's Caroline. No, she's not with Nate."

"Oh. I thought she was."

I feel a crackle in my chest. "Nope," I say cheerfully, but then add, "Why did you think they were together?"

"Oh, maybe they're not. I just heard them arguing in a cabin doorway when I left the train. They didn't see me."

My heart twists as I remember that I caught Caro and Nate in that weird tense conversation when Max and I reunited with them on the hike. It struck me as weird because Caro and Nate don't have a relationship. Max and Nate—yes. Me and Nate—obviously. But Caro and Nate—nothing. I mean they're friendly, know each other well, but not friends. Never hung out independently of me. I rationalized what I saw as Caro telling him to give me time. Berating him for the breakup, maybe?

"Did you hear what they were arguing about?" I ask.

"Yeah, of course I did." She nods. "No one pays attention to kids. They didn't even notice me. They were talking about Dubai. My classmate went to Dubai last year."

Dubai? Suddenly it clicks, that Nate has been in Dubai often the past half year because of business and trying to get Rima and Youmna out of the country. And that Caro went there on business, too, a couple of months back. My heart sinks right down to my toes.

"Yeah, he said, *Rory can't find out*." She looks at me.

I nod, not able to speak.

"I shouldn't have repeated that."

"No, it's okay," I manage. "I'm glad you told me. What else did you hear?"

"Well, the girl—Barbie—said, *I have to tell her*. And the man said, *You can't*. And the girl was quiet. And the man said, *What if it's in the book?* And the girl said, *Well, the books are gone now*. And then she said, *But . . .*"

"But . . . ?" I hear the word slice the air but hardly feel my lips eject it.

Chiara shrugs. "I got sort of bored. I kept walking after that. I shouldn't have listened, huh? Papa always says, *Non ascoltare le conversazioni private*." She does an excellent imitation of a stern Gabriele that would make me laugh, if I didn't feel like crying. "That means, *Don't listen to people's private conversations*. But I can't help it. Because sometimes they're really interesting."

It can't be. Caro and Nate? No. It can't be. There has to be another explanation other than the horrible, obvious one my mind has conjured up.

"Did they—" I venture, but stop when I see Chiara's face scrunched up. She's put her unfinished gelato on the bench and is rubbing her chest.

"I think—I think there's something wrong with me!" She peers under her shirt, scratching her skin raw.

"Yeah?" I peer too, even though I'm far more absorbed in my head, in the facts my brain is trying to make sense of. "Like a mosquito bite?"

"No, I feel like my chest is going to explode!"

I wonder if it's a bit, an act, but then I see her face, which is suddenly immensely childlike and contorted in pain.

"Explode?" I say uncertainly. "What do you mean?"

"Like fireworks." She bolts to a stand. "I need to—I don't know— there's something wrong! Do you ever feel like your whole body is going to explode?"

Now I feel a bit panicked, at this babysitting job I didn't sign up for, that has suddenly confronted me with Chiara's life in peril. "Your dad is almost here," I tell her. "He'll—"

"You texted him?" She isn't in too much pain that she doesn't say it quite accusatorily.

I blush. "I'm sorry. Grown-up rules. I had to."

"Well, whatever, but we can't wait around for him! Look at me!" She points, and suddenly I see them—red welts spackling her chest. What the hell? I'm afraid that something is seriously wrong. And that I've been a catalyst to it, as Chiara's unwitting babysitter.

"We have to go now!" she shouts.

Before I can think, before I can come up with a reasonable plan, Chiara takes off—sprinting, really—back toward the train.

CHAPTER TWENTY

Rory

I'm back in the Roma Suite—a place that's starting to feel like the inside of a nightmare. My eyes skitter around the space that now seems confoundingly small, my shakerato glass miraculously cleared, along with the condensation on my nightstand it left behind. Marco's done efficient work, but I wonder if he also removed some of the air in the place. As I pace around, contemplating this bizarre train trip, I feel suffocated. Everything is gold and crystal and lacquered wood, every fabric luxe brocade, and yet it feels like around every gold curvature, every brocade bend, is a new betrayal. A boulder barreling toward me. And there's no way out. What could possibly be next?

The boulder flattening me, turning me to dust, that's what. Nope—not sticking around for that.

A tap on the door, pressing pause on my thoughts. I open it, and there's Gabriele, his lips quirking in a tiny, sheepish smile, like I've caught him in a walk of shame.

"*Mi dispiace tanto*. Thank God you found her." He enters cautiously and throws a hand through his thick dark hair. "I'm so sorry, Rory. This daughter of mine, she's—"

I wave a hand. "It's fine. Seriously, Gabriele, it's totally fine. These things happen."

He grimaces. "With her, it happens too often. In Rome, though, she knows not to go past the Tiber and to come home before dark. This time it's not okay. What if the train had left without her? What if she'd been kidnapped, *dio non voglia*." His eyes fritter around. "Is she hiding? Where is she anyway? *Chiara!*"

I motion toward the bathroom. "She's toweling off. A fire ant got into her shirt. Stung her all over. I've been bitten by them before and it's pretty horrible."

"A fire ant? Oh. *Formica di fuoco*. They are beasts."

"Beasts. Really did a number on her chest. She's going to be itchy for a few days. I had Neosporin, but she may need steroid cream, too."

Gabriele nods. "Thank you. There's a doctor on board. I'll take her. She's so lucky you were there."

"Oh, I don't know. That girl of yours is capable. She took off running. If I wasn't following her, she would have found some stranger to let her use their shower. She's strong. Resourceful."

I smile, a bit sadly, because I recognize that. No fault of Gabriele's, but a girl who grows up without a mother—no matter how fantastic her father—has to learn to mother herself.

I sit at the banquette, trying to keep the smile on my face but unable to stop the loop in my head of what Chiara told me before she was attacked by the fire ant.

Gabriele goes to the bathroom and knocks on the door. There follows a steady stream of Italian—nothing I understand, but starting fiery on both sides, and then ending with Gabriele on his second walk of shame to join me at the table.

"Is she okay?"

He nods, sighs. Rubs his stubble.

"Are *you* okay?"

He exhales a heavy breath. "She's so wonderful, you know? But sometimes I feel like I'm . . . *il giocoliere*. . . ." He extends his arms and turns his palms up, facing the sky, then paddles them like he's tossing imaginary balls.

"A juggler?"

"A juggler." He smiles, but I can see it's an effort.

"Well, I think you're doing an incredible job. She's a special kid."

"She is." He half smiles. "You know, she regularly invites people over to dinner—the butcher, a docent at the museum—and then lets me know when they'll be coming. Sometimes only an hour before."

A giggle shoots out of me.

His smile fades. "And what about you? How's the trip? This is supposed to be about you, with Chiara and me in the background, but we've got it all switched around today."

"The trip is amazing," I reassure him, trying to smile, but my lips no longer feel like complying. "I mean, it's amazing, yes, I'm grateful. But it's also crazy and, honestly, awful. And I'm starting to get angry. Like, this feels like a setup."

"A setup? Ulterior motives, you mean?"

"Yes. Maybe. Today we all brought our books to the beach in Monterosso, and they were stolen from our chairs."

"Your books? You mean, *The Cabin on the Lake*?"

"Yes! Stolen. Caroline did it. Took them, I mean. I saw a copy in her bag when we got back. She denied it, but——"

"Your *friend* Caroline?" He arches an incredulous eyebrow. "But why would she— *Oh*."

That *oh* speaks volumes, answers a question I've been chewing on. So he knows about the contents of Ginevra's letter. I'm not sure if I'm angry about that, that he's responsible, in part, for this smoke and mirrors trip, or comforted that I'm not facing it alone. Both, I guess. "It's true then? What Ginevra is accusing Caro of?"

He shrugs. "I know as much as you do. The embezzling. But still, why would Caroline steal the books?"

"Ginevra must have put stuff in the book about what Caro's been up to. And she saw and didn't want me to find out." I don't say the additional rationale I've just deduced——that if there's something between her and Nate, she also could be worried the affair lives in the pages of the book. The affair. God. Maybe it does. Maybe *that's* what I missed. Everything feels so unwieldy, like a tangled necklace I'll never manage to unpick. I *need* to read that book again.

"I see." Gabriele's brow furrows. "But she knows you'll get another copy. I can get another for you easy, when we're off the train. And taking them doesn't stop the book's publication, or you eventually reading it. So it's very weird. Maybe it was a fan who took the books. Ginevra has a lot of them, you know. Many quite strange."

"I saw it in Caro's bag," I say harshly. "I know what I saw."

"Okay." He's quiet. But I don't know if he believes me.

I think whether to mention the boulder, and my finicky doubt as to whether it was actually a fluke accident, but I wonder if I'm starting to sound crazy. I don't want Gabriele to think I'm losing it. So instead, I opt for, "Hey, do you know why Ginevra wants me to go to Le Sirenuse when we get to Positano?"

"I don't know. She didn't tell me all her plans. But . . ."

"What?" His face scrunches, like he's trying to decide whether to tell me something. "Please. Please tell me whatever it is."

"I truly don't know anything about Le Sirenuse. But Ginevra's sister lives in Positano. Her name is——"

"Orsola." I remember vaguely, the few times that Ginevra mentioned her. Ginevra's twin.

Gabriele shrugs. "I don't know if that has anything to do with it."

"I see."

Ginevra's twin sister lives in Positano. What in the world could that have to do with anything? I consider telling Gabriele that I'm planning to go see Ginevra tomorrow when we stop in Rome, that I am speculating—spinning out, maybe—that she could have been involved with the adoption I recently discovered. But something stops me. I trust Gabriele, as much as I trust anyone right now, I suppose. But I need to take back control of this trip. And somehow, I feel he knows more than he's letting on.

"And Nate? What's going on with him? Are you back together?" Gabriele smiles pleasantly, a smile that I can't see behind to decipher what he's getting at. If he's asking casually, or if he cares about the answer for more selfish reasons.

"Back together? No." A memory flashes—early on when Nate and I were together, after we met in Ann Arbor. I took him to meet Papa, who had an old Grand Marquis at the time. Like a long cop car. It was so smudgy and dirty and Nate offered to clean it. Papa insisted on helping then, and I remember the two of them now out on the driveway, dipping into the soapy bucket, laughing, cleaning Papa's car.

"He wants to be back together," I tell Gabriele, "or he says he does. But——"The thing Chiara told me, about Nate and Caro in Dubai, is still ricocheting through my brain. They couldn't have slept together. They wouldn't.

But something is flaring in me that says maybe they did. I'm not ready to talk about it yet. Not aloud. Not with Gabriele.

I need to be alone. To think. My head is pounding—all the conflicting thoughts. Young Nate, with a healthy Papa, when life was simple. Nate and Caro, kissing each other on a movie screen hosted by my spiraling mind.

"I'm really tired," I finally say with a small, apologetic smile. "I think I need to rest a bit before dinner."

"Yes." Gabriele nods. "Chiara—*andiamo!*"

As they filter out, there are more apologies from Gabriele, and Chiara requesting that I set up a meeting between her and Max, declining to say about what, only that she wants to talk about how she and Max can help each other. I promise to try to arrange a meeting. As she leaves, Chiara says, "Tomorrow would suit me."

"She's a star," I tell Gabriele as we hover in the doorway.

"That's one word for it." But he smiles. Then he surprises me by pulling me into a tight hug.

I'd forgotten—his spicy orange scent that feels like it harks from another era, his arms that encircle me tightly. He runs his thumb over my back assuredly, communicating he needs not a thing from me. Just giving. Just *having* enough to give, without depleting his own stores.

We slept together one time. It was first sex, so you'd think fumbling and nervous laughter. Tentative unbuttoning. But it was hot. Not earth-shattering necessarily, although I'm old enough to know that sex can ebb and flow and change. The way he held me, though—that was the earth-shattering part. Nate is a great cuddler, but we both gravitated toward our separate sides for sleep. It was like that since the beginning, and I thought I was good with it, that I needed space, that I wasn't the type to conjoin in bed. But Gabriele, he just held me. Not tightly, squeezing the life out of me. Softly. So softly and nicely that I heard myself humming throughout the night—like a thousand mini-orgasms but all felt in my heart, appreciating how nice and homey and right it felt.

I realize all of a sudden that I've been hugging Gabriele for a very long time. I let him go, force my body to inch away. I smile ruefully. "Thanks."

"Why?" he asks. "I should be the one thanking *you*."

"Oh . . ." I blush. "For being a friend now. For the hug."

He nods. "Hugs come free. The friendship, too."

"Thanks. I could use them both now."

"They're yours. Anytime."

Then Gabriele goes, and I watch him trail Chiara down the hall. I close the door, swivel around, and ease myself slowly to the ground, my body still tingling from our embrace. I wrap my arms around my knees and rest my head atop.

What was that?

Eventually I lift my head and stare at the glass mosaic on the wall for a long time—long enough that my eyes feel pulled into the green and pink glass, swimming inside them. Then the room refocuses. I pull out my phone, dread building in my chest. I scroll to Caro's Instagram. To that shot of her at the Burj Khalifa, in her white sunglasses. May 24.

I take a deep breath, consider if I don't just want to shelve this. Forget what Chiara told me. Forgetting would make for such an easier life, wouldn't it? But somehow I know it—I didn't sign up for the easier life.

My heart drums in my ears as I jump over to Nate's page. He posts a lot for a guy, a noninfluencer. A few fundraisers, for human rights injustice type things. Otherwise architectural shots, stuff in nature, animals. A caterpillar, even. (*A caterpillar got the feed, and you haven't posted one of us in months?* I remember asking, laughing. *Look at the close-up! It's a cecropia moth that can grow to be four inches*, he said, zooming in, awestruck.) If I cruise down his feed, there are indeed shots of us that he hasn't erased. I know this because since our breakup I've blocked him, then unblocked, then muted, then unmuted, all the while scanning his feed, peering at those old pictures of us for illusory clues.

But today I'm not looking for evidence of my past with Nate. I'm looking for other evidence; and when I see it, I freeze. It's a video of a pool—just the water shimmering, nothing else. But the location is tagged as Dubai. And the caption says simply, "Breathe in, breathe out."

Posted on May 24.

CHAPTER TWENTY-ONE

Nate

We board a Venetian-style taxi boat from Portovenere across Le Bocche strait to Palmaria—a tiny triangular island with marble caves and apparently abandoned bunkers from the Second World War. It's evening now, too dark to see any of that, though, and our mission is food, in a charming trattoria apparently beloved by celebrities from Spielberg to Streisand. The atmosphere on the boat is tense, almost bizarre—we're different people than we were on the trail through the five towns, and I'm trying with my best Fabrizio Salvatore impressions to pierce Rory's stony silence, the grim set of Caro's jaw. To no avail.

We dock on a long wooden walk lit up with votives, and a waiter seats us on the upper terrace at the rail overlooking the sea, romance oozing from the place's every pore. The waves lap the shore below, I can practically taste the salt in the air, and the lights of Portovenere twinkle in the distance.

Perfection, or a veneer thereof. Everyone busies themselves with the menu, avoids each other's gaze. What happened? What has made Rory so clearly angry all over again? It's like the possibility that sizzled after I told her I wanted her back was all in my head.

Could she possibly think that I took the books?

Could she think that—?

No. *No.*

But then again, Rory is sitting next to Max, giggling almost pointedly with him about stuff that happened when they were kids, asking him if he wants to share the bollito di crostacei, with lobster and shrimp, as their main, when she well knows that Max is finicky about shellfish and I would have happily gone in on that. Sure enough, Max says no, but does she want to share the grilled fish; and Rory hesitates for a moment, but then shuts her menu and says yes. When I know—*know*—that she'd never forgo lobster for simple grilled fish unless she was avoiding speaking to me.

"Hey, look," I tell Rory, fishing for an opener. "There's Mr. Pom-Pom. His face has gone from red to purple at this point."

"Wonder what tirade I can arrange for him today," Rory says, no ironic smile to be found.

Still, we watch him at his neighboring table for one, struggling with an object, a blue and white china canister. He mutters something unintelligible into the wind. Suddenly, he hitches open the canister, stands, and begins to scatter gray dust over the rail into the sea.

"Is that . . . ?" Rory asks.

"Oh my . . . *pfffff*," I say, as some of that dust flies at me. I recoil, immediately brush at my face. I spit a few times into my napkin. When I surface, I say, "Ashes." I duck.

"What?" Max asks, not having yet cottoned onto the scene, and then he gets some himself. I stay low, below the table line. "God, you look straight outta the coal mines, Maxie."

The waiters have now glommed onto what's happening, and hasten over to have words with Mr. Pom-Pom, who, by his sharp, skewering tone, does not sound pleased to have his ceremony interrupted.

We're all a mix of horrified and laughing, scrubbing at our faces with wet napkins. "Still think he's a minion paid by Ginevra Ex?" I ask Caro.

She rolls her eyes. "He's unlikely, that's for sure."

"But if he's Ginevra's lackey, shouldn't he be operating more on the down-low?" Max asks.

At that we all erupt in laughter. Something unfurls in my chest, and I find myself laughing the hardest. Maybe this dinner is going to be all right, after all.

Our waiter brings out our antipasto, crowding the table with a veritable feast on plates covered in pastoral lemon prints. There's stuffed mussels, anchovies, shrimp salad, penne with scampi, and spaghetti with the local ripe pesto, all artfully arranged, with sprigs of herbs and citrus wedges. The waiter uncorks a bottle of crisp Ligurian white wine and swishes it into all of our glasses—well, except Caro's. She's not drinking this trip.

I know why that is. Why her alcohol intake lately has been nil.

"So how was everyone's afternoon postbeach?" Rory asks, her tone no longer imbued with any lightness from the ashes-in-our-faces absurdity.

I push down the anxiety in my chest. "Good! I was dead, though. All that sun and wine and limoncello. I needed a nap after."

"Oh, yeah?" Rory asks, and now I know for certain I'm not imagining it, her unmistakable subtext. Like she knows I am lying.

Dumb answer, Natey-boy. The woman dated you for ten years. She knows you don't nap.

"And what about you, C? A *nap*, too?"

My unease grows as I realize Rory could have heard us arguing. Fucking hell. How dumb of us to speak so publicly in the hall. Heat creeps up my neck as I consider what that means. That Rory could have heard my words, but even worse—seen what was written on my face.

But it's not like Rory passed by—I know she didn't. We're not that oblivious or idiotic.

"No, I didn't nap," Caro says. "I had to deal with the office, take care of a few work things."

"Oh, the *office*. You had to take care of stuff with the office. Right."

"I did," Caro says, looking genuinely surprised. "That's what I did, after you came by and borrowed that dress."

"You mean, after I saw *The Cabin on the Lake* in your bag."

"What?" I sputter.

"What . . . you saw what?" Max asks.

"Mm-hmm, news flash. Caro took the books. I saw a copy in her bag."

"When you were searching in my room," Caro says in a strange, high-pitched tone. "And you don't know what you actually saw."

"Are you saying I need to get my eyes checked?" Rory asks, her tone so scathing that I feel whiplashed. "Because last appointment, I'm pretty sure I was told I had twenty-twenty vision."

My eyes bounce back and forth between them. This isn't what I expected. Not at all.

"I'm saying . . . things are not what they appear."

"Well, that's the first honest thing you've said. Because you are definitely not what you appear, C."

I suck in my breath. "What's up, Ror?" I finally venture. "What are you trying to say?"

Her eyes flare with anger. I have been twirling a forkful of pasta but now I stop and hover my fork over the plate, my appetite vanished.

"Well, let me tell you . . . yes, let me tell you *all*. I had a really interesting afternoon, even before I saw the book in Caro's—"

"You're wrong, you're so wrong, Ror. . . ."

But Caro is silenced by Rory's skewering gaze. "When we got back from the beach, I talked to Papa, which was . . . you know."

No, I don't know, I want to say, but I want to know, want to be there for her. I want to say it forcefully, so she understands how much I care, how much I love her, but that would be a demonstration for me more than for her. She doesn't want me to be the one who comforts her now— it's blazingly obvious.

"And then I saw the book. Whatever. I'll get another copy from Ginevra." Rory shakes her head. "And I know what's in it, Caro. I *know*."

"What?" Caro asks, pushing back. "What are you talking about? What's in it?"

Rory glares at Caro. "Please. Like you don't know."

"I—I don't."

Rory rolls her eyes. "Just stop. We'll do this later. There's another thing—another betrayal—that's cut ahead in the line." Now she moves her eyes to me, a hard, level gaze that makes me shrink back. "Because, after my talk with Papa, I went for a walk to clear my head and while I was out, I ran into Gabriele's daughter."

"Gabriele?" I ask, surprised. Maybe she doesn't know. My heart surges with preliminary relief.

Rory rolls her eyes. "Yes. Gabriele. The guy who's arranging our whole trip. Who set this whole evening up."

"Right." *Him.* "I forgot his name." Goddamn it, that annoyingly competent guy who looks like an Italian Tom Cruise in his prime. I know Rory slept with Gabriele, because she told Caro, and Caro told me. When we were both drunk, in a hotel bar with so many gold surfaces it put the Orient Express to shame. In Dubai.

"Anyway, his daughter, Chiara, ran away from the train this afternoon. It was this whole thing. So there I am, talking her down, and she happens to tell me how when she was leaving the train, she saw a couple arguing."

My chest constricts with fear. Shit. Holy shit, shit, shit, shit, shit. Fuck.

"Yes," Rory says, looking straight at Caro. Defiantly. "You and Nate."

Max shakes his head. "Caro and Nate arguing? That's what she thought she saw?"

"Not thought, Max," Rory says. "She definitely did."

"Okay. . . ." Max swipes a clump of pesto from his lower lip. He's clearly puzzled but not finding the information catastrophic like his sister does.

I can't speak. Move.

"Chiara recognized them obviously. She saw us all the first day in the bar car. But she heard them say *Rory can't find out.*"

"Rory can't find out," Max repeats skeptically. "Rory can't find out what?"

"It had to do with Dubai," Rory says, quietly now. "That's all Chiara heard."

"Dubai." Max frowns. "Who went to Dub— I don't get it. What does Dubai have to do with anything?"

A table behind us erupts in cheer—I instantly recognize the mealy laugh. It's that big brute of an Italian man whose family took our chairs and possibly also our books, who boated over with us for this dinner, and seems to be in peculiar lockstep with our group. But he's a blip on the scene right now because, Dubai. Rory knows. Or she doesn't know everything, but she knows enough. My fingers finally detach themselves from my fork, but it doesn't feel like I am running the show, operating my appendages.

"Oh God," Caro says, her face now one giant plea. *No,* I'm beseeching Caro, but words refuse to follow. *We can save this. We can turn it around.* However, I've glimpsed the car crash, and it's all four of us in the crash. Already pounded, scorched, limbs twisted in agony.

"You were in Dubai." Max claps his hands in realization. "For that conference."

"And Nate was, too," Rory says, her voice venomous. "On May twenty-fourth."

Oh God. Oh God. Oh God.

"Nate was there, too?" But Max's face is still placid.

"I've been wanting to tell you," Caro says, and now she's speaking only to Rory. "I've been wanting to tell you ever since. I'm so sorry, Ror. I never meant to do it, or keep it this long. . . ."

"Do what? Keep *what* this long?" Max asks. "I really don't get it. . . . Nate . . . *bro*— What is she talking about?"

Caro keeps her eyes fixed on Rory, doesn't look at Max—shit, I can't look at Max, either. Max—who has loved Caroline since I first met them both. Who has pined after her, his gaze ever fixed on her, following her with lovesick obviousness, whether she has a boyfriend or boy-something by her side, or whether she's single, just flirting with a bartender, trying to get a rise out of him. I've known—always known—that Caroline loves Max, too. That for whatever strange reason, she's held herself back from being with him.

Max has always called me bro, a moniker that early on I found flattering, albeit a bit contrived, because he started using it soon after Rory and I started dating, before we were even close. I grew up with brothers, but Max, of course, didn't. He didn't have many male friends, still doesn't, but we got along. He's the smartest guy you've ever met, has interesting things to say, interesting perspectives, and he's a great listener. Immediately, Max adopted me into his fold, drove me to the airport each time I had a job interview, was my biggest champion to Rory. Treated me like his real brother, and I came to feel the same about him. We've been in touch, too, since the breakup, with Max always telling me he was sure Rory and I would find our way back together.

Max loves me, and I love him, and I've been torn up in agony over betraying Rory, without realizing that I've betrayed Max, too.

Now I do realize it. I've betrayed Max, too.

I take a deep breath, summon words, but Caro gets there first.

"Nate and I slept together when we were both in Dubai a couple of months ago. It was a huge mistake! A total—"

"A *total* mistake." Fucking hell! My body flushes with heat, the fire creeps up my neck—onward to inferno. "After we broke up, Ror. It happened *after*. Even though that's not an excuse."

"It was after," Caro says quietly. "You guys weren't together. Not that it makes it any better. I was at such a low point, Ror. I—I can't even explain it. Nate was on a work trip, too, totally random that we happened to coincide, and I—I was in such a bad place, and I . . ." She coughs, doesn't laugh her inappropriate stress laugh. "I've never regretted anything more."

Her eyes beam me daggers.

"Same," I say. "Deeply same."

Rory is silent, staring out at the calm, black sea.

"We were broken up," I say again, hearing myself plead, trying to regain some moral ground. "And I was in a horrible place, too. It meant nothing. It meant less than nothing."

Although on that note, I know I'm still lying. It didn't mean nothing. Not to me. But it *should* have meant nothing. My girl's best friend. It should have meant nothing. But I guess I always had a little crush on Caro. Meaningless. And when we slept together, maybe I hoped it would be forgettable. But it wasn't. Not for me, at least. Which is the worst part. Not that I'd confess that now. I'll take it to my grave, unless—unless Ginevra Ex knows. Unless she put it in the book. My chest tightens again, contemplating that inconceivable thought.

"It meant less than nothing is for sure," Caro says.

"I see," Rory finally says in a voice that is terrifyingly void of emotion. I'm still blazing hot all over, furious that Caro's confessed it, furious even more that it happened. Why did this have to come out? Why couldn't our one horrible, stupid night stay private?

I know why. All roads lead back to fucking Ginevra Ex. Spinning out, speculating whether she knew. Whether she put it in the book—and how much. Mine and Caro's whispered conversations, trying to discern if we needed to get ahead of it coming out.

"You slept with Nate. . . . You guys *actually* hooked up?" Max's eyes flicker over to me, his face white and still.

"It meant nothing," I hear myself say weakly, again. Even though you can't sleep with your ex-fiancé's best friend—with the girl your essentially brother loves—and have it mean nothing.

"It's why—one of the reasons why—Caro took the book," Rory says briskly. "Because she thought Ginevra found out about their affair and put it in her story."

"It wasn't an affair! It was . . . once. And I didn't take the books. Literally . . . that's not what . . . It didn't even cross my— Ror, I didn't." Caro stares at her hands like they are foreign objects of which she can't make sense.

"Mmm," Rory says. "Right."

"Ror . . ." I stretch out a hand. She jerks back. I retract my hand, feel utterly pummeled myself.

"I can't believe you both . . . I just . . ." Rory's voice rises, and she half stands. For a moment I wonder if she'll do something crazy, like flip the table over.

Then the man who flung his ashes all over us swivels around from his neighboring table. "Some of us are trying to have a pleasant evening without your hijinks."

"Without *our* hijinks?" I can't help but shout. "You just covered us in—" I stop as he recoils, suddenly looking haggard and sad, and I regret my outburst. I hear murmurs from the patrons nearby and hang my head. God, this is all spiraling. I wish I could melt through the floorboards.

"Sorry." Rory nods an apology to all our spectators, and when everyone returns to their food, she takes a shaky seat. "Caro, I can't believe *you*," she says in a whisper. "You above all."

Caro above all. My breath catches at my place in the ranking.

"I never would have thought this could be possible." Max blinks rapidly. "Aliens landing, a meteor striking . . . sure . . . better chance than Caro and Nate . . . than Caro and Nate . . ."

"We'll explain," I say. "You have to hear the whole story. You'll understand, if we tell you the whole story—"

"I don't want the whole story!" Rory fires back in a quiet hiss. "What, you think I want the details? When you reached for her hand . . . how you *fucked* her nice and slow . . ."

"It wasn't like that, Ror," Caro says quietly. "It wasn't like that at all. It was . . . bad."

"Horrible," I agree, feeling punched in the stomach from Caro's assertion. "The stupidest thing I ever did. And least satisfying."

"For me, too," Caro says defiantly. "For me, most definitely, too."

"Sure. Uh-huh," Rory says. "I still have one question, though. And it doesn't have to do with which one of you satisfied the other, and how, because, gross. Seriously gross." She mimes a finger down her throat.

Max frowns, presses his lips together; and I find myself holding my breath, hoping he won't cry. Max can't cry. Somehow, that out of everything I can't handle. Now I regret all the stuff I said, going down that road. Better not to get into any details at all. We were supposed to keep this quiet. No one was going to ever know. We could have lied our way out of it. I'm so . . . *angry*, even though I know I'm not entitled to be. But Caro and I . . . we had an agreement that we wouldn't expose this! We could have gone to our graves without anyone the wiser. And I could be with Rory, and Caro could be with Max.

Life could slot us into the pairs that are basically ordained. And now everything is messed up. And I can't imagine how I'm going to reverse this level of damage.

"You can ask me anything, Ror. Of course. Oh God, I'm so sorry." Caro's cheeks stream with tears. "You can't imagine how sorry. I swear, I was always going to tell you, but in person. I couldn't do it on the phone. I've been sick over it. Seriously sick. I'll tell you anything you want to know. Anything. Literally anything." Caro's relief is blatant—relief at being out with this secret, relief that Rory hasn't gotten up and exploded and declared their friendship over. She and Caro are best friends, but more like sisters—closer than any best friends I've ever seen. Genuinely there for each other, supportive, not the jealous types.

But it doesn't really matter that we were broken up or that we're sorry, does it? There are things you can't undo.

"You're pregnant, Caro, aren't you?" Rory asks.

"Pregnant?" Caro asks quietly.

"*Pregnant?*" I ask, because—oh, *no*. No, no, no, no. This can't be happening. "You're pregnant? But . . . no . . . you can't be."

"Actually, she can," Rory says in a scathing tone. "Wake up, Nate. And you've lost weight," Rory says, returning the brunt of her anger to Caro. "You're hardly eating. You're definitely not drinking. Ordering mineral water at lunch. If you're pregnant, and you guys are hiding it for some later, like, revelation, just tell me now. Rip off the fucking Band-Aid now."

"I'm not pregnant," Caro stammers. "Definitely not. You're wrong. I mean, I get why you think I could be, but you're totally wrong, Ror. I've been so torn up about what I . . . what we did. Maybe I've lost a few pounds from the stress. Not that I'm trying to make you feel sorry for me. Not at all. I—I don't trust myself with alcohol anymore. Not since . . . but no, I'm not pregnant. Definitely not."

"Definitely *not*," I add, eyeing Caro. She shakes her head at me, which is a huge relief. *Huge*. I gulp in air.

"So *not* pregnant." Max raises his glass, drowns it. "Just sex. Just Caro and Nate having . . . *sex*." He laughs, a strange laugh that bumps across my bones.

"I'm really sorry, Max," Caro says softly. "I'm so sorry."

"Me too," I say. "Guys . . . I . . . shit. I'm—"

"A piece of shit?" Max volunteers. "Yep. I'd say so." Then he waves over our waiter with aggressive hand motions.

"Well, I don't care who's joining me, but I for one am gonna need another drink!"

CHAPTER TWENTY-TWO

Rory

Nate tries to follow me back to my suite. Insists on accompanying me in the boat back to the train, even though I scream, "Get the fuck away from me."

Every time I say *fuck* it feels delicious, and then terrible. Eventually I shout, "Fuck you, fuck you," right outside the bar car bursting with revelry, and it's like that screech when the music halts, and all eyes come predictably to rest upon us.

Not my finest moment, but honestly, I feel pushed to the brink. I walk in a manic rush, past the Italian couple who stole our chairs, who now give me a serious case of the heebie-jeebies. Doesn't matter that they're bedecked in their finest, there is something overwhelmingly sinister about them. And they're always there, right around every turn! They smirk at me as they pass—well, the dislike is mutual. Then I peer back, infuriated that Nate is still trailing me to my suite in the guise of my safety. When, really, he's doing it for himself! How unsafe can I possibly be on this train populated with bazillionaires and tons of staff milling about? When we finally arrive at my suite, I don't address Nate, don't even acknowledge his existence.

"Can you please keep everyone out?" I ask Marco. "That includes *him*." I gesture toward Nate without giving him the satisfaction of even roving my eyes his way.

By the fumble of his hands as he unlocks my door, Marco is clearly befuddled. "Can I get you something, signorina?"

"No, I'm fine, *grazie*."

"Nothing? Hot water? Perhaps you'd like some brandy?"

"No, *grazie*."

I'm nearly in my suite, but Marco blocks the entry. His eyebrows crease in concern. "A doctor? We have a doctor on board."

"No. If you could keep everyone out, please, that would be doing me a great service."

Then I appraise the suite, feel a slight claustrophobia as I prepare to step inside. Is it possible that I've been on this train a grand total of one day? It feels more like a hundred years. And there are still two nights left. Two endless, excruciating nights, with people I thought I knew. People I thought I loved. Where else am I going to go, though? Off the train? That's an idea, actually. But at the sight of my beckoning bed, I sigh and force myself over the threshold. I shut the door, heave myself on the bed, and curl into a ball, the insanity of my life squeezing on my lungs.

I'm catapulted back to the blow of Papa's diagnosis. How after the doctor said Alzheimer's, even though I'd suspected it for a while, I wanted to scream, to rail against a God in whom I wasn't even sure I believed—but I had to be strong for Papa, for Max, who both had emotions in spades. I consoled, I peptalked, I unleashed every optimistic take I had in my arsenal. It was only after, when I returned to LA, with Nate out of town, that I could feel it, the rumble threatening to erupt from within. And I just said a loud no and drove straight to work. Dove headfirst into reporting on some crisis or another. I convinced myself I was doing the noble thing, the strong thing.

I remember now what my meditation teacher said on the retreat: *You can't rise from the ashes unless you first allow yourself to burn.*

Finally I cry. The biggest, deepest cry I ever remember feeling, or allowing.

Nate . . . Caro . . . Papa . . . the adoption . . . my career . . . everything I thought I was, I'm not . . .

When the tears ebb, I grab my phone. I thumb to the album I haven't yet deleted, titled *Nate* with a red heart emoji. I scroll—my fingers know what they are doing, where they are going. Fifteen or so rows down, they stop, hover, zoom in on a shot of Nate sleeping, with his baby curls unfurling against golden muscles, where he looks like a toothy crocodile. A sweet, vulnerable crocodile. Mouth stretched open, midmorning light bisecting his face, big sturdy hands resting at his sides. Right now, through the screen, I can almost see the rise and fall of his chest, hear the occasional snore rip through a still morning.

I always marveled at the peace of his slumber. Whereas I tend to ball myself up, fists curled into my cheeks, I was in both awe and envy of Nate's ease—his defenselessness.

I would just stare at him sometimes, a lot of times, when I would wake up to pee or because it was too cold or I'd had a bad dream, and he would start at my movement but then settle back into his impenetrable cocoon. As I watched him, I felt above all joyful that he was mine. That I was his. That this part of my life was wrapped up, tied in a bow, deposited in a vault. Certain. I felt safe with him, that was the startling thing. I didn't feel safe, necessarily, growing up. I feel guilty at even permitting that thought access to float across my brain. Perhaps it wasn't Papa's fault or Max's, but mine. In the story I invented about my childhood, I was the girl Salinger wrote about, holding the whole world together. With Nate, I could lay my head on his chest and exhale. I remember after I took his crocodile picture, how he grabbed me close. Called it creepy, my obsession with staring at him asleep.

I protested that it was merely my hobby. Some people crochet. Others watch their boyfriends sleep.

He laughed, claimed he was going to start charging me by the hour. But I knew he was pleased. Who doesn't like to hear they are admired, lusted after, even when they've got their head lolled back and a stream of drool out their mouth?

Okay, then. Enough diving back into moments that no longer exist. And I've done the crying thing. Gold freaking star. Where did it get me? All I feel is strange and vacant. I place my phone face down on the side table, and that's when I hear a knock at my door.

Great. Thanks a lot, Marco. I'm not entirely surprised, though. There's probably a stipulation in the employee manual about not heeding guests' requests when they appear manic.

I creep closer to the door, but I know instinctively who is waiting outside. Sure enough, when I whip open the door, it's her.

My former best friend.

e〜

We face each other with exceeding formality.

"Ror," Caro says, extending her hands across the table, like she actually expects me to meet them with my own. "I'm so sorry."

"Mmm. For what, exactly?"

"Sleeping with Nate. Of course. But . . . there's so much I haven't told you. I've been in a horrible place." She says it in a quiet way that rings of truth. But, like, why should I care? She slept with Nate, stole the books, and she's also embezzling from my brother's company.

"I know about your horrible place. I know *exactly* what you still haven't told me."

"You do?" Caro hesitates, plays with my whistle, which I've left on the table.

"Yeah. Ginevra told me. She had private investigators—did you know that?"

"Max told me." Caro laughs. "Sorry. That's totally crazy. She's like a wild conspiracy theorist who lives in a bunker."

"Wild or genius. And I can assure you she doesn't live in a bunker but a lavish apartment in Rome." I don't add the sarcastic, gossipy thing I might have, if we were our normal us, that the apartment is also a shrine to Sophia Loren. In fact, I am almost shocked at my voice, oozing with contempt. But I can't excise it from my tone or my heart. "Regardless, let me just say, what the investigators found was pretty illuminating." I stand, walk over to the tiny closet where I stuck the letter Ginevra wrote me. When I return, I fan out the bank statements. "Recognize these?"

Caro's arranging her hair back in a clip, but when her eyes catch on the statements, her hands flop to her sides. "My bank statements? But how—how in the world did she . . . That's . . . I don't get it. Did she, like, steal them?"

"I don't know. I don't know how, but that's not really the important thing, is it? Because you're obviously embezzling from Hippoheal. How could you, C? How could you do that to Max? To Papa? The company is all for him, you know? What Max is doing . . . what you're taking is actually from Papa. Making it less likely that Max will be able to cure him. I don't understand how you can live with yourself."

She stares at me, eyes darting from me down to the statements and back again, but not speaking. Dumbfounded. Stunned, it appears, at the evidence of her crime.

"How could you?" I say again. "And I mean, I get why you took the books, to make sure there's no evidence, but I—I don't even know who you are."

"How could I?" she repeats in a monotone. Not denying it. "*Embezzle* from Max. Take the books. Right. How could I?"

"So you don't deny it. Stealing from the company?" My voice drops to a whisper. Part of me hoped—believed—she would deny it.

"Deny it?" In the strangest flat voice, she says, "Why bother? You seem to know everything, then."

"I think you should leave," I finally say, feeling all my disbelief whoosh out of me, leaving something quiet and sure behind. "I just . . . I'm too angry. You must know, though—I'm going to have to tell Max."

Caro pales. "Please . . . give me a couple of days. Until the end of the trip, at least. It's not what you think. I just need a few days. Give me a few days before you talk to Max. Please."

She looks so pitiful, so out of sorts, that I hesitate for a moment. I start to feel bad for her, to want to hug her, to make things okay. Then I remind myself—this is a person who slept with your ex-fiancé. Who stole the books and then lied about it to your face. Who is stealing from your brother.

"Until the end of the trip, that's all." I shake my head. "I thought you had so much more integrity than this. You really should be the one to tell Max first."

"Right. I should tell Max that I'm embezzling from him." Caro's tone is so strange, so bland, almost devoid of emotion, that it puts me off-kilter.

"Why did you do it, C? If you needed money, you could have asked Max. He's loaned you money before."

"I could have . . . *asked* him for money. I mean, sure. Whatever you say." It feels almost like she's mocking me.

I shake my head. I'm confused about all of it. Talking to her right now—it feels like a whole lot of meaningless words and zero answers.

Caro shakes her head. She walks to the door, turns the knob.

"Ror?" She turns back.

"Yeah?"

"I love you. I'm so sorry for everything. I need you to know, I really love you. I love your family. Truly."

"You'll understand if I can't say I entirely believe you."

She nods. "I hope one day soon you will."

"You have a strange way of showing it. Your *love*."

"Yeah." Her shoulders budge up. "I should have done it all differently. I can see that now." She gazes around almost aimlessly, like a child who's gotten lost at the mall, and my heart pangs at the memory of the little girl at school who was indeed lost. Who never had a family to guide her, to hold her. Just us. Just me, Papa, and Max. And now we Aronovs appear to be exiting her life, one by one. Guilt shivers through me. It's Caro—my sister. But why should *I* feel guilty?

I can't be her person now.

But I'm suddenly afraid, because this really isn't like Caro—sleeping with Nate, stealing from Max, taking the books, now utterly defeated. Looking like she'd be fine if life chose to run her over, leave her on the side of the road for dead.

Suddenly the train starts rumbling. Right. We're off. By morning, we'll be in Rome.

Caro and I stare at each other for a long moment, then she slips out without looking back. I want to slam the door, or my brain wants me to do it, make a real statement, but instead, I peek out and peer after her, watching her walk down the corridor slowly, desolately, with tiny sobs that quake her frame.

And as I watch her, all my emotions seep out of me—the anger, the hurt, the indignation—and I just long for my friend. I suddenly want her to run back and hug me a smidge too hard, to sit cross-legged on my bed and eat through my stash of gummies and listen to the lunacy of this train ride. To help me see it all straight. I almost shout after her to wait, let's talk, let's work things out. I need her. I need us.

And I want her to give me the book back. I need to see it for myself. What it says that she risked everything to conceal.

But she doesn't look behind, and I suppose that's for the better. Because she's betrayed me and my family in excruciating ways.

And what's that thing Papa used to say?

Sometimes you have a blind spot for the people you love most, so that they can convince you of wild things—so you even start believing the earth is flat. One day, though—it might take a very long time—but eventually you will realize the earth is indeed round. And then you will have a choice to make. Because for some people, it's easier to keep on living forever on their false flat earth.

I wonder who or what Papa was talking about. What experience in his life lent him such a wise conclusion. Too bad I can't ask, not anymore.

Maybe he's right, though. Maybe Caro had me entirely fooled. Because of her, I thought the earth was flat. And all I feel at the moment is excruciatingly sad that after today, I have to live on an earth I now know is round.

CHAPTER TWENTY-THREE

Ginevra

Three Months Before

Let's talk about Nate."

A week into interviews, and thus far, Rory had spoken around him. Ginevra had walked Rory through enough of her childhood, darted between Max and Ansel, delved thoroughly into Rory's career. But Nate remained the elephant in the room.

Rory sighed, discreetly checked her phone. The time flashed: 7:56 in the evening. The interval, already, of the *passeggiata*. Through the windows directly opposite, Ginevra could glimpse indistinct people milling out in the piazza, a blur of glossy shoes and sport jackets, pigeons fluttering above the fountains, the sky gone violet.

"I could be violating labor laws by keeping you this late." Ginevra smiled, but she didn't follow it up with *You may go*. No, this conversation was pressing, overdue. If she wanted to finish formulating her entire plot, she needed this part done.

Rory smiled back. "I signed up for long hours." She sipped her wine— Ginevra had opened a very good Bordeaux. Ginevra followed with a healthy sip of hers.

"Nate and I met in college, my senior year. We were at Rick's, a dive bar. I was a waitress, and he was with his buddies. I brought them over this shark bowl. It was our signature drink. Disgusting." Rory grimaced. "Like radioactive blue. You were supposed to put your hand to your forehead, like—"

"A shark's fin." Ginevra smiled.

"Yes. You've done one before?" Rory's eyebrows quirked in surprise.

"*Oddio!* No." Ginevra didn't say she'd read about the shark bowl in an article about Rick's in Ann Arbor, in which she'd also learned that the bar was named after the one in *Casablanca*.

"Right." Rory smiled. "I can't quite imagine you at Rick's."

"I can assure you I've never been." Ginevra laughed. "So you gave Nate the shark bowl, and let me guess, was it love at first sight?" Ginevra could almost feel it, all her senses submerged in a foreign pinky glow.

But to Ginevra's surprise, Rory shook her head vehemently. "God, no. I figured he was a total frat boy. Entitled. Cute, I'll give him that. Baseball cap—"

"What color?" Ginevra asked, scrawling.

"Light blue. And he had his collars double popped." Rory's face pinched in distaste.

"Double popped?" The article hadn't mention that phrase.

"It means you wear two different collared shirts, and the collars stand up even more. You could also triple pop. The higher the number of pops, the bigger the douchebag the guy. It was a late-aughts thing. I don't think the double pop is anywhere close to still on trend."

Ginevra wrote furiously. This was the stuff—good atmospheric color to sprinkle in.

"Nate and his friends asked me to do the shark bowl with them, so I did. Good for tips, but I pretended to drink. You get good at it, pandering to groups of rowdy guys. Anyway, the night wore on, and I barely noticed Nate, but when I finished my shift, I saw him on the phone outside. And he was almost—I dunno—crying."

"Crying?"

"Not exactly crying, but he kept saying, *Is he going to be okay?* in this really terrified voice. And I didn't know what was said on the other line, but he didn't have a jacket on. So he was, like, shivering, with bare arms, although good that he had that extra shirt for insulation." Rory smiled sadly.

"That used to be a joke of yours?" Ginevra guessed.

"Yeah. Anyway, turns out his brother had overdosed and was at the hospital. Later I found out it wasn't the first overdose. I offered to drive

Nate there. And Nate tried to refuse, said he could drive just fine, but he was clearly in no state to be behind the wheel, so I took him."

"Nice of you."

Rory shrugs. "Anyone would do it." ·

"I don't quite think so." But Ginevra decided to leave it at that. "So you bonded in the car?"

"No. He white-knuckled the door handle and kept saying, over and over to himself, *This is my fault.* So finally, after a very long ride of him saying that, I said, *Did you give him the drugs?*"

"And Nate looked at me, all surprised. I think it was the first time he really noticed me. I wasn't my most attractive, let's say—hair pulled back, sweaty from the night. Outfit all black that concealed Shark Bowl splashes. But when he looked at me, I felt—"

"Something."

"Yeah." Rory nodded slowly. "Something, I guess. And Nate said, *No, I didn't give him the drugs, but I've been preoccupied.* And then he told me stuff. Like, I learned he'd grown up in DC and all over the world, because his father was a diplomat, but then when his father retired, they moved to my same area of Michigan, where his mom's from. Like a thirty-minute drive from Ann Arbor. That's why Nate decided to go to grad school in Ann Arbor, when he got into programs at Columbia and Georgetown. He told me that he was getting his master's in international relations, and simultaneously working remotely for a think tank in DC, basically full-time. I was so surprised, because, like I told you, I pegged him as this douchey frat boy, and he was anything but. I asked him about the double-popped collars, and he groaned and said one of his buddies had told him it was cool. Then he pulled the collars from his neck and said he felt like he was being strangled by them!"

Rory smiled, but then it quickly faded. "He told me that between school and work, he hadn't had time to check in on his family. He hadn't gone back home to visit in a month. Then he said that maybe he'd been glad for the distraction. The excuse. I could tell there was something deep there. Then Nate said, *I'm the only one who can keep Garrett in line.* That's his brother. The younger one."

"What did you say then?" Ginevra asked.

"I said—" Rory stopped. Her face shaded. Ginevra could tell there was something there. Something important.

"You said you understood," Ginevra supplied.

Rory looked away, toward the framed photo of Sophia Loren, but then finally returned her gaze. "It just came out. I didn't even know I felt that way. That I felt responsible for Max like that."

"Not only for Max." Ginevra had pieced a few things together. "For your father, too."

"In a way. I mean, they weren't addicts. It feels a little ridiculous, the comparison. I had a great father. *Have*. And Max, he's—he's the best brother I could imagine. Truly."

Ginevra didn't record it. Instead, she found herself scrawling her signature, over and over, the same way she always did, with artistic flourish—a circle swirl hanging down from the *a*. Everything Rory had said was swimming, perhaps drowning, in Ginevra's brain. It all felt familiar in a way she could vaguely pinpoint. Needing to convince yourself so badly on one front, because without its fundamental truth, the world collapses as if it were made of sticks.

"But," Ginevra finally said, the feeling still gnawing at her.

"But . . . sometimes they needed me in a way that felt like too much. I told you about Max, and the kids bullying him. . . ."

"Yes. But your father? He needed things, too?"

"He did." Rory nodded. "If I'm being honest. To you and myself." She told Ginevra then about Ansel's money problems, about paying bills herself, about how she got into the habit of taking rolls of toilet paper from school and hiding them in her backpack, then depositing them in the bathrooms at home, so Ansel wouldn't have to purchase them.

Sadness surged in Ginevra. Anger, too. Mostly at herself. The feeling that she wished so badly she could gather that little girl into her arms. How she wanted to make it better—how she *should* have made it better.

"You never went hungry, though, did you?" Ginevra finally asked.

"No. Honestly, Papa was amazing. He worked so hard. Maybe some of our financial difficulties were in my head. I always had everything I needed. And maybe I didn't need to pay our bills—maybe I should have left it to Papa to figure out, because he always did."

"It's important to feel needed," Ginevra said, realizing it struck a chord for herself, too, but not in a way she thoroughly understood.

"Not as a child." Rory shook her head firmly. "As a child, you don't want to feel needed."

"That's right." Ginevra heard her voice hitch.

"You want to feel loved and like you are perfect just for being your pure self," Rory said.

"Yes." Ginevra couldn't prevent it—the cascade of her father's voice returning to her after all this time. *La mia belleza*, he always said, cradling Orsola's head to his chest in uncharacteristic physical touch. And Orsola soaked it in, radiant.

Domenico never called Ginevra his beauty. Not even once.

You want to feel loved and like you are perfect just for being your pure self. Yes. Rory had summed it up quite perfectly. The ideal childhood. If Ginevra had learned anything from her main characters, it was that pretty much no one had one.

"So what happened—you went to the hospital with Nate? You stayed with him?"

Rory bit her lip. "It was awful—his brother was in a coma. His younger one," she clarified. "Garrett. Nate's older brother has Down syndrome. It was like, a total mess. His parents were a mess. And when we arrived, before his parents spotted Nate, I just watched him, this supposed frat boy I'd written off, and he squared his shoulders and, like, made himself toughen up, and he went in there, almost . . . This sounds ridiculous, but almost like he was going into war. And then he hugged and reassured and said positive things, and talked to the doctors, and I saw how his parents could let go, could lose it, because Nate had assumed control. He's good in war zones, too. That's where Nate shines. In a crisis."

"It impressed you," Ginevra said.

"It made me sad. But, yes, it also impressed me. And I suppose I saw Nate as a person you could lean on."

"Yes. You were looking for a man like that. Makes sense." So little in life did, so it was nice, pleasing, to tease out the things that did. "And then what happened?"

"And then I stayed there with him, got his parents waters and stuff, and at some point Nate came over to me, and he started to say how he couldn't thank me enough, and I could go now, could he pay for the gas, and I don't know what came over me, but I said, *You look like you could use a hug.*"

Ginevra felt tears poke at her eyelids. What a wonderful girl Rory was. Ansel had done well with her. With both of them.

"What did Nate say?"

Rory crunched down on her lip. "We hugged for I think the longest hug I've ever had in my life. After, he stepped back. He was kind of embarrassed, I think. And he said, *Thanks, Rory. I'm okay now. I can take it from here. I really appreciate everything you did for me tonight. For basically a stranger.*"

"And you said?" Ginevra asked, even though she already suspected what followed.

Rory smiled sadly. "I said, *You're not getting rid of me yet.*"

Silence for a while, as they both absorbed it all. That's one thing Ginevra had learned—big feelings needed big room to breathe. You couldn't flit from one emotional land mine to another. You needed to give main characters space. Time. Cushioning.

In the silence, Ginevra played with her burgeoning plot, slid ideas out of little file folders and shifted things around. Later, she might reread *The Mirror Crack'd from Side to Side* for inspiration. German measles as the cunning clue that unwound the mystery for Miss Jane Marple. Or *Death on the Nile*. The victim as the murderer. Utterly ingenious. There must be a reason those books called to her again. It was worth investigating. Over her career, Ginevra had received many negative reviews, but the one that stung most called her "derivative Christie."

It stung most because, perhaps, there was a kernel of truth to it. Ginevra knew her strengths—she could come up with brilliant plots, modern ones. But she needed her ready-made characters fanned out before her, and she needed a grand twist.

And there were only so many twists. Dame Agatha had basically siphoned them all!

But there was a saying with story—around five basic stories exist. Every bestseller has recycled one of them.

The victim as the murderer. Yes, that one was intriguing. What does it mean to be a victim? Isn't that what Ginevra and Rory were cycling around this whole conversation?

No, Ginevra wasn't derivative. She'd done the best with the hand she got dealt. With the mistakes she had made. With the path she'd decided to walk down, despite the consequences.

Oh, the consequences.

But derivative, no. It wasn't a crime, after all, to marinate in a little genius, repackage it for the entertainment of millions.

Or if it was a crime, then fine, Ginevra was guilty. Add one more strike to her long list.

CHAPTER TWENTY-FOUR

Rory

I'm back in Rome, swept into the crowds, anonymous. Fourteen-year-old boys on *motorini* whiz past, the heat far thicker than when I left it, every inch of my skin slick with sweat. My sandals crunch over green glass bottle shards that haven't yet been swept up from the cobblestones. The throngs of tourists have soared, with the sounds of chattering English on every corner, clear American accents belting out "*Ciao!*" making me cringe, because as anyone who has spent enough time in Italy knows, *ciao* is what you say to your best friends—too familiar for a shopkeeper whom you've never met, for whom *salve* or *buongiorno* is more appropriate.

I hasten across the piazza, past pharmacies with their glowing green plus signs, where I've learned you can't get cleaning supplies or birthday cards, only medicine. I pass little shops called bars that aren't places to buy alcohol, like in the United States, but rather coffee and gelato shops. I pop into one for a macchiato—sit at a table and watch the world happen for a bit. There aren't to-go cups in Italy; and so for a few minutes I stare and sip, as everything from the past couple of days swishes around in my brain. When I finish, I set the empty cup on the bar, feeling thoroughly Italian. I find myself smiling—half a year ago I couldn't have imagined it, spending months in Rome, even knowing the culture a bit. It's an adventure I never anticipated. Then my smile fades. I couldn't have anticipated the other stuff, too.

It's still so incomprehensible—that Caro betrayed me. Nate, too, yes, but my anger is more acute with Caro, to be honest. It's more than the fact that she was my best friend, my sister. I've been mulling it over, dragging my tongue around this feeling I have like it's an aching tooth that Caro has always lived in some way to please me. It's not a fun vantage point to examine, and perhaps I've avoided it, because of what it says about me: that I've enjoyed it. Maybe it stemmed from Caro never having a solid family, that she went above and beyond to avoid harming her connection to ours. But she's stood up for me at every turn, dropped everything to fly to California when Nate broke up with me and I lost my job. She's whisked me away for surprise spa weekends that I wondered how she could truly afford. She's comforted me and listened to me, to the littlest things on my mind. But Caro's a hard person to probe, to get her to spill the littlest things on hers. For Caro, things are usually great, great, great, even when she's sunken into debt, even when her career isn't quite working out. It's like she hasn't wanted to need my help or to admit that things weren't going swimmingly. Maybe she finds it easier to be private and upbeat, to push down her troubles, pretend they don't exist. And I suppose I've had so many troubles of my own that they've naturally dominated our conversation these past few months. Maybe I missed signs, though, maybe I should have probed more. Because I've never wanted a friendship centered around me. Still, I wonder whether, like Max sometimes accuses, I do have a tendency of attracting the limelight. Whether I positioned myself as the star in our friendship, without realizing?

How could she do it, though? Stealing the books and denying it to my face when I saw the evidence with my own eyes. Sleeping with *Nate*. No matter that we'd broken up, it's such a deep betrayal. And it doesn't mesh with my friend, who is the most loyal, caring person I know.

Well, it's unlikely I'm going to logic this thing out. Sometimes shitty things happen for no reason. Exhibit A: Papa having Alzheimer's so young.

I leave the bar, then weave down Via Condotti. The famed shopping avenue is already bustling at ten in the morning. I pass Bulgari and Cartier, Gucci and Prada, all the luxury stores fanning out from the Spanish Steps, catching glimpses through the windows of the impeccable saleswomen wrapping items with their traditional painstaking care, where I know it would not be unusual to spend fifteen minutes waiting as they tenderly fold tissue paper and select beautiful boxes and bows. At the Barcaccia fountain, I ascend the Spanish Steps toward the church bell towers that hover over the iconic expanse. I'm in one of the most famous parts of Rome—of the world—and yet I'm in a sulky, but blessedly caffeinated, mood as I hurry toward Ginevra's apartment.

I've told Gabriele I need time alone and asked him to pass it along to the others. The others being Nate and Caro, although I didn't explain the reason to Gabriele. I've told Max as well, said I'll try to meet him at the Colosseum later, where Ginevra's arranged a group tour. We're all scheduled for the Sistine Chapel in the morning, and the Pantheon, both of which I've frequented more than once in my months-long stay in Rome and am opting out of this round. Max said he wasn't sure if he was going to join the morning tour—that he might wander Rome on his own. He looked tired this morning, his under eyes bruised half-moons, which I thoroughly understood, since I, too, passed the night in fitful sleep.

Max and I shared breakfast in his suite, a few carriages down from mine. We flaked off pastries and drank cappuccinos, speaking circles around Caro's and Nate's betrayal. We talked instead of Papa, how I'll go to Michigan soon to visit, how I'm thinking about training to become a meditation teacher. Max reminded me how talented I am as an anchor, how I can't give up everything I worked for—a speech that sits in my stomach like cement.

Worked for. I did. So hard. Maybe I want it to be easier now, I said, and he shook his head, offered me a job with his company, any job at all. I smiled. Declined. I almost told him then about Caro's other betrayal, about the embezzlement, which she didn't even deny, but then I didn't. I'm saving what I know, for now. Funneling all my energy toward confronting Ginevra. I considered texting her again, giving her notice of my arrival, but I've decided not to. She told me, when I was her main character, to feel utterly at home in her apartment. She even showed me how to access her spare key in the lockbox in the electrical closet, in case I arrived for a session when she wasn't yet home.

I need answers. A whole lot of answers. But will I get them? So far all I know is Ginevra has set me on a collision course on this train with the people closest to me. She has something planned for me in Positano, although I have zero clue what. She's not going to spill all now, just before what I am starting to suspect is a carefully crafted end—will she?

On the other hand, the books have been stolen. That can't be what she intended, especially since I know Caro took them and not some minion Ginevra hired for PR purposes. Ginevra will give me a new one, I assume. Or will she? If she's still planning something sinister, if she was involved in that boulder crashing toward me, then I can't take anything she says or writes at face value. Again, I remember that strange feeling that came over me after I speedily read the book. That there was something off in its pages. Was it the embezzlement or the affair—or a fact about my birth mother?

Is Ginevra my mother? It's such a crazy notion. And if she is, will she even tell me now, before the journey she's set me on concludes?

Truth is, I'm a little sick at what I'm considering. Hoping Ginevra will be home.

Hoping a little bit more that she won't be.

e

Ginevra lives on a leafy street in a rather unassuming historical, crumbly building that you wouldn't suspect of housing the world's most famous author. I punch in the code, then enter to a foyer that smells vaguely of recently freshened paint. The building has no elevator—just pink marble steps Ginevra ascends, huffing like a smoker. She's not even yet sixty, but she climbs up so laboriously that I've wondered if she worries that one day she will have to move to a more accessible place. More likely, I've thought, she'll buy the whole building and install an elevator. She's lived in the apartment since her thirties, she said. And she's not a person who I imagine easily navigates change.

I take the stairs in leaps, two steps at a time. Then, once I reach the second landing, I hesitate outside Ginevra's door with its brass lion knocker, but no other evidence—not even a nameplate—that the beloved author lives inside. Then I rap twice. I hold my breath, awaiting the heavy footsteps. The face swimming in chins. The eyes warm, but with a swampy film atop, muddying the brown. Ginevra is the type of person who looks to have lived fifty lives. Funny, I've always thought, that she needs main characters at all.

Authors often repackage their own traumas. I interviewed another author on air once, far less successful than Ginevra, and she told me, *You can't know your characters unless you truly know yourself.*

I asked Ginevra about it, in one of our later interviews when I still had a job. About whether she agreed with the other author's credo.

Ginevra replied, "I know myself all too well. I know pain in my deepest corners. That's why I have main characters, because their pain doesn't provoke me. I can remain objective. Playful. Creative. I believe that an author who exploits only her own pain—who repackages her traumas—cannot see beyond her own borders. My way of creating may be unorthodox, but no one can dispute that it works."

It was a neat explanation, but as I stand here, I wonder if all Ginevra's success does indeed prove that it works. And even more, I wonder about Ginevra's pain.

Whether, somehow, its origin is me.

e~

No answer. I've knocked multiple times, and Ginevra hasn't come. I feel quite certain she isn't home, since usually when I arrive, her throaty voice quickly signals her onset. I draw a deep breath. Am I really going to do this?

Yes. I head over to the electric closet, peer inside, then punch in the code to the lockbox. The door springs open, and I grab the key. Yes, I'm going to do this.

I quickly unlock the door. "Ginevra," I call, stepping inside. "It's Rory. Are you here?"

The steady hum of the air conditioner is my only reply. I walk slowly past the curved wooden benches and the bronze sculpture of a naked woman with her knees up to her chest, past the jade marble entry table on which a nineteenth-century silver candelabrum is perched.

"Ginevra?"

The air is thick with Ginevra's signature perfume—Sophia Loren's favorite, Jean Patou's *Joy*, melding jasmine with roses. But she's not here. I feel pretty sure of it at this point.

Am I really doing this? Am I really breaking into her place? After Caro's? It's becoming a pattern.

Past the foyer I go, toward the dining room, with its long black lacquer table dotted with blown-glass roosters. The curtains are pulled, so unlike my other visits here, no light flushes the space, offering even more certainty that Ginevra is out. The place is far more suffocating without daylight streaming in—like a 1960s museum to Sophia Loren, with even her photo contained in a round frame on a side table, a close-up of her lovely face from when she was in her thirties, like how you would display a lover or a child.

I hang a right toward Ginevra's study. I've never been inside that room, only past the heavy wooden door on my way to the powder room. The author gave me a grand tour at the onset of my employment, even showed me her bedroom, with its eighteenth-century four-poster, painted Italian headboard, and muted pastel chinoiserie. In her closet, she unveiled the frothy custom Dior gown that Sophia Loren wore in 1966 on the set of *Arabesque*, and the cream embroidered dress Sophia wore in 1955 on the balcony of a Byzantine palazzo. It was the first time in all my years of knowing Ginevra that I saw her spark with genuine enthusiasm. She smiled as she told me how she bid on Sophia's old dresses at auction, how even pieces of the furniture in the apartment had once belonged to her idol. It seemed quaint to me, if a little sad, that Ginevra lived inside a shrine to a woman she'd never met. It was a metaphor of sorts, I intuited, to her life spent spinning stories about other people—that seemingly contrary to her aged patina, to her astounding success, Ginevra must have lived so little, experienced near nil, that she needed main characters to help her craft exciting tales.

Who was Ginevra, really? I remember thinking.

I still don't know. I'm not even sure now if *she* knows.

On completion of the tour, when we were back in the living area, I asked Ginevra to see her study, where her books get written— the one door I noticed she passed by without showing me inside. But Ginevra simply smiled and said, "That's a private space, just for me. We creatives . . . we get quite superstitious about the things that work. And what works for me is keeping my office private."

Now I hover outside the door, my eyes darting around for any concealed cameras. Ginevra has never seemed like a security freak, but still, she's wealthy as all get-out. Someone of her status might collect a few stalkers or grifters, right? No cameras, though, not that I can spot.

I twist the knob, but then pause. What I'm contemplating is such an enormous invasion of privacy. What has Ginevra done, after all, other than ameliorate my career catastrophe and send me on a once-in-a-lifetime trip to boot? Try to resolve things between me and Nate with, as far as I can tell, benevolent intentions? Expose Caro's alleged crime in a gracious, private way, leaving me the discretion to handle it as I see fit? All my other conjectures are exactly that—unproven.

But then I swallow hard, feel a sudden hardening of my resolve. I am not anyone's puppet. Not Nate's, not Caro's. And certainly not Ginevra's. I signed up for three months of being her main character. But my contract is over. I'm not her main character any longer. This is my life, and I need to regain control over the script.

CHAPTER TWENTY-FIVE

Rory

Ginevra's office isn't anything special, mostly in line with the rest of her apartment. A bit more playful—a hunter-green table with myriad drawers and blond wood legs; a coral lampshade on a twisted gold base. The vibe is, as the rest of the place, decidedly 1960s, with the sole concession to modernity a massive Apple computer and keyboard.

On the table is something I recognize: a bound manuscript of *The Cabin on the Lake*! I contemplate what to do. Reading it over again will take hours, time I don't currently have. I need to get out rather quickly, in case Ginevra returns. But I can't take the book, can I?

I hesitate but then grab it, stuff it in my bag, my mind already conjuring explanations—*You weren't answering, so I wanted to check that you were okay. I went inside, heard rumbling in the office. You weren't there, but I saw the book, and ours were all stolen. So . . .*

Oh, scratch it all. If it comes down to it, I'll deny I was ever here. The Mystery of the Disappearing Bound Manuscript is the least of my problems.

I bend over the computer monitor and wiggle the mouse. A password prompt illuminates on the screen. Am I going to break into Ginevra's computer? My fingers tremble as I type in *Rory*.

Nope. I grimace, then change it to *RORY*, all caps.

Doesn't work. My fingers hover over the keyboard. Not sure if I'm relieved or disappointed.

I sift through my brain for anything else relevant to Ginevra, any dates, her birthday. Nothing. Oh! Then I remember her sister. Orsola.

I try *Orsola*, both lowercase and then all caps, but nope.

Okay. Need to move on. I begin opening drawers, rifling through items, trying to move quickly and keep everything in its allotted spot. Ginevra is a pack rat, clearly. Her house is stuffed, but not quite hoarder status—her furniture like crowded teeth that still somehow fit into a person's mouth. Her drawers, on the other hand, are packed to the brim: a jumble of pens and yellow legal pads with their margins jammed with her now-familiar scrawl, her unique swirly signature that I've seen her doodle countless times. I identify several notepads as constituting rough drafts of books published decades before. One drawer boasts only purple pens, probably thousands of them. Purple: her favorite color. Ginevra told me that once and it stuck, probably because it is one of the few things she has ever told me about herself in full transparency, in all our years knowing and interviewing each other.

I kneel as I get to the bottom row. It strikes me that nothing I find is of a personal nature. Office supplies, old drafts—but no pictures of family or friends. No mementos, accolades, awards. It's like Staples in here. Sterile.

Until I get to the last drawer, on the bottom right. I pull and am completely unprepared for what I find: a mass of newspaper clippings and yellowed newsletters, old pictures. Stupid announcements—kindergarten graduations; bar and bat mitzvahs; high school senior blurbs in the *Detroit Jewish News*.

Every last clipping and photo spotlighting Papa, Max, and me.

I sift further through the drawer, staggered by what I find. A school photo from when I was six, clinging to the chair back like I was terrified of the photographer. Max on the pontoon, reading a hefty science book, while beside him I'm rubbing Coppertone sunscreen onto my stomach. Papa at the wheel, his ankle sock tan lines visible even in muted nineties instant camera film, his smile boisterous, sucking the marrow out of life. Photos I've never seen, capturing not only people but mementos. Reams of science fair ribbons awarded to Max. A ceramics certificate that bears my name. I vaguely recognize a photo of a neighbor's basement where I took the lessons; we ate graham crackers and emerged with strange lumpy clay figures that Papa proudly displayed on our secondhand credenza.

So many questions skewer my brain. Synapses begin to fire; disparate threads connect. The original interview—how I was chosen to spearhead the feature on the renowned Ginevra Ex. It's beyond clear now: She knew me. She must have asked for me. Because why? She knows Papa. She's my mother?

If she's my mother, then why did she give me away? Why did she follow me my entire life, all the dumb milestones, but stay away? Why did she so innocuously drop my adoption into my lap, but not tell me it was she who gave me up? Why is she back now, and sending me on a trip like one of her twisty book plots?

She's made a game of my life, and I must be near the climax. Fury bubbles in my throat. What does she think—that a storybook resolution awaits a few chapters away? That I'll be grateful to her? Fall at her feet in delight?

Call her fucking *mom*?

I am still kneeling, the parquet beneath my knees nudging at my bones, as my fingertips continue to dig through the detritus of my life. The room starts spinning, the light blazing in from the piazza attacking my pupils, little black sparks fuzzing in my vision. I realize I am panting, almost gasping for breath, so I swivel around, shifting onto my butt, letting the desk prop up my back.

As I shift, my eyes catch on the sherbet-orange stuffed chair across the room, winged by a gold stool. On the stool is a silver picture frame, and I feel myself rising, lunging—grabbing it in my hands.

Staring in complete disbelief. Inside the frame is a picture of two girls, both with long dark hair. They are twins—that fact is immediately evident, as is the relative time period in which the photo was taken. The seventies or eighties, by the vintage quality of the shot, the swingy floral dress adorning the girl on the right, and the violet pussy-bow top and flared jeans sported by the one on the left. The girls aren't embracing, just standing beside each other, arms rigid at their sides. The one on the right isn't conventionally beautiful—she has an aquiline nose and slender limbs, but her eyes are almost bulging, outsizing her face. When I peer closer, bring the photo right up to my eyes, I can discern that makeup has been artfully spackled to her skin, partially concealing craters and acne. It's her smile, though—cold, thin. Strange to see a smile in someone so young so devoid of warmth, of joy.

Smiles tell stories. Deep ones.

I am reminded of how, during COVID, Caro went out with a guy she met in a Rite Aid, who was wearing a mask when they got to talking in line. She was excited for the date—he was tall, had dazzling blue eyes. A total ten. But when they got to the restaurant, and he took off his mask, Caro was stunned. She called the moment of truth the "Mask Reveal," a close cousin to the "Penis Reveal," whose results Caro always reported upon whenever she started dating someone new. The Mask Reveal was a more palatable letdown, but nonetheless disappointing for Caro that day. Rite Aid guy had a weak mouth. His front teeth were pronounced, like Chiclets. She was immediately repulsed. And the few-second impression Caro got of the guy was immediately transformed—not just by the bottom half of his face, now visible, but by his energy, his brash treatment of the waitstaff, how he only left a 10 percent tip.

The girl on the right in the photo isn't ugly so much as plain. The acne-riddled skin, the slightly bulging eyes—I recognize it all. I've spent endless hours with the woman the girl grew into. Ginevra.

The girl on the left, on the other hand, is stunning—she's slender, too, but with kind eyes and a warm smile, giving the feeling that if you cut her open, you'd find sunshine inside.

I can't see all her features, though, the girl on the left. Because her pretty face, her wide, friendly smile, is marred by a black Sharpie *X* slashed over her face.

Even more shocking, the reason breath still feels elusive: The girl on the left is familiar. I know her—or I know of her. About her. Zero doubt lingers in my mind.

The girl on the left, the beautiful one, with a giant permanent-marker *X* singed on her face, is the woman I know as Sandra Lowenstein. As the love of Papa's life. The woman who left us far too soon.

As Mom—to both Max and me.

CHAPTER TWENTY-SIX

Ginevra

Moscow, 1980s

On the drive from Sheremetyevo airport into the Moscow city center, Ginevra Efrati pressed her forehead to the window, riveted by the whiz of ugly concrete monstrosities. Finally—a glimpse of mysterious Russia.

Thus far, Ginevra had juggled dueling perspectives on the place: one from Tolstoy and Dostoyevsky, the greats, illustrating life in the days of the tsars, Ginevra's perspective formed as much from the admittedly tragic content of the pages as from the cozy library in which she read them; and the other perspective inherited from her father's frequent diatribes consuming their dinnertime about the cruel Soviet Union and its particular hardships for the Jews. Ginevra was twenty-two, but still young enough to be sucked into the romance of travel—she wasn't sure yet which perspective of this place would manifest in her reality.

Orsola sat in the middle of the back seat, sandwiched between Ginevra and their father, smoothing her stiff sky-blue dress. It was a nice dress, albeit not her stunning silky one with its full skirt smattered in lemons that Orsola couldn't find when they were packing for the trip, even though she'd torn the bedroom apart in a frenzy, searching for it. Still, Orsola looked fresh and pretty in a replacement dress that seemed to Ginevra almost a brazen attack of cheerfulness on this sad gray country, whose skies were already pelting rain against their windows. Ginevra, on the other hand, wore a gray shift dress—well, she and Orsola were, as always, distinguishable. In energy, too. Where Orsola was almost unenthused about this trip, content with her vibrant life in Rome, Ginevra brimmed with excitement: to explore the world beyond their hometown, to meet and mingle with people of this foreign place that so dominated international conversation.

Ginevra's stomach rumbled, reminding her she was ravenous. At the airport, in the great wide hall where the Efratis had waited in an endless customs line, an officer had confiscated the family's cheese and sausage on the premise of hygiene. And the big fat booming man had not even waited for them to leave before taking a hulking bite of the sausage. Thankfully, the officer had not confiscated the many other items the family had transported: tallit prayer shawls; yarmulke; Western books potentially deemed antigovernment; siddurs; postcards of scenes in Israel. In order to enter the country with such loot, Domenico had negotiated with the officer, slipped him rubles. Still, hunger was apparently beyond bribe, as the officer had nonetheless seized the edible portion of the Efratis' supposed contraband.

Ginevra's father was a professor of Jewish studies at the prestigious Sapienza University of Rome. His specialty was ostensibly Italian Jewry, the oldest in Europe, dating back to 200 BCE. But Domenico Efrati had lost his entire family in the Holocaust—of his parents, two older brothers, and three younger sisters, Domenico was the sole survivor. Impossible for his experience in childhood not to shape a man. And shape Domenico it did. He studied, rallied, absorbed history through his pores, gave rousing speeches, collected donations. In the day-to-day, with his daughters, he was weary of life, often somber. But give him a cause— Jews to save—and he was transformed. Fiery, persuasive. Sure, he could pander to the community with fervent tales of prominent Jewish Italians, but his true passion—the genuine aim of his life's work—was to help the world's persecuted Jews.

In Domenico's mind, Jews had a moral responsibility to save one another—because, by and large, no one else in the world could be relied upon to do so. The Holocaust had borne out this conclusion with certainty. And this is how Ginevra's father, who had set foot outside of Italy only so far as the concentration camps, came to spearhead the cause of

Soviet Jewry. In the seventies and eighties, Ginevra knew well the plight of the Soviet Jews, because it was a frequent topic at the Efratis' dinner table. Ginevra knew about Sharansky, various Soviet Olympic defectors; she and Orsola even proudly wore big Star of David necklaces carved with the names of famous *refuseniks* to spotlight their plight.

Now they were going to help in person. To tell these Jews who were isolated and alone, imprisoned behind the Iron Curtain, that they had not been forgotten. To clasp the hands of these persecuted Jews and assure them that the Efratis—and many others outside the USSR—supported their plight. And to provide them concrete support, too—to take down their names and addresses and try to get them out.

The entry visas, extensive paperwork—all had by now been painstakingly produced. Three weeks in Moscow. But the Efratis almost hadn't set off.

A month before they were scheduled to depart, Domenico had complained of tingling arm pain over dinner; an hour later, an ambulance rushed him to the hospital, as he'd suffered a heart attack. It was terrifying for the twins, who traded off waiting at his bedside, after he'd survived the surgery but remained in a precarious state. Now he had been cautioned by his doctors against making the trip. But in his characteristic defiant last word, Domenico had said they were going. He would give up his beloved butter and wine and steak, he would rest and take a little walk every day; but his mission wouldn't be deterred, and his daughters were certainly capable of fulfilling it in his stead.

"Moscow is organized in circles," Domenico said as the rain continued to drill down the window panes. "We're in the inside circle, now. Look, *piccoline*, Bolshoi Theatre."

Ginevra stared out at the blur of ivory pillars.

The driver said something, and Domenico translated—the only one of the Efratis who spoke Russian. "That was GUM department store. See the lines, *piccoline*."

Indeed, Ginevra did—lines stretching around the block of people with shoulders slumped forward, but otherwise dressed finely, looking not dissimilar to Romans.

"It's horrible weather to be waiting in line," Orsola said.

Ginevra silently agreed.

"Well, when there is a line, you join it," Domenico said. "That's the Soviet way. The stores are largely empty. Empty shelves. Lines. Lines. Doesn't matter what it is, if it's for sale, these people will get in line to buy it."

"Without even knowing what they're waiting for?" Ginevra asked.

"Yes," Domenico said. "Could be lipstick, perfume, toilet paper. In a communist country, supplies are extraordinarily scarce. The philosophy is: You buy what there is, and after, you'll sell it for more than you paid. There are different stores for tourists, with more things on the shelves. That's what I've heard."

"Look at that man," Orsola whispered to Ginevra, pointing to a tall blond man in flared blue jeans and the black platform shoes that were the height of cool. "He's gorgeous."

Ginevra felt herself bristle. Leave it to boy-crazy Orsola to spot a guy when they hadn't even yet stepped foot in Moscow. But then Orsola smoothed her dress and her beautiful face looked flushed and hopeful, and Ginevra felt a wash of shame. She was jealous, as usual. She wanted to say something kind, conspiratorial, like twins were supposed to be, giggling into the night, sharing about crushes and makeup. But the Efrati twins had never been that way. They'd always had separate friends, their own secrets and dreams folded up and deliberately hidden from sight, as if the other might steal or exploit them.

"There are gorgeous men in Italy. Gorgeous men is not what we're here for," Ginevra said, hating herself. She was grumpy and envious. Orsola didn't deserve it. What had she done but be born beautiful and kind and with all the ideal femininity? No doubt the Muscovite men would flock to Orsola the same as the Roman ones did. The other day, Orsola had declared Roman men too provincial, too obsessed with their mothers. Russian men were bound to be a whole new species. Russian men were basically the only reason Orsola hadn't mounted an anti-travel-to-Moscow campaign.

Domenico nodded his chin to the right. "Red Square. Can you believe it, *piccoline*? We're here. We're actually here."

Three heads craned toward the vast expanse paved in cobblestones over which loomed the red-brick clock tower with its black imposing face, and beyond it, the bloated domes of the famed Saint Basil's Cathedral looking almost like hot air balloons that got stuck atop steeples. Suddenly, an inch from their car marched a man in a severe navy uniform with a glossy black cap, his eyes narrowed as if he could see inside and had found the Efratis lacking in some respect.

"Is that KGB?" Orsola asked in a whispery voice.

"No," Domenico said. "If it's KGB, be sure he wouldn't advertise it. But we did just pass Lubyanka."

"What's Lubyanka?" Orsola asked.

Ginevra knew what it was—KGB headquarters. Where enemies of state were taken and never seen again.

"We're almost at our hotel," Domenico said, evading Orsola's question. Ginevra watched her sister return to a smile—how nice that life blessed her so, that she could have a not-pretty thought and quickly forget it.

Ginevra's not-pretty thoughts collected, decayed.

"We're here," Domenico announced. "Hotel Metropol."

The rain had let up, and everything began to sharpen, revealing the town's unexpected old-world charm. Ginevra felt a thrill run over her. Moscow! And the Metropol—the grand historic hotel in the center of town that had been there since the days of the tsars.

When Ginevra had informed her colleagues at the library that she was going to Moscow, their foreheads had creased in confusion. A few had asked if it was safe. Another had said: *Is Moscow quite as far as Sicily?*

Already a battalion of doormen were making way for the Efratis' car.

Their driver said something again in Russian, his tone harsh. As Ginevra already knew, he was in all likelihood a KGB informant.

Before they left Italy, Domenico had sat the girls down, given them a primer on life in the Soviet Union and the precautions the Efratis would need to take. In order for foreign tourists to receive visas to the Soviet Union, they had to sign up as organized tourists with an Intourist guide—who would also be an informant to the KGB. The Efratis would be monitored every step of the way. The KGB would likely bug their hotel rooms. Domenico wasn't well enough to rigorously tour, but the girls would go out, on alternate days—one to stay with Domenico, the other to explore, with the family's ultimate aim to help any Jews they could find. Free time away from the Intourist guide would be restricted, but Domenico had heard that bribes could soften this rule, incentivize the guide to turn a blind eye, especially useful if the twins wanted to mingle with Jews at the synagogue. In this aim, the Efratis had packed their suitcases with Marlboro cigarettes (in case their guide was a man), and perfume, lipstick, and pantyhose (in the event of a woman), all items that were nearly impossible to buy in the Soviet Union, unless procured on the black market, or if your father was high up in the government and you got access to special stores. Domenico had puffed on his cigar, explaining to the girls that although they could circumvent some rules, they could not underestimate the KGB. The KGB followed foreigners; the girls would be monitored within the hotel, as everyone from the door staff to butlers would be KGB informants. Sure, the Efratis would have a bit of a pass because they were Italians. The Soviets were more ruthless about tracking Americans. But if for some reason one of the girls met a Jewish man—

For Domenico, it would be unthinkable to consider anyone other than a Jewish man as a suitable husband for his daughters.

"If you met a Jewish man," he'd said, "it is quite possible he could be tailed by the KGB, and surveillance on you would increase. Jews are innately suspected as being Zionists and thus persecuted by the Soviet regime."

Now, as a doorman reached out to open their door, Domenico gripped both girls' forearms with strength that surprised Ginevra. He whispered, "Remember we're here to enjoy and to do good work, *piccoline*. But we must endeavor to invite no trouble. We are not here to make *friends*."

"Of course, *babbo*," Ginevra said.

Domenico nodded. "Do you understand what I'm saying, Orsola? *Niente scherzi*."

No funny business.

"What kind of *scherzi* would I possibly get into?" Orsola asked, doe eyelashes fluttering.

"Oh, I don't know," Domenico said. "Except that I do know." He looked at his daughter sternly, but then his look disintegrated to fondness as it always did in the face of the daughter who assumed the spot as apple of his eye. Envy swelled in Ginevra, threatened to release from the dam. With great effort, she pulled it back off the precipice.

"How about, no falling in love? Not in Moscow," Domenico said absently, searching through the papers in his coat jacket.

Silence, as Ginevra watched a brief shadow pass over her sister's face.

"Okay," Orsola said, her tone cheery. "Don't worry, *babbo*. You think of such wild, improbable scenarios."

Domenico frowned, and Ginevra thought he was about to say something stern, about how those scenarios were not wild at all, and Orsola was quite naïve, but then he half smiled, apparently convinced.

Ginevra, however, was not convinced. As the Efratis exited the car and were swept into the shabby luxury of the hotel, with its plush red pre-revolution carpet and furniture and the gold-braided uniforms of the reception staff, she thought about what her father had speculated. Its possibility clunked up against her organs.

Ginevra knew her sister, and she knew—theoretically, at least—men. She'd covered for Orsola with their father countless times, when Orsola stayed out late, galivanting on the back of some boy's *motorino*, and in that endless weekend Orsola had gone off to Genoa with that junior professor, and Ginevra told Domenico that Orsola was volunteering extra hours at the hospital.

Where Orsola went, romance and dramatics followed. As ever, Ginevra wondered what a different life it would be with Orsola's commanding beauty, to walk through the world with footsteps that made marks, and attracted besotted male attention. Like Sophia Loren.

Instead of a person whose footsteps hardly made an imprint, with plain, off-kilter features at which no one glanced twice.

It made sense that Domenico's worries focused on Orsola. Fat chance, after all, that Ginevra was at risk of causing trouble in the realm of love.

Their Intourist guide was named Olga—chipper, midforties, in scuffed cream pumps and a tan trench coat, with deep lines creasing her forehead and yet, paradoxically, lips both plump and rosy. Olga ushered Ginevra and the rest of the tour group around Moscow at a clipped pace, always telling them to hurry while flashing a winning smile, like she alone was going to sell these tourists on the Soviet Union's prowess and superiority—or be shot for failing at her mission.

At the spectacular Bolshoi Theatre, Olga led the group through the ornate auditorium, explaining proudly how it was from this theatre itself that, in 1922, the formation of the USSR was proclaimed. Beside Ginevra shuffled an American tourist named Harold from a place called Minnesota. Harold was in his midsixties, and as kindred spirits do, he and Ginevra had already identified each other as not just one of their fellow sheep tourists. She and Harold had begun to quip at each other in whispers.

"Notice she didn't say that shortly after the revolution, the government almost closed the theatre," Ginevra told Harold as they traipsed past red velvet curtains with gilded rope trims that shrouded the VIP box which, during performances, housed the top government premiers.

"Yes. They wanted to eliminate every element of the bourgeois culture. Thankfully they didn't fully succeed. Although they are still trying valiantly to rewrite history. Olga's primary job seems to be to prevent the tourists from actually seeing anything."

Ginevra smiled and nodded. She didn't fully agree, although she understood the sentiment, understood that, of course, they were being shown a particularly cultivated image of the USSR that wasn't necessarily representative of real life. Still, Ginevra was fascinated by everything: Red Square and the Kremlin a block from the Efratis' hotel, the Kremlin Armory with the largest collection of Fabergé eggs worldwide, even the queue to see Lenin embalmed in his open tomb. Sure, as they shuffled forward in line, Olga dramatically rewrote the impact of the revered revolutionary on the history of the world, to omit the millions who'd died brutally at his hands and his orders—far more murdered by Lenin than even Hitler himself. But for Olga, Grandfather Lenin and Father Stalin were on the level of Jesus—or perhaps above. An equivalent somehow to God himself.

Still, Olga's was a talent Ginevra admired—the ability to fictionalize anything. And Ginevra didn't have to love Lenin to appreciate standing in line to see him, to be awed by this society that was so different from hers, to study people in line—the man who kissed his daughter's forehead and called her *zaychonuk*; the couple who bickered, their low tones belying a conversation that appeared intense—and imagine spinning stories out of their little characteristics.

Ginevra was a student of people. She loved observing them, scribbling character traits and conversation snippets in the notebook she kept tucked in her bag. She was good at English, as was Orsola; they learned it in school. Ginevra loved that she could spy on American tourists, hear what they were saying. Orsola loved that she could converse with cute American tourists. For both girls, it would come in handy in Moscow. Neither spoke Russian; English could be a common language. Meanwhile, Ginevra was also a student of history, utterly fascinated by it. She'd read of the horrors under Lenin and Stalin, the Jewish Doctors' Plot, the millions of lives annihilated in the Soviet Union—a country whose borders stretched so far and wide it was almost incomprehensible when one viewed it on a globe.

It was late April now, the air carrying far more bite than in Rome, where artichokes and strawberries had already started to appear at the farm stands. Olga hustled the group toward the Revolution subway station. After a ten-minute walk, the group descended into an ornate station. To Ginevra it almost looked like a theatre inside—mint-green walls, dark granite, bronze statues, even chandeliers. She was impressed. Rome's public transport was nothing like this. Her father had explained before the trip that the Soviet capital they would be privy to see would be smoke and mirrors. Moscow was the showpiece of the entire nation—every Soviet citizen longed to live there, because its stores were less empty, its employment opportunities more robust. However, citizens needed a permit to even live in Moscow, unless they were born there, enrolled in school there, or fortunate to land the admiration of a Muscovite native, renowned for their marital prospects. The glorious capital was crafted as such to please the government elite who lived there, and also to display to tourists Soviet greatness. Still, little cracks slid past the veneer—for instance, the Efratis' hotel. Apparently one of the nation's finest, it sometimes lacked hot water.

All of the Soviet peculiarities aside, Ginevra's enthusiasm hadn't yet wavered. This trip was the most exciting thing to ever happen to her— spirited away from the sadness that she now realized blanketed their Rome apartment, from the shameful envy that always assailed Ginevra, coveting her sister's beauty and charms. From the inadequacy Ginevra felt every moment of her life: that she wasn't beautiful, that she never had any success with men—that although it was never spoken aloud, her father expected Orsola to marry well. And the inference that Ginevra, steadfast Ginevra, without marital prospects, would care for him as he descended into old age.

Now Ginevra was freed of it all, freed of her twin, freed even of her father, as she wove through crowds, bumping against fashionable women wearing pantyhose, men in fine suits gripping the day's *Pravda*. As the group waited on the platform for the train, Olga chattered about how lucky they were—*positively blessed*, Harold the American teased with a twinkle in his eye—to be in Moscow for the First of May festivities. Apparently, there were parades and military demonstrations, but Olga exuded anticipation and fervor, like they'd been invited to lunch with the queen or to the launch of a spaceship to the moon. Toward the afternoon, after a nice-enough lunch at a restaurant called Belgrade facing the Foreign Ministry, with blintzes and a strange drink called kvass, which tasted like sour beer, Ginevra went to the restroom. In the stall, she glanced around and toward the ceiling for a hidden camera, before rummaging in her handbag and reassuring herself that her antistate materials were still accounted for and tucked away. She was allowed to possess them herself—at least she believed she was—but it would be a crime to distribute them.

They were deemed religious artifacts—a prayer shawl; Leon Uris's *Exodus*; postcards from Israel, the Zionist state the Soviets abhorred.

Ginevra closed her handbag and it percolated through her—the danger of what she and her family were planning to do. She was a little afraid, but no part of her considered turning back. Her father's entire family had perished in concentration camps. It was horrifying to Ginevra that Jews suffered under this regime, persecuted. For the first time in her life, a smile lit in Ginevra's soul, a fire kindled by something other than her beloved books and the escapism they provided—kindled by the prospect of helping her own people. Doing what she could so Soviet Jews could live freely as they desired.

Ginevra returned to the group, wrangling her face into a picture of innocence. It didn't matter. As usual, no had even noticed she was gone.

When the tour group began to head back to the Metropol, stopping for Olga to expound upon points of interest en route, Ginevra peeled off early. She announced she wasn't feeling well, that she was heading back to the hotel. Olga nodded at Ginevra, the briefest nod, a direct consequence of the two pairs of pantyhose Ginevra had slipped her in the morning before breakfast. Ginevra walked briskly the half mile toward the Moscow Choral Synagogue on Arkhipova Street, whose location her father had described. She tried to look like she belonged, like she was any other Soviet citizen hustling home from work. But Ginevra never felt that she quite belonged—and all the more acutely here, in this gray place, with unsmiling people and amorphous KGB agents lurking in the abyss.

At first, she thought she'd gone the wrong way and prickled with worry, but then Ginevra relaxed as she glimpsed the massive neoclassical yellow-brick temple pinned down by a cascade of white pillars, a truly gorgeous building especially in contrast to all the brutalist Soviet block housing Ginevra had thus far observed. The synagogue was built pre-revolution, when Judaism was more or less tolerated by the tsars, even if in practice, antisemitism raged and pogroms targeted Jews—Cossacks with sabers plundering Jewish villages, slashing Jewish throats. Ginevra slipped up the stairs, through the wooden doors with Hebrew script and stained glass windows, and was immediately absorbed into the majestic space.

Ginevra swept past rows of blond wooden pews, up to the ornate white marble ark surrounded by towering menorahs. As she wove through the huddles and the people milling about, hearing a smattering of languages—Russian, Ukrainian—suddenly all her excitement fizzled and the only sound in the place was the thrash of her heartbeat. Why had Ginevra volunteered—pushed, in fact—to be the first of the Efrati twins to get out into Moscow? She should have let Orsola test the waters. The leader, the extrovert, Orsola was the one always making friends, attracting people.

To assuage her nervousness, Ginevra rummaged in her bag for one of the prayer books she'd brought and began to pray the Shema Yisrael, which she found she was saying in unison with the boy—man—beside her. She didn't dare look over at him, and she didn't question why. But if she had to guess, it was because she typically avoided eye contact with men. She'd

never had success in that area, and had steered quite clear of the male species altogether since middle school, when Stefano Avolio had found out she
had a crush on him and made fun of her in front of their whole class.

Ginevra was perceptive, though. She didn't look at the boy in the pew
beside her, but she took his energy into her awareness, let her gaze drag
out to her periphery and absorb snippets of his shape, voice. She pegged
him in his late twenties, a bit older than her. Well, that wasn't a boy anymore. That was a man.

When they finished, to Ginevra's surprise, the man said in English,
"You are American?"

Ginevra turned over her shoulder, to spot the American he was assuredly speaking to. But she saw no one.

"You." Now he tapped her shoulder, took her eyes into his piercing
blue ones, which did something to Ginevra she'd never experienced. She
could compare the sensation only to what she imagined it would feel like
to be stung by an electric eel—a jolt that electrified her entire being and
would surely lead to her imminent death.

When unbelievably it subsided and she again felt capable of breath,
Ginevra said, "What did you say?"

"I said, you are American, no?" He smiled then, and the electric eel
feeling returned.

"No . . . *cioè* . . . I am not. Not American, I mean. I am Italian. Italy.
From Italy." She'd forgotten how to speak a sentence in one sweep.

"I see." He smiled again. He didn't have perfect teeth—neither white
nor straight. But his smile was utterly perfect, Ginevra thought. Kind and
broad, a smile that was ready to swallow all life had to offer, a smile with
which life would assuredly cooperate, because of course life cooperated
with beautiful smiles, beautiful people. Ginevra stared upwards at this
tall specimen of a man who stood several heads over her, so her own head
hardly reached his upper chest.

"Hello," the man said. "My name is Anatoly." He stuck out a big hand
with long delicate fingers. "Anatoly Aronov."

CHAPTER TWENTY-SEVEN

Caroline

We are at the Vatican, my senses under full-scale assault. Art, people, colors, patterns, words, smiles that feel like tiny darts to my injured heart. Our tour guide has so many words, so many smiles, and I can tell she wants me to reciprocate them.

I stray back. I don't have words for her, let alone smiles.

The floors swirl in mosaics, the walls crammed with beauty. On another day I would snap photos for the Gram, but I can't be bothered. Posting things, adding filters, arranging a pleasing grid—all of it seems trite. Like the dumbest, least meaningful thing a person could do.

Different languages chatter on by. Bodies shove mine.

I slip, falter, steady myself. No one notices.

Max is ahead, chattering with our guide, with Gabriele and Chiara close at his heels. Both Rory and Nate decided not to join our tour—small blessings. I still can't believe . . . I'm still so overcome with shame that Rory knows. And anger at Nate, especially over what he said to me on the hike, when Rory and Max were wrapped up in their intense conversation. Nate and I went ahead and revealed our mutual fears about whether Ginevra Ex could have put our affair in the book. Then Nate admitted that even though he loves Rory, even though he does truly want to be with Rory, our night together meant something to him. He admitted he'd always harbored a bit of a crush on me. I made it perfectly clear to him: It meant nothing—less than nothing—to me!

So, yes, I'm quite happy Nate and Rory opted out of today. I considered it myself, but I've felt so strange, so unreal, like a ghost in my life, that I worried more about what I might do if I roamed Rome alone.

Max hasn't spoken to me. Not a word since I admitted I kissed Nate. I am a ghost in more lives than just my own.

Gabriele glances back at me, his eyes creased in concern, asking if I'm okay. I nod. I try to smile. I fail.

The fervor of this place adds to the feeling of unruliness thrumming in my veins. Like I could wander away and decide to jump off a bridge. Or push someone off.

Someone in particular.

And I'm not sure which option is more appealing.

I've been to Rome three times before, each on my own. I am a city girl, really, ironic given that I've never lived anywhere other than suburban Michigan. I contemplated it when I was younger—the usual suspects of New York, London. Even Chicago. But I got a job at Nordstrom after college, and I liked it. I liked styling, and I liked blogging and posting to Instagram. I liked the convenience of strip malls, the manicurist and Starbucks barista who knew my nail preferences (square with a hint of oval) and coffee order (quadruple-shot iced Americano with almond milk and one pump of sugar-free caramel). I enjoyed the almost fluorescent greenery of my hometown, running along the lake, and reliable traditions, like the Dream Cruise in summer, when vintage cars parade down Woodward and I gather with friends to watch and drink beers.

I suppose I've always liked being comfortable. But it's a paradox, because I've also always wanted to escape. So I used to solo travel, to Lebanon, to Bahrain, to Georgia. And if I needed to pass through Europe, I'd finagle a stopover in Rome. I prefer it to Amsterdam, to Madrid, to Paris.

My preference starts with the Italians themselves, especially the southern ones. Romans, versus the more uptight Milanese. Southern Italians are messy, but rooted in the ancient. Their streets aren't sparkling clean; any spare surface is riddled with graffiti. And yet around every corner is a hulking two-thousand-year-old pillar. The people are loud and boisterous. I am not loud and boisterous, so it's funny that I gravitate to them, but I do. I admire their verve, perhaps I envy it. I like that Rome is gritty and its history unparalleled, along with the most fantastic art, architecture, fashion. Sure, Paris has Chanel flats and classic tweed jackets, but Italy has excess. Gucci and family dynasties. Mafia. Intrigue.

Paris is pretentious, Amsterdam, seedy. Rome is a bit barbaric, it is true—you can almost see the blood spilled across the Forum, imagine the emperors stomping around Palatine Hill. The city doesn't pretend to be refined.

And in the Colosseum, on our schedule for the afternoon, you can almost hear the roar of the crowds. The stampedes. The frenzy.

I would do practically anything to see the ruins of a Roman temple. To me it goes along with loving beautiful, unusual things. I covet a panther ring as much as obscure Roman ruins. It's more than beauty and rarity, though. If I had to pin it down, it's the chase. God, how I fucking love the chase. For me, satisfaction lies more in the process of achieving something than the having of it.

But today, as I trudge through the Raphael Rooms, I can't muster any excitement for the chase.

"Caroline, you are okay?" Gabriele lingers back to fetch me.

"Fine." Strange for me, who leaps to make others comfortable, that I can't produce a more emotive reassurance.

"We are almost at the Sistine Chapel." He says it with a smile, well-intentioned, surely. Like I can possibly enjoy it. Like my eyes can take in beauty, like I deserve to stand in the vicinity of Michelangelo's genius.

I stop—bodies weave around me, assaulting me with their awful perfume and BO.

Unexpectedly, I hear myself say, "Did you know Michelangelo was so miserable painting the Sistine Chapel that he wrote a poem about his misery?"

Gabriele starts. I can tell his jovial face doesn't know how to assimilate my darkness.

"Sorry." I spot a bench, sink down. "I need a little rest. I'll wait out here."

"You sure?" Clearly he wants to pitch me on the fresco of God's finger reaching toward Adam. How it's just a few more steps. I'm almost there.

Almost there is the crux of it. I've had it so often in life—almosts. Nearlys. Just around the corners . . .

None of it matters. None of it counts. What counts is what is here and now.

I'm tired down to my bones. My cells have no zing, no charge.

I give up. Raise the white flag. Hands in the air. Surrender.

"I'm sure."

Gabriele nods, then gives me a sympathetic smile and returns to the group, slipping his arm around his daughter's waist. I watch their backs all file into the chapel.

Max doesn't turn around. Not even once.

e

I'm still in a daze after my rest outside, and I follow the group to lunch. Honking, people crossing the street as traffic flows, drivers swerving an inch from bodies. Swearing, from both sides. Whoever has the right of way is decidedly unclear. Suddenly I'm jostled by the crowd. I fling forward, nearly swan dive into cement.

I manage to right myself and forge on, my vision glazed, not paying attention to lights or signals.

"Caroline!" A screech, then I feel Gabriele's grip on my arm. "Caroline, didn't you see that car?"

"Oh." I peel my sweaty hair off my forehead.

"It almost hit you."

"Oh. Well! If it's your time, it's your time." I realize I sound manic.

Gabriele looks at me peculiarly, doesn't respond.

We lunch at a spot that's supposedly the best. At this point I expect nothing less of the illustrious Ginevra Ex. Our waiter, Giuseppe, hands us laminated menus in a three-ring binder and a burgundy leather cover— so many pages it's like reading a book, pictures and words swimming in my vision. I close the menu, ask Gabriele to order for me. He does. Platters of pizza appear, pastas. Rigatoni alla gricia. Then a dish with pork—Gabriele doesn't know I keep kosher. I tear bread, swirl it in olive oil, swallow bites of pasta from my fork, not tasting, just eating to avoid Max's gaze. To avoid the guide's harmless questions. When I don't answer, blatantly ignore her, she resorts to flattery. Your ring! *Che stupendo.*

I fumble with words, saying something but nothing, then excuse myself to the restroom before the guide can elaborate, pin me down for more. It's obvious she wants a good rating at the end of this day—that she views me as the one potential holdout. Ginevra probably gives her good business, refers her, has paid her bazillions. I wish I could say: *Leave me alone, and I'll sing your praises until the end.*

When I emerge from the stall, Gabriele's daughter is at the communal restroom sink, looking in the mirror, smoothing her frizzy red hair. I smile at her, rummaging for her name.

"Chiara!" I exclaim as I remember it all of the sudden, ashamed that I've been touring with her all day and have been so lost inside my own problems that I haven't made an effort at conversation. Kids intimidate me, though—so much personality. So much conviction! And they can see right through anything false. "Are you having fun today?" I ask.

Chiara frowns. "I live in Rome. It's not like I haven't seen the *Vatican* before."

"Fair enough. Well, we'll be on the train again soon enough." I apply pale pink lip gloss, then press my lips together. I spot Chiara looking over longingly. "Do you want to try some?"

"Papa wouldn't like it."

"Ah. Too young for makeup." My parents never cared—I was lucky if my dad grunted my name, let alone gave a thought to my welfare, and whether makeup would contribute to it.

"Not too young! He lets me have makeup, within reason. He wouldn't want me to share your germs. He's a neat freak." She sighs.

"Oh, I see," I say, nearly laughing. "Well, I think I have a fresh one in here." I rummage in my bag, indeed find a spare for when mine runs out. "Here, you can have this."

"Really?" She snatches it, cradles it to her chest. "Oh, wow. Oh, thank you!" She applies the gloss and appraises herself in the mirror, tilting her head one way and another.

"You look beautiful. The pink really complements your outfit." She's wearing a pink denim dress.

"*Che figo!*" Chiara gives me a great, wide, genuine smile. "That means cool."

"*Che figo!*" I say, and follow her back to our table.

Then, my mood lifted, I can almost enjoy our dessert that Giuseppe delivers: something called tozzetti that look like biscotti. We make declarations about best meals and returning soon. Gabriele pays the bill on behalf of the author. We leave, walk the cobblestoned streets toward Trevi Fountain. Back in the thick heat, with everything swirling in my head, my mood plummets again. Every time I've been to Rome, I've thrown a coin into the fountain's turquoise depths and imagined for a moment that my life was as cinematic and charmed as Audrey Hepburn's in *Roman Holiday*. Believed, drunk the Kool-Aid, that maybe wishes do come true.

But I've never been to Rome in July on what is resolutely the worst day of my life. The city boils with tourists; and not a lingering cell within me, a solitary atom, can get behind wishes coming true. I squeeze my fists tightly at my side. Is everything in my head? I almost don't trust myself to maintain perspective anymore. Suddenly I wish fervently that I could poof—disappear. I want off this ride . . . off the fucking train . . . off this life. . . .

Gabriele and Chiara have parted from us, back to check on their apartment, I think is what Gabriele said. See their dog, water plants, wielding *ciaos* that felt like slaps.

Max throws a coin into the fountain over his shoulder. He closes his eyes briefly, and I allow myself to stare at his long dark lashes that kiss his skin. I blink away a tear. It's all changed. . . . It's all spiraling out of control. . . .

When Max opens his eyes, he looks right at me, jaw square. "You gonna make a wish?"

"He speaks," I say with a half smile.

He doesn't smile back.

"We're on a short schedule. We need to get to the Colosseum. And Rory texted a second ago. She's gonna meet us there."

Great. I know I should be happy about Rory joining, seize the opportunity for more apologies, but the truth is, I need a little space. From Rory and also from the intensifying guilt I feel in her presence. I wish I could zap myself away—away from this fountain, and away from that godawful train, where the walls are closing in on me.

"So don't you want to make a wish before we go?" Max is practically shouting, but still his voice is faint over the gushing waters.

"I guess." I open my wallet, rummage for a coin. Max is watching me. Our guide is watching me, too.

A wish comes. I send it helplessly to God along with the coin, flicking my wrist toward the water. It travels far, almost to the ivory statues presiding over the fountain. I find I am a little bit pleased with myself.

"What did you wish for?" Max asks as we turn to leave, weaving through a group of American tourists, easily identifiable from the blinding white of their sneakers and their T-shirts plastered with the words *Italy* and *Rome*.

"Anything good?" Max's voice isn't kind but also isn't angry—just neutral, bland, like vegetable broth. Even though I know there is nothing vegetable broth about his feelings now, but for now, out in the open, he keeps them tucked away.

I think about telling him my wish, really putting everything on the table, initiating the frank conversation we need to finally have. But then I chicken out.

Instead I say quietly, "I wished for something that probably not even God has the capacity to fix."

CHAPTER TWENTY-EIGHT

Rory

The Colosseum is its typical crowded self, but as I overhear a tour guide cheerfully declare, not yet at prepandemic levels. Max isn't answering my call, and I'm not about to try Caro. Max said they were in the upper level, but then he stopped responding. For a moment, I hesitate—wonder why I'm even here, why I'm voluntarily opting to put myself in Caro's path. But, no, I want to see Max and tell him what I discovered. Even though—and I'm still processing this—it might impact him, too.

Sandra Lowenstein was in that picture.

She must be Orsola, Ginevra's twin sister. The one who lives in Positano, where tomorrow Ginevra has orchestrated a strange lunch date for all of us. The beautiful and good sister, from Papa's fairy tale. Though—why does Ginevra hate her sister so much as to keep a photo with an *X* over her face in her office?

What does it all mean?

I need my brother—my lifeline on this strange, twisted trip.

Thankfully Ginevra's advance ticket and private tour got me hop-the-line access, and both Max and Caro are still on my Find My Friends. I follow Max's dot, not pausing to linger at the massive arena that extends underground, where all the gladiators, slaves, and animals would congregate before a fight. I did that tour on my first week in Rome—when everything in my life still felt relatively shiny, optimistic.

I was heartbroken about Nate, scared about finding a new job after the main character gig ended. But still everything made relative sense. Now nothing does.

I hustle past little group clusters, my thoughts mingling with the myriad guides bringing the stadium to life in a smorgasbord of languages.

Ginevra Ex. X over her sister's face.

So callous. So . . . bizarre.

The beautiful sister is the good one. The ugly sister is evil!

"The stadium could house fifty thousand people at one time. . . ."

Is Orsola my mother? Is she Max's mother, too?

How did Papa even know the sisters?

"The largest and most complex amphitheater of the ancient world. . . ."

Ginevra knew everything about me and Max. She watched us grow up from afar. . . .

How did she get all those mementos from our whole life?

Why did she gather us all on this train? For evil reasons? Or benevolent ones?

"Built under Emperor Vespasian in 72 AD. . . ."

Caro and Nate . . .

My breath is hard going as I mount the stairs, pushing past the slow couple ahead. I veer right to follow Max's dot, still blinking in the same place. There are far fewer people in the upper arena, mostly VIP tours, but I hasten ahead until suddenly I am jostled sideways, into a stone wall.

"*Scusi, scusi!*" It's that Russian couple from the train, the woman with her head buried in a guidebook. I rub my smarting shoulder as they file blithely past. God, can a girl get a few hours without any of these train people?

Now I pass exhibition displays, Nordic tourists navigating with audio sets. My pace slows. What was I rushing for? Why am I even meeting them now? I've visited the Colosseum multiple times since coming to Italy. I don't need—or want—to face Caro now. Strange how three months apart—by far the longest separation since we met as kids—has mangled our friendship. Did she become a different person in that time? Or did I? All I know is we feel more and more like strangers. . . .

It's for Max that I'm here. It wasn't any easier—any less of a betrayal—for Max to find out about Caro and Nate. And I guess I came to the Colosseum for my own sake, too. Because I need to confide in my brother, talk through the things in my head.

I dial Max again, but the call goes to voice mail. I swivel, my vision a whizz of concrete, travertine, and marble. Where are they?

My attention is diverted by an elderly man stooped over a cane, talking about the events that led to the building of the Colosseum.

"Nero's palace," he says, "was located exactly here. When Vespasian came to power, his decision to build the Colosseum here could be seen as a gesture to return an area of the city Nero had acquisitioned for his own use to the people."

"Nero was discredited at the end of his life, wasn't he?" asks a gentleman in his midfifties, the type you see always beside the guide, asking questions as much for the answers as to hear himself sound intelligent.

"Yes. Very much so. He murdered his stepbrother, his first wife, her sister—then he killed his new wife, too. He removed anyone he perceived to be in opposition to him. The people held him responsible for the great fire in 64 AD, and tides began to turn. Eventually the senate declared him an enemy and ordered his execution. Nero tried to bribe the officers of the Praetorian Guards to help him, but—"

"He ended up committing suicide, didn't he?" the eager tourist asks.

The guide nods. "Yes. But Nero didn't want to. His instinct to live was strong. One of the Praetorian Guards asked Nero, *Is it so terrible a thing to die?*"

"*Is it so terrible a thing to die?*" the tourist echoes. "Well—"

I don't stay for his contemplation. Chills spring down my arms.

I push through the group, and finally free of the crowd, I spot Max and Caro. Just the two of them—no guide in sight. No wonder I couldn't find them. They're in a corner marked off for renovation, surrounded in tape and blockades. Caro is up on the ledge, and Max is a few feet behind her.

They clearly shouldn't be there. How did they even get up there?

I scan the area for an access point, realizing they had to surmount the barrier. I start to go that way, a strange fear circling my stomach. Caro is standing beneath an arch, up against a pillar, close to the edge. So close that if she steps farther out . . .

"Guys!" I shout, but I'm still too far, and my voice bounces off the stadium walls, doesn't travel. "Max! Caro!"

They're both facing out, toward the street, their backs to me, so I can't see what they are saying, but something about their setup is odd.

Something about the scene, their being in this area that's walled off, their stilted body language, strikes me as . . . terrifying. Suddenly Caro glances over her shoulder, back at Max, and I start at the twisted look her features assume, the pain leaching from her eyes.

Max reaches a hand out toward Caro, but she doesn't step back. In fact, she almost seems to pitch forward.

I start to run.

"Caro!" I scream.

CHAPTER TWENTY-NINE

Max

Caro doesn't speak—just shakes, full body shakes, until we get her back on the train.

Her room is tiny, not a suite like mine or Rory's, not spacious enough to fit a banquette, table, and a bed simultaneously. So two attendants arrive to effectuate the transformation typically done at dinnertime: turning the banquette into the bed. I stay with Caro, and Rory fetches the doctor on board. Once the bed is unveiled, Caro wraps herself in the huge navy bathrobe embossed in the Orient Express's compass rose jacquard weave. She drags the hood up over her head, giving her the appearance of a member of one of those elite university secret societies. Skull and Bones. Then she eases herself onto the bed, curls into a ball, and faces the window.

The doctor arrives, and Rory and I squish together like sardines to accommodate him. The doctor asks Caro to remove the hood, then he slips his stethoscope in beneath the robe. Finally, he declares that she's fine, *fisicamente*.

"Physically," Gabriele translates from the hall, as there's zero added room to squeeze in with us. He's just arrived, having been summoned by Rory, I presume. Or else the author has a hidden camera on us. I wouldn't be shocked at this point, given what Rory told me briefly in the cab. About the drawer full of stuff from our childhood. It's bizarre.

More than that. Creepy.

"It was a panic attack, no doubt. But she should be checked out further." The doctor indicates his head. "*Terapista*."

"No!" It's Caro's first word since Rory and I helped her down from the arch, from the dizzying heights above the piazza. "No therapist. No. I'm fine. I wasn't trying to . . . do something to myself! I just needed space. I couldn't breathe in the crowds, the heat. It was a panic attack, like he said. Please don't overreact. You can all leave me alone. I just need a bit of rest now."

"But, C." Rory sits on the bed. God, Rory's a champ. Still so caring, putting aside her anger—her very legitimate anger. "You were so close to the edge. You almost—"

"I'm fine. Honestly. I'm tired, and I was just hot—I needed space. There were so many people, and I felt . . . I— Now I need all of you to leave. Please . . . let me close my eyes."

I look at Rory, jerk my head. Caro's *not* fine, no matter what she says. She almost—

She almost jumped, is what I want to say. But it was obvious enough.

"C, why don't you come rest in my room?" Rory says. "It's bigger, you'll be more comfortable—"

"And then you can monitor me?" Caro asks. "I'm fine. Really." She laughs—not a high-pitched, awkwardly timed Caro laugh, but a lower one, bitter. "I'm not about to pull down the curtains and off myself, if that's what you're thinking."

I frown. "God forbid."

"C, we're just worried about you," Rory says.

"Are you?" Caro asks, sounding genuinely unsure. "Are you, or would all of you be better off if I wasn't here?"

"Caro!" I say. "That's ludicrous. You're being crazy. Really. I understand that you're"—I rummage for the right word—"upset at yourself for . . . sleeping with Nate, but you're going way overboard. The important thing is you were honest."

"Really? Are you all happy I was honest? Is honesty *truly* the best policy?" She sounds so strange—so undone. "Truly. I want to know."

"Look, C, I can't lie and say I'm not upset about what I found out," Rory says. "And . . . you know."

Silence. Caro knows *what?*

"But so much is going on right now with me that has nothing to do with you," Rory says. "I . . . please . . ."

"Do you forgive me?" Caro asks, almost desperately, her voice muffled by the pillow, into which she has stuffed her face.

Rory looks at me helplessly. I shrug. I have no clue what's right here. Honesty and lies seem almost the same thing—and entirely beside the point.

"We forgive you," I finally say. "Of course we do. You're family, C."

Caro doesn't answer, just makes a grunting noise.

"Look, we'll leave you, but I'll be back to check in on you in a few," Rory says. "Max is next door, and I'm around the corner. Call me! Or—" Her eyes search around in desperation, landing on the guard's whistle on the table. "If anything—if you—"

"If I have a single dark thought, I'll holler." I can't see Caro's face, but I know she's smiling. I can picture it exactly—her beautiful smile—and the image strikes my system with blunt force, like a blast of cold air on sensitive teeth.

"Okay," Rory says doubtfully. And then we do leave.

"What happened out there?" Rory asks once we're in my room. "At the Colosseum, I mean?"

I pour vodka into an art-deco-inspired Murano glass with hand-painted amber and navy geometric motifs. I plunk a few ice cubes in from the bucket.

"Join me?"

Rory shakes her head. Then says, "Oh, what the hell."

"A double," I say, making hers and then handing it over. "Just what the doctor ordered." I clink her glass. "*Nazdarovya.*"

"*Nazdarovya.*"

We sip, and trade aahs back and forth. I crack my neck. What a day. What a fucking day. What a trip.

"What happened?" Rory asks again.

I settle on the bed, stretch my arms behind my back. There's another satisfying crack, and then it's gone—the relief fleeting.

"I honestly don't know, Ror. We had a guide—"

"Where was Nate? And Gabriele and Chiara? Weren't they all supposed to be on the tour, too?"

I shrug. "Gabriele and his daughter were there for the earlier part. But Gabriele had stuff to take care of. Said they'd meet us back on the train. And Nate didn't join in the first place. Not sure where he went. Haven't much cared. You know?"

She exhales deeply. "Okay, so where was the guide when I found you guys? And how did you get to that part that was all shut off?"

"We went up with the guide, you know, to the top, and she was talking about—oh, yeah—she was telling us about all the holes in the stadium—"

"Holes?"

"Yeah. You see them everywhere. Apparently, they used iron to shore up the structure, the emperor back then, I mean—"

"Vespasian."

I smile. Rory is so smart. Maybe I get more credit for that, between the two of us, given Hippoheal, but my sister is brilliant in ways that I'm not. She retains information; she can ask the smartest questions, remember the smallest facts. Speed read. The station never should have fired her for such a stupid mistake. What blazing idiots.

"Anyway, there was a shortage of iron in later years, and so the Roman people pillaged the iron from the gaps."

"Got it. So . . ."

"Right. So I don't know, at some point, I realized Caro had disappeared. Completely wandered off. And I told the guide to stay where she was, and I went off looking for her, and then, I don't know, the way that you spotted us, probably, I saw her, and it looked—it looked—"

"Like she was gonna jump," Rory says quietly.

"I don't know. I really don't. Maybe it was just a panic attack like she said." My stomach swishes, and a panicky feeling returns.

"You worried, though—that it could be—that she could be thinking about . . . hurting herself." She shivers. "That was your instinct?"

"Yeah. I guess. I started running toward her, but I didn't know what exactly to do. I was wishing I'd read more—we had a training at work—it's why we keep the windows sealed. I remembered they'd said intervention is always the best choice, even if you're worried about making it worse. So I got up close to her, and she told me to go away. That we'd all be better off if she was gone, and she didn't want to stay around to ruin our lives anymore."

"That's what she said?" Rory rubs her eyes. "Jesus."

I nod. "And I was trying to reason with her. God, Ror, we were so high up. She could have——"

"She didn't." Rory sounds like she needs to convince herself as much as me.

"She didn't. But, Ror, I'm scared she's not okay. I'm really scared."

Rory heaves a deep breath. "Me, too. I've never seen her like this. It's so crazy. Caro's always been——"

"Full of life."

"More than that. Steady. Stable. Like Papa in a way."

I realize it for the first time, the similarity between them. Neither is stable in the financial way, but Rory is right. There is something earthy to them, rooted. Dependable.

I shrug. "No one is immune from mental health issues."

Rory nods. "Tomorrow we'll be in Positano. We need to get her real help. And last night was probably the worst possible trigger. Having to tell us about Dubai. I mean, it was . . . I can't believe she did it, but it proves what a dark place she was in. Although I still don't really understand why. I need to get to the bottom of it. As much as I—as angry as I still am—Caro loves us. I know she does."

I nod, bite my lip. "We're her family."

"The only one she has. Maybe I wasn't . . . maybe I should have been——"

"You can't beat yourself up, Ror. Caro is okay. And you had reason to be furious."

"Still, family is supposed to be there unconditionally."

"Loyalty is everything," we both say in unison.

"But I don't think Papa was contemplating someone in the family sleeping with another's ex." I laugh dryly.

"He's not *just* my ex," Rory says, the pain branded on her face.

"I know. Of course, Nate's more than an ex. And he really regrets ending things. I believe him about that, at least." I find myself scowling. "Even if I've also learned that he's a total ass."

I wonder briefly if Rory will still contemplate taking Nate back after this trip. I would have said no, that certain things would be unforgivable, but this trip is challenging that, making me wonder if boundaries have gotten stretched—if we all haven't contemplated things we wouldn't have conceived.

"And there's—" Rory stops. An odd look comes over her, then fades.

"What?"

"I don't know. It's *a lot.* Max, why do you think Ginevra had all that stuff about us?"

"Because she's planning something sinister?" I chuckle. "Tonight, when we're asleep, she's gonna pop out of the darkness like Chucky, with a knife?"

Rory frowns. "Seriously."

"I'm being serious." I shake my head. "This trip is bonkers. Getting more bonkers by the minute. So I honestly have no clue why your author I've never met has science fair awards from when I was eleven in her drawer."

"The beautiful one and the ugly one. The sisters." Rory drums her fingers on the table. "That has something to do with it. I just don't get it yet. I don't get how it all fits."

I shake my head. Rory's pushed this theory of hers already, but I hardly understand it or remember Papa's childhood fairy tales.

"I need to go stare at a wall," Rory says. "And meditate."

"Go ahead. Sounds like a good idea to me. You're really dedicated to this new habit."

Rory blushes. "I'm trying. It's like . . ."

"I know. Zen. Staring at trees in the wind."

She pokes my side. "Don't you think I'm less intense than usual?"

I laugh. "You're still pretty intense!"

"Ha." She laughs. "Fair. Listen, will you—"

"Yes, of course." I drain the last of my vodka. "I'll go check on Caro."

"Thanks. She needs us right now. It's just . . . I have so much in my head . . . and I wanna call Papa, too."

"I got it. Send Papa my love. Caro'll be okay. Don't worry. It's been a full-on trip, for all of us. I don't really think she'd . . ."

"No, I don't think so, either." We sit in quiet for a few moments. Then Rory reaches over a hand to squeeze mine. "What a vacation, huh?"

"What a vacation. Do you feel like for all the dollar signs, it should be more . . ."

"Spacious?" Rory offers.

I smile. "Bingo. I'm getting sick of running into that old, crotchety man every time I open my door."

Rory laughs. "What, you don't want more ashes in your face?"

I laugh, too, and shudder. "Please, no. And the Californians. So chipper, with all their therapy . . ." Rory and I exchange a mischievous glance.

In unison, we both declare, "Ira!" and spear imaginary hiking poles in the air.

"That won't get old," Rory says.

"Not ever."

Rory squeezes my hand. "What would I do without you? I'm beyond glad you're here, Maxie."

"All for one and one for all. And extra, because I gotta have your back for Papa, too."

"Love you, BB." Rory comes in for a hug.

"Love you, LS." I tug her closer. Men aren't supposedly big on hugging, but I always have been. I've sunk into Papa's hugs, Rory's. Caro's. I haven't always felt the most lovable. Strange, for sure. But I have so much love in me, so much that is bursting to get out. And anyway, no one would ever describe me as your usual suburban Michigander, with the respectable job, who got married at twenty-six, starter home at twenty-eight, popped out two point two kids by now. But I've come into myself, blazed my own path.

Rory stays inside my hug—for the first time I wonder if she likes it, too, or if our long hugs are because she knows I need them. My sister's hair is a soft familiar fluff, poofy from the humidity, wafting the spicy scent of the Orient Express that seems infused in the air, as well as in the shampoo and soaps that are lined up so perfectly uniform in our suites. I always forget how small my sister is. Deceptively so, because she's stronger than me. Maybe she was once braver than me, too, but I'm brave now, as well. Daring. Serving the Aronov name well. I hope—I know—that's what Papa would say, if he were still capable of expressing himself fully like that.

My heart throbs as my sister detaches from my grip, and I watch her slight frame slip out my door.

CHAPTER THIRTY

Ginevra

Moscow, 1980s

"He-hello," Ginevra stammered, face-to-face with the most breathtaking human she'd ever encountered. Speaking to her now, his name and other foggy words that he expected her to reciprocate.

"Ginevra. That's my name, I mean. Nice to meet you, Anatoly. It's a pleasure."

She felt proud of herself for managing to eke out that sentence.

"The pleasure is mine." Anatoly took Ginevra's hand in his and shook it solemnly. "Would you like to——?" He gestured up, toward the balcony with trees of life painted on the walls.

"Oh? Yes." Ginevra followed after the man as if swept by an unseen force. She passed through the aisle, up the stairs near the front door, her heart thwacking her chest. Finally, she had the bandwidth to take in her companion, not worry that she would be observed assessing him. He was dressed similarly to the boys in Rome—flared blue jeans and platforms. He had thick black hair brushed across his forehead, which she caught a look at when he turned and flashed a smile.

"Just checking you're still there."

"Still here," she said, shocked at the fact of it herself.

He was hands down the most handsome and magnetic man she'd ever seen.

She tried to root herself back to earth as they mounted the stairs. *He*

*knows you are a tourist. He probably wants something from you—help to get out
of the Soviet Union, or he suspects you have goodies in your handbag.*

Upstairs, Anatoly led Ginevra over to two wooden chairs in a vacant
corner. Immediately he sat and leaned forward, propping his elbows on
his knees in the manner of a man who was comfortable in his surroundings because he was innately comfortable in himself.

"I don't bite." He smiled, gestured toward a chair.

She smiled, too. "I know."

"You don't know." He shook his head, serious now. "You never know.
You shouldn't trust anyone in this country. Anyone can be KGB, or a KGB
informant, ready to report on you." He snapped his fingers. "Quick you
are in Lubyanka. Never heard from again."

"Oh!" Ginevra hovered over her chair in a squat, stopped herself from
a seat.

He must have realized he'd frightened her because he said, "Not me. I
am neither a KGB agent nor an informant."

"How do I know you are being honest?"

He laughed, a beautiful guffaw that warmed her insides in the cool
synagogue. "Well, first, I am Anatoly Aronov. All my blood is Jewish
blood. They don't let Jews in the KGB."

"Wouldn't that be something KGB would say?" Even as she said it,
she'd relaxed, though, was teasing him. She was shocked at her ease, her
surprising lack of awkwardness.

"Fair enough." Anatoly leaned back, crossed his arms over his chest.
"Truth is, I could be a *stukach*. An informant. The KGB is masterful at
recruiting them. Even Jews can be informants."

"Jews against Jews?" Ginevra asked, mouth agape. That was unthinkable. You had to help one another, especially your own brothers.

Anatoly shrugged. "When they threaten you and your family, there is
often no other choice. But it breaks down trust in our society. It's why
the greatest Soviet pastime is to say *shhhh* anytime anyone starts to criti-
cize the government or talk about religion. Because your neighbor, your
uncle, even your brother, could be a traitor. So I'll leave it to you, then,
to determine if you can trust me. We can listen to anyone, hear anything,
but in the end, we only have our wits. The wisdom within to tell us if
someone speaks the truth. Or if they lie."

Ginevra smiled uneasily. The wisdom within—what did that even mean? Ginevra had fearful thoughts, mean thoughts. Deep swells of love, too, especially for her sister and father. And for multitudes of strangers, like the dreary shopkeeper who always looked like the day was too heavy to handle or a little girl turning in circles in a piazza. But wisdom—Ginevra wasn't sure.

"I am not a *stukach*," Anatoly finally said. "I shouldn't have teased you. You weren't born in this hell. You don't understand the humor we prisoners have about our jailers."

"Is it that terrible?" Ginevra asked.

The smile disappeared from his face. "It is. It truly is."

"How?"

"You really would like to know?"

"I really would."

And so he told her—about his father's tragic death when Anatoly was seven, about the kids who beat him as a child for being Jewish, how he never had enough food to eat or clothes to keep him warm.

He started to tell her about his military years, and then he stopped. "Oh, it's not an unusual life. I am singing you a sad song. But I am not a victim."

But Ginevra was already hooked—on this man, on his sorrowful life, a life that made her feel sad, yet impossibly charmed.

Then Anatoly told Ginevra about his mother's sudden death a few months before.

"She had a stroke. A bad one. She was gone before I even got back to Zhitomir to say goodbye. She died alone. I am an only child, and I should have been there. She died alone," he said again. "I haven't said that to anyone. I don't know why I am telling you."

Ginevra put her hand over his and didn't even realize she'd done so until her eyes took it in. She waited for him to extract it, but he didn't. And she didn't dare move it. It was the happiest home her hand had ever had.

"And what about you?" he finally said, looking up with a smile Ginevra could tell he didn't feel. "Any sad stories to match mine?"

"Not to match yours," Ginevra said quietly. But she told him then, a little, about how her mother had died in childbirth, and her father and her sister blamed Ginevra—even if they didn't speak it aloud.

"I think it is the things that are not spoken aloud that are the loudest," Anatoly said, and Ginevra nodded.

Ginevra began to tell him the truth, about Orsola—how she was so beautiful and desired—but then Ginevra didn't want to sully the conversation by introducing him to a sister who would sound infinitely more appealing than her. Ginevra told him, instead, how she loved writing and dreamed of becoming an author. How she read voraciously, and Anatoly shared that he did, too, even though Western books were all but impossible to procure. His eyes lit up as he shared that a few years back there had been a bicentennial exhibition for American Independence in Sokolniki Park, and after waiting for four hours in the downpour, he'd gotten his hands on a copy of the Declaration of Independence. He'd stayed up late into the night, translating, absorbing. It had struck him like an object crashing from the sky, the enormity of the revelation. *All men are created equal and given inalienable rights to life, liberty, and the pursuit of happiness.*

"Can you imagine it, Ginevra? All men are created equal. Do you have the same principles in Italy?"

"Yes, I suppose we do." She thought about it, amazed that something she'd taken for granted—freedom—was the thing Anatoly most coveted. But she almost told him that she didn't know if she agreed that the freedom the Declaration of Independence contemplated was really true.

Because Ginevra had a twin sister and their prospects in the world were not equal. It wasn't fair to say they had been created as such.

Anatoly straightened up. "I shouldn't have said that before."

"Said what?" So much was percolating through Ginevra's mind, more to process in an hour with Anatoly than in years of regular, routine life in Rome.

"When I asked if you had sad stories to match mine. No one has a monopoly on pain. Least of all me."

"I didn't take it that way. Your English is very good, by the way."

He smiled. "I learned it in elementary school, and now I take lessons, because I dream to move to America. What about you—does America appeal to you, too?"

"Appeal, sure," Ginevra said slowly, speaking honestly, but realizing she hadn't much considered it. "What do you mean, as in to live there?"

"Yes." His eyes were focused on her, like he cared about the answer to the question, like maybe he was even puzzling out some future the two of them could have.

Oh, she was being absurd.

"I suppose I could imagine living in America as much as I could imagine living anywhere," Ginevra finally said. "Rome is"—she tried to put a finger on it—"home, I guess, but not because I chose it. It's a wonderful place, of course, but it would be a different thing to choose your home. Maybe I wouldn't take it for granted so much. Appreciate it more. Contrast always makes you see things differently."

Anatoly nodded, a faint smile on his lips, and Ginevra felt her heart soar, because she could tell he approved of her answer. "Contrast does that indeed." He lowered his voice. "When I am out of this place, I shall never take freedom for granted."

Ginevra thought about that, and her realization she didn't feel so wedded to Rome. That, despite her father and Orsola there, perhaps she wouldn't even choose it as her home. America, though? Could she really fathom it? Her future felt foggy—that was the truth. It had always been so: a great fog she couldn't see past, to discern what would be.

Suddenly a midforties man ascended the steps to the balcony, and the hairs on Ginevra's neck prickled. The man walked over to the rail.

"Is he KGB?" she whispered.

"No."

"How do you know?"

"KGB doesn't come inside, but they are across the street, always monitoring."

"He could be a *stukach*, then. An informant." She was proud she'd remembered the word. She watched the man, her heart twitching.

"Could be," Anatoly admitted. "It is dangerous to break off from your group, you know. You are a brave woman."

"I pretended I was sick. I gave my Intourist guide two pairs of pantyhose."

"Ah." He smiled. "So why did you come?"

"To Moscow?" she asked uncertainly.

"I can guess why you came to Moscow," he said. "Adventure. Seeing Soviet marvels. I meant why you came to the synagogue."

"My father is a professor of Jewish history. We wanted to come to tell you and other Jews that you are not alone. That we will help you however we can. And I have things in my bag. Things I'd like to give you."

"Oh." Anatoly blushed, looked touched.

"But . . ." Something else burned in her throat. She couldn't quite believe her daring as she said it. "But I think I really came to the synagogue to meet you."

The week progressed with a joy Ginevra had never known, either before or since. One day she would tour with Olga and the group, and the next day Orsola would go out. Even the days Ginevra stayed with her father in the hotel, Domenico noticed something was different about her, telling her fondly, "This gray place is doing you well, *piccolina*."

Ginevra returned to the synagogue and saw Anatoly again. She told him she would do everything she could to get him an invitation from fake relatives in Israel to help him apply to leave the Soviet Union. This time, Ginevra recorded Anatoly's address in her little book that she hid in her underwear bag when she was sleeping. Then when she'd finished writing it down, almost without thinking she added her swirly Ginevra signature on the bottom of the page, with the curly circle hanging down from the *a*.

"You sign your name so distinctly. Your signature is almost a piece of art."

"Really? I never thought of it that way. But my sister has tried to imitate it and she's never been able to. When you're a twin, you have to have something that's all yours. My father has always said I got the creative genes in the family."

Anatoly smiled, and Ginevra did, too. They spoke for hours. This time Anatoly told Ginevra about his violinist career, and how he dreamed of playing at the Bolshoi. They even took a walk, over to a café on Kutuzovsky Prospekt that Anatoly said was too expensive for regular Muscovites, so it was empty inside. Ginevra said she was treating—she was delighted to treat. The waiter gave them menus that read like books, with endless items listed, but each time they tried to order, the waiter shook his head and said they were out. Finally, Anatoly asked: What *did* they have? Eclairs. So Ginevra and Anatoly ate eclairs. Anatoly moaned over the deliciousness, the crumbs hanging off his lips, and Ginevra joined in to extol its praises, even though she thought Roman pastries superior.

Then Anatoly asked Ginevra what she'd be doing two days after, which was the First of May. Ginevra understood from the way he said it, like something sour and painful to entertain in his mouth, that he detested the day and what it stood for. Ginevra said that their group would be going to watch the parades in Red Square—and that it would be Ginevra's day out touring, and Orsola's day in the hotel, staying with their father.

What Anatoly responded startled her—that he'd met her sister at the synagogue.

Ginevra felt instantly cold all over, off-kilter, especially when Anatoly added, "You are twins, yes, but you are distinct. Very different."

Because of course, all her life Ginevra had known she was different.

But then Anatoly cycled back to the First of May conversation, and Ginevra filed it away—that he'd met her sister, but appeared unaffected by it. *Grazie a Dio.* Anatoly said then that he had to march in the parade, in the civilian part that followed the military rendition. Ginevra said, wow, she would look for him. And he said, "How about you meet me after?"

"Is it safe?" she asked. "I mean, KGB . . ."

"It will be the safest place to meet. In fact, everyone will be so swept up in their excitement over the communist machine. No one will notice one Jew and one tourist—"

"Also a Jew," she reminded him.

He nodded. "I know who you are, Ginevra. And I can guarantee you, no one will pay us any attention at all."

So Ginevra did meet him, at their appointed time, in the middle of Red Square, having stolen away from her group fairly easily, as Olga was absorbed, riveted to the reviewing stand with all the communist leaders.

"How was the march?" she asked Anatoly, looking up at him in awe—incomprehensibly handsome in his smart black suit.

"Oh, fine." He shrugged. "A loose kind of march."

"What was the whole thing? I couldn't understand anything anyone said."

"Ah." He smiled. "We approached the reviewing stand, you saw it, above Lenin's mausoleum?"

She nodded.

"Well, did you see Gorbachev?"

"Vaguely. There are so many people."

"Yes, well, we all shouted, *Progressive forces around the world unite against the evil capitalists!*"

She smiled at his obvious facetiousness.

"And then you heard it? *Ooo-rah!*" He imitated it with dramatic force.

She smiled. "I heard it. Our group chimed in."

He rolled his eyes. "They don't even understand what they are saluting, eh? Sometimes I feel like I'm in a movie, you know? And we're all just actors saying our lines. That's how this whole country feels."

She thought about it. "I know what you mean." Then she was surprised to hear herself follow it with "I feel like that sometimes, too." She didn't elaborate, but the whole picture of her life flashed back at her—taking care of her father, their dusty apartment without much laughter. "Writing is the only time I feel really *me*, but my father doesn't support it. Doesn't think I'll ever make money of it."

"I'd love to read your writing." Anatoly smiled. "I bet you're as good as Dostoyevsky."

She smiled. "I wouldn't go that far." But a pleasant feeling settled in her, like a stream lapping at rocks beneath a gentle sun.

"You know," said Anatoly, "it was my first time seeing Gorbachev."

"Was it . . . exciting?"

"Exciting? No. He's hardly something exciting to see." Anatoly laughed, like that was an absurd question. "He's better than the others, at least, provides less fodder for jokes. Brezhnev, for instance—we had many jokes about Brezhnev."

"I want to hear."

"Well, there's one." He smiled. People jostled by, and Ginevra moved closer to let them by. In doing so, she brushed up against Anatoly's chest. A jolt went through her.

"It's a teleprompter joke," he said as Ginevra was still feeling the jolt. "Someone knocks on his apartment door, and Brezhnev comes to the door, and pauses. He's uncertain what to do, what to say. Then he reads aloud from his teleprompter: *Who is there?*"

Ginevra giggled. "That's funny."

Suddenly Anatoly was solemn. "I'm really glad you came to meet me."

"I'm glad I did, too."

Indeed, for the first time ever, Ginevra's mind had begun to cycle forward, somersault into fantasies of what life could be. She and Anatoly, in America. Because he was determined to live in America, the land of freedom, the land of the Declaration of Independence he so revered. She would go, of course, with him. It would be difficult to leave her father and sister, but for love—a love she never could have fathomed she'd attract—she would leap.

But then one evening, a week and a half after the Efrati family had come to Moscow, Ginevra's fantasies were swiftly severed.

Ginevra and Orsola were finishing up breakfast in the fancy hotel dining room with its huge painted glass dome. A harpist played as people helped themselves to the buffet. There were scrambled eggs and pancakes, which were decent, but the juice didn't taste like juice—just water with sugar. Still, Ginevra savored it like it was the finest wine, so was the cloud she was floating atop. Domenico had eaten with them and had now gone back upstairs to rest. It was Orsola's turn to tour today, and she looked lovely—in cream trousers and a yellow silk blouse with a jaunty scarf around her neck.

"You look happy," Orsola said to her sister, and it was funny, because Ginevra had been thinking the same thing of her.

"I am," Ginevra said. And then she debated telling her sister about Anatoly. She hesitated, because the twins weren't the conjoined type bandied about in Western lore. They very deliberately lived their own separate lives. Ginevra had always felt Orsola was a little ashamed of Ginevra, of her looks, her shyness, but maybe that was unfair—because Orsola had never given her reason to think so. Had never said a mean word to or about Ginevra, other than that one unfortunate conversation with their father to which Ginevra had overheard all those years before. About Ginevra being responsible for their mother's death in childbirth.

"I met someone at the synagogue," Ginevra said, picking up the sugar water and sipping it to distract her thumping heart. "A man."

"Oh!" Orsola clapped her hands. "Did you? That's funny!" She paused. "Because I did, too!"

Something cold swept over Ginevra, prickling all her little arm hairs.

"What's his name? Oh, Ginevra, this is exciting! You never talk of boys."

"It's not like that," Ginevra said, even though it was, but suddenly she regretted saying anything to her sister. "I don't like him. I just met someone, you know, to help. That's all."

"Oh. Okay, well what's his name?"

A sick feeling gripped her entire being. "Anatoly." She held her breath. She knew, of course, from Anatoly, that his path had crossed with Orsola's. But perhaps Orsola wouldn't even remember meeting him.

"Oh! Oh, that's so funny. I met him, too. Anatoly—tall with dark hair and gorgeous blue eyes, right?"

Ginevra nodded, sick dread settling in her stomach. "He's a violinist."

"Yes! I've been meaning to tell you, in fact, but . . ." For a moment she looked almost apologetic, like she felt sorry for Ginevra. That was the look—pity. Now Ginevra's stomach felt composed of cement. "I met him, too. Well, more than that—he didn't say?"

Ginevra shook her head, or at least felt her neck move her head. She didn't feel like it was she directing it, like she maintained any control over her body anymore. She felt divorced from herself, almost floating above.

"Oh." Orsola nodded, flushed pink. "Well, in fact, we've been meeting in secret." Her eyes shone. Her sister never looked more pure or happy when in love—and Ginevra had seen her as such many times.

"Meeting in secret?" Ginevra stammered.

Orsola nodded. "He took me ice-skating. He took me to eat." She laughed. "I've been giving so many tubes of lipstick to Olga that soon we won't have any left."

"When?" Ginevra heard her voice—hoarse—and tried to convert it to nonchalance. "When did you meet him?"

"Oh, a week ago? When we got here, the first day I went out. I didn't tell you because I didn't want you to be like Papa and tell me it's dangerous and that I should stop being boy crazy. But this is so utterly different from Gino . . . from Pietro. . . . Wait a minute." She studied Ginevra's face. "You don't *like* Anatoly, do you?"

Suddenly Ginevra felt converted to a marionette, manipulated by strings to swivel her head right, then left. Indicating no. No, she did not like the man who'd apparently become besotted with her sister. Because what else was there to say?

"Oh, good." Orsola smiled big. "Yesterday he played me the violin, and, Ginevra. It's crazy, but I feel like it's the first time in my life that I'm actually, truly, falling in love! Why a man in Moscow? I don't know. But already, we are talking about how to get him out. How he can come to Italy, perhaps. *Al cuore non si comanda*."

The heart wants what the heart wants.

Orsola's beautiful bright eyes gleamed, shooting hearts right out of her pupils, which landed as daggers in Ginevra's own.

Yes, Ginevra thought—wasn't that saying true, deeply so? She'd add a corollary, too: *And of course, the heart always wants Orsola.*

CHAPTER THIRTY-ONE

Rory

"Papa!" His face blinks on the screen—reassuringly vital and tanned. If you didn't know he was sick, he'd be the older man you'd pass on the street and think, *I want to be that sprightly when I'm older.* I know Suzette makes sure he sits outside by the lake, gets some sun, and buries his bare feet in the grass like he loves.

"*Privyet,*" he says, his smile neutral. It's a quick, sickening blow—he doesn't recognize me. Besides, Papa never speaks to me in Russian. I know *privyet* means "hello," both by context and overhearing Papa in Russian mode at the diner. But he didn't teach it to Max and me; he wanted to move on from his past, become thoroughly American. Russian dragged him back—but now, here it is.

"And who might you be, beautiful lady?"

I try to maintain my smile, but my lips struggle with that big ask. This has happened before, of course, his not knowing who I am, but it stings like new.

"It's Rory!" Suzette says.

"Rory?" Papa shakes his head, laughs. "Rory is little. A child! Where is Rory?"

The phone clatters, and I hear a rustle. I know what is happening.

"Look, there she is at four, and six," Suzette is saying, distant. We made Papa scrapbooks for this reason exactly—photos from when Max and I were kids.

"Beautiful," I hear Papa say reverentially. "My Rory is beautiful."

Emotion swells in my throat as I listen to Suzette flip through the pages—try to get Papa's mind to accommodate me as a grown-up. It's common with Alzheimer's patients; they remember the past so much better than the present. So the theory is, as our social workers have counseled, that by showing Papa photos of me through various stages, he will witness the trajectory of my aging and recognize me now, all grown up.

This has happened a few times previously, and it's worked—but there's always the chance that this time it won't.

"Rory at college graduation," Suzette says.

"We ate at Pizza House after," Papa replies.

"Yes!" I shout. "That's right, Papa. We had chipatis."

I hold my breath as they page through my first office; my first time on air; and then, finally, he's back.

"Rory!" Papa smiles broadly, as if he's only just answered the phone. "It's you!"

"It's me." I hover closer to the screen, drink in the smile of a father who knows me again, aware that soon he may not. That next time, he might not be capable of following the bait.

"Where are you, Rory?"

I swallow hard. "Italy, Papa. I'm in Italy, with Max."

"Oh, wonderful! I'm so glad you and your brother are together. It's so important to me, that you are always close."

"We are, Papa. You never have to worry about that."

"I didn't have a brother or sister. I was an only child. The best gift I ever gave you was each other. And then you both have Caroline. I'm so pleased you have her, too. How *is* Caroline doing? I haven't seen her since . . . in . . ."

"Caro's good, Papa. You won't have seen her recently because she's in Italy with us, too."

"Oh, wonderful, wonderful." But his eyes dart around. I can tell he's growing more confused.

I try to bring him back. "It's like you said, though. Max, Caro, and I are always there for each other."

His smile fizzles as he struggles to maintain it, and I'm scared he's losing the connection—that in a moment the synapse that holds me in his brain, that recognizes me, is going to misfire.

I open my mouth, then close it again. Is it fair to him to even try to probe? I shake my head, knowing I at least need to try.

"Papa, you know that fairy tale you used to tell me and Max when we were kids? About the duke and the sisters."

I see the recognition dawn, but it's not joyous, I realize for the first time. "The good sister and the evil sister. And the duke—the duke who was in love with the good, beautiful sister. He met her on the lake, isn't that how I told it?"

"Yes. Exactly, Papa. Exactly. Can I ask you—"

"You can ask me anything, Rorachka." My breath lapses at that childhood nickname I'd forgotten. He hasn't called me that in years.

It feels so fragile, this conversation. Like one wrong sentence on my part, one push too hard, and the tenuous thread connecting us will snap.

"The fairy tale, the duke on the lake, the twin sisters—it sounds a bit like *Swan Lake*." I never realized it, never even thought of the connection until now, until it spits out of my mouth. But the more my brain turns it over, the more I wonder if I'm onto something. If *Swan Lake* has something to do with Ginevra, even though I'm determined not to drop her name again, remembering how much it agitated Papa last time. But maybe this line of questioning will feel less intrusive to him. Help him to tell me a detail that might shine light on it all.

"Was the fairy tale based on *Swan Lake*, Papa? Or something else? Is it a true story that happened to you?"

"*Swan Lake?*" It comes out of him fast and angry. "I wasn't talking about *Swan Lake!*"

"Okay, but—"

"It wasn't *Swan Lake!* Not at all! You're wrong! She's wrong." His head swivels, his blue eyes wild.

"Papa, I'm sorry. We don't have to talk about this anymore." I'm trying to say it calmly, soothingly, but I'm shaking.

"Not *Swan Lake!* You don't understand. The duke always knew, Rory! The duke always knew!"

"What does that mean? The duke always knew?"

But Papa disappears, and Suzette's face seizes the screen, her jaw firm but her eyes apologetic.

"Rory, I'm—"

"I know." I swallow hard. "Tell him I love him. Tell him Rory loves him."

Suzette smiles sadly. "I will, sweetheart. But I don't need to tell him. He knows."

Then she goes. Leaving me to curl up in a ball—infinite thoughts pulling at my brain, begging to be unlocked. Beseeching me to make connections that I am finding it quite boggling, quite impossible, to make.

All the while feeling very eerily sure there are major things I am missing that are right in front of my face.

I rub my forehead, briefly flirt with a nap—is that what I need? No. I spring out of bed, grab my phone that is charging on the malachite table, check the screen. A text from Ginevra, completely ignoring the many urgent texts I've sent in the past couple of days. Simply saying:

Ciao, bella Rory! All will be clear tomorrow at Le Sirenuse. I promise.

Yours, Ginevra

My frustration with her shoots to fury. When I finally get to speak with the author—whether she's my mother or not, my aunt or not, best-selling beloved freaking superstar or not—I'm quite positive I'll pop off. My gaze flits to the banquette table, to the copy of *The Cabin on the Lake* that I took from her office. I'm itching to read it again, to figure out what's been nagging me. What my brain flagged but hasn't yet deigned to clue me in on. But I don't have the brain space right this instant for plopping in bed and spending hours reading on a potentially needle-in-the-haystack search. I'm too on edge. I need a release. A massage . . . a workout . . . sex . . . or at least a drink . . .

I riffle through the itinerary. The blasted itinerary. Nate was right, at the start of all this. Ginevra Ex is the puppeteer, and we're her puppets. Private chef's dinner at 7:45 p.m.

No, thanks. Dinner with Nate and Caro? I'll pass. I'll quite pass on that. I'm officially done following Ginevra's plans. Time for some of my own.

I quickly change into a black midi skirt and flouncy off-the-shoulder matching top. It's an outfit I wore with Gabriele on one of our few dates. I felt powerful when I saw the look on his face when I arrived, but even more so when I gazed into my own eyes, like now. Somehow in all this, I've aged, grown. I like the person I'm becoming; who maybe isn't a news anchor; who meditates every day; who can be broken open, cracked, split, but still moseys on.

Well, maybe not moseying, but one foot in front of the other, at least. Still standing. Papa would be proud. It's the Aronov way.

I grab my key, wave to Marco on my way out, ducking off quickly before he can ask what he can do and start to offer up his litany of suggestions.

Max and Caro are two carriages over, next to each other. I'm fired up as I stalk over there, thinking it's another example of Ginevra plotting us like one of her books. Arranging little meet-cutes for the couples bound to get together. Although—can't imagine she's trying to couple Caro off with Max, but then, maybe she is. She invited Caro on this trip, after all, even after suspecting that she's embezzling from Hippoheal.

I hesitate outside Caro's door, trying to pull myself together, summon the wherewithal to put my anger toward her aside and focus on my friend who clearly has lots going on of which I had no clue. I knock on the door softly, wait a few seconds. No answer. Fear begins to drift across my chest, clench on my lungs. What if—what if Caro—

No, I can't go there in my head, but hell, I have to go there. Why did I leave her alone? Why did any of us believe her excuses and leave her in there all vulnerable? My hand is an inch from the wood, about to rap harder, break the door down if I have to, when I hear a click, and suddenly Max's face pops out from the neighboring cabin.

"I thought I heard something." He rakes a hand through his hair, and for the first time, I am startled to notice silver threads amid the black.

"Have you seen her?"

"Yeah." Max nods. "She's resting."

"Is she—I mean, Max, do you think . . . ?"

His shoulders budge up a touch. "I think we really need to get her a doctor tomorrow."

"But do you think . . . like, will she be fine through the night? Will she . . . ?"

I just don't get it. I can't believe this is Caro we're talking about, although I know theoretically that suicide doesn't spare anyone. That there's no "type" to which suicidal thoughts attach. And I suppose it makes sense—I've been absorbed in my own stuff, but Caro's been through the wringer, too. Even if both situations are her own making: sleeping with Nate and stealing from Max. Poor Max—he doesn't even know the latter yet. Now is not the time to tell him, though. I don't have the strength to add more tumult to my list.

"I think she'll be okay, Ror. Till Positano. Plus we'll check on her. I've already given her my key, told her to come at any moment in the night, if she needs me. And I'm gonna bail on dinner tonight. I've asked Francesco to order dinner to the room. I have work to do anyhow, and then I'll be close if Caro wants to talk, and to check on her, in case . . ."

I exhale deeply. "You're the best."

Max shrugs. "She's . . . you know what she is to me. . . ."

"I know."

He loves her, of course, but neither of us needs to speak it. Love—their kind of love, the type I thought I had with Nate, too—it just exists, breathes, an organism unto itself.

"How can you forgive her so quickly?" I ask him. "For sleeping with . . ." My tongue lingers on the word, rejects it.

"It was a mistake." He smiles sadly. "I don't think it actually meant anything. And we've all made mistakes. Except for you, maybe."

I groan. "Oh, I've made plenty. You're the perfect one. Not me."

"Papa would disagree. He's always seen you as perfect."

"Really?" I'm surprised to hear it, the way Max has perceived things. To me, Max could do no wrong—always winning awards, the best grades, succeeding. And now, with his Alzheimer's vaccine, he's poised to save millions of people, billions. Papa, most important.

"Well, I'm not so perfect anymore. News career down the toilet and all."

"Oh, I'm not worried about you," Max says.

I cock my head, surprised. "Seriously? You're not? Because I am. After this trip, I literally have zero income. Zero security. I don't even have a home anymore."

"No, I'm not worried. About other people, I might, but you? No. You always land on your feet. The sky is beyond the limit for you, Ror. When we were kids and Papa said he could see you as a news anchor, I could visualize it, too, but . . ."

"What?" I move closer to Max to let a couple squeeze by, surprised at everything he's saying. I want, *need*, to hear the rest of it.

"Well, I could also imagine so much more for you even. You could be the president, Ror."

"The president!" I laugh. "Shut up."

But he doesn't smile. "Seriously. I read a little of the book, you know. Before all the copies got stolen. What you did when the kids wrote Maxie'sTinyOne on my locker—I never knew that."

I blush. "Oh. That was forever ago. That was nothing. I was a kid."

"It wasn't nothing. It wasn't. It's . . ." He shakes his head, his face flushed with palpable emotion. "Pretty remarkable, is what it is. You were always brave, Ror. So much braver than me. There's no way that kid—the one who did that—doesn't land on her feet. And maybe . . . maybe the path you're on will lead to something Papa couldn't have foreseen in his crystal ball conch shell. You know?"

I feel a catch in my throat. "Wow, thanks, Maxie. That—that's really . . ."

"Of course." He pulls me in for a hug, kisses the top of my head. "Hey, Ror," he says, when I pull back, "you know that thing you said about not having a home?"

"Oh. I didn't mean like a roof over my—"

"No. I just wanted to tell you—that you always have a home. With me. You have to know that. Please don't forget that."

"I won't," I tell him, and smile at my brother. "Hey, I'm gonna—" I point down the hall, toward the bar car and then mime throwing one back.

"Enjoy." He laughs. "I'll toast you from my room, when I'm on the phone with my lab director."

"And you'll—" I point to Caro's room.

"Of course." He nods.

"If—"

"If she even so much as blinks the wrong way, I'll get you. How's that?"

"Thanks. Have a good night, BB. A good, uneventful night. We could use one of those, don't you think?"

Max snorts—an involuntary snort like Papa makes sometimes, too. "We *could* use one of those, indeed, Ror. A good, uneventful night to you too, LS."

CHAPTER THIRTY-TWO

Nate

I'm sitting in the bar car, nursing my second Casamigos on the rocks. No one's around—none of my group. Those three have seemingly placed my existence outside their periphery, but still, not ordering a vodka neat felt like some kind of knife to them all. The Aronovs, at least, for whom vodkas neat are basically a religion.

Screw them, Max and Rory! For turning on me, when I didn't actually do anything wrong. It's not like Rory and I were together when the dumb thing with Caro happened. It's not like Caro and Max were together either! Ever, in fact. So screw them all— and to top it off, screw Caro, too. For outing our stupid fling. The most regrettable night of my life.

All that anger flitters around, then shoots back like an arrow at my heart. Screw *me*! That's who I'm really angry at, if I'm honest with myself. Max and Rory have every right to be enraged. And in spilling things, Caro was only trying to be a good friend. An honest person. The way I should have been.

Screw *me*. I've always tried to live with integrity, and now I've betrayed the people I love most.

I appraise the now-familiar patrons: the lady with the yardstick posture, swathed in purple silk; the Italians from the beach who are either Ginevra's spies or a picture-perfect family, the kind that laughs too much, making you doubt it could possibly be real.

God, get me off this train. If I never have to see any of this lot again in my life, I'll be a happy man.

I stare into my tequila, my ears buzzing with my own agitation, my silent self-attacks, my eyes stinging from sudden tears that reignite the traces of sunscreen that caught inside them earlier. Serves me right. I saw Rome in a hot, lonely blur—pacing from ruins to ruins, aggressively trying to distract myself from reality, attempting to take in all there was to see, in what was supposed to be a romantic city. A destination Rory and I had flirted with for our honeymoon.

I rub my eyes, blink several times, trying to dislodge the sunscreen, and the room sways a bit, like I'm on a cruise ship instead of a train. Are we moving? No. The itinerary says we don't start moving until midnight, and it's still light outside. Hours left to occupy. All alone . . .

I shake my head. How could I do it? How could I do it to—

Rory! She's appeared at the door, in all her gorgeous Rory-ness, her eyes bright and her hair long and wavy like I love, her top a bit more skin baring than usual. I feel myself ache for her, arch toward her, like a plant starved of sun.

I watch her scan the place for a spot. It's packed, like the entire train jammed into one carriage, even as people have slowly started to filter out to dinner. And I watch her eyes latch onto me—disappointment flashes in them. Transfers to me.

But then to my surprise, Rory walks over and plops down beside me. When I muster the courage to look over at her, it's not disappointment I read on her face, but something else. Not friendly, exactly, but more relaxed, her lips straight, if even a little upturned. I feel something in my chest settle. She eases her tote bag off her shoulder, and a surprising item spills out onto the sofa—a copy of *The Cabin on the Lake*.

"You got the book back?"

"Oh." She slips it back inside her tote. "I found another one. Long story."

"You saw the author in Rome?"

"No. Not exactly. I—" Her face darkens. "Does it bother you that I have the book?"

"No!" I realize what she's inferred. "I didn't take them, Ror."

"Yeah. I know. Caro did. But you worried the affair might be in it."

"It wasn't an affair! It was one stupid night."

"Whatever. Whatever you say." She raises her hand, flags over a waitress. "Vodka neat, *per favore*," she says.

"With Zyr, if you have it," I say with her, as it comes out her mouth.

She rewards me with a tiny smile.

"You're staying? You're gonna have a drink with me? Not banish me to Timbuktu? Tell me to get the hell out of this carriage, off the train? Out of your life? Because I would understand if you do."

She crosses her legs and a kneecap pops out of the slit in her skirt, then the rest of her leg slides out, even the top up by her hip, not golden from the sun like the bottom part. My heart lurches. Rory quickly shifts her skirt around so it covers everything again.

"We were broken up when you slept with Caro. I don't have much of a leg to stand on."

That throws me. "Yes, but . . . I mean, you—"

"I'm still mad at you both! Don't get it twisted. If you were going to sleep with anyone, why her? And why did she pick you? It's . . . messed up." She shakes her head. "But honestly, there's so much going on right now that I . . ." She looks down at her hands.

"What's going on? What are you talking about?"

When Rory looks up again, her eyes are shining. If I didn't know her better, I'd say they were on the verge of tears. "I just could use a friendly face right now, Nate."

"You have me. You always have me." My arm budges, wanting immediately to sling itself around her shoulders. I'm so overwhelmed with relief that she's said what she said, that she doesn't despise me.

"Yeah?"

"Of course," I say, and then unexpectedly, she burrows herself into me for a hug that recollects thousands of others—a hug my body remembers. I smooth her hair as oceans of relief and love overwhelm me. What I had with Caro was fleeting, a hot flame, yes, but it's all flickered out. I want Rory. She's the one. The love of my life.

And yet still, as I rock her in my arms and as all the familiar ways I am soothed by this amazing woman flood my senses, I can't help the niggling sense that there is space between us that didn't exist before. Not miles. Not feet. Perhaps not even inches. Maybe a little centimeter that has wedged itself in there, and yet as I'm marinating in the rightness of hugging Rory again, I am also acutely aware of this new space. Aware that it is amorphous, tiny—maybe even just a figment of my imagination.

Still, with every second that ticks by, the space between us seems to balloon.

I shake my head, pull her closer, resolve to close the gap. To do anything—anything at all—so that we are back to NateandRory again.

CHAPTER THIRTY-THREE

Rory

If you had told me when I walked into the bar car that I was about to get overserved with Nate, to gorge on oysters and caviar and cheese plates together, and eventually to leave arm in arm, to invite him near midnight back to my cabin for a nightcap—I'd have said, "Zero chance."

And yet here we are, teetering out, giggling hysterically. As we weave our way through the packed carriage, with meager space between bodies, fabrics and textures accost me. My ankle grazes the sharp black sequins of a woman's flowy pants; feathers tickle the back of my neck. Near the door, I accidentally knock into the Russian hipster guy, sending what looks like a Jack and Coke sloshing over the edge of his goblet. He shoots me a peeved look, and I return a sloppy smile.

"Sorry! Put another one on my tab. I'm—I'm . . . the Roma Suite!" I finally say triumphantly. I stop a waitress who is balancing a tray of drinks. "Can you please get that gentleman another Jack and Coke on me?"

"It's not a Jack and Coke. Please, do not bother," he says to the waitress.

"Come on!" Nate nudges my arm toward the door.

"I should have figured, not a Jack and Coke—not on the Orient Express! Not nearly bougie enough. I'm sure he was drinking . . ." I fumble for those fancy names on the menu.

"A beetroot hopper!" Nate says.

"Yes! Or a grapefruit delight."

"A flower breeze."

"No. No. . . ." I can hardly get the words out I'm laughing so hard. "I got it! He was drinking a spicy zombie."

"Bull's-eye." Nate smiles, and his smile shoots through me.

Everyone else is a vague blur—eyes on me, scowls, but it's all tempered by the nice buzz that has settled in my body. A calm, lovely feeling that has permeated me for the first time in days.

"Live a little!" I say cheerfully to all of them. Then I stop. "Oh wait, I forgot my bag."

"I'll get it." Nate ducks back into the fray.

When he goes, the Russian guy is still brushing off Coke droplets from his bomber jacket.

"I really am sorry," I call over to him. "I'll pay for your dry-cleaning bill."

He shrugs, peeps a smile with surprising blinding white teeth. "It's okay. Lucky girl yesterday, eh?"

"Lucky?"

He points at me. "That big rock. We saw it all. We were hiking right above you. It was loose. It went down the hill. We tried to stop it. We ran after it. . . . It is very lucky." His eyes roll upward. "You must be on God's good side."

I halt, suddenly shaky. "No one pushed it?"

He laughs. "Pushed the rock?"

"Yes?"

He laughs. "No one pushed it." Then his laugh disappears, and I notice his pink-pixied girlfriend weaving through the crowd, scowling. She must have misinterpreted our conversation as me trying to flirt with her man. God, maybe she even thinks I spilled on him intentionally. I spot Nate, raise a hand to flag him. He shoots toward me, weaves his arms through mine, and steers me toward the door.

"What was that about?"

I open my mouth to tell him—the boulder was an accident after all. Not Ginevra Ex, or her minions, or the darker places my mind has even gone that it could have even been Caro who pushed it. Maybe I'm inventing all my suspicions, after all. Maybe all my fears are in my head. . . .

Unless the Russian guy was lying. Unless *he* is Ginevra's minion, and he deliberately raised the subject endeavoring to mislead me. My eyes flit over at him—he's staring at me, talking furtively with pink-pixie girl.

I'm spinning out. I must be spinning out.

"What?" Nate presses, his shoulders stiffening.

"I think I might be a little bit drunk," I finally say, deciding I don't want to talk about the boulder. For a blessed moment, I'd like to forget all of it.

Nate grins. "Me too. This reminds me of—"

I summon back cheer. "God, I was just thinking it, too!"

"The Erewhon night," we say in unison.

Nate and I are decidedly not Erewhon people; we're more the Kroger types. And we're also not the type of people who had frequent drunken nights, but we once did get very good and drunk at an Olive Garden, of all places. (Bottomless breadsticks are my jam.) And I was so thirsty driving home that we made the Uber stop at the first place we came across, which was Erewhon, the fanciest, most ridiculously overpriced grocery store, catnip to most of LA, acolytes of Goop, who love nothing more than to spend twelve dollars on an alkaline water.

Nate's laugh shoots out of him like a projectile. "I'll never forget it. You'd had so much to drink that you were basically communing with the squirrel outside. I got you your water—the cheapest one they had, at least."

I laugh. "Not alkaline, thank you very much. But that squirrel was so cute. And clearly hungry."

"I remember. You actually made me go back for carrots."

"Oh my God, I did. I really did." I double over, but not before a flash of purple catches my eye. I straighten up, suddenly more alert. But the flash—the plum-colored fabric with feathers, swishing in the hall—has gone. Into a cabin. I shake my head, disoriented.

"What?" Nate stops.

I continue down the hall, eyes darting between the doors. Which one did she—?

Was that—?

No. Couldn't be.

"What?" Nate asks again.

I shake my head. "Nothing. I thought I saw . . ."

"What?"

"Who?" I correct him carefully, my tongue mulling over the two words I'm about to eject, yet stopping myself from slipping them out into this night. Stopping myself from allowing those two words to drain this mood I'm in—this silly, happy, finally relaxed mood, with my problems distant, finally not dogs pouncing at me, demanding my attention and resolve.

"What? I mean, *who?*" Nate follows my gaze, but it's too late. Whoever that was, she's gone.

"Never mind. Come on, let's go." I pull him in the other direction, but can't help one last glimpse over my shoulder. Still, there's nothing—no motion in the hall. Just all the glossy wood and the din of conversation and cheer emanating from the bar car.

I shake my head, try to shake it all out. There's no way anyhow. My mind must have been playing tricks on me.

But as Nate kisses my cheek, pulls me in the direction of the Roma Suite, a discomfited feeling settles in my stomach.

If I wasn't so drunk, if I didn't know it was impossible—I'd almost swear I just saw Ginevra Ex.

CHAPTER THIRTY-FOUR

Caroline

I jolt in my bed, startled at the sudden pulse of movement beneath me. Seconds later it occurs to me: It's the train en route again. Must be midnight, departure time to Positano, if I remember correctly from the inane itinerary. My eyes flitter to the clock inlaid into the bar and confirm it, what appears to be one thick black line hovering at twelve. The train jerks onward, soon smoothing into a steady pace. Seconds pass, and you'd hardly notice it now——the movement has become a constant, a part of reality you no longer question but blindly accept.

I swipe at my eyes, pry away the crust from old tears. Dried. Gone.

I'm not sad anymore, I realize, nor distraught. I'm something entirely else.

I sit up and it flashes through me——standing on the edge of the Colosseum, at dizzying heights. Kicking a pebble and watching it skitter down. So very far down, until colliding back into the earth. Stepping back from the ledge, my heartbeat berserk, the panorama of Rome stretching out into forever——at least the extent of forever as I could see or imagine exists. Feeling the rustle of Max at my back, his shirt grazing my skin.

As close to me as my next breath.

I shift atop the bed, and as I do, my thigh comes down hard on something metal. I wince, wriggle it out.

Max's key. He gave it to me, of course, instructing me to come see him next door if I needed anything. Anything at all. Suddenly, in a bout of fury, I fling the key toward the door. It lands with a tepid crash on the parquet.

I catch a glimpse of my reflection in the mirror panel right across. My hair is mussed, my skin red, crisscrossed in pillowcase creases. But my face is hard and firm. Spontaneously, I give myself a tiny salute.

I exhale deeply. Can I do this? Can I really, really do this?

My tiny jolt of bravery goes as fast as it came. The Colosseum returns to me—the heart-thrashing intensity of being up so high. So close.

All that talk of suicide, all that chatter my mind shoveled away. Funny how they missed it, how Rory did at least, when she murmured with Max in the car back on the way to the train. Stuff they thought I didn't overhear. The thing is: It requires some measure of courage to commit suicide. To actually do something about your feelings and problems. Not to drown them out any longer.

I stumble to my feet, slap my hands on the table, intentionally hard, inviting the sting. No more. I stare at my palms, pink and tingly. A buzz builds in my ears.

No more. I can't handle it anymore!

All of a sudden, I feel my child self slip before me, a sad, meek mirage. Coming toward me, nearer, nearer, until she's an inch from my nose, Little Caro startling me, her contours I'd lost, been desperate to shed. Little Caro—I see it now. She's courageous as all get-out! That sweet little girl. Tears soak my cheeks once again.

I realize that for a long time I've tucked Little Caro away. Instructed her to rot. Die. Thought critically of her. Invented stories that weren't even real.

Told myself if she were different—better—*good*, her parents would have been different, too.

No longer. I stand up, retrieve Max's key ring, swirl it around my index finger. Then I remember something. Suddenly I rush around the room, palming surfaces, eyes darting about. Where *is* it?

I dive into my suitcase, toss it off the stool it's perched on. I turn the carrier over, spill all the contents onto the floor, digging through things, flinging aside lingerie and silk dresses—not finding it. When I surface, I am dazed. I notice a pair of underwear on a lamp. Fear mounts in my chest. Where the fuck is it?

And then I spot it—a tiny pile of metal on the little table. I walk over and retrieve it: the whistle that came in our welcome kit. Rory was wearing it as a necklace the first day, which I found cute, but not the type of fashion statement I'd typically make.

I loop it around my neck. I'm not wearing it as a fashion statement now.

My mind whirls and swirls, reshuffles thoughts among their file folders.

I *am* courageous—or I'm going to try to be, at last.

CHAPTER THIRTY-FIVE

Rory

Kissing Nate is exactly how I remembered. Hard. Firm. Urgent. His hands moving in all the familiar ways, grazing my sides, gripping my butt, stroking my hair.

For a long time—for ten years—I thought there was entirely one way to kiss, one way to have sex: the way Nate and I did it.

I loved that way, I was ready to sign up for an eternity of our tried and true. But then I kissed Gabriele. Then I slept with Gabriele. It's not to say that Gabriele was the be-all and end-all, not to say I ranked him higher or lower than Nate. Just that he was different. He was caramel praline ice cream when I'd been quite ready to sign myself up for pistachio for the rest of time.

Now I remember, pistachio ice cream was insanely delicious. Maybe, truly, my favorite of life.

But caramel praline was pretty epic, too.

All thoughts of ice cream evaporate from my head as Nate moves me back toward the bed, our mouths locked, clearly feeling victorious in a match we didn't even expect we'd be playing, communicating, *Yes, we are good at this! Oh, yes, we know how to do this!* In swift, terse motions, Nate tugs my shirt up and off, then pushes down my skirt so it pools around my ankles. Then he's back kissing me, urgent. I'm hungry, too. Pulling his shirt upward—irritated when it stalls over his head. Tugging, tugging, until his lips are on mine again, and he's lifting me up, drawing me against his chest. I wrap my legs around him, noticing that he's already shed his pants—when he did it, I'm not even sure. Caro and I always joke about it—how men can be Houdinis with their clothing: now you see it, now you don't. Just Caro's name bounces up against organs, a pain to my heart, my stomach, then blessedly fizzles from my mind. I run my hands over Nate's arms—his biceps are my favorite, smooth ivory skin, a graze of a tan . . .

As I suck gently on his neck, he says, "Ror . . ."

"Yeah?"

My name—it's a plunk down to earth, a shock out of my tipsy joy, a hole punch in what we're about to do, what my body is communicating it *quite* wants to do.

I continue sucking on his neck, trying to slip back inside this, trying not to let the thoughts invade, the ones that are suddenly knocking insistently on the door.

Nate slept with Caro, and now you're going to—what—pretend that didn't happen?

Do you even want him back?

Do you really want this?

"I want this!" I say, and then start when I realize I've said it aloud.

Even in the darkness, I can make out Nate's crooked grin.

"Well, I'm glad to hear that. I want this, too. But, Ror . . ." There's movement, his skin detaching from mine, his shape lowering to the ground.

"Wha— Nate, what are you—?"

"Shit, can you even see me?"

"Not really," I admit. But suddenly I have an inkling as to what he's doing, and my whole body has seized up, frozen.

No, no, no, no, no.

"Wait! Don't turn the lights on."

"I know." He chuckles. He knows how the light kills my mood. Not because I don't want him to see my body, or because I don't want to see his, but unless it's candlelight, there's something too bright and bracing about artificial track lighting. (When Nate and I first started dating, he'd always try to turn on one of those awful lava lamps right before sex, until

I convinced him to leave it out on the sidewalk for a guy whose girlfriend actually enjoyed being lit up like a Christmas tree.)

"No, I mean—" How to say it? "Are you—are you about to . . ."

He laughs again. "It's like the first time I proposed. . . . You wanted to micromanage the whole thing."

I manage a dry laugh, but my head is whirling. "You're trying to propose again? Is that what's going on?" I cross my hands over my chest, even though it's dark, and he's seen my boobs probably a hundred million times.

He stands, pulls on my arm, leads me to the bed. He fumbles in his pocket and out comes a familiar velvet cushion box visible in a trickle of moonlight through the nearly drawn drapes.

"You brought the ring?" I hear myself stumble over the words. "I can't believe . . . you mean you planned—"

"I hoped. Like a lovesick loser, I guess. I don't want to just sleep together, Ror. I want you to say you forgive me, that we can really be together again."

He pops open the box, and I stare numbly at my old ring glinting in the near-dark, almost more striking without competition from the light. It's stunning, still the exact ring I'd pick—a simple one-carat round diamond on a thin gold band. I loved wearing it—to be honest, I felt very LA, even if it was far smaller than most diamonds in La-La Land. And I loved the story the ring told—that I had been chosen by a wonderful man, that my life was set, resolved, in this all-important category.

I realize it now, thinking back half a year, how important it was for me to feel like my life was filed, in good order. Career, check. Man, check. I never stopped to question whether the contents of the files were right. I was just happy that they were filled and slotted away.

"Ror, will you marry me? Please. Say you will. Say you'll wear the ring again. I want to marry you more than anything."

"I—I don't—"

Suddenly the train jerks forward.

"Oh, we must be moving." Nate places a hand on my knee, the ring hooked on his forefinger.

I stare at it, feeling woozy. "I need water."

"I'll get it." He crosses to the bar. The train settles into its steady pace.

"Can you believe we'll be in Positano soon? The end of the line?" he asks, his back to me, as his shadow twists open a cap, and I hear the liquid spill out.

"No, this trip seems like the longest trip of my life." My eyes catch my bag that I dropped by the door in the frenzy of our kissing. Now that we are on our way, and Nate's re-proposed, and my head is pounding, now that I've remembered that I have *The Cabin on the Lake*, which I'd really like to reread, now the wisdom of our hookup—everything it represents—feels like it's morphed into a question mark.

Morphed into a question mark . . . or something else, I realize with a thud.

Morphed into an *I need to be alone*.

"Ror?" Nate's back with a glass. I accept it, chug. My mind is churning, wondering how to deal with all this, when suddenly there's a rap at the door.

"Yeah?" Nate sounds peeved. "Who's there?"

"Probably Marco with more mints for our pillows." I feel a surge of relief, hop out of bed, drag my top and skirt back on. Nate laughs, but puts his pants back on. I fling open the door, suddenly eager for light to invade.

Gabriele appears in the doorway.

"Oh, hi! *Ciao!*" I'm startled, and I hear it in the stutter of my greeting. I flick on the light on the panel on the wall and blink my eyes as the room illuminates.

"*Ciao*." His smile shifts from easy to weary, and I swivel, following Gabriele's dark eyes lock onto Nate's. And vice versa.

Gabriele fixes back on me. "I'm sorry . . . I'm really sorry for interrupting."

"You're not! We were just—"

"You don't have to explain anything to me, Rory."

I nod slowly, but I feel like I do.

"I wanted to check on you. I saw you and Nate in the bar car, and I didn't want to disturb. Only wanted to make sure you made it back to your room okay and—"

"She made it back quite okay, man," Nate says, crossing his arms over his bare chest. "As you can well see. So we'll wish you good night and—"

"No," I say softly, then force it out louder. "No. I mean, Gabriele, thanks for checking on me. I'm fine."

He nods curtly. "I'll see you in the morning. After we get off the train, a car will pick us all up. You know you have the reservation at Le Sirenuse at one."

"I know. About that. Do you . . . ?" I'm on the verge of asking him again if he knows the motive behind this mysterious reservation. Maybe even tell him about what I found in Ginevra's apartment. But to say it would involve Nate, too, and probably hours of subsequent speculations.

"Yeah. Le Sirenuse. See you tomorrow, Gabriele. *Buona notte.*" I shoot him a sheepish smile, but he only nods and rubs his beard, his face expressionless. Then he ducks out and the door clicks shut behind him, leaving me and Nate in the too-piercing light.

"Nate, I . . . look . . ." I run a hand through my hair, unable to coax myself to meet his gaze.

"I get it." Wearily, he slips the ring back inside the box. When he looks back at me, he's not mad, but a sad that I feel, too. "A guy's gotta shoot his shot when he has it, you know?"

I place a hand on his forearm. "I don't . . . we drank too much. My head is spinning, and I still haven't exactly . . . you and Caro, I mean—"

"You haven't forgiven us." He sits on the bed, wiggles his feet back into his sneakers. "I get it, Ror. I'm not saying you need to. I mean, you should take all the time—"

"It's more than that. I haven't even told you what happened with Caro at the Colosseum. . . ."

His eyebrow arches. "Caro? At the Colosseum? What do you mean?"

My chest stiffens—what I saw returns, and the panic that set in as I ran toward her. I shake my head. "I'll tell you tomorrow. Just, it's been the longest day, and I don't want . . . I mean, if you and I—I want it to mean something, if we sleep together, you know?"

He wiggles his head through his shirt and the material swishes back down over his abs. "I wouldn't want to force you to do anything you don't want to."

"I know. So let me just . . ."

"Sure." He stands, stuffs his hands in his pockets. Then he kisses my cheek. "Sleep tight, Ror. If you need anything . . ."

"I know where to find you." I stand in the doorway, watch him disappear.

Marco's nowhere in sight. Thankfully, I've noticed the stewards stop keeping such vigilant watch in the night. Not that I'll have such privileged problems after tomorrow.

I return to the room, the lights still stinging my eyes, the space in disarray, like fun was had.

Well, fun was *almost* had.

I lick my lips, still tasting Nate, my mind running in circles over it all. I'm not tired . . . no longer drunk exactly, but jittery, like there is little chance sleep will give itself over.

My eyes rove the room, then catch on my bag—*The Cabin on the Lake*. That's it. The book is the key to everything. I *know* it.

I grab my new copy, sprawl out in bed, and prop the cover open, praying to the gods of Laci and Candace, Benedict and Eddie that with this read, I'll puzzle things out.

CHAPTER THIRTY-SIX

Caroline

It's nearly two in the morning when I finally knock. I accomplish two hard raps before my confidence folds. I consider ducking back into my room.

No. Not now. Not anymore.

I add one final loud knock.

The hall is quiet, devoid of bustling passengers, although distant revelry filters from the bar car, competing with the drum of my heart. I touch the guard's whistle looped around my neck, then dig my fingernails into my bare thigh. I glance down, register for the first time that I'm wearing a matching pale blue silk pajama set. That if anyone were to see me, waiting here, for *him*, they would form a distinct picture in their mind about what was about to go down.

Footsteps. I cough. The now-familiar scent wafting through the Orient Express—wood, leather—is wringing all the breath from my lungs.

Or maybe it's just being on this enclosed train, after everything that's happened. I almost opened my window before to guzzle in fresh air. But as I undid the catch, I stopped myself. Something about the train whizzing through the countryside, the wind gusting in my face—it harkened back to the Colosseum. Being on the edge. Pushing things too far. To their limit.

I watch the doorknob turn.

Things are already pushed to their limit. There's no way around that anymore.

The door cracks open, revealing a face whose twitches and planes I know well. He smiles—a sad, strange smile.

"I figured it would be you."

CHAPTER THIRTY-SEVEN

Max

I step by to let Caro pass, then I close the door, do the lock. I turn to face her, glad I had the foresight to tell Francesco he could have the evening off. That, after my dinner service, I wouldn't be needing him tonight.

"You figured it would be me?" Caro asks. "Really? That surprises me."

My phone flashes on the table. I glance at it briefly, then turn it over.

"I told you to come if you needed me."

"I don't need you. And you know that well and good. All that suicide talk . . . what you probably told Rory. It's ludicrous, Max."

I sigh. "Why don't you sit?"

"I don't want to sit." She crosses her arms over her chest, stands awkwardly in the middle of the room. I could crack a joke—Caro hates standing around awkwardly. Feels self-conscious, taking up space like that. It's a trait we used to share until I started Hippoheal. Until I realized that the spotlight feels quite warm and nice. Suits me.

"Okay, well, I'm going to sit." I lower myself down, but then I have a better thought. "How about a drink first?"

"We need to talk, Max. You can't wriggle out of this conversation like you always do. Like you did yesterday, and again at the Colosseum."

I walk over to the bar, give her my back. Pour, cubes, gulp. When I return, I say, "I'm not wriggling out of anything, Carolina." I wink at her. I'm pretty sure I'm the only one who randomly calls her that.

"You only call me that when you're trying to wriggle out of something."

I arch an eyebrow. "Or into something."

She doesn't smile. Doesn't sit either. "It's the middle of the night. I didn't come for jokes."

"Okayyyy." I place the glass on the table. "No jokes, and no . . ." I motion my head toward the bed.

"Jesus, Max." She scowls. "No."

"Okay. That's a no. Anyway, you slept with Nate. If you were coming for that, it's probably his door you'd be knocking on."

"You're mad. I knew you were mad, and that's why I've let it go this long. I was trying to give you space. I was trying to—I don't know—let you cool down. But *I'm* mad! I'm freaking out! And honestly, Max, Rory *knows*. I can't do this anymore."

I falter, almost lose my footing. "Rory knows what exactly?"

"She knows. She knows about Hippoheal."

An avalanche loosens, starts tumbling toward me. Still I try to remain as outwardly calm as I can muster. "What exactly does Rory know?"

"Well, she thinks *I'm* embezzling from you. The author had a private investigator—got bank statements and stuff. Rory *knows*, Max. And the author does, too."

The avalanche settles. Fresh crunchy snow in towering drifts, blocking the door, but we're still alive on the inside. "Okay, so she doesn't really know. She doesn't know—"

"That your vaccine is a *fraud?*" Caro finally sits, crosses her snowy white legs. "She doesn't know. Not yet."

"Stop. Stop! You know—"

"I know what? That I'm not allowed to speak of it, not even when we're just the two of us? That I've promised to never tell? Well, I'm done, Max."

"Done? Done doing what?" Words are torching my tongue, making everything feel like fire.

"Done keeping your secrets. Done hiding it all. The vaccine isn't working, and what's more, it's harming people." She ticks off on her fingers, her panther ring glinting as she does. "Rashes covering their bodies, encephalitis, loss of vision."

"Stop. Stop saying that!" I take a sip of my drink and squeeze my eyes shut, willing myself to calm down.

Except, didn't I expect this? Didn't I intuit that things were heading toward this?

"I can't anymore." When my eyes flit open, Caro is staring at me, dead in my eyes. Not like the rest of the day, when her eyes darted around, landing on anyone—anything—but me. "I'm sorry, Maxie. I love you so much. You know that. But I can't keep this anymore."

"I just need more time! With a little more time, the lab will get the formulation right. We're so close to a cure. And then it's going to save Papa! It's for him, C. I need more time for him!"

"No." She leans forward. "No, Max. *No*. You can't use Ansel as your bargaining chip anymore. You know I love him. He's like a father to me, too. But you're not going to save him. You have to face it."

"I *am*," I say back evenly. "Just because you don't believe. You think people didn't believe Jonas Salk, too? Thought he was crazy. Anyone's crazy until they succeed."

"I . . ." She shakes her head, fumbles with words. Of course she does, because I'm right. And every time she goes down this road, she has to contend with her own guilt. That she herself is trying to snuff out Papa's last chance.

"No, Max. You've been saying this for a year. Ever since . . . ever since I—"

"You were never supposed to even *be* in the lab. Spy on Katerina! Talk to the lab team behind her back. You're in sales. You're not a scientist, Caroline. You never have been."

She frowns, but not a frown of upset. More in the neighborhood of pity—which pops something inside of me, makes my chest fizz.

"You didn't even have clearance to go inside."

"Well, I *did* go inside the lab, Max. We can't change that now, can we? Anyway, let's not erase history here. It didn't start with me snooping. It started with me overhearing Operation Kazuka. You should have picked a better code name—you think I wouldn't know what that meant? And it's not like I went looking for the whistleblower in your data department. Manny came to me on his own accord, and honestly, Max, *what*? You thought you'd order them to fudge the data going to the FDA, and no one was going to spill?"

The fizzing in my chest is cratering. Turning volcanic. I grip the table. "They signed NDAs. All of them, fucking Manny, too. You think I spent so much time on research—so many years of my life—to come this close and then not save Papa? You think that's what I've done?"

"You're not going to save Ansel," Caro says, standing, coming closer to me, her face wrenched in anger, more fiery than I've ever seen her. More fiery than I even knew she was capable of. "Max, wake up! You have to face it! Make things right. Enough already!"

"No. You're wrong! I need more time. It's so close to working. . . . It's so—"

"It's not! If you don't fix things, admit what you've done, then—"

"Then what? You're going to turn me in?"

"Yes," she says simply. "Yes. I've given you a year already. People could die, Max! Die. D-I-E."

"Who *are* you?" I ask her, shaking, unable to fathom that this horrible person is my sweet, even-keeled Caro. The girl I've loved for as long as I can remember. "Who even are you?"

Her head whips back to me. "Who are *you*? Literally, who are you? I don't recognize you. Ansel would be ashamed, Max! He would be so ashamed of the path you've taken!"

"Shut up, shut up, shut *up*! Papa would *not* be ashamed. I'm trying to save him!"

"Well, you're not saving him. And you're hurting others. Face it. You have to face it!"

What she's said echoes excruciatingly in my ears. It has been echoing, in fact, since she said it the first time.

Yesterday. And again today. At the Colosseum. But somehow, in a softer way. Now she's abrasive, hurting my eardrums, pain in my heart. And another feeling building in my chest that's not pain, or at least it's not sadness. It's anger. It's fight.

"I know! You told me that already. That I'm another Elizabeth Holmes. That Hippoheal is going to be another Theranos if I—if *you*—don't put a stop to it now."

"And you erupted on me! Like it was my fault. I thought . . . for a moment I thought . . ." She shakes her head furiously—reminds me of a dog emerging from the lake, trying to rid itself of its sopping wet.

"What? What did you think?"

"Ow!"

I realize now that I've reached over for her wrist. That I'm twisting it. That I'm strong—not jacked like Nate, but strong and far bigger than Caro nonetheless.

"You're hurting me, Max."

I try to let go, but I find that I can't.

"What did you think when we were standing on the edge of the Colosseum?" I ask her again.

"I thought . . ." She winces, still trying to detach her arm, but failing. "I thought . . . maybe . . . you were going to push me," she whispers.

A scary silence grips the room.

"I was. I almost did. But then Rory showed up."

She reaches down for her whistle, nearly gets it to her mouth.

But I'm one step ahead of her.

"I love you," I whisper in her ear as I cover her mouth with my hand. She tries to scream, but I clamp it harder, using it to press her body back against mine. Then I release my other hand that's been gripping her wrist and fumble on the table next to us where a knife rests on the fruit plate. The one I used earlier to cut a mango. Surprisingly sharp.

I grip the knife in my palm and recall the story in the author's book. How Rory went with a knife to defend my honor from those bullies at school. My fourth-grade sister, with enough courage to wield a knife at boys a head taller than her. It bolstered me, that story. Made me remember I'm not that weakling anymore.

My heart is racing as I twist Caro closer to me.

"Fuck you, Caro!" I hear myself shouting, but I am powerless to stop it. To stop anything that comes after this point. "Why did you have to turn on me? I really did love you! That's the craziest part. I thought it would be easier, when I found out you slept with Nate. But it's not easier. I still fucking love you! But—it's not enough. You see that now, don't you, C? The fact that I love you is no longer enough." I shake my head, because truly it does boggle the mind.

Boggles mine at least. How two things can be true at once: I love her deeply, and yet I very much want her dead.

CHAPTER THIRTY-EIGHT

Rory

I'm about to switch off the lamp, put this crazy book about me down. Admit defeat. Because I've reread more than half of it with painstaking attention and still have zero clue what's been nagging me. And I'm exhausted to the bone. But, no. I grab a Coke from the minifridge and strengthen my resolve. I'm an Aronov. I don't easily give up, not when I truly want something. So I caffeinate and continue reading, and finally my eyes reward my persistence by registering a detail on page 224. Two words.

Operation Kazuka.

I gasp, because suddenly it smacks me, that odd sensation the first time I read the book. And now I can pinpoint exactly what it's arisen from.

Operation Kazuka.

See, Papa was pretty strict. We always had early curfews, rules about boys and girls mingling unsupervised. I wasn't in the popular crowd, not too fast, but I had crushes, flirtations. Parties I wanted to go to. Max wasn't in the partying scene, at least not in high school, but he always backed me up if I needed help. Papa had this system, where instead of waiting up for me, he'd set an alarm clock and leave it in the hallway. I had to get home before it would start blaring, to switch it off.

But sometimes I'd call Max and say, *Operation Kazuka.* And he'd turn it off for me.

And that one time I threw a party when Papa was out of town—and then discovered he was coming back early—Max was ace. We kicked everyone out, gathered up all the red Solo cups. Filled the half-drunk vodka handle back up with water and prayed Papa wouldn't notice the dilution.

Operation Kazuka. I forget who invented it, or when . . . Max and I used to chew reams of that pink Bazooka bubble gum that was popular when we were kids, and one of us was staring at the wrapper when we spun it into our sibling code.

I bolt to a seat, understanding fully now why I found it so jarring on my first read to stumble across that phrase in the book

I didn't mention it to Ginevra Ex. I know—*know*—I didn't. That I wouldn't. Which means she must have overheard it from Max. But I can't imagine him offering up that story, either. We pinkie swore on it, vowed sibling code. We were always loyal about those types of things. Especially Max—anything family related assumes *Sopranos*-level devotion. Only Caro knew what our code meant, impossible to hide it from her, as she was practically an Aronov herself. And anyway, we haven't used it in years—*decades*. I'd venture that even Nate doesn't know *Operation Kazuka.* Which means the only way I can imagine Ginevra gleaning onto our code—and finding it catchy enough to include in the book—is if she overheard it.

If Ginevra overheard Max using it. Say, to his assistant. I can easily imagine it: *No, Ramona. Please tell John that's in the file for Operation Kazuka.*

Is Max involved in something fishy? Dishonest? And so . . . what, he read the book and knew full well that if I latched onto what Operation Kazuka means, I'd infer the import behind it?

But what the hell? What could my brother possibly be covering up?

Suddenly, sheer dread fills me head to toe, and I wonder if I know.

e~

My brain is whirling, forming links between facts that were previously disparate, innocuous.

How Max is so fast to say work is *great, great*—but how in the past year at least, Caro's face does something strange as he says it.

That Max and Caro were arguing at the Colosseum.

That Caro is embezzling from Hippoheal . . .

That Max's motive in life has always been to make Papa proud.

So different from me. Sure, I became a news anchor, like Papa foretold. Whether it's because of him, because I valued his opinion more than anyone's, or whether he truly saw what was best for me, I'm no longer sure. The chicken or the egg . . .

But I know that I've done things that displeased Papa—moving to LA, smoking weed in college. (He found a stash in my bag when he was looking for mints, and his reaction was as though I'd started a nuclear war. Apparently smoking weed in the Soviet Union was considered on par with shooting up heroin.)

And while I hated upsetting Papa, or disappointing him, it didn't shatter me like it did Max. Max has always needed more of Papa—been splintered by his opinion. The two of them riling each other up, making little things mean more than they do. And on the flip side—Papa's approvals could be overwhelming, a torrent of praise and affection. Max always lapped it right up. I don't know why, but I enjoyed it yet always needed it less.

I sift through all the separate pieces but none of it gels. And *Caro* took the books, not Max. Unless . . . could Caro and Max have taken them together . . . but why? If Max was somehow involved, because of a thing that he needs to conceal, then what's he covering up? Something with the vaccine? I freeze, as the scene at the Colosseum replays in my mind.

Caro at the edge, Max behind her. Me screaming, running—them both looking my way. Then Caro shaking, practically catatonic in bed.

What am I missing?

Another snippet from the book floats up toward me. A memory Ginevra teased out of me, that she included in its pages. She'd asked if Max had any negative qualities—I suppose because she'd realized that, to me, Max could do no wrong. I've always looked up to my brother. Who in the world now wouldn't? But I told Ginevra that as we got older, Max could have a temper if he felt threatened. And I thought of the Robinsons' dog next door. Davey. How he was found dead on our street, struck by a car. A hit-and-run. Never solved. Except I had my private thoughts, which I shared with Ginevra in a moment of vulnerability and truth. That I always suspected Max had done it. We lived on a quiet cul-de-sac. Only us and the Robinsons. And Max hated that dog. The feeling was mutual.

No one spurred Davey's barking like Max. Davey was a nothing to me—little, yappy, jumping on you, constantly frolicking out on the street. But Max hates dogs. He was scared of Davey and didn't like admitting it. Max was seventeen when Davey was run over. Max had recently gotten his license, started driving Papa's car. I never knew for sure he hit Davey. Told myself I was crazy. But the Robinsons froze us out after that, never invited us again to their annual summer barbecue or asked me to babysit, and I could intuit they shared a similar suspicion to mine.

I didn't tell Ginevra that story, of course. I told her one far more innocuous. In loyalty to my brother, I even painted over the hard edges of it, too.

Truth was, every once in a while, Max erupted in this scary, venomous way. And you didn't want to be in his striking path when he did. That's simply fact, a part of our childhood I don't dwell upon much and would gladly erase. In the days of Maxie'sTinyOne, Max seemed almost paralyzed by fear and stress, his reactions suspended. Like he was afraid to access them. But in later years, his anger unleashed, flowed free. I remember in middle school, I accidentally shuffled up his important science papers, and he released a torrent. His face shaded red, spit flying into my face, and he raised his hand like he was going to strike my face. For a moment I was truly terrified. He stopped himself, but I can still summon back that feeling—genuine fear of my brother.

If I sift through my memory, there are other incidents. Once I even thought Max was going to hit Papa! He was so angry, mouthing off, spouting vitriol about how Papa didn't really love him, and Max was the forgotten child. Papa's crime? Failing to make a Zhitomir salad for Max's birthday dinner. But Papa had worked double shifts the day before. Max could only see red, though. But most of those times are buried in cobwebs. Things I wrote off as one-offs, flukes. And I never actually witnessed my brother being violent to another person.

My chess set thrown in the lake, okay; but when it came down to it, Max wouldn't harm anyone. Especially not me or Caro. Right?

I stumble out of bed, throw on sweatpants and a tee. I need to see Caro. Talk this through. I don't care that it's the middle of the night. Maybe I'm being crazy, maybe I'm inventing scenarios that don't exist, but I have this awful feeling I'm missing a big puzzle piece. And that Caro can help me slot it into place.

I burst out my door, then still. It's quiet in the hall—just the low rumble of the train churning forward. Something about the vacant hall is eerie. No people, no stewards, even, only the cool, almost over-oxygenated air. The dead of night on the Orient Express. I rub my arms, realize goose bumps have sprouted all up and down.

I walk fast toward Caro's room.

CHAPTER THIRTY-NINE

Caroline

Y ou didn't even defend me when Rory accused me of taking the books."

"Huh?" Max is standing over me with a knife, its silvery jagged edges illuminated in the dim light. My heart thrashes in my chest. This can't be real, and yet it is. I shake my head—maybe I'm dreaming. That this is a dream is the only thing that would possibly reconcile it.

"The books. The author's books. *You* stole them. Not the Italians, not Nate—and not me. *You.*"

Beyoncé—of all things—is playing softly on Max's Bose speaker on the table, odd in this room that feels like I've been transported to the Turkish Grand Bazaar. Especially this song: "Cozy." The exact opposite of how I feel. I strain, struggling to release my arms twisted behind my back. Max tied my hands with something, his tie, I think.

He eyes me, then heads toward the door, his back to me. Now's my chance—I don't think, just lunge, aiming my shoulder toward the knife at his side.

He swivels and suddenly I feel something hard connect with my stomach. His fist. Excruciating pain follows, like he's bowling strikes, using me as his lane.

As I writhe on the floor, my vision blurs with the Lalique crystal panel formed into flowers, inlaid in the wooden wall. I am vaguely aware of the door clicking open, then closed.

"There." He's in my face now, dragging me up. His blue eyes meet mine—the ones I daydreamed about a thousand times, fixed on me from under the chuppah, as I walked toward him, into our beautiful new life. He deposits me on the bed face down with a thump. My body throbs against satin, my vision swallowed up in stars. It hurts, physical ache, but the shock of it all is far more acute.

Max hurting me, Max trying to hurt me.

"Yes," he tells me, panting. "We've been over this. I took the books. I didn't hide it from you, C. You know I couldn't have anything out there about Operation Kazuka."

"Exactly." I try to twist my body so I'm facing back up, have better access to air. I finally manage to roll over. "You were worried Rory would read it. That she'd realize something was off, if Ginevra knew that phrase. You probably should have been more careful when Ginevra was interviewing you. Because I'm not the one who let Operation Kazuka slip. *You* are."

Max shakes his head furiously. "Shut up about Operation Kazuka!"

But I can't keep quiet. Not anymore. "It's why I knew immediately you'd taken the books. After I read the Operation Kazuka line, and then they went mysteriously missing, it didn't take a rocket scientist to figure out who took them. And I wasn't surprised you'd kept a copy . . . had it like a trophy in your room after the hike—"

"It wasn't a trophy! You're twisting it all up. You know I needed a copy for legal, to get them involved. Ginevra's not gonna risk a lawsuit, not for one phrase that's meaningless to her. She'll take it out. Or change it. I don't care. I needed to make sure that in the meantime, Rory didn't see it. And cut the innocent act, C. Once you knew I'd kept a copy, you practically begged me for it."

I inch back from him. "I didn't beg you."

"You did. And you *lied*. Said you just wanted to see how it all turned out, make sure there were no other surprises. *Lies*. You were protecting your own ass. Yours and Nate's, and your sick affair."

I'm quiet, because on this point he's right.

"So it was justice that Rory caught you with the book. That she is sure it was you. It works." He nods, whispers to himself. "It's perfect."

It pinches my heart when I realize what he means. "This is insane!

Please, Max, think about all this logically. You won't get away with it. You know you won't!"

"There's no other way." He bites his lip, looks childlike for a second, sending ribbons of hope at my chest. But then his face reassumes its determined bent.

I scream, a rip-curdle sound, but as I do, the train bleats in tandem, letting off one of its shrill, screeching puffs through the smokestack as the locomotive rolls over the track. In a moment, Max is on me again, clamping my mouth, the knife blade against my biceps. He hisses, "I'll use it. Don't make me use it."

I'm crying now, into his hand, which he once used to hug me and hold me and weave into my own. I'm not tough like I wish I were. Like Rory would be, if she were in my shoes. Oh God, he really means it. He really wants to kill me. I understand that on a base level now, that he's not playing around, trying to get me to shut up for longer, like buying me off with those payments.

"If you scream again, no one will hear," Max murmurs into my ear. "Your room is next door, after all. Empty. I gave Francesco the night off. Just put the Do Not Disturb sign on my door. Next door on my other side's the supply closet. Everyone's sleeping anyhow."

"Ansel wouldn't want this! You know that. If you actually stopped and thought. And what do you think—you're going to kill me? Stab me? And get away with it?" I wriggle on the bed, trying to wrangle out of the tie binding my wrists. If only I can get my hands free, slip the whistle in my mouth . . .

"Honestly, I'd rather not stab you. And I won't unless you force me to." He walks to the window between the bed and table, fiddles with the catch.

What is he . . . ?

A horrifying thought seizes my brain.

"You don't mean, you can't possibly m—"

"You tried to kill yourself earlier at the Colosseum. No one will question when you return to finish the job."

A loud, long, primal roar rips out of me.

Max is on me again, his hand clamped on my mouth, the knife in front of my face.

"Shut up, or this will go very quickly," he hisses, his blue eyes blazing. "I said I don't want to kill you with a knife. But I will. Don't fucking test me again."

I go very still. "What—no—if you kill me with a—knife, you'll never be able to cover it up."

He shrugs. "I wouldn't need to cover it up. It would be self-defense. Pretty obvious."

"What—how would . . . ?"

"Well, you're embezzling from me. That's what Ginevra thinks. That's what Rory thinks, too—glad you told me all that. The money's in your account. The bank statements are crystal clear. Let's be honest, it's going to be so cut-and-dried that they're not going to look into who made the actual transfers. You came to *my* cabin. I threatened to expose you once and for all, and you attacked me with a knife. You tried to silence me. So . . . anything that happens after that, well, me fighting back—it can all be explained."

I'm sobbing now, thrashing. "No one will believe you," I manage through my tears. "No one will believe I came into your room and threatened you."

His eyes flicker toward the window again. "I think you're wrong. I think they will believe it, and I think you think so, too . . ." He nods his head at me, at the shriveling mess I've unraveled into. "But I told you—I don't actually want to stab you. And I won't, if you make this easier on yourself."

"No one will believe I threw myself out your window, either!" I choke out.

"Oh, c'mon, you know they will. I gave you my key after all."

"I forgot your key in my room. I knocked when I came over here."

"Oh." He shrugs. "That can be fixed. I can grab it from your room—after. So you came in with the key and . . ." He points beside me to the bed. I notice now it's rumpled; he must have been sleeping when I knocked—the silk damask throw pillow askew against the wall, the ivory brocade coverlet in a heap on the floor. His eyes shoot back in his sockets as he thinks. "You came in, slipped into bed with me. But you were still distraught, and while I was sleeping . . ."

My breath stalls in my throat. "Please—and you didn't hear?"

"Maybe I did hear, and I tried to stop you, but you were already—" He makes a slash at his throat, and I gasp. He frowns. "Or if it's too farfetched that you killed yourself in my room, then they'll have to believe you did it in yours." He dangles my key—the one to my room, that I brought into his. He turns it in loops on his forefinger. "After, I'll go to your room and open your window."

I still at the plausibility of all the stories he's weaving, stories that, in a chilling way, feel like they could somehow pass muster. "My DNA is all over your room. And your DNA is all over me."

"Well, you came over before, I guess. I left you my key. Everyone knows you nearly jumped—you needed soothing. Oh, this is hard for me, too, C! This sucks. It's all your fault! You're the one pushing me to this! Don't you see it, C? Don't you see that you're responsible for all of it!"

His face is puce with rage as he reaches for me again. I wiggle back, try to burrow into myself. He's right. They're going to think I jumped. *Rory* is going to think I jumped. And she's going to be left behind . . . all alone . . . with her brother. A monster. My eyes fill with fresh tears at the thought of Rory—dealing with me dead. Believing I killed myself because I'd betrayed her and betrayed Max. I did betray her is the thing. The tears clog my throat, my nose, obstructing my breath. I did betray her, and all I want is to make it up to her. Explain how it happened . . . the stress I've been dealing with . . .

Rory—she's my best friend. My soul sister. The thought of never see- ing her again pries me apart, bone by bone.

"Please don't, Max!" I try to swipe my cheek against my shoulder, but the tears keep falling, sliding. "Please don't do this. I love you. We'll figure this out. I won't say anything to anyone! Just . . . please—"

"Own your part in this, C!" His breath tunnels at my face, his eyes still fiery. "You didn't mind when I paid off your debts. You didn't mind pocketing my bribes. But when it came to protecting me, you were out so fast you—"

"I didn't *take* your bribes!"

"Oh? You're telling me you didn't take the money that went into your account every month, ever since you figured out Operation Kazuka?"

"What was I supposed to do?" I hear myself pleading. "I couldn't figure out how to pay it back. How to stop it from entering my account. I told you a million times I didn't want it!"

"Didn't stop you from buying that panther ring." My heart settles dully in its cavity. Because on that point, he's right.

"I'm weak," I whisper. "I've made mistakes. But you have, too. And I swear, Max. I didn't want the money. I only kept it to give you more time. To give Ansel more time. I only kept it because it kept appearing in my account, and how was I supposed to send it back?"

He laughs bitterly. "You could have refused. Told me you didn't need bribes to keep my confidences."

"Your confidences? Please." Anger is a geyser now up my throat. "You're the one responsible for this! Stop trying to shift the blame to *me*! Can't you see that you're hurting people? That this can't be right, if you think you have to hurt me to get where you want to go? You can still stop, Max! It's not too late."

"It *is* too late," he says in a cold decisive way that makes my chest rigid with fear. He hefts me up and clamps his hand over my mouth once again. He switches off the speakers, so even Beyoncé's muted, comforting voice departs, leaving me all alone with him. I scream into his palm, trying to bite him but not managing to, and all I can hear is my heartbeat in my ears and the thrash of my body, trying so hard, but so unsuccessfully, to whip out of his grip.

Suddenly I feel my body shift in the air, horizontal, and the tie he's used to bind my wrists spring free. Then there's a sudden burst of air.

I'm startled as it gusts into my face—and even more so as my torso crushes on the sill below and I am shoved forward, straight out into the black night's abyss.

CHAPTER FORTY

Rory

The first thing I notice is Caro's door open an inch. My mind tumbles over why. A couple filters down the hall, black suiting and a swingy pink dress, bowled over laughing, almost impossibly carefree. Gripped by foreboding, I manage to step back, allow them berth to pass. They do, stumbling down the hall, eventually disappearing from sight.

Then I burst into Caro's room. I don't know what I'm expecting to find but it's decidedly not this. Nothing neat and orderly; it's all in peak disarray. Suitcase upturned, clothes exploded around. A pink lace thong is caught on a lampshade. The sheets are rumpled, the covers a heap on the parquet, a toothpaste glob melded to the porcelain sink. It even smells musty, like a sealed space where a sick person has convalesced.

"Caro?" I call, but it's immediately obvious she's not here. It's not my first rodeo; I know there's nowhere in this tiny space a person could hide.

I spin around slowly in the room, my mind whirling but not gripping on to anything substantial. Spinning stories, though—Caro on the Colosseum wall, appearing poised to jump. And now she's disappeared, in the middle of the night.

Where could she possibly be?

Suddenly, the train jolts, and I stagger, nearly tip over. We're twisting around the mountains, it looks like, as I watch the countryside whoosh by, the moonlight an eerie spotlight on the abandoned industrial buildings we're streaming past. My heart drums my ears, my brain working frantically—surfacing with diddly squat—when I hear a strange noise.

At first, I think it's the air conditioner, or generator. Except it's not a steady rumble, but a faint sort of bashing. Then I hear—I think—a screeching noise.

I hold my breath. Listen again, hard. Nothing.

I walk the length of the room, squatting on the floor, staring up at the ceiling. Then I walk back again, the journey completed in a couple of terse steps.

What in . . . ?

I hear the screeching again, and suddenly, buoyed by instinct alone, I press my face against the window. Something flashes in my vision. An arm.

It's gone as fast as it came, but I swear it was an arm.

I fumble with the window, manage to shove it open. When I peer to the left, in the direction of what I think I saw, I am greeted by a sight more horrifying, more incomprehensible, than anything I've ever witnessed.

It's Caro, propped halfway out of the window next door, her eyes wild, pooling sheer terror, her fingers propping a silver whistle in her mouth, as she blows on it wildly.

Her eyes register me—surprise, relief? The whistle detaches from her mouth.

"Caro, hang on! Just hang on!"

I anchor my lower half against the wall and reach out to grab her. But our hands barely brush, fail to connect. She's thrashing—thrashing against something.

Against someone.

When her eyes connect with mine, I am staggered that inside them isn't simply a plea. She mumbles something, but I can only read her lips.

I'm sorry.

That's what, incomprehensibly, I think she says.

And then she's gone, writhing, back partway into the neighboring cabin.

Max's cabin.

I retreat inside, panting, adrenaline and fear surging through me.

Max is trying to kill her.

It hits me with a thud; the whole world collapses on my chest. There's no other explanation for what I just witnessed. Maybe it has to do with Hippoheal . . . or . . . there isn't time to sift for the why.

My eyes dart around. Without much thought, operating on cold, clear instinct, I grab the hefty crystal ice bucket from the bar. Then I spot a key on the floor by the door. I grab it and read the insignia: The Istanbul Suite.

Right. I remember. Earlier, Max gave Caro his key. In case she needed him . . .

I duck out the door, feeling almost robotic. But strangely, scarily alert.

I slowly turn the key to my brother's suite, aware only of my racing heartbeat and the frozen, eerie silence.

Then a scream cuts the stillness.

No. No, no, no, no. no. NO.

The lock gives itself to my key. I open the door. Step inside.

CHAPTER FORTY-ONE

Rory

It's the stuff of sheer nightmares: My brother's back to me, trying to shove my best friend out the window. Caro's legs flailing in the air—unmistakably her legs. Long, blindingly white, with the birthmark in the shape of a crescent moon in the place her butt meets her thighs, visible beneath her silk shorts riding up her hips. One of her legs is thrashing, trying to kick back at Max, and one is fumbling to anchor the top of her foot against the windowsill.

"This is all your fault, C! You brought this on yourself. And this isn't a fight you have any chance of winning. Not anymore."

"No, don't!" But my plea emerges faintly—barely audible in the backdrop of their battle. "Max! Please. Max, stop. . . ."

My brother doesn't turn. Instead, I watch him pry Caro's foot from the windowsill.

I walk closer toward them. Walk the plank, as Caro's legs stop their jerking. Become unnervingly still.

I want to say it louder, demand that Max stop, again—but what if he doesn't? What if he gives Caro one last shove? What if he turns on me . . . ?

I need to knock my brother out, incapacitate him until help can arrive.

My brain gives up on thought, fires up my arms, propels them up, up, up. An utterly horrifying crack follows—not loud. You'd think loud.

I lunge for Caro's hips, wrench her back inside with superhuman strength.

A scream. It takes a beat before I realize it's mine. I stare in horror at the crystal ice bucket skidding across the floor.

Covered in blood.

CHAPTER FORTY-TWO

Ginevra

On an ordinary night, Ginevra found sleep uncooperative—but on the Orient Express, with the culmination of long-spun plans in sight, sleep was wholly elusive. Ginevra exited the Venice Suite, began to roam the corridors. It was a bit risky; she could run into any of the four, but she thought not. The Fab Four, as she'd begun calling them to herself, in almost singsong glee, imagining at each moment of their trip where they'd be, eating what delectable bites, in what sublime settings, on her perfect itinerary. She smiled. They'd be sleeping now, and at this point, Ginevra supposed, even if she saw them, even Rory or Max, she could proffer an excuse. Say all would be clear tomorrow.

Or, actually—today! In Positano.

So Ginevra swished down the hall in her floor-length plum silk robe with feather trim on the sleeves, feeling almost—nearly—strangely—happy. Almost, as close as she'd ever felt, to beautiful.

It had to be said: The robe was absurd attire. But if you couldn't jaunt around the Orient Express in a feathered silk robe, then where, really, could you? One should suck out the marrow, delight when it was possible to do so. Because life could be tragic and crushing, so why not wear a ridiculous robe when you were able, if it gave you small pleasure?

Before she'd left her suite, Ginevra had given herself a rare, thorough appraisal in the bathroom mirror. And for once, she hadn't hated what she'd seen. Maybe it was the end of this journey in sight—the tantalizing jewels that tomorrow held, the culmination of her long, fraught plans.

Or maybe it was simply that, at last, Ginevra had achieved the peace and equanimity of Sophia Loren that she'd long desired. In a recent interview, Sophia had talked of, inexplicably, how she'd never actually liked her looks. But the part Ginevra could relate to—strive to relate to, at least—was that when Sophia looked in the mirror, she no longer saw her negative aspects, only her good ones. Because—*It's about what you do with your life, isn't it?*

Easy to say you no longer saw negative in the mirror when you were Sophia Loren, staring at your stunning self, wasn't it?

But still, Ginevra found wisdom and even solace in the quote. Because somehow, staring into her own eyes, Ginevra could see her goodness, her striving. She could have given up long ago, folded her hand. Maybe she had in some ways, but she hadn't fully. Here she was, still fighting, still loving, or trying to, after everything.

And now—finally—Rory and Max were as far as a stone's throw, and the potential of joy, of real, true, unadulterated joy, was nearly as close as her next breath.

Yes, Ginevra was positively blooming, full of little seedlings about to sprout into a veritable garden, when she passed the Istanbul Suite. Ever since she'd boarded the train in Rome, rendezvoused with Gabriele, settled into her prebooked Venice Suite, the specter of the Istanbul Suite had loomed in her mind. She hadn't dared stroll past it, not in daylight, at least.

Her whole self was still one great smile when she grasped that something was awry.

The door was ajar.

She stopped a bit past the door, mystified. Then she heard it—cries. Feral cries.

Her heart stilled in her chest. She turned back, made for the door, her chest twitching with something cold and unfamiliar . . . yet also familiar. . . .

After all, Ginevra Ex had an instinct for tragedy. She cracked open the door, feeling as though she were opening her own coffin. Preparing to slip inside.

She gasped at the scene: wind gusting through an open window, and two hysterical women cradling one motionless man. His eyes were closed, but his head looked strange. It took Ginevra a moment to decipher why. His dark hair was matted, all wet and crimson.

"No," she croaked, and felt herself crumple to the floor.

CHAPTER FORTY-THREE

Ginevra

That Afternoon

The car was ice cold, its speed excruciating slow as they navigated Viale Pasitea.

"Your villa will have everything you need. We were lucky to . . ." Gabriele stopped; the sentence toppled off a cliff.

Lucky. No. No luck in any of it.

Ginevra knew Gabriele had been about to say they were lucky to find the villa at such short notice. That it was high season. Positano was booked. Ginevra had prebooked rooms at Le Sirenuse for everyone, but Orsola was staying there.

No, Ginevra couldn't face Orsola yet. . . .

Ginevra stifled a sob. Images filled her head—Max on the ground, desperately trying to wake him, shake him, rouse him back to life. The train grinding to a halt. Medics, police. A stretcher. A sheet over his body, then inched up over his face. Like he never was.

Like he'd never even existed at all.

Ginevra's knee knocked against Rory's as they sailed over a bump. She looked at the girl, really looked at her, managed to focus upon something outside her own grief. The girl was motionless, staring straight ahead.

"Ginevra?"

"Yes?"

"Are you my birth mother?"

Rory still stared straight ahead, out beyond the window onto the fancy shops lining the one-way street, the charming hotels with balconies brimming with flowerpots, the tables spilling out of the restaurants at which Ginevra had dined—each a pleasant memory, posing for photos with the chefs, photos that now bedecked walls.

Ginevra had imagined showing them proudly to Rory, to Max. Ginevra's second home, this town. She'd been coming to Positano for decades, ever since Orsola moved from Rome.

"No," Ginevra finally said. "I'm not your birth mother."

Rory nodded. Caro rubbed Rory's shoulder with her long, pale, aristocratic fingers. On Rory's other side, Nate kissed the top of Rory's head and gave a pained exhale.

"So then . . . your sister is my birth mother, isn't she? Orsola?"

Ginevra gasped. "How do you know about Orsola?"

"I just . . . I just do."

Ginevra swallowed hard. "No," she finally managed. "Orsola isn't your birth mother, either."

"What . . . I don't get it. . . . I don't understand—"

"It's Max," Ginevra finally said, and the truth of it briefly stunted her of breath. "I'll tell you. I'll tell you everything you want to know, everything you deserve to know. When we can sit and talk properly. When we've had time to . . ." *Process things*, was what she'd been about to say. But how could something this horrific—this final—ever be processed?

Rory finally turned to Ginevra, gazed at her with startled green eyes. "Max?"

"Yes." Ginevra instructed her neck to bob her head. "Yes. I am Max's mother."

Ginevra's lungs gasped for air. "Max is—was—my son."

CHAPTER FORTY-FOUR

Caroline

Two Days Later

I'm out on the terrace, staring into nothingness. Or not nothingness, exactly, because I'm vaguely aware of the pergola woven in greenery, the infinite Gulf of Salerno below, lapping against craggy cliffs, and the cascade of pastel-hued houses baked into the mountains, all punctured by staircases hewn from ancient stone that weave up from the sea.

Not that I've climbed them. Nor left Villa Angelina at all. None of us have. It's been all I can do to force myself to eat. To convince Rory to, as well. And to get through all the police business . . . giving statements . . . reliving that horrific night . . .

So far the board of Hippoheal has held off on all-out grilling me, but they're aware now of Max's fraud—the vaccine causing harm. I've had to fend off investors, board members, and employees—all expressing cursory condolences for Max's death and then fiendish in their desire to discuss, to try to predict how all this is going to crash down on their shoulders.

I've buried my phone in my bedside drawer. There will be recriminations, but for now I'm too heartbroken. Too angry—at myself. Coming down from the worst night of my life.

Still, Villa Angelina is certainly not an awful place to recover from the man you loved trying to murder you. To grieve his death. To participate in all the reconstructive exercises your mind has ordered up, rummaging through all the ways you should have done things differently.

Suddenly a sound filters toward my ears, and my chest roils with familiar fear. It takes a few moments for me to register what the sound is—the door off the terrace sliding open.

And what it's not—Max opening a window to shove me out of a moving train.

Footsteps against stone. Then Rory lowers onto the plush taupe cushions beside me.

"How'd you sleep?" I reach over to stroke her hand. When she doesn't react, I linger for a few beats, then retract my hand, aware at how my skin snaps back when it detaches from hers.

"Didn't," she finally says. "You?"

"Not much, either."

"Maybe we can have a sleepover tonight."

"Yeah? You hate sleepovers. Like in the same bed?"

She bites her lip. "Every time I close my eyes, I see him, C. Just his back. I see myself walking toward him with that ice bucket. It was so heavy. . . ."

"I know," I whisper. I want to say more: *Thank you for saving my life.*

I'm so sorry.

I wish it had been me.

It sickens me, that last thought swishing in my head. Because as I probe it, I see I don't actually mean it. It's my natural instinct, I suppose, to minimize myself to make it easier for someone else. Like, for Max. I nearly subsumed myself entirely to conceal all his lies. And struggling for my life out that window, I realized I want to be alive. I want it desperately.

Rory sweeps her hand roughly through her hair. "I don't know how I'm going to live with what I did, C," she finally says.

"What you did was protect me. What you did was save me."

"But I shouldn't have hit him so hard. And maybe if I'd have . . . called out louder. Tried to convince him—"

"No. He could have turned on you, too. The knife—he had it in his pocket still. We don't know what more Max was capable of."

"We don't know." Rory stares out at the terra-cotta planters brimming with rosemary. "That's the thing. We don't know. We don't know if he would have seen sense. If I could have convinced him . . ."

"We never know, *cara mia*," says another voice from afar, amid another bout of glass door scraping open. "That's the strange and cruel thing of life. We never know how it would have gone if we'd done one tiny thing differently."

I swivel to see Ginevra in ratty purple sweats, her purple-red hair a wild mop. I don't know what I expected of the famous author mourning—maybe head to toe in black, with a black lace veil shrouding her face, and even black Jackie O sunglasses. Nope. She looks terrifically shabby and utterly sad. She sinks down into a chair on the other side of Rory, stares listlessly at a lemon tree. She dabs at her eyes with a handkerchief.

"Yes, it's what I deserve, I suppose. To never know. What a purgatory. I'll blame myself for the rest of my life. I don't think I'll ever be able not to." Rory says it almost violently, like she's trying to convince Ginevra of this, to make it easier on Ginevra somehow.

I hold my breath, because I'm not sure which way this will go, how the author will react. We haven't much seen Ginevra in the past couple of days, what with the police having endless questions, and the villa being cavernous, each of us retreating into our rooms, our own shock and grief. But Max was Ginevra's biological son. It's still an enormity to process. And we haven't yet gotten the whole story, all the hows and whys.

Still, I've gleaned from our limited interactions that the author cares about Rory, but nonetheless, strictly speaking, Rory *is* the one who killed her son with a crystal ice bucket. Defending me.

So I'm not so sure that the author doesn't blame Rory—and me. That she's not here wishing it were one or both of us who died in his stead.

Which is why I'm surprised—shocked, really—when Ginevra says, "You are not to blame, Rory. You are not to blame one bit. Please promise me you won't blame yourself. Stop it right *now*."

For a few long moments, there is only the tweet of a few magpies. They chirp and dance on the magenta bougainvillea that climbs the pillars pinning down the terrace.

"I killed him," Rory says. "I—"

"You're wrong. You are very, very wrong," Ginevra says, and for a terrible beat I am certain she is going to correct Rory by saying that *I* killed him. That I should have exposed his wrongdoing earlier, and by failing to do so, I catalyzed everything that followed.

She'd be fair to say so, I think, for the billionth time since that night.

But then Ginevra says, "I killed Max." Her voice dribbles over his name, fades into air that suddenly hangs stiflingly thick. "I killed my son, and let that be the end of it. I arranged it all—this trip on the Orient Express for you four. I told you, Rory, that Caroline was embezzling from Max. I didn't contemplate—it didn't occur to me—that those payments could be something else entirely. I had good intentions, it can be said. Yes, I did."

Her face crumples in. "But good intentions mean nothing. *Non tutte le ciambelle riescono col buco.* Not every doughnut turns out with a hole, you know?"

"No." I have no clue what that means.

"Not everything turns out as planned. But I suppose even that is absolving myself of responsibility. It's just—sometimes things go horribly awry. More than sometimes. In my case, often. That is what I have learned in a life that has been long and difficult. I wanted everything! I wanted this trip to be perfect. I wanted to make amends, to meet my son, to meet you, Rory. I've thought of you as my daughter your entire life. I know it sounds crazy, but I have."

"I don't understand," Rory whispers.

"Yes." Ginevra nods. "Well, you wouldn't. I will tell you. There is another saying we have that keeps running through my mind. *Chi troppo vuole nulla stringe.* You don't know what it means, do you?"

"*Grasp all, lose all.*" Ginevra's voice crackles with emotion. "I wanted it all. And so I have lost it all. This has been the theme of my whole life. I don't know why I thought it would be any different this time."

"I still don't understand," Rory says.

"No. Well, I suppose it's time that I tell you." Ginevra gazes back toward the screen door. "Perhaps you'd like to find Nate, have him here for this? Perhaps Caroline can get him."

"Does the story involve Nate?" I ask.

"No. I just thought Rory might want his support. For him to . . . do the things men do. You know, when they love a girl."

I find the statement odd, the sentiment, too. It's like Ginevra is talking in theory about men, without having ever experienced one. Although maybe, on reflection, she hasn't. I did a little poking around about Ginevra

Ex when we did our interviews. She's never been linked to anyone. No partner, no romance, as far as I could discern.

"No," Rory says. "No. We don't need to get Nate. I have Caro here." Her eyes flitter over at me, and I nod, feel my chin tremble.

Maybe Rory doesn't hate me. Maybe—just maybe—there is a chance she can forgive me, for that horrible night with Nate. For how badly I fucked everything up when I found out about Max's fraudulent vaccine— for keeping the information to myself this whole year. For how fighting for my life ultimately cost Max his.

Ginevra nods. "Okay, so you are ready, then, Rory? The story I want to tell you goes pretty far back. To Moscow, 1987."

"You knew my father in Moscow?" Rory's eyes widen, mirroring my own surprise.

"*Sì*. I met Anatoly—Ansel now—in Moscow. And my sister met him, too. My twin sister. Orsola."

"She lives here, doesn't she?" Rory asks. "In Positano. That was our lunch date? I mean, the person we were supposed to meet at Le Sirenuse?"

"Yes. So you figured it . . . yes. We were all going to meet at Le Sirenuse. I was going to tell you and Max everything. That was my plan. Best-laid plans, eh?" Ginevra grimaces. "You've puzzled it all out, then, Rory, have you?"

"Not really. That's all I really know. And Orsola, does she know what happened, then?"

"No." Ginevra shuts her eyes, clamps down on her lip with her teeth. "She doesn't know yet. . . ."

"About Max?" I don't know why I'm surprised—I know nothing about this Orsola—but it's been all over the press. "Doesn't she watch the news?"

Ginevra flutters her eyes open. "My sister? No. No, that's not necessarily . . . no, Orsola doesn't much care for the news. I just told her there was a delay with the train. She won't have heard yet. And I'll have to tell her. But I needed to be alone with it first. I still can't . . . It's difficult to . . ."

No one speaks for a while. Then Rory asks, "Will Orsola be sad? I mean, about Max . . ."

"Yes. She will be devastated. You see, Max was as much her child as he was mine."

The statement snags on my brain, doesn't amount to much sense. After all, why have twin sisters across the world been so invested in Max's life—and in Rory's?

"I don't understand," Rory says, echoing my thoughts.

"Yes. I will tell you everything now, and then you can judge it all for yourself."

"I don't want to judge you," Rory whispers. "I just want the truth."

"Well, the truth you shall have. And trust me, Rory. You will judge me. As well you should. I deserve all the judgment in the world. And an eternity more."

CHAPTER FORTY-FIVE

Ginevra

Moscow, 1980s

Ginevra folded a dress and placed it inside her suitcase with the same listless fatigue that had pervaded the latter part of her trip to Moscow—ever since Orsola had informed Ginevra that she was in love with a Soviet Jew named Anatoly Aronov.

And in the days following the revelation, Ginevra felt as if in her sister's eyes, in her moony mannerisms, Ginevra was reading a book she wanted to burn: a flip-book of her sister falling in love, and feeling deeply loved in return.

Ginevra's eyes skittered over the shabby, ornate room: the turquoise, orange, and cream carpet that clashed perplexingly with the paisley fabric of the couch; the minibar, empty because apparently the Metropol hadn't yet obtained the import license it required to bring in foreign-made soft drinks and the like; and then beyond the bed that Orsola and Ginevra shared, the window onto Red Square, where it was currently drizzling.

According to weather reports, it was meant to rain all week.

Ginevra felt shame at the feeling that arose in her: satisfaction that tomorrow, on Orsola's last day of touring, she wouldn't be able to skip down the streets with Anatoly. They'd have to live the last keynotes of their love with an umbrella over their heads.

Although there was something romantic about huddling together beneath an umbrella, wasn't there?

A desolate feeling pervaded Ginevra that not only did she feel heart-broken, but she envied others their joy. What had she thought after all, that a few hours spent with Anatoly Aronov had erased her meager looks, her quiet, unassuming self? Had transmuted her to a woman worthy of great love? Could light a candle compared to her vivacious, beautiful sister?

No, that was the worst thing of all. That ever since Ginevra had over-heard that conversation between her father and sister, ever since she'd realized she was the cause of her mother's death, probably even earlier in her life still, she'd never felt worthy of great love. More than that—she'd known in some deep, awful pit inside herself that she'd never ascend to experience the love others took for granted. Or if she did, it would be a love with its conclusion akin to Romeo and Juliet—love subsumed by tragedy. That was what Ginevra had felt since she was a little girl, a foun-dation of tragedy that underpinned her existence. The polluted soil feed-ing her. But God wasn't available for replanting. This was the soil she got. Best be happy with it, try to create a garden from the weeds.

Sometimes it was really hard, though, to exist in a garden without flowers.

Through the window, the rain sloshing down the panes, Ginevra could glimpse all the tour groups queuing to see old man Lenin em-balmed in his tomb. Ginevra had left her tour early, feigning illness again, which ever since Orsola's revelation about falling in love with Anatoly, felt acutely accurate. Ginevra was ill—her heart throbbed, excruciating pain. Today the group had gone outside Moscow, to Zvenigorod, a quaint country town, but all Ginevra had wanted was to escape.

Not till now, back at the hotel, did she realize she only ever wanted to escape the borders of herself. An impossible thing.

She drew aside the gold brocade draperies shrouding a part of the window. As a consequence of moving the draperies, dust stormed her nostrils. She coughed, sighed a long, hollow sigh, staring out at all the people—even lovers down there in the drizzling rain, kissing beneath canopies. It was the USSR, gloomy and desolate, but still people loved and were loved in return.

Not Ginevra.

She drew the draperies back so she didn't have to stare out again into everything she was missing. Then she sat on the bed and was feeling profoundly sorry for herself when a knock sounded on the door.

Ginevra turned, confused. Orsola was with their father today, which meant she spent the day three floors below in his room, shuttling him to meals, sometimes ducking out with him to a café or a local sight if he felt up to it. Ginevra knew the routine because she did it herself every other day this trip. But perhaps Orsola had forgotten something, a raincoat or galoshes.

Ginevra went to the door, flung it open, expecting to see her sister.

But her sister was not standing in the entry. Instead it was the last person her mind could have conjured up.

It was Anatoly Aronov.

He was dressed like a chef, with a white coat and a tall white hat. Rain droplets clung to his long eyelashes.

"What are you doing here?" she stammered.

He removed his cap and fixed his blue eyes on hers. "I had to sneak in. They are listening." He pointed a finger toward the ceiling, his eyes rotating up.

"What? I don't understand. I—"

"The rooms are bugged. And I'm not exactly beloved by the KGB, let's put it that way." He spoke softly, but he paired the terrifying statement with a smile. A smile like his showing up here wasn't the craziest thing in the world. Like he expected her to be joyful. To welcome him in.

Ginevra didn't understand. She didn't understand anything at all. Until suddenly, she did.

Anatoly thought she was Orsola.

He'd come for Orsola.

"Can I come in?" he whispered. "I paid off the woman by the elevator." He was referring to the rigid, unsmiling woman at her vigilant post, meant to keep tabs on the tourists on the floor. A KGB informant—a *stukach*. Ginevra had also paid her off numerous times. "I promise I have nothing indecent on my mind. Only seeing you. But we shouldn't talk. Just—I know you're leaving in two days. I wanted to see you."

Right. If Ginevra had any doubt at all, that confirmed it. She hadn't told Anatoly she was leaving in two days. Orsola must have informed him. Which made sense, of course. Orsola and Anatoly were in love. Ginevra should be flattered, even, that this spectacular man had mistaken her for her sister, on cursory glance.

Ginevra was suddenly grateful she'd switched off the lights, drawn the drapes, that there was no sun to torch her features, make the slants of her face apparent where Orsola's were delicate curves.

She should tell him she wasn't the twin he thought she was.

But as he entered the room, shedding his chef's coat, revealing a pale-blue button-up with a hint of chest hair sprouting out atop, she couldn't breathe—let alone speak.

He came over to her, tipped her chin up so her eyes met his. "We can't talk, but can you read what I'm saying to you in my eyes?"

His touch sent electricity down her bones.

She managed a slight nod. She didn't say it was so dark that she could barely see his face, that shadows were obscuring it. Then before a thought, an analysis, a preliminary recrimination, could invade her brain, his lips met hers, and her brain became entirely beside the point. Her heart was the conductor of this symphony; and as they kissed, her heart wound itself into a frenzy. It wanted more and more and more.

Ginevra's fingers went to the buttons of Anatoly's shirt and began to undo them. It wasn't an act of courage, of daring—rather, it felt as natural as breathing. The next obvious step.

He pulled back. "Are you sure? I didn't come here expecting—"

"I'm sure," she said loudly, assuredly—then stepped back. Maybe he didn't want this? Maybe he'd realized who she was?

But he just smiled, pulled her back to him, and she returned to the work of unbuttoning. His hands danced down to her hips. He hooked his fingers beneath her waistband, his touch like honey on her skin.

"You are beautiful," he whispered.

Suddenly she knew what it was like to be a silk dress, satin sheets. Sophia Loren.

What it was like to be Orsola.

Coveted. Comfortable. Relaxed in the knowledge that you are desired. That you will eternally be desired.

A twinge of remorse. How horrible a person was she, to take this from her sister?

Horrible, maybe, but for once, Ginevra wanted the best. Wanted it all. Wanted Anatoly.

They undressed each other, fell onto the bed, and Ginevra lost all sense of time and even who she was. She *could* have been Orsola. She could have been anyone, really, even Gandhi or God. And the only thing she knew was that this couldn't be wrong.

That she'd willingly live with the consequences for the rest of her life. No matter what they would be.

An hour later, when Anatoly left, making her promise to come see him at the synagogue the next day, Ginevra lay by herself on the rumpled sheets. She could still feel him on her skin, smell him on the pillowcase, and she tried to savor it all as the world crashed back down around her. As her skin sprang back to its solitary self, eliminating the indent of his finger pads, accustomed again to an existence without his touch.

She was a fool. That's what she was. As common as the next silly girl lusting after the boy she'd never get to have.

But worse. To merely think herself silly was minimizing the evil of what she'd done. Ginevra had deliberately slept with the man her sister loved. She'd misled him. A word floated into her mind: *rape*. Wasn't it as bad as rape, what she'd done?

She was a horrible, jealous sister. She'd acted spontaneously, reprehensibly. Sometimes she did. Usually she was restrained, but then in rare frenzied fits, she couldn't help herself. Like Orsola's dress—the lemon-print one Orsola had been so excited to wear in Moscow. Orsola didn't know it, of course, but Ginevra was responsible for its going missing. Orsola had saved her money for it, looked so lovely and glowing and curvy, courting the attention of every eyeball around. And Ginevra hadn't been able to stand it—the flagrant contrast between her sister's charmed life and Ginevra's own inadequate one. In a fit of rage, she'd pilfered Orsola's dress, taken scissors to its silky fabric, then buried the shreds in a garbage bin blocks from home. After, on her walk back, Ginevra had felt like the most grotesque person on the face of the earth.

Now Ginevra shivered, held herself, shaking, choking on her own tears. Feeling like that grotesque person all over again. And yet, she still couldn't fathom the consequences.

How high a price she'd have to pay.

CHAPTER FORTY-SIX

Rory

Clanging church bells cut the silence that is thick with Ginevra's revelations.

Even though I've just heard about my father and Ginevra—about their intimate moments, about the author's incomprehensible betrayal of her sister, of my father—I can't help but feel sorry for Ginevra. I know that feeling, after all, when your skin longs for its pair, hates to return to its solitary self.

I press my feet into the swirly Majolica tiles, cool under my soles. "That's not the end of the story, though, is it?" I finally ask Ginevra.

"No. No, it—"

"You were pregnant." It comes out harsher than I intend. I knew it already, of course, but I didn't know the how, and now I'm finding it difficult to restrain myself. My grief over Max is pooling, overtaking things. My anger—at my brother, but also at myself. And now I have a new target, a new person to blame for all of our misfortunes: Ginevra. The person who sent me on this twisted journey. Who has played us all like pawns on her chessboard.

"Yes," Ginevra says, not meeting my gaze.

"What happened next?" I feel Caro put a hand on my mine, but her touch burns. I flinch, pull my hand back to my own lap, can tell without glancing over that Caro's hurt, but I think it's more. There's something needy in touch—I witnessed it in Ginevra's story; I understand it in my own. And right now, I can't contend with anyone else's needs. I can only try, however imperfectly, to satisfy my own.

Now I need the truth.

Ginevra sighs and something slips over her face. Something impenetrable that I realize I've seen in Papa's eyes, too—back before Alzheimer's, when on the rare occasion an innocuous trigger would catapult him back into his past.

"I didn't see Anatoly after we slept together. In fact, I never saw him again. The next day, Orsola went out on her tour. I stayed with Papa. I knew she'd go to see Anatoly. Of course—our last day in the city. I worried—no, *worried* is the wrong word. I was terrified out of my mind that my sister would figure out what I'd done. That she'd tell my father, too. That Anatoly would make a reference to sex, that he'd touch Orsola in an illustrative way. When she met us for dinner, though, she was all smiles. I didn't dare ask her a thing. Not until the airplane—not until I could see the clouds. I asked her if she was sad to leave Anatoly, and she said that yes, she was, but we were going to get him an invitation to leave, and soon he'd join her in Rome.

"Then my sister said, *You're awfully interested in Anatoly, Ginevra. Don't tell me you developed a bit of a crush on him.*"

"But she was joking," I say. "She didn't really mean it?"

"Oh, she meant it. But she was joking in the way that she knew it wasn't reciprocated. So she could smile about it. Because he did not reciprocate my feelings." Ginevra shakes her head ruefully. "Obviously."

I nod. Sentences form on my tongue, hang unspoken in midair. *That must have been so hard for you to have pretended to be your sister to sleep with him. But even more so, it must have been so hard to part from him—to never get to say goodbye, to remember his kisses and his embrace, and know that part of life was over.*

I don't say it, though. I'm not so generous, I suppose, because I can't just see Ginevra as a misguided girl. She slept with my father, pretending to be the woman he loved. I am not an uninterested party.

But still, I remember what it felt like when Nate broke off our engagement. How I didn't shower for days because I wanted to keep the scent of him on my skin.

"What did Ansel mean, about the KGB listening in?" Caro asks.

"Oh." Ginevra shrugs. "He was a Jew and a bit of a troublemaker. His place was ransacked once by KGB agents, looking for what they called Zionist materials. He dressed as a chef to come up to my room because he didn't want to be identified. And they *were* listening; they did bug hotel rooms of foreigners in those days. And citizens could be rounded up for manufactured infractions. Maybe it seems like he was being overcautious, but when you saw your friends and family shuttled off to Siberia, imprisoned in the basements of Lubyanka—well, it paid to be safe."

Ginevra pauses. "I've often wondered if that day would have gone differently if he hadn't been so worried about the listening ears. Because when language can't be resorted to for communication, bodies become the vehicles."

She hangs her head. "Or maybe that was just my excuse. Trust me, I'm not looking for absolution, least of all from you, Rory."

"I can't give it, anyway." I manage a half smile. "It's my father you deluded. And I still don't know the rest. When you realized you were pregnant . . ."

"Yes. Well, it wasn't even a month later that I knew. The signs were immediate. Suddenly meat made me sick. The sight of raw chicken—the smell—sent me rushing for the toilet bowl. I lay awake at night, feeling paralyzed, although to be honest, I wasn't surprised. I deserved this. This was my punishment for what I'd done. I thought about aborting the baby, finding some back-alley way, but every time I contemplated it was a sucker punch. I had loved Anatoly—for me it had been real. The realest love I'd ever known. He hadn't reciprocated it, no. And our baby was born of my deceit. I couldn't get around those facts, but still, that baby was born of love, too. Mine. And Anatoly's—he'd told me in one of our early conversations that he dreamed of being a father."

"How did you tell Orsola?" I ask, feeling sick imagining it, that scared girl, hating that sympathy is bubbling in me for Ginevra, even though she brought it all upon herself.

"Well." Ginevra peels a chunk of purple-red hair from her face and tucks it behind a wilted ear. "Orsola realized something was off with me. There was a little twinly intuition, I suppose. She asked if I was sick, and I said that, in a measure, I was. We were at dinner with my father. I'd made amatriciana. I knew I couldn't hide it. I was going to have this baby. I hadn't yet thought beyond that, but I knew in my soul, I had to have this baby. It all spilled out—fast. I couldn't look them in their eyes. I remember the shock. The anger. The disbelief."

"Orsola?" I ask. "She must—"

"Orsola was silent." Ginevra swallows hard. "My father was the one blowing up. I'd never seen him so angry. He was Mount Vesuvius. And all of a sudden, he started clutching his chest. The left side."

"No." I cover my mouth with my hand, because I can intuit now where this story goes.

"Yes," Ginevra says simply. Her shoulders budge up, her face painfully childlike. "He had a heart attack. Another. A big one this time. He died in the hospital a couple of hours later."

Ginevra's father. That would be Max's biological grandfather, I realize.

"Yes. Yes. I killed my father. That's how the story went. Can't rewrite it, after all. Make it any different. I stole my sister's love, and then I killed my father. Those are the facts."

Ginevra's mouth sets in a grim line and she brings her fist down hard onto a teak side table, as if she is a dictator of centuries past, pronouncing her own guilty verdict.

"I might as well have killed myself, too. But after my father died, I never felt like I deserved to exist at all."

e~

The chef calls us for lunch. Nate joins, too, asks what happened, his eyes flickering with concern. Caro pulls him to the side of the terrace by the pool. I figure she's filling him in, but I don't have the energy to join, chime in. Instead, I watch our feast filter out. I can't summon the appetite to eat, although I note bitterly that Ginevra doesn't suffer the same affliction. She eats almost ravenously: grilled branzino, pasta al pomodoro, a Neapolitan babà for dessert. And as always, Ginevra imbibes prosecco like water. I count two refills of her glass before I lose track.

I watch everyone eat, watch forks enter mouths and retreat again, stare out at the turquoise perfection of the day that is trying valiantly to pull me out of my spiraling thoughts.

Finally, I say, "You didn't finish the story. You just gave baby Max over to my father? Just like that?"

"Oh." Ginevra puts her fork down, chews. Watching her do so is revolting—fish juice on her lips, flakes in her teeth. Then Ginevra sighs a sigh so emotive it has worlds inside it. "Not just like that. To tell the truth, I was so mired in my grief, mourning my father, knowing I'd killed him. I desperately wanted to give the baby to my sister. Maybe even that was selfish. I wanted to make everything up to her in some way. What other way existed than giving my child to her? I wanted her plans to proceed. The life she and Anatoly desired, I wanted them to still have it. I suggested that Anatoly still come to Italy, that they raise the baby as theirs. But Orsola wouldn't hear of it. After she knew what I'd done, after I became pregnant, she said she couldn't fathom a life with Anatoly anymore. That I'd ruined it, sullied it. Destroyed it.

"And of course, I understood, or I tried to. During my pregnancy, Anatoly received an invitation to leave the Soviet Union. He was denied by the government, became a *refusenik*. But he made a big enough stink that eventually he got to leave. He understood by then what had happened in that room at the Metropol Hotel, how big a blunder he'd made, mistaking one twin for the other. Orsola filled him in on everything. I was so ashamed that he knew. But my grief over my father's death overshadowed it all. Orsola said Anatoly wanted the baby to raise on his own, in America, and I was so numb. Of course, I agreed. When I gave birth, I didn't even hold him. I couldn't. If I held him, I feared I'd never let go. Instead, I handed him to Orsola, and she took him to America."

I nod numbly. "Max."

"Yes. Your father named him. Your father was—"

"*Is*," I interrupt.

Ginevra nods. "It's not the Alzheimer's that makes me talk of him in the past tense. For me, he's long been in my past."

I open my mouth, about to say, I found all the clippings, all the photos—that clearly Papa hasn't been in her past but communicating with her all these years.

But then Ginevra says, "He kept in touch with Orsola. Sent her pictures that she'd share with me." Ginevra smiles sadly. "She loved Ansel, you know? He was the love of her life. I always thought she made a mistake, that she didn't go to him, that she didn't raise Max as hers. But she couldn't do it, and I understand that, too. Instead, we soaked in the pictures, mementos."

"You sent money, too, didn't you?" It spurts out of me, surprising myself. But all of a sudden a picture is forming—a clearer picture of my childhood that in hindsight I realize I never quite understood. Sometimes those overdue bills arrived, and I would worry like crazy that we were going to be evicted, have to live in a homeless shelter, or eat Spam, but then somehow, things would be fine and Papa would even buy us extras, special items, like he was suddenly flush with cash. I remember having the childish thought that my babysitting money stuffed into those envelopes had made the dent, gotten us over the hump of hard times.

Ginevra blushes. "I did send money to Ansel. It was my pleasure and joy to do it. My responsibility, too. Orsola was our go-between. I always felt it generous of Orsola, to let me stay in her life. If our roles were reversed, I'm not sure I would have found the same generosity. And it was kind of Ansel, inordinately kind, to allow me to share in Max's milestones, and in yours, too, Rory. To allow me to provide for you children in some way. Even though, he was always clear about it, he wasn't going to rest on his laurels and take handouts. He worked hard."

"Very hard. Until his Alzheimer's worsened, he was still doing double shifts once a week." Emotion swells in my chest. "I don't understand something else. I thought the past few days you might be my mother, or maybe Orsola was. So—"

"Who is your mother? Yes." Ginevra sighs. "I felt so horrible when I asked you about your adoption and realized you didn't know. It never occurred to me, I suppose, that Ansel didn't share it with you. Although I knew from Orsola that he hadn't told Max the truth . . . about me . . . And why would he?" She says the last part loudly. If her words were an object, they'd be a knife she was aiming directly at her own heart, like she deserved it.

"Why would he tell Max a painful truth—that his mother was still alive and wanted him, but couldn't be with him? That the woman who should have been his mother—my sister—was thwarted from such. Why tell such a terrible story to a child? No, it makes sense your father invented Sandra Lowenstein. And it makes sense now, to me, why he continued the fiction with you, Rory. I'm only sorry to have shattered that."

"So my mother—my birth mother—who is she?"

"Like I told you, I think she was a woman from your father's diner. A teenage girl. I remember vaguely hearing of it from Orsola. A girl who wasn't ready to have a child. Your father was a sort of mentor to her, I think."

"Not . . . I mean, he didn't . . . ?"

"With a teenage girl? Your father?" Ginevra frowns. "Come now, Rory. You know, he would never."

"I know," I whisper.

"No. I am certain of this—Ansel isn't your birth father." Ginevra must note the sadness stamped on my face. "I'm sorry to break that to you."

"No." I try to brush it aside. Not like I wanted Papa to have had a creepy affair with a teenage waitress, but the confirmation that he isn't really my father, not by birth, is painful. I swim through my memories, through all the sweet waitresses who cut me extra slices of halvah. One of them . . . one of them is my mother. Probably she's alive, possibly even still in Michigan. I shove the information back into my recesses. I can't deal with it now.

"I guess that clears things up." I stare at my pasta, unable to fathom dragging it into my mouth.

"Clears things up in an insane way," Caro says.

"In an insane way. Yes. Except—I have one more question, Ginevra."

"Anything, dear."

"Why me?" I still don't understand. "I'm not your child, then. Why did you and Orsola care about me at all? Why did Papa send you both pictures of *me*? And this train trip . . . yes, I understand now, you wanted to meet Max. You wanted to take him to meet your sister. You wanted to save his company ostensibly from Caro. But why involve me? And why invite Nate?"

I say it so quickly, before I remember he's sitting here. "Sorry, Nate."

"It's fine." He waves a hand. "You deserve all the answers now. I'm certainly intrigued myself."

I nod. "I even understand inviting Caro, to fix stuff at Hippoheal. However misguided that was."

Ginevra clears her throat, sets down her fork.

"But inviting Nate, that was for me. It means you cared about me, that—"

"That I wanted you to have the perfect trip? Well, I did. I understood that Nate wanted you back, and I didn't want you to miss your chance at love. You think when you're young and beautiful that it will come again, but I saw it with my sister—it didn't come again. She mourned the loss of Ansel her whole life. Oh, sure, she had men wound around her fingers. Wining and dining her, buying her pretty bags and jewels. But she didn't love them. And I didn't want you to let love stream through your fingers. I didn't want you to lose your great love. And I wanted Orsola to meet you at last. I knew that would mean a lot to her. And all my life, I suppose, I've tried to make things up to my sister. Not that I ever could. Not that anything would ever be enough. But I suppose I can't stop trying."

"But *why*?" I'm still not seeing through the weeds. "Why did you and Orsola care about *me* at all?"

"Oh." Ginevra stops. She looks right at me with such a tender, loving gaze that transfixes me. I'm embarrassed, ashamed, of the feeling that bubbles up—that this is what a mother's gaze is like. That I never knew it, never felt it. That even having shed my childhood long ago, I still somehow want it.

"Oh, I'm surprised . . . no, it makes sense you don't understand. I thought it was rather obvious at this point. I've thought of you like my daughter ever since Ansel adopted you. Orsola has, too. We love you just as much"—Ginevra's face crumples—"just as much as Max. I'm not sure if it's because I loved Ansel, or because I loved Max, that I came to love you. I forget now if it was instant, right when I heard he adopted you, or if it took a little time to grow. All I know is that I've loved you for a very long time. And Orsola has, too.

"I thought it so perfect when I planned this trip for you all—that it would end in Positano, where my sister lives. Because of me, she has lived a difficult life. Oh, sure, I have tried to make it nice for her, materially so, once I realized success with my writing. I bought her a villa in Positano, where she always dreamed of living. I buy her clothes, bags—whatever my sister desires. It doesn't, as you can imagine, make up for what I did. But I still do try. And I figured—when Ansel was lucid, well, he could determine not to tell Max the truth of his parentage. That I am his mother. It was Ansel's right not to refer to a far-off mother when I could not be a true one in Max's life. But now that Ansel's Alzheimer's has progressed, I thought this the right time to tell Max the truth. To introduce you both to Orsola—the love of your father's life. And I knew that it would make Orsola's heart soar to meet the children. . . ."

Ginevra croaks with a cry. I take it all in, stare mutely ahead.

"Yes, well. That was my plan. My horrible fucking plan."

I've never heard the author curse before. I watch stupidly as her anger—all directed at herself—pings through her.

"Well, there it is. I regret many things in my life, as you now know, Rory. But I'll be honest: One thing I will never regret is the fact that I've spent my life watching you from afar. I'll never regret thinking of you like my own child. And I'll never regret loving you."

Ginevra stops, and her face suddenly softens, like her admission has exorcised something. "I'll never stop loving you, Rory. Even if you never want to see or speak to me again.

"And that, my dear, is that."

CHAPTER FORTY-SEVEN

Rory

Car's here," Nate announces at the rumble of an engine in the circle drive.

"Whose car?" I ask.

He shrugs, zips up his carryall. "Ror . . ."

"One sec." I draw a breath. I know—have known—he wants to talk. Have *the* talk.

I watch the concierge—who came as a package deal with this insane villa—outside, conferring with the driver. When the concierge returns, she says, "Transportation to Naples Capodichino for Signorina Caroline and Signore Nate."

Caroline emerges down the staircase, crosses the terra-cotta foyer, and stops beside me in the entry, beneath the frescoed dome.

She squeezes my arm. I allow it to be squeezed.

"We're okay?" she asks.

We've already talked—ad nauseam at this point.

"We're okay," I confirm, surprised every time I say it that I actually mean it. It doesn't mean that it doesn't still hurt. That everything that happened this week won't take a very long time to process and heal. But Caro is my sister—always has been, always will be. And we all do things we wish we could change, make happen another way.

I flash back to the moment when I launched a crystal ice bucket into my brother's head. I brace myself on the oak entry table.

"Really, though. Are you really okay?" Caro leans over to hug me, and I allow myself to be hugged.

"Yes. No. . . ." We break apart.

"Hey, Ror, are you sure . . . ?" Caro gestures at Nate, her cheeks turning pink. "You sure it's okay we're traveling together? You know it's only to the airport. . . . It means—"

"Nothing. I know. It's fine."

"Not just that it's fine, Ror. Because, honestly, we can take separate cars—"

"Please don't."

"Ror . . . " Nate is at my side.

"Okay." Caro's eyes flitter from Nate back to me. Her phone blips, and she studies it.

"More news?"

She looks up a bit guiltily. I know she's been hiding it from me—what they're saying on all the main channels, in the gossip rags, too. Last night I finally did a Google search, and it was pretty horrific. Not just the bare facts, that my brother died at my hands. But also how deep his fraud went. That one patient in his study died under mysterious circumstances. Circumstances that will now be thoroughly investigated. It's bizarre; I can remember participating in the frenzy on the other side. Like when the Theranos scandal hit, as a reporter, it was gold. But now I'm a sister.

And what makes everything even more excruciating is facing up to the fact that Max's vaccine doesn't work. That it won't—will never—cure Papa.

"I'll handle everything," Caro says, standing up straighter now. "You can count on me, Ror. And I'll see you in Michigan. Love you so much."

"Yeah. See you in Michigan. Love you, too."

Caro squeezes my arm, then disappears into the white Mercedes.

"Ror, are you sure you're fine on your own here?" Nate sweeps a hand through his curls.

"Yes. I'm fine, Nate. I've *been* fine on my own, for months now."

"I know." He gives me a sheepish frown. "I—I don't know what to say. I want to be here for you now. With . . . you know—"

"I know." I need him to stop, before he says my brother's name. I just need to get through this day. Then get on a plane, go see Papa. Break the news—I can't fathom how—that Max is gone.

That I'm responsible for his death. There goes that crushing sensation across my sternum, like an elephant stampede on my chest.

"Ror, do you think . . . is there any chance left for us? It's not fair of me to ask you now, is it?"

"But you're still asking it," I say softly.

"Huh?" He cocks his head, his brown eyes surprisingly warm. It's like I'd forgotten that Nate is kind, that he cares about me—reinvented things, maybe. When he left me, gave up on us, it was easier to reimagine him as the devil incarnate.

I sigh. "*I don't know* is the answer to your question. It's really all I can do right now to put one foot in front of another."

"Of course! I mean . . . that . . . of course you . . . but when you're back in LA—"

"I don't know that I'm going back to LA." I put all my stuff in storage. Of course, I thought I'd return. I've lived there for a decade, practically the whole of my adulthood.

"You'll find another anchoring job, Ror! You can't give up on your dreams."

"I don't know if they *were* my dreams."

He looks mystified. "Of course they were your dreams. You've been working toward being the main anchor on an evening news show ever since I met you."

"I don't know." How to explain it, that I'm not sure if I've wanted this because it was a pure desire, or if Papa planted the seeds and I ran with it? "I'm thinking of taking a course to become a meditation teacher."

"Really?"

I smile faintly at his tone.

"Not disparaging it. Not at all. If that's what you want. But, like, isn't that more a . . . side thing?"

"Not if I want it to be a full thing. There's so much stress out there— wars, fights. I covered it every day, and it starts to seep into your pores, you know?"

"I know."

I nod. Of course. Of anyone, Nate knows deeply what I mean. We had that in common, our common mission to try to make the world a better place. But since the meditation retreat, I can't stop wondering if there isn't a different angle to come at it from.

"If we want a happier world, I think we need happier people. And meditation dissolves stress. It makes you feel a little brighter and shinier when you come out of it. More optimistic." I pause, wondering if he thinks I'm being trite or naïve, and then decide I don't care. "Anyway, I don't know exactly what I want to do. That's the point right now. All I do know is I don't want to be anyone's main character again. Okay? I need to write my own script."

"Of course. Okay, of course. I just . . . I'm here, Ror. I really . . . I want us back. I want you to forgive me, for cracking when I should have stayed strong. For Caro . . . that was the dumbest—"

"I forgive you," I tell him, and realize I mean it. "But—"

"Is your *but* about . . . Gabriele?" Nate grimaces. "I mean, I know something was up between you two. I have to ask."

"He's texting me, I'm not going to lie. Obviously, he is. Checking in after all that's happened. We're friends, Nate, and beyond that, I have no clue. To be frank, it's really none of your business."

"Right. I lost that privilege, didn't I?"

I don't answer. Instead, I watch him fiddle with that ratty bracelet that's still on his wrist. The one that I wove him. It makes me smile slightly, but it doesn't change how I feel inside. That now I need empty space, freedom. To be beholden to no one but myself. To build my life back brick by brick, allowing for the possibility it's all going to look different when I choose it anew.

"Nate, do you know KonMari?"

"No. Should I?"

"It's that minimalist woman, Marie Kondo. She has a Netflix show. She teaches you to get rid of your stuff."

"Okay?"

"Well, the way she does it is you have to go through your closets and drawers. Lay it all out—everything you own—on the bed. And then assess if it sparks joy. If you want it back in your life."

"Oh," he says flatly. "So you're saying you need to lay me out beside all your bras, basically, and decide if I spark joy?"

"I guess," I say quietly. "I need some time."

"I never should have . . . " His eyes cast down. "I wish I could erase the last four months. The last four months *never* should have happened."

"Well, they *did* happen. They did, and I—" I break off, thinking of Max, and the loss and guilt and immense sadness barrels at me.

"I wish I could take your pain away."

"I know." I try to shove it all back, away, until I'm alone, until I make it through this day. Meeting Orsola—the love of Papa's life. This day is important, and I want to be present for it.

Nate smiles his crooked Nate smile—sad, familiar. "Well, I'm here, Ror. And if you decide I spark joy, you have my number. I'm not going anywhere."

"Nate!" Caroline's back in the entry. "We need to go." Her eyes flit at me. "And, Ror, the car taking you and Ginevra to Le Sirenuse is here."

"Right." I take a deep breath. "Time for us all to go."

I hug Nate, but I don't sink into him—not like before. Then I watch my best friend and ex-fiancé walk out the door.

CHAPTER FORTY-EIGHT

Rory

The ride to Le Sirenuse is short, Ginevra tells me. Ten minutes, not more. The car gently rolls forward, and I gaze out at all the little gates and awnings punctured by more bougainvillea than I knew existed in this world, let alone have ever seen. Ginevra folds her hands in her lap, twists one of her fantastic rings—this one with hulking ruby gemstones—up toward her knuckle, then down again.

"When we get there, we'll have to climb many steps to the entrance." She shrugs. "That's how they do it in Positano. You'll be okay?" Her eyes flit to my espadrilles.

I nod. Think that the more apt question is, will she be okay with the climb? She's relatively young, in her late fifties, but she wheezes when she walks. Even though Papa has Alzheimer's and is older than her, she seems by far his senior. Like any verve she once had evaporated long ago.

Well, now that I understand what happened—what she did—I can sort of understand.

No. I can't understand. So much is churning in me that I haven't begun to deconstruct.

"Rory, I need you to permit me something. A favor, I suppose."

"What?" I ask, hearing my harsh tone but feeling unable to excise it from the next part. "Don't you think you've asked a lot of me already?"

Ginevra's head jerks back. "That's fair, but what I meant is . . . the favor

I want to ask . . . is that I'd like to take over payments for your father's care. It's expensive," she says carefully. "Employing Suzette around-the-clock. And other aides may be needed over time, or even . . ."

"Even a care facility down the line," I slowly say. I haven't wanted to contemplate it, but most Alzheimer's patients proceed to a stage where they require it.

Ginevra nods. "And now that Max . . . Well, it's unlikely Hippoheal will have the funds, so I thought—"

"Oh, wow, Ginevra. I can't . . . I don't know what to say. I mean, that's wildly generous to—"

"It's nothing." Ginevra half smiles. "It's what I want to do. For Max's father. For your father. For the man I loved. Nothing will ever make up for what I did. I know that. I'll have to live with it. But I'd like the burden of his care not to fall on you. It's nothing to me." She waves a hand. "The money, I mean. Please let me do this."

Something lifts off my shoulders that I can't even say I didn't know I was holding—because I knew. It was weighing on me, a burden I didn't want to voice, because what a thing to focus on in the aftermath of Max's death. But how was I going to pay for Papa's care? And although I'm proud, I'm not too proud to refuse Ginevra's help. Because I can even see that her assuming the payments has a strange circularity to it. It feels right.

"Okay. Yes. Thank you. Thank you so much. I can't—"

"Just because I'm doing this, it doesn't mean I expect you to forgive me." The author shifts in her seat, grips the leather door handle as if it's a stress ball. "This is what I want to do."

"Okay, then. Still, thank you."

"You're welcome."

We sit in quiet for a bit. "Does she know now?" I finally ask the author. "Your sister, I mean. Have you told her by now that Max . . . that—"

"No. Still, not yet. She deserves to find out in person." Ginevra twists another ring—an emerald. Her hands are studded in colorful rocks, almost geological oddities unto themselves.

"Does Orsola live at Le Sirenuse?" I ask.

"Temporarily. Her villa is undergoing renovations now."

"Huh. So you're putting her up at the fanciest place in town."

So much to make up for. And no matter what Ginevra does, it will never be enough.

"I mean, I know you said your sister doesn't watch the news, but maybe she'd have heard about . . . Max around town? I think it was a pretty big thing . . . locally."

Ginevra's eyes flicker with something—derision? But then it passes as quickly as it came. "No, my sister doesn't care much for current events. Nor do the people she surrounds herself with."

I process that. I am curious—more than curious, all of a sudden—to meet this woman whom my father loved. He kept a picture of her all this time. This is the woman he wanted Max and me to believe was our mother. If I know Papa, and I do, he must have found her worthy of the title.

She must have been something, Orsola, to make my father fall so hard and fast that he never married.

Suddenly a thought strikes me, and I reach for my phone.

"I don't . . ."

Ginevra's face creases with concern. "What? You are nervous to meet her? My sister? Don't worry—she will love you. She will be so happy to see you. Regardless of Max . . ."

"No, it's not that." I thumb through my photos, land on the one I just remembered. "This is awkward to say. I hope you won't be upset."

"With you? I couldn't be."

"Well, when the train stopped in Rome, I wanted to see you. I was angry at you, to be honest. For sending me on this crazy trip. For telling me I was adopted but giving me no more information. And the books were stolen . . ."

"Max."

"Yes. I wanted another copy. A lot of things. I figured you might be home."

"Oh. I boarded the train in the morning."

"Yes, well." I breathe in deeply, then show her the picture that I snapped, when I was at her apartment. The photo in the frame that I now understand was of Ginevra and Orsola Efrati, with a vicious permanent marker X over the beautiful one. An X on Orsola's face.

"I broke into your apartment," I explain fast, when I make out

Ginevra's dismay. "I'm sorry. I knew how to get in, with the key, the code. You weren't home, and you weren't responding to my texts, and I wanted answers. I'm really sorry. I know it's a huge breach of privacy, but . . ."

Ginevra's hand goes to her throat, her eyes still fixed on the picture.

"It's okay, *cara*. I understand. I understand quite well why you did what you did."

"Okay, but . . ." I gather courage. "But I just realized—I still don't understand something."

"What's that?"

"The *X*. Why did you put an *X* over your sister's face? You were the one who deceived *her*. Not the other way around. So I don't get it—what did Orsola do to you to make you deface a photograph with her, and then frame it?"

Ginevra glances up at me, perplexed. "But I didn't put an *X* over my sister's face. You're mistaken, Rory. I put an *X* over my own."

"You . . ." I study the picture again. "But that makes no sense . . . that . . . I don't understand. . . ."

"I didn't put an *X* over my sister's face. I put it on my own. I wanted to cancel myself out. I guess my whole life, I've felt so guilty and ashamed. I never wanted to let myself off the hook. Forget what I'd done. I suppose, like Ansel, I took a new name, too. Ginevra Efrati became Ginevra Ex. And I wanted it in my study, facing me every day. I didn't want to let myself live one day forgetting it."

"But you were beautiful." I point to the picture—undeniable as it is. "*You* were the beautiful one!"

"You're mistaken. Look." Ginevra points to the girl on the right. "My sister was always the beautiful one. Even my father always said so."

We both stare at the picture, but it's clear to me now—Ginevra was indeed beautiful. "Maybe your father said so not because he thought she was *more* beautiful than you, but because he was trying to convince Orsola of it, and he didn't think he needed to convince you." I remember how Papa would always bolster Max, tell him he was brave, pump him up. He didn't say it to me—but then I didn't need him to.

"The beautiful sister and the ugly sister . . ." I say slowly.

"Oh, yes. You told me about it in our interviews. The fairy tale Ansel used to tell you as a child."

"I think I told you the basic gist, but maybe not the intricacies." I fumble for them, the words slipping out fast. "In the fairy tale, there's a duke, and he comes across two sisters. One is beautiful and good, and one is ugly and evil. The duke is in love with the beautiful sister and he tries to be with her. Papa used to invent all these ways the duke got thwarted, which I found hilarious as a child. But the ugly sister is evil and controls the beautiful sister. And in the end, the duke and the sisters all wind up alone. Yes—I remember the ending. The evil sister locks up the beautiful sister in the tower and throws away the key."

My conversation with Papa on the train flies back at me. *The good one was the beautiful one. The evil one ruined it all!*

He said something else, too. What was it . . . ?

Ginevra shakes her head. "I'm afraid I don't understand what you're trying to say, Rory."

"You were the beautiful sister," I say slowly. "*You* were the one my father was in love with."

"Oh." Ginevra pales, laughs. "That's not true. You're very wrong."

I stare at the photo as it all coalesces in sickening clarity. I clap my hand over my mouth.

"I asked Papa the other day if the fairy tale was like *Swan Lake*, and he said it was the opposite of *Swan Lake*. He got agitated. He kept saying the duke always knew! The duke always knew! I didn't understand what he meant, but now I do. In *Swan Lake*—"

"The prince is fooled by the substituted girl," Ginevra says slowly, her face perplexed.

"Yes," I say softly. "But Papa was telling me that he wasn't fooled. He always knew which girl was which. He knew you were the twin who opened the door at the Metropol. Did you ever even see Orsola and my father together?"

"Did I see . . . ?" Ginevra croaks, her eyes rolling back in their sockets. "Did I? It's so long ago. No. We toured on different days. We were caring for my father. . . ."

"Orsola must have met my father, too. And when she found out you cared for him . . . when she saw the love written on your face, she decided to take it from you."

"No. That's . . . no, she couldn't have done."

I'm suddenly certain. "She did."

"Orsola . . . no, I can't believe . . . I wasn't beautiful!" But I watch it dawn in Ginevra's eyes, the possibility, however slim, that maybe she was.

"You were." I reach over and squeeze her limp hand. "You were. The picture is the proof. Even if you didn't think so, you were gorgeous. And Papa had a picture of *you*. He called you Sandra, but he wanted Max and me to believe you were our mother. He wouldn't have done that unless he loved *you*."

I study the picture again, and suddenly I have a realization. "And your favorite color is purple! I *knew* that." My vision blurs with the young, beautiful girl wearing the violet top, a girl who had a world of possibilities open before her, but never even knew when they all got closed off, one by one. "I should have known it was you." And the girl on the right—Orsola I now know—is wearing a cheery floral dress. Ginevra is so not a cheery-floral-dress person. Even the items she's bid upon from Sophia Loren's collection have some measure of gravitas.

I made such a snap judgment that the beautiful girl in the picture wasn't Ginevra. I figured it couldn't be her—the seeming sinister machinations of the train trip; the fact that, now, aged and having suffered for many years, Ginevra is not conventionally beautiful. The *X* over her face. Why, after all, would a person deface a photo of herself—cancel herself out?

Now I understand. It's something that only a person with deep reservoirs of pain and self-hatred could do.

Ginevra is still shaking her head, her face ghostly white.

"Yes." I'm breathless, my heart still yammering at my chest. "Your sister must have manipulated you. In the most horrific way. To give up your own baby. To forsake the man you loved. To believe you were responsible for your father's death. To provide for her all her life, making you believe you owed her. You didn't steal your sister's life. She stole yours."

"No, it's not possible, it's just not—"

"She maintained the contact with my father." I feel frenzied to piece this together, but also achingly sad at the story we're unraveling.

"Yes. Orsola told me from the beginning that it felt like a dagger in her soul to even imagine us together. That she couldn't withstand our staying in contact. So I didn't. At the beginning, he called me. Sent me letters. But

I hung up on him every time. I ripped up his letters. It was about Max, I figured, or trying to convince me to fix things with Orsola. And Orsola said that even though it was painful for her, she would prefer to keep up the contact. Ansel would send her photos, mementos, and she'd pass them to me, too. I helped out, gave money sometimes, but always through Orsola. In the end, the letters stopped, and so did the phone calls."

We stare at each other, stricken. "Papa wanted to be with you. He tried. Calling you, letters, but Orsola must have been spinning her tale. He couldn't visit," I puzzle out. "He didn't have any money, and he was trying for citizenship. He wouldn't have been able to leave the US after having immigrated so recently. Plus, he had Max."

Ginevra shakes her head. "I don't know. I don't know what to think. All this time, I assumed he despised me, or at best, pitied me. . . ."

"He didn't. He must have loved you." I'm now as sure of it as I am of anything. "I wonder why he didn't visit you later, though. Why he didn't try to get you to see the truth. In person. Once he could. Maybe Orsola did something. Thwarted him somehow."

Ginevra bites her lip. "I spoke to Ansel only twice after I left the Soviet Union. I remember the last time clearly. Max was six. Ansel had adopted you a couple of years prior. There was a problem with a wire I'd sent. We needed to coordinate on the phone, and so I didn't tell Orsola, I just called him. And on that phone call, Ansel told me something I never understood. He said, *We have one thing in common, you and I. We both constructed our own prisons.*"

I gasp.

Ginevra looks at me, eyes misting up. "I can't believe . . . he loved me. If you're right . . . if . . . he really must have loved me, didn't he?"

"He really must have." I hold her hand, feel it tremble.

"He went to America," she murmurs, staring straight ahead now, dazed. "He always wanted to go to America."

"Yes. What does that—"

"Orsola—when she told me their plans, she kept saying Anatoly was going to come to Italy to be with her. It rubbed me in some way. Odd. Because—"

"Because Papa always wanted to go to America. Yes. Ever since he got a copy of the Declaration of Independence in that pavilion exhibition."

Ginevra nods. "America was in his heart. Not to say he wouldn't have gone to Italy for"—she chokes over the word—"love. But it struck me as strange, that's all, how Orsola was so adamant about his plans. I guess I didn't question it. I suppose I've never really questioned much of anything my sister has said. Oh!" Her face sparks with something, then she grimaces.

"What?" I ask.

The car grinds to a halt. "When I was pregnant, pretty far along, I spoke to Anatoly on the phone. That was the first of our two calls. He'd just arrived in America, and he tried to tell me he loved me, that I should come join him with the baby. I scoffed. I thought that of course he was only saying those things because he wanted to make sure I was going to give him the baby. And I told him the baby was going to be his, not to worry about that, and never to contact me again. Then I slammed down the phone. *Dio mio.*" She presses a hand over her mouth, eyes wide. "He wrote me all those letters. . . . He called me so many more times. I ripped up every letter. I hung up on every call."

I glance over at the author's tormented face and am certain I mirror it with my own. "Papa didn't just say he loved you because of Max. He must have said it because it was true."

Suddenly the driver turns. "We've arrived. Le Sirenuse."

There is nothing I want more than fresh air right now. The atmosphere in this car is thick, surely stifling us both.

Still, I say, "It's probably not the time right now, to see your sister, don't you think?"

Ginevra removes her hand from mine. Her lips set tightly together. "On the contrary, Rory. I think now is the very perfect time."

CHAPTER FORTY-NINE

Rory

Le Sirenuse has a siren-red exterior that opens into a quaint but luxe old Italian foyer—tan tiles punctured by turquoise and navy ones; a reception desk made of old weathered wood behind which room keys hang on pegs, harking back to another time.

Ginevra marches toward the elevator, the fastest I've ever seen the author move. I rush after her and slice out my hand as the door begins to close.

I slip inside. Ginevra's gaze hardly flickers at me. She presses the top button.

"Want to venture a guess where I've booked my precious sister in?"

Her voice is dull, almost robotic—so different from the Ginevra I've come to know, the Ginevra with warmth, if a little odd.

"A suite, I'm assuming? Ginevra, I really think we should . . . I don't think *now*, when you're angry—and of course you would be, I'm not trying to minimize what you must be feeling, because I'm incredibly angry, too—but I don't think now, exactly, is the right time to meet Orsola. I mean, shouldn't we cool down, both of us, before seeing her?"

"*No*. I don't think. And, yes, you're right about the suite. The premier suite in this place. A two-bedroom apartment—because one-bedroom would be too tight for my sister's lavish tastes. A terrace facing the sea, overlooking the manicured gardens. Want to guess at how much a place like that costs? Costs *me*, I mean."

"A lot?"

Ginevra laughs a scary, crackly laugh. "Five thousand euros a night. So, yes. *A lot.*"

The elevator dings, and off she goes, her short sturdy frame striding purposefully down the bright white hallway with its cross-vault ceilings and cheery tiles with navy swirls.

"Ginevra, I don't—"

But she's already knocking—hard, insistent raps—and by the time I reach Ginevra, the door has opened, revealing a striking woman whose plasticky face looks supremely irritated.

"*Stai scherzando?*" I see her spot me, light spark in her eyes. She switches to English, still with an air of being imposed upon. "I was coming. You didn't need to make my eardrums bleed, Ginevra."

It takes a moment for it to set in who this woman—Orsola—reminds me of. At last I come to it: Donatella Versace. It's the same long platinum blond hair, the fake orangey tan. A face-lift, no doubt. Orsola is short like Ginevra, but that's about where the similarity ends. Where the author is hefty, all clad in black, her sister is tiny, with arms as flimsy as spaghetti. She is wearing an outfit wholly at odds with her age and the laid-back, old-money surroundings of this charming hotel. Instead, from her moss-green flared, vaguely see-through pants to the matching crop top spilling out cleavage, she screams new money.

More accurately, new money, courtesy of her sister.

My heart is pounding as I approach her—this woman my father has warned me my entire life is evil, who so callously and knowingly set out to ruin his life and her own sister's. Who stole my brother from his mother.

Would Max have acted differently toward the end if he'd had a mother to care for him?

Orsola leans toward her sister to cheek kiss, but Ginevra flinches. She steps back. Orsola looks momentarily stymied, but then straightens.

Ginevra motions to me. "This is—"

"Rory Aronov," Orsola supplies. She doesn't even hide it—pursing her pumped-up lips and giving her eyes free rein to rove over me, head to toe. "Yes, you're Rory. Of course. Ansel's Rory." Her eyes widen with obvious false cheer. "It's so *wonderful* to meet you, darling."

She kisses me, once on each cheek, and I am too dumbfounded to protest. Instead, I am engulfed in her thick floral perfume, but also her natural, pungent, almost mildewy scent that has inexplicably survived the dousing.

"Where is the boy?" Orsola asks. "Max," she adds, as an afterthought.

Ginevra doesn't answer. I can imagine it's all she can do to follow this horrible, manipulative person into the suite she has paid for.

Even putting aside all I now know, it's clear enough from briefly meeting Orsola—there is no way, not ever in a million years, that this woman would have captivated my father. Papa is too smart, too perceptive. Too loving, too full of integrity. He would have seen right through her.

It was Ginevra who was weak . . . understandably under her sister's spell . . . traumatized at a young age . . . impressionable.

My mind swishes with all the incomprehensible things. We shouldn't be here. It's too soon. Too raw. After all Orsola did, all we've finally understood . . .

Something surges in me—I fucking *hate* this woman.

And if I feel that, then what is cycling through Ginevra's mind now?

The author and her sister trade ostensible pleasantries. They've switched to Italian, so I can't understand what they're saying.

"Rory." Ginevra glances at me. "My sister and I are going to go out on the terrace. We have a few things to catch up on, before . . ." She indicates pastries and coffee and fruity alcoholic drinks arranged artfully on a table. "Then we will have coffee and treats. Lemon granitas, too. Delicious. We'll all have a fine *gab*."

She's clearly speaking facetiously, with an aggressive calm that I find terrifying. Orsola doesn't seem to notice. She's used to, it seems, focusing most of her attention upon herself.

I sink down into a couch slipcovered in pale blue damask. I take in the room, almost impossibly sunny and pleasing, at odds with Orsola, the ugly, evil woman who has now been fully unmasked.

I'm staring at the terrace, at the white cast-iron chairs and table and the endless wash of blue that suffuses the horizon. The painted church dome we could see from our villa, too, but closer now.

The voices on the terrace ratchet up in volume, angry Italian. Vicious Italian, even.

My eyes flicker, focus—and that's when I see something tumble over the thin white lattice rail of the balcony. Not just something: a body.

Followed by a scream, and then a loud crack.

e⁓

Minutes later, I am standing beside Ginevra in the property's lush gardens. Orsola's crumpled shape lies at our feet in a tangle of juniper bushes, her shimmery green outfit camouflaged by the foliage. It's evident she's dead, simply by her body's unnatural twist. But I knew it even as we rushed down; no one could survive a fall that high.

Sirens begin their din in the distance.

"What did I do? What did I do?" Ginevra's shaking, her eyes darting around. But it's only us for now, though I hear voices in the distance. I called an ambulance, of course, after it happened. And the staff on the property will no doubt be descending soon.

"How could I do it, Rory? What did I just do?"

"What did your sister say?" I ask. "What—"

"Orsola admitted to everything. She was almost . . . smug—yes, that's the word." Ginevra stares numbly at her sister's body. "She was running her charade the whole time. Our whole life. She had me eating out of her hand ever since I was a kid. Like a dog. Obedient. Not questioning anything. She even told me—she even said that she wrote to Ansel eventually after the whole ordeal, pretending to be me."

"Pretending to be *you*? I don't understand."

"Yes! Telling him I didn't love him. That he needed to stop contacting me. She was worried that eventually I'd cave, that I'd listen to Ansel's pleas, read his letters, believe him that he loved *me*. So Orsola had to thwart it, prevent it at all costs."

I shake my head, trying to make sense of what she's saying. "But why would Papa believe it was you writing that letter? He knew how evil Orsola was, how she'd manipulated you. Forging a letter from you wouldn't be out of fathomable bounds when he knew what she'd already done."

"She had me sign my name on the letter! Your father knew my signature. It's specific."

I nod. I've seen her doodle it countless times, with that distinct swirl at the tail of the *a*.

"He knew my sister couldn't imitate it. And yet, in those horrible months after my father died, Orsola and I had to sign countless documents. Bills, estate things. She slipped them in front of me, one by one. I was practically catatonic with grief. I didn't pay attention to what I was signing. She wrote Ansel a letter from me to get him to give up on me, and manipulated me into signing it myself! She admitted it all. She took it, Rory!"

My breath feels all hoovered up—the horrific facts, but also, the body at our feet. "Took what?" I finally manage to ask.

"My family. The family I could have had. But I killed her!" Ginevra's voice crackles with pain. "How could I do it? To my own *sister*. To my twin. How could I just push—"

"She jumped," I tell the author quietly. "I'll say I watched her jump."

The sirens grow closer. Ginevra says, "I'm not her main character any longer."

AUTHOR'S NOTE

This book is very close to my heart, as the Soviet storyline and the character of Ansel are loosely inspired by experiences had by my father and his parents. My father, Alex Goldis, was born in 1950 in the town of Zhitomir in Ukraine, then a part of the Soviet Union. My father is Ukrainian, but his identification card stated only that he was Jewish. Thus illustrating his status, and the status of all Jews, in the former Soviet Union: precarious and persecuted.

My grandmother Khana Vinarskaya hid in a cellar during frequent pogroms as various Jew-hating factions went door to door with sabers, murdering Jews, including my great-granduncle. Later, my grandmother escaped the Nazis on the last train out of Kiev, but her parents, Itta and Azriel Shpiegel, opted to stay behind. They were subsequently murdered by the Nazis in mass graves outside Zhitomir. My grandfather Shimon Goldis, originally from Beltz in present-day Moldova, lost his entire first family early during World War Two and was sent to a Soviet gulag in Siberia for the duration of the war. He died when my father was a small child, so we don't know the details of what happened to him there, only that it was horrific.

Practicing Judaism was illegal in the Soviet Union, and so my father and his family maintained their religious rituals in secrecy, fearful of exposure and punishment. Throughout his young life, my father endured much antisemitism, from the bullies who beat him as a child for being a *zhid*—the derogatory term for a Jew—to the ones who did the same after he was drafted into the Soviet army, where antisemitism was systemic and condoned by the top brass. There were quotas for Jews; they were kept out of the best universities and relegated to few professions. The totalitarian Soviet regime has been inherited by the present-day Russian government, whose atrocities against Ukraine we are now tragically witnessing.

My father always dreamed of leaving the Soviet Union, and the signing of the Helsinki Accords in 1976 opened a narrow but perilous pathway for a small number of Jews to get out. My father attended university in Moscow, and like Ansel, he approached Jewish tourists at the Choral Synagogue to attain an invitation to leave, after which he applied to emigrate. But he was denied, converting him to a refusenik—the term given to Jews refused the ability to leave, and thus deemed traitors of the Soviet state. Consequently, my father was tailed by the KGB and fired from his job. My father could have been jailed or sent to Siberia, like many refuseniks of that time. But he refused to be silenced or to go quietly; he staged protests, was interrogated by the KGB, and was finally allowed to depart. So my father left the Soviet Union with twenty-six cents in his pocket and a burning desire to experience the liberties described in the Declaration of Independence that he so admired. Through his perseverance, courage, hard work, and positive and grateful attitude, he created a beautiful life in America. He has never taken his freedom for granted.

Ansel is a fictional character, and his personality, profession, illness, looks, qualities as a father, and storyline are wholly inventions of my imagination. However, Ansel's trauma from youth, the tragedies that befell him at the hands of the brutal Soviet regime, his refusenik journey, and the constant barrage of antisemitism against him are all drawn with near identical contours from my father's experiences.

As antisemitism now spikes in terrifying ways across the globe, it is not hard as a Jew, as the daughter of my father, and as the granddaughter of Khana and Shimon, to imagine what could happen if this antisemitism continues unchecked. My grandmother's constant refrain was to say *Shhhhh* to my father. She was terrified that if the Soviet government were to discover their rituals of practicing Judaism, or if my father were to speak out against the regime, that he could be taken from her, or her from him. My grandmother shrank into her little corner of the world; she couldn't speak out for fear of death—hers and her family's. But thankfully, at this moment in time, I do not have to fear for my life to write this book, and to shed light on some of the injustices that they could not. And so I have.

ACKNOWLEDGMENTS

Hugest thanks to my agent, Rachel Ekstrom Courage. You are a phenomenal advocate and the best partner I could wish for on this literary adventure. What a joy to work together, and I am so excited for everything to come.

Thank you to my spectacular editor, Lara Jones. You caught all my blind spots and saw exactly what this book needed. I am so grateful for your astute edits and genius ideas, and for making the whole process so seamless and also such fun. And how lucky am I to have an editor with a degree in Italian to correct all my Italian gaffes!?

My heartfelt thanks to the wonderful team at Atria/Emily Bestler Books. To Emily Bestler, Libby McGuire, Dana Trocker, Megan Rudloff, Dayna Johnson, Hydia Scott-Riley, Karlyn Hixson, Morgan Hoit, James Iacobelli, Paige Lytle, Shelby Pumphrey, Jason Chappell, Dana Sloan, Nicole Bond, Abby Velasco, and everyone on the sales, audio, and education/library teams, thank you for championing my books, giving them the most stunning art, layout, and audio, and helping me make them into works that I am proud to send off into the world!

To my fantastic foreign rights agent, Heather Baror-Shapiro, and TV/film agent, Tara Timinsky, thank you for being such stellar advocates for my books. Thank you to Alessandra Shapiro for letting me pick your brain on all things Italian culture. And to John Hooper for your exemplary and indispensable book *The Italians*. Thank you to my cousin Gil Grant for helping me with medical accuracies—any errors are mine! And a special thanks to the Venice-Simplon Orient Express for the luxurious train inspiration vibes, from which I let my imagination run wild and took a few design alteration liberties.

Thank you to the authors who've blurbed my books—your endorsements and support are so meaningful, and I wish I could hug each of you in person in thanks. To the very best critique partner, Nicole Hackett: it's so fun to get to walk this path together. To the uber talented, kind, and supportive author friends I've met along this crazy journey—I cherish each of you. Thank you to the fabulous bookstagram community: your creative, gorgeous, generous posts humble and thrill me, and it is such fun to get to chat with and get to know you all in the DMs, too. And to all the wonderful booksellers and librarians: while I live abroad and don't often get to see you in person, I am bowled over by your support and look forward to visiting stateside to meet more of you. My deepest thanks to my fabulous readers; your messages and emails touch my heart, and I am so grateful for each of you who picks up one of my books! And thank you to the very best friends and family, including my wonderful aunts, uncles, and cousins, who support me, cheer me on, order copies of my books to distribute to their friends, send copies to their PR connections, and even decide to be deliberate walking advertisements, walking casually down the street with one of my books in hand face out so that passersby will take note. (Love you, Tor!) I adore and appreciate you all beyond measure—you each have such a special place in my heart!

Thank you to Jas for lending Nate your Italian alter ego, Fabrizio Salvatore, keeping a stock of my books at AAI, and being the most supportive and loving brother. And to Suz, for being my first and best reader who provides the smartest and most on-point edits—no way would my books be what they are without you, the other half of my writing brain! I am so particularly grateful for how you helped me hone and improve the parts of this book that contain some of our own family story. You two are not only my siblings but my best friends in the world, and it's been that way from the start. We may often live on different continents, but I immeasurably cherish our phone and video chats and our time together when we get it. And thank you to Nadav and Arica, the best bonus siblings a girl could ask for. When I think about what I want to say about you two, the word I am looking for only exists in Hebrew—*firgun*. It means you always lift me up and celebrate me in such touching, heartfelt ways; I am the luckiest to call you both my brother and sister. And to the best nephews and nieces in all the land, Liad, Reagan, Griffin, and Noa—each of you is so special to and beloved by your Auntie Jac.

To my Bubsicles: ever since I was a kid, I've wanted to be an author, and you've shared that dream and belief in it right alongside me. You bought out the *Sweet Valley* section at Annie's Bookshop, took me to the best teachers, and have told me innumerous times, with the certainty only a grandmother can express, about how much better my books are than fill-in-the-blank stratospheric bestselling author. I adore you, Bubsicles—thank you for loving me so hard and believing in me so big. And thank you to my beloved Zadie—I feel you with me always, and I know you are so proud of all of this.

To the most wonderful parents: you celebrate and champion me and all my books, but this one in particular carries both of your strong influences. Mom, we had some of my favorite brainstorm sessions in the pool, as you let me talk through all the twists of this plot. Thank you for answering my every call on basically the first ring—you are the most caring mom I could imagine. And Dad, not only are you MWF (my wonderful father) and my most hardworking salesperson, making sure that every golf buddy and men's club member buys a copy of my books, but you have inspired this book in an enormous way. As I wrote in my author's note, your courage and strength through some of the cruelest and most difficult obstacles are present in the character of Ansel. Though you are very different from Ansel as a person and a parent—you always made me feel so secure growing up, for instance— I gave Ansel some of the experiences and hardships of your childhood through which you persevered. (And I gave Max your proclivity for issuing very precise specifications when ordering your custom Zhitomir salad.) Thank you for ensuring that the parts of the book set in the Soviet Union are accurate to the tiniest detail, and for sharing with me—and my readers—why the atrocities committed there, and now happening in new ways in Ukraine at the hands of the Russian government, must be stopped at all costs.

And finally, thank you to my grandparents I never got to meet, Khana Vinarskaya and Shimon Goldis. I never had the opportunity to listen to your stories, and so I will never fully know the contours of your suffering, but I know this for sure: your potent legacy is your love for each other and your love for my father, and how, when you had so little, you still gave so much to those who needed it. That is the inheritance with which you have blessed us, your steadfast commitment that, even in the face of the worst evil and darkness, love and light and goodness will prevail.